INDEXING
REFLECTIONS

OTHER TITLES BY SEANAN MCGUIRE

INDEXING
REFLECTIONS

———

SEANAN
MCGUIRE

Published by 47North, Seattle

www.apub.com

Amazon, the Amazon logo, and 47North are trademarks of Amazon.com, Inc., or its affiliates.

ISBN-13: 9781503947740
ISBN-10: 1503947742

Cover design by Megan Haggerty

Printed in the United States of America

This book is dedicated to everyone who asked me
"What happens next?"

I thought that you deserved an answer.

Forbidden Doors

Memetic incursion in progress: estimated tale type 312 ("Bluebeard")
Status: UNRESOLVED/IN ABEYANCE

Ciara Bloomfield squinted at her reflection. She looked reasonably professional, especially by the standards of the organization she worked for: Sure, suit jackets over ruffled pirate shirts were unusual, but she had notes in her file that explained the choice. Her pencil skirt was long enough to be appropriate, and her sensible heels would make it possible for her to run for her life, should it become necessary. Which might well happen, given where she was going.

"I think I need to make an appointment at the salon." She bent forward enough to get a look at the crown of her head. "My roots are growing in."

"I love your roots," said her husband automatically. He didn't look up from his spreadsheet. She didn't expect him to. Their relationship was a healthy one, built on mutual respect, shared interests, and her never unlocking the door to the garage.

"Most people's roots don't grow in blue," she reminded him, turning away from the mirror. "Will you be all right without me?"

"I'll finish this report, go down to the shipping yard to check on things, and order a pizza for dinner," said Giles. He offered her a quick, toothy smile. "Don't go into the garage while I'm away."

"I wouldn't dream of it," said Ciara. She crossed the room to kiss his forehead before heading out. It was time to get to work, and it wouldn't do for her to be late on her first day.

# # #

My day began—again—with half a dozen bluebirds beating themselves to death against my bedroom window. They were determined to wish me a good morning, and they'd been getting better and better at getting past the bird-safety nets I'd installed in an effort to save their featherbrained little lives. The sound of their bodies hitting the glass and rebounding into the bin Jeff had set up to catch them was almost soothing, at least until something larger hit the glass. It squawked on impact.

I groaned, not opening my eyes. "Please tell me I didn't just kill a falcon."

"Technically, you don't kill any of them," mumbled Jeff. He sounded like he was about half as awake as I was. He was not an early riser. His story tended to keep him up at all hours of the night, making him a champion of sleep deprivation and inappropriate napping. I hadn't realized that before we'd become a couple; I'd always assumed his constant availability was the result of a strong work ethic. It wasn't. It was insomnia, and a thousand midnights spent staring at the clock and fighting the urge to start making shoes.

"I know, but they wouldn't be here if it wasn't for me." I rolled over and squinted at the clock. 5:45 a.m.—at least this time they'd waited until it was almost time for my alarm before beginning the avian assault.

"Once upon a fuck me running. I'm getting up. Do you want me to wake you in an hour?"

"If I say yes, will you actually wake me?" Jeff sounded plaintive. He'd been sleeping more regularly since he'd moved in with me, largely because I wasn't opposed to picking him up and carrying him to bed when I felt he'd been up too long. He'd given me permission to do exactly that. The upside of this arrangement was that he was better rested and hence better able to cope with a world that spent a lot of time trying to kill us. The downside was that he'd learned I would let him sleep through almost anything, just to be sure he was getting enough rest.

It was all sickeningly domestic, and if there was any redeeming quality to our relationship, it was that Jeff was no Prince Charming and I was no dainty little maiden. He was one of the Shoemaker's Elves, and I was a princess, and while there had been hundreds, if not thousands, of people like us through the years, I was pretty sure we were the first ones to fall into bed together. He couldn't make me a Queen, and I couldn't buy him socks without risking him breaking up with me, but we were making things work. Surprisingly well, in fact.

There was probably a betting pool at the office on how long we'd last, and Sloane was probably organizing it, using her "Bed, Wed, Behead" chart. I wasn't bothered. She'd earned the right to have a little fun.

"I'll wake you," I promised. "But if you get up now, you can join me in the shower."

Jeff reached for the nightstand, recovering his glasses. "I'm up," he said.

I shook my head, smirking, and got out of bed.

The hallway carpet was covered in wildflowers. Jeff stopped to squint at them, and then sighed. "Blue lupines," he said. "Today's the review, isn't it? I wonder what the connection is going to be."

"Did you swallow a botany book while I wasn't looking?" I opened the hall closet, taking out a pair of towels and passing one to Jeff. "Most men can't identify the flowers growing out of the carpet without at least a little more effort."

"Most men don't date women whose presence causes flowers to grow out of the carpet," Jeff countered. "I like to know what to expect. You're like a horoscope in horticulture."

"I'll be sure to put that on my business cards," I said.

Jeff laughed.

We met at work. We're both agents for the ATI Management Bureau, an organization dedicated to keeping stories from eating the world. It's in our motto, even: *In aeternum felicitas vindactio.* Defending happily ever after. For most people, fairy tales are beautiful things, meant to be encouraged and enjoyed, and I guess that's an easy position to take when you're the one wearing the glass slipper or kissing the princess. For the people in the way of the narrative, fairy tales are deadly, capable of rewriting reality in order to get what they want—and what they want is rarely good for anybody who's not on the short list for a happy ending. Fairy tales are not for children, and they don't care who dies. They never have.

Jeff and I, along with the rest of our field team, worked hard every day to keep those memetic incursions from destroying reality as we knew it. Like most of the members of our team, we had a strong personal stake in the fight: we were both on the ATI spectrum, making us living fairy tales. Jeff was a type 503, a Shoemaker's Elf. If the narrative had its way, he would have worked his fingers to the bone making shoes for strangers, all to teach some asshole the importance of respecting your hired help. It was a relatively rare tale type, and one that made him extremely well suited to working with our cleanup crews and in the Archives. I, on the other hand, was something more common and more dangerous. Aarne-Thompson tale type 709.

Snow White.

Until recently, I'd been holding my story at bay, living with the symptoms but not the fully fledged disease. Then our former dispatcher decided to play Storyteller and put me in a position where the only way to save myself and my team was to embrace my story. I'd been living with the dead-white skin, the blood-red lips, and the suicidal songbirds since I was a little girl. Now I had a solid connection to the fairy-tale forest where all the Snow Whites who'd ever lived existed, and I was spending half my dreaming hours trying to get a handle on what I was going to be for the rest of my life.

At least I didn't have to worry about princes. Jeff and I had started our relationship before I had fully manifested, and he understood the danger princes represented to me. Between the two of us, we were always on our guard. Nothing charming was going to get anywhere near me if we had any say in the matter.

I'd always expected manifesting my story would mean that my life was over. Instead, it had coincided with a lot of things I'd never thought could happen. I had a boyfriend serious enough that he was *living* with me, not just visiting once a week until he ran in terror. I was talking to my brother again—really *talking* to him—more than once a month, and for more than five minutes at a time. I was even getting along with Sloane, which was a minor miracle if anything was.

We were going to be okay. Or at least, we were going to be okay if we survived the review, which was by no means guaranteed.

I stepped out of the shower and grabbed a towel, wrapping it around my head. "At least I don't need to worry about fixing my makeup," I said, keeping my voice forcedly light. "Nature has supplied me with sufficient lipstick and mascara to kill a legion of fashion models."

"Yes, and if you put on blush, you'll look like you have a fever," said Jeff as he turned off the water. "May I still suggest a little eye shadow? It'll make you look less like a storybook character, and that could be important."

I sighed. "You're right. I wish you weren't."

"I know," said Jeff, and left the bathroom.

I sighed again and got to work. Jeff's story had been active for years, and he understood how to work with the Bureau's regulations better than I did. If I wanted to stay a field agent, I needed the people in charge to believe I was still on the side of the human race, rather than standing on the side of the story. It wasn't going to be easy.

Adding a few dabs of eye shadow made my reflection look perfectly made-up, if unnaturally pale. I looked at myself for a moment, trying to will color out of my lips and into my cheeks. It didn't happen. It never happened.

I turned out the light as I left.

# # #

We pulled up in front of the office ten minutes before we were due, a box of donuts riding on the seat between us. I slid our plain black SUV into the designated space, and watched, unsurprised, as the woman who'd been sitting on the curb rose and stomped over to meet us. Not walked: literally stomped. It was her primary means of locomotion, and had been for as long as I'd known her. She moved like she was mad at the world and wanted to make sure it knew.

"Morning, Sloane," I said, sliding out of the car and pushing the donut box toward her. "Cruller? It's the only baked good that sounds like 'cruelty.' You know you want it."

"You're not taking this seriously," she snarled. "If you were, one of you would have taken a taxi. You want to give them an excuse to split us up? Huh? Because there are easier ways." She glared at me.

Sloane Winters had been with the Bureau longer than anyone else I knew—possibly for centuries, if her throwaway comments were meant to be taken seriously. She was five feet, eleven inches of rangy, easily angered Evil Stepsister, with the bad attitude and trust issues that came along with her story. Her hair was currently bleached ice white, and dyed with streaks of toxic green and bloody red, making her look like a walking poisoned apple. It went well with her outfit: red plaid skirt; black tank top with a bleeding-heart logo on the front; and, of course, big stompy boots. Always the big stompy boots.

I continued to hold out the donut box until her expression softened.

"You really got me a cruller?" she asked, opening the lid.

"I really did," I confirmed. "An apple cruller, even." I couldn't stop the shudder that moved through me on the word "apple," half longing and half revulsion. Apples were my heroin. That didn't stop my mouth from watering at the thought of biting through their crisp skins and feeling their flesh against my tongue.

Every Snow White knows an apple will be her downfall, just like every Sleeping Beauty knows to be careful of spinning wheels, and every child of the Juniper Tree knows to watch out for oaken chests. And it never helps, because those are the things that draw us. They're our magnetic norths, unique and terrible and inescapable.

"Cool." Sloane took the cruller. "You need to take this review seriously, both of you. I get that you feel like you're invincible right now, but that's the story talking. Bureaucracy trumps narrative any day, and bureaucracy can say that we can't afford to have an active Snow White on a field team. You're a security risk, Henry."

"Jeff's been on the field team for years," I said.

Sloane took a bite of her apple cruller, eyes narrowing as I shivered. When she swallowed, she said, "Jeff's never been allowed to lead a field team. He's compromised. Now so are you. Not only that, but you have weaknesses he doesn't. He isn't vulnerable to princes the way you are."

"If it makes a difference, I did prove vulnerable to princesses," said Jeff, adjusting his glasses with one hand. I wrinkled my nose at him.

Sloane rolled her eyes. "You two are gross," she announced. "Now come on. I need to make some popcorn to eat while I watch you getting fired." She turned on her heel and yes, stomped away, putting so much force into each step that it was a wonder she hadn't broken an ankle yet.

"Do you think she has downstairs neighbors?" mused Jeff as we followed her. "I bet her landlord has to rent at a discount. She's probably in someplace rent controlled. She'd be moving every six months otherwise."

"She's been in town long enough," I said. None of us had ever seen Sloane's home. Apartment, house, or converted storage unit, I had no idea—although I suspected house, given how little she liked being around other people. Sometimes it was all she could do to keep herself from murdering us, and we were some of the few people she seemed to almost *like*. I couldn't imagine her having close neighbors. Not without a basement and a body count.

Jeff snorted, but didn't say anything. We were too close to the doors. Casual conversation could be monitored and, given the day's purpose, could be used against us in a court of human resources.

The ATI Management Bureau was built in a repurposed biological-warfare research lab. It was fitting, in a sideways manner: fairy tales were memetic warfare, and we were constantly looking for ways to lessen or eliminate their influence on the human race. Our Archives contained copies of every known variant on every known story, and were being updated constantly to better prepare us for what we might wind up facing in the field. Our armories were packed with weapons both commonplace and cuckoo. Most princes could be stopped with a tranquilizer dart. For the ones who couldn't, we had cloaks woven from lentils, bridles of gold, eggshell boxes, and more. So much more. For each common story like Snow White or Cinderella, there were a hundred less common ones, like the Juniper Tree, or the Three Princesses of Whiteland. Every story required a certain set of conditions to get started, and a certain sequence of events to end. Unless it was averted, of course. Aversion was our stock-in-trade.

Jeff and I swiped our badges and made our way through the old air lock to the hall. The few people who were there looked at us sympathetically, and didn't stop to talk. Everyone knew today was my team's review, and the word on the street was that at least one of us—probably me—was going to get benched. It didn't matter that I'd embraced my story for the sake of my team, or that we'd all have died if I hadn't eaten that apple and manifested as a full Snow White. I was a story now, and as a story, I couldn't be fully trusted. I might never be fully trusted again.

Sloane was in the bullpen when we arrived, sitting squarely in the middle of her desk, which was used more as a chair than it ever was as a place for filling out paperwork. She had eaten half her cruller, and was waving the remainder tauntingly in the face of one of our other team members: Andy Robinson, a hulking mountain of a man who was looking more and more inclined to snatch the pastry out of her hand.

"Do you want a donut, Andy?" I asked, setting the box down on my desk. "Where's Demi?"

"Henry!" He lit up as he turned to face me and my burden of sugary goodness. "Please tell me you got me a maple bar. I would kill for a maple bar right now."

"I got you a maple bar," I confirmed. "Where's Demi, she asked again, with slightly less patience?"

"Not here yet," said Andy. "She was taking the bus this morning, since her car's still in the shop. She's got at least five minutes before we all wind up fired for failure to report." He stood and walked over to my desk, where he began investigating the contents of the donut box.

"See? I'm not going to be responsible for things going horribly wrong. It's going to be a group effort." I picked out a plain cake donut and dropped into my desk chair. "You should all have more faith in me."

"We do, or we would have requested reassignment weeks ago," said Andy. His voice was unexpectedly grave. I looked up, startled. He shrugged. "Me and Mike, we're looking into adopting a kid. You know how expensive that is? How above reproach you gotta be before they'll even consider your application? And that's assuming you're a straight couple. Black man married to a white man . . . the deck's already stacked against us. I need to be the guy with the good, stable government job.

Makes it more likely that the agency reviewing our application will go 'whoa, better not discriminate against this one, we'll get our asses sued.'"

"I'm sorry," I said. "I didn't think about that."

"It's cool," said Andy. "Just don't think for a second that Jeff's the only one who has your back. He may be the one who goes home with you, but during the workday, we're all here for you as much as he is."

"That means a lot. Thank you." I took a bite of my donut to keep from needing to say anything else. I was swallowing when there was a commotion from the mouth of the bullpen. I smiled without turning. "Demi's here."

"I'm here!" called Demi, half a beat later. A skinny Latina rushed past me, dumping her things on her desk. A flute case protruded from the edge of her duffel bag. "Am I late? I'm not late. I have," she checked her watch, "fifteen whole seconds!"

"You do," I agreed. "Have a donut."

"Oo, donuts," said Demi. She moved to root through the box. I sat back in my chair, feeling a little better about our chances. The gang was all here. If we stuck together, we could survive anything.

Demi Santos was our newest, youngest member. Like me, and Jeff, she was ATI active: she was a Pied Piper, and could accomplish almost anything with the right sheet music. She was also the strongest argument for taking the team away from me. Birdie Hubbard, our old dispatcher and unexpected enemy, had been able to use Demi's story to turn her against us. Having a Pied Piper gunning for you wasn't a fun experience. I don't recommend it. Demi herself was a generous, thoughtful, compassionate girl, but once her narrative got involved, all bets were off.

Snow White wasn't such a sweet, delicate story either, once you started digging into the monomyth. It began with bluebirds and true love, but it ended in sacrifice and blood on the snow. I could do a lot of damage if I ever let my narrative take over. The Bureau would be within its rights to minimize that damage by pulling me away from the front lines. It was up to us to convince them that leaving me where I was would be a better idea.

"Excuse me?" The voice was pleasant, female, and unfamiliar. I turned, already starting to rise. There was only one person I didn't know who could reasonably be expected to be approaching my team today. Everyone else in the building was avoiding us like we'd contracted a bad case of the plague.

The woman at the mouth of the bullpen was short, curvy, and dressed like the accountant of a pirate-themed restaurant. I'd never seen anyone combine a ruffled blouse with a pencil skirt and striped tights before. It worked surprisingly well, maybe because the woman looked so comfortable. Her only jewelry was an antique-looking brass key, worn on a black velvet choker. She had ash blonde, salon-perfect hair, but there was something wrong with it, something about the roots.

Deputy Director Brewer was a foot or so behind her and to the left. He didn't look pleased. That was nothing new. The deputy director never looked pleased if he had any possible way to avoid it.

"Hello," said the woman. She was smiling. That made me nervous. "I'm Dr. Ciara Bloomfield, from Human Resources. I'm here to perform a full evaluation on your team and determine whether there's anything the ATI Management Bureau can do to help you keep functioning at your best. Is Henrietta Marchen here?"

She knew I was a seven-oh-nine; it was written all over my files, going back to my birth. It was still nice of her to pretend she couldn't tell on sight. "I'm Henrietta Marchen," I said, dropping my half-eaten donut back into the box. "Pleasure."

"The pleasure's all mine," she said. "Would you like to come with me?"

No. "Sure," I said. I cast a reassuring look back at my team, who didn't look reassured at all, before I followed Ciara out of the bullpen.

# # #

We wound up in one of the interrogation rooms. I wondered whether Ciara realized the mirror behind her was a two-way, designed to allow for observation. I decided she had to know. If she was high up enough in Human Resources to be doing employee reviews, she would have encountered this sort of setup before.

She waited until I was seated before producing a file and setting it on the table between us. "I want you to feel safe in this room. Whatever you say is entirely between us here."

Between us, and whoever was on the other side of the glass. I leaned back in my seat and just looked at her. I was aware of how disturbing my appearance could be to people who weren't used to dealing with me: There's a reason almost all representations of Snow White add a little color to her skin. "Dead white" is not a shade humans are supposed to come in.

"Now, Henrietta, according to your file, you prefer to be called 'Henry.' Is that correct?"

"Yes," I said.

"Is there a particular reason?"

I forced myself not to sigh. "I've manifested the coloration associated with my narrative since birth. I've never been capable of going outside without sunglasses and high-proof sunscreen. Most of my medical issues in grade school stemmed from my 'forgetting' to reapply before recess, because I was trying to be like all the other kids." The rest of my medical issues in grade school had arisen from the other kids. They had a finely tuned sense of what was right and what was wrong, and when I'd failed to be the Snow White they thought they were entitled to—when I was brash and bossy, instead of meek, sweet, and inclined to bake cookies for everyone in my class—they'd been more than happy to show me the error of my ways. Because nothing says, "gosh, I wish you were nicer" like kicking your classmates in the teeth.

"I'm afraid I don't follow," said Ciara.

"I didn't want to have an old-fashioned name to go with being considered 'funny looking.'"

"This didn't have anything to do with your brother?" Ciara looked at me earnestly. "According to his file, Gerald Marchen started insisting on male pronouns at the age of eight, and was living full time as a male by the age of fourteen. Did you choose a male name for yourself out of solidarity?"

"Yes," I said. I didn't hesitate. I was sure there was something in my file that confirmed exactly that, possibly clipped to a note from my adoptive father, Andrew Briggs, one that went into detail about how I'd perverted and twisted my sister into becoming my brother in my attempt to escape from my story. Mr. Briggs had never been able to cope with the fact that Gerry had always been male: that it was his body, not his brain, which was in error. "Gerry was experiencing severe emotional distress in both our home and school lives. At home, he had to wear dresses and play with dolls, even when he was begging to be allowed to wear jeans and climb trees. At school, he was being called by a female name constantly, by both teachers and students. When we both adopted a male nickname, people just thought the Briggs twins were being weird again. They tolerated our weirdness better when we did it in unison."

"You didn't experience emotional distress over being called by a boy's name?"

"No. Why would I? I was born female, I grew up female, everything around me was constantly approving of and reaffirming my gender, even if it was in tiny ways. I got to use the right bathrooms. I got to line up with other girls. On our birthday, I got dolls and teddy bears and toys that said 'you are a girl.' Even if I didn't want them, they affirmed my gender identity. A name couldn't take that away from me. Gerry didn't get any of those things. He got the whole world telling him, every day, that his idea of who he was wasn't right. I got the opposite of emotional distress. I got to know that me having a boy's name meant my brother didn't have a girl's name. He got one thing, and I helped to make that possible."

"I see." Ciara made a note. "Did you feel betrayed when he escaped your story? When the narrative started seeing him as male, and turned all its attention on you?"

"No," I said.

Ciara tilted her head, seemingly waiting for me to continue. When I didn't say anything, she made a note on her pad and said, "There are people in Human Resources who are concerned that your recent activation will lead you to sympathize with other actives over those who have been averted or do not appear on the spectrum, even as you showed more sympathy for your brother than for the other students in your class who may have been made uncomfortable by having a little girl insist she was actually a little boy. How do you respond? Can you be sure you won't favor your own kind over the nonactivated?"

I stared at her. Literally stared, my mouth hanging slightly open as I tried to process what she'd just said. I took a breath to respond, and stopped. There was nothing I could say that wouldn't get me into trouble. Better for me to keep my mouth shut.

There was something about this Ciara woman that put my teeth on edge. It wasn't the questions she was asking, oddly—I was willing to bet those had come from somewhere up the chain of command, and she was at least *trying* to ask them with empathy and compassion. They were horrible questions. They made me want to punch whoever'd written them. This woman didn't write them: she was just doing her job. No, it was something about her hair, something I should be seeing, but wasn't.

Then she tilted her head, and I finally saw.

"Blue roots," I said. "Are you a one-three-eight dash-one, or a three-twelve?"

And Ciara smiled. "What do you think?"

"You can walk, you can talk, and you're wearing a shirt you stole from Captain Hook. I'm betting three-twelve. Averted or abeyance?"

"Abeyance," Ciara said. "I'm happily married to my Bluebeard. He said 'don't go in that room and I'll give you whatever you want,' and I took him up on it. He loves me."

"He's a murderer." I didn't know why I felt compelled to point that out: I just did, like there was a chance that she wouldn't know.

"I'm his first wife," she said. "I may have triggered his story when I agreed to marry him. As long as I never use this," she fingered the key around her neck, "he never starts killing. Can we really punish people for what they might do?"

I looked at her, and slowly, I smiled.

# # #

"Here." Andy pushed the coffee into my hand as I joined him in the viewing area. I shot him a sidelong look. He shrugged. "You looked like you needed it. She pretty much chewed you up and spat you out. All those questions about Gerry? I expected you to start swinging."

"She's just doing her job," I said. "I don't think she wrote those questions." I glanced at the mirror, which was a window from this side. Ciara was greeting Sloane, who looked about as happy to be there as I'd been. "Odds that Sloane punches her in the mouth if she gets invasive?"

"I don't think so." Andy's expression leveled out, becoming almost neutral. "I did some digging when I heard we were going to get reviewed. I didn't want to be caught flat-footed, you know?"

Sloane was taking her seat. Ciara, looking much more nervous than she had when it was her and me, sat down across from her.

"Makes sense," I said.

"Remember how Sloane said something about being a track runner once, and we all assumed she'd been on the track team in high school? I got to wondering about that, so I had the folks down in records pull everything I was cleared to see. One of them was a report from 1908, right after this area got its first office. It mentions 'the unpleasant Miss

Winters and her ongoing crusade against respectability and good behavior.' I checked the roster. There's never been another Miss Winters, and women weren't allowed to compete in track and field until 1928. Whatever Sloane meant, it wasn't a high school track team." Andy looked back to the window. "Sloane's older than we ever thought she was. She hasn't been canned or shipped off to live with the other fairy-tale villains. That means she must be better at dealing with things like this than we want to give her credit for."

". . . right," I said, after a long pause. I'd suspected Sloane was older than she looked for a long time. There were things she'd said, ways she had reacted, that tended to imply a long, long life, all of it spent fighting against the story that wanted to define her.

It must have been very difficult, being Sloane.

Andy pressed the button that would broadcast the conversation going on in the other room. Ciara was talking. "—opinion, do you feel Miss Marchen is overly inclined to put the needs of individuals on the ATI spectrum above the needs of individuals who are *not* on the spectrum?"

"In my *opinion*, the snow bitch has always been too soft on the stories," said Sloane. I tensed. She continued: "If it was up to me, we'd kill them all. Princes, princesses, goosegirls, it doesn't matter. Slit their throats and let Grimm sort them out."

"So Miss Marchen shows mercy when it isn't warranted?"

"No," said Sloane. She leaned forward, putting her elbows on the table, and nodded toward Ciara's files. "You have a write-up on me in there?"

"You know I do," said Ciara.

"It probably says something like 'Sloane Winters is impulsive, temperamental, and poses a possible danger to herself and others. While she is a highly effective field agent, the need to team her with individuals who will balance her moods cannot be overstated. Her aggression is often focused toward individuals who suffer from placement on the ATI spectrum. Recommend she be working with or under one or more individuals who show increased empathy to people in that situation.'" Sloane's smile was sudden, and seemed to contain too many teeth. "There's probably a lot of correction fluid on the second to last sentence. 'ATI spectrum' is pretty new language. Not what we used to call people like you and me."

"What was that?" asked Ciara, sounding horrified and fascinated in equal measure.

"Cursed. They called us cursed, or story touched, or both, and they said I always had to be paired with a princess or a second son, because otherwise, I'd burn down the world." Sloane kept smiling. "I think Henry's too soft because I think you're all too soft. Let me slit a few throats and see how the fairy tales back off this region. If you're not willing to do that, Henry's what I need to keep me under control."

"Damn," breathed Andy. "Girl's a menace."

"She knows what she is, and she makes sure she doesn't take it out on us," I said. "That's the definition of a hero in my book."

On the other side of the glass, Sloane was still smiling. "They've taken my muzzles away before," she said. "That should be in your files too. Take a look at how that always ends, and get back to me, huh?"

# # #

Sloane sauntered into the observation room like she didn't have a care in the world, and scowled when she saw the coffee cup in my hand. "I came for coffee," she said. "If you have consumed all the coffee, I am going to straight-up fucking murder you, and drink a latte out of your skull."

"You forgot to mention poison," I said, taking a sip from my cup and making an exaggerated "mmm" face before turning my attention back to the window. Demi was stepping into the room. Out of everyone on my team, I was most worried about her. Not because she was going to slip and say something she shouldn't: because she had been as victimized by Birdie Hubbard as I was, if not more, and we were still figuring out where her fault lines were.

I had known I was on the ATI spectrum from the time I was born. Skin as white as snow was a pretty big indicator. But Demi . . . her world had been perfectly normal, up until the day Sloane had crashed into her music theory class and dragged her out by the arm. She'd been given no warning of what the world wanted her to become: she hadn't even known the Bureau existed until we'd dropped her off the deep end and told her to get to work. We hadn't been fair to Demi in a lot of ways. We'd done what we had to do in order to save the world. Sometimes I wasn't sure she could forgive us for that. After all, *her* world had essentially ended the second she saw Sloane's smiling face.

"I'm trying not to poison people this week," said Sloane. "I figure it'll make it more surprising when I spike your food with ground glass." She sashayed more than stomped to the coffee machine and snagged a cup. "So what, are we having a party in here? Andy, what are you doing? You haven't had your review yet."

"Yeah, I have," said Andy. We both turned to stare at him. He shrugged. "I'm not on the spectrum, remember? HR sent a normal auditor yesterday afternoon to ask me a bunch of questions. Which were nowhere near as invasive as the ones you people seem to be getting. I mostly got 'do you worry about being killed by your coworkers,' and 'are you interested in moving up within the Bureau.' That sort of crap."

"I don't think questions about murder are normal in most agencies," I said. "You didn't tell us you'd already had your review."

"Yeah, well, I didn't want to make you self-conscious before you'd had your brain picked." Andy sipped his own coffee. "I can't do much to make this easier. That was something I could do, and so I did it."

"Thank you." On the other side of the glass, Demi was rattling off her full name and looking at Ciara like she was afraid the other woman was going to unhinge her jaw and swallow the diminutive Pied Piper whole. I grimaced. "Better start another pot. Demi's going to need it when she gets out of there."

"I think chamomile tea might be a better bet," said Andy.

I pressed the button to let us hear what was happening.

"Now, Demi, I understand that your awakening on the spectrum was triggered by Agent Winters," said Ciara, looking down at her notes. "How did that make you feel?"

"Um," said Demi. "Like I was losing my mind, or being pranked, or maybe both. For a long time, I thought this was all some sort of a really lousy joke, you know? Like a reality show on MTV, only probably not MTV because fairy tales aren't edgy enough. Only I never signed any waivers, and then I saw things that couldn't be real, and I guess I came to terms with it. I didn't have much of a choice."

"Ah, yes, choice." Ciara turned a page. "Were you given a choice about whether or not to become active?"

It felt like my heart stopped in my chest.

We had been facing a pathogenic Sleeping Beauty scenario, an airborne narrative that could have taken out the entire city, maybe even the entire state. There are variations of the story where the kingdom, not just the castle, goes to sleep. If our target had been living one of those variations, we could have lost the *country*. So I'd done what needed to be done. I'd sent Sloane to find me a Pied Piper, someone who could pipe the disease into rats and send them off to drown themselves. She'd found Demi.

Sloane was supposed to be the villain of our team, but I was the one who'd insisted Demi be handed her flute and told what to play. I was the one who'd looked at a scared teenage girl and forced her to become a fairy tale. If I had the same scenario to run over again, I would do the same thing. I would destroy Demi's life over and over, if that was what it took to save the world. But if they already thought I was favoring fairy tales over regular people, how was this going to look?

"Yes," said Demi. "Agent Marchen explained what would happen if I didn't. My family lives in this city. My grandmother lives here. I love my *abuela*. If there was something I could do to save them, I had to do it, no matter how bizarre it sounded. I didn't really believe what she was telling me, so I guess on some level, I didn't give informed consent, but she did her best to make me understand, and I'm not sorry. I've saved a lot of lives."

"You've also endangered some lives, Demi. Birdie Hubbard was able to subvert your story, and you did some damage. How does that make you feel?"

"Sad," said Demi. "Like I failed. But not like my team failed me. They didn't set me up to be taken, and as soon as they knew I was gone, they started trying to get me back. Henry made sure I didn't have to go away for rehabilitation—she got me back on the field team. My family wouldn't have understood if I'd disappeared. I owe her a lot for that. She didn't have to do it. It would have been easier to let me go."

Easier, yes, but not better, especially not since Demi was active because of me. I sipped my coffee, trying to pretend I couldn't feel Andy looking at me.

"Shit," said Sloane. "Who knew the kid was so good at telling stories?"

"Not me," I murmured. Demi wasn't lying—quite—but she was twisting the truth like a beanstalk, turning it into something she could climb.

"I see." Ciara made a note. "Do you feel like Birdie was in the right for wanting to let the narrative take over? There are more people on the ATI spectrum than most would suspect. Letting the narrative do as it likes might have some positive effects."

"With all due respect, ma'am, you can tell that to the dead." Demi frowned. "I may be a Pied Piper, but I know where most of the stories would be casting their peasants. My friends and family deserve better than a supporting role in some princess's happy ending. And if the narrative tried to turn someone I care about into a Cinderella or a Katie Woodencloak, I would find a way to kill it where it stood."

"Katie Woodencloak—that's not a name I hear often," said Ciara. "Where did you hear about that story?"

"Our archivist gives me homework. I do it, ma'am, because I want to be better at my job, and because I never want anyone to get the drop on me the way that Birdie did, ever again." Demi's expression hardened. "I'm still me when I'm the Pied Piper. I've always been a Pied Piper, I just didn't know it. But when Birdie twisted my story around to make me bad, I wasn't me anymore. I was an idea somebody else had. I didn't like feeling that way. If knowing more about stories most people don't remember can help keep me from ever needing to feel that way again, then I'm happy to learn."

"I see." Ciara made another note. "You were planning to be a concert flautist before all this started. Has that changed?"

"Since I don't want the entire audience to follow me home, yes," said Demi. "I'm going to stay with the Bureau. I'm going to learn everything I can, and someday, when the Bureau says I'm ready, I'm going to have my own field team. It turns out I like saving the world." Demi's smile was fleeting but sincere. "I think I could wind up being pretty good at it if you give me enough time with the right people."

"Do you feel that your current teammates are the 'right people'?"

Demi glanced toward the two-way mirror before focusing on Ciara and nodding firmly.

"Yes," she said. "I really do."

# # #

"We're almost out of coffee," said Sloane.

"That's probably a good thing, since I'd like to sleep again this century." I looked down into my empty cup. I couldn't help wishing I had something to put in it, like more coffee, or better yet, whiskey. This whole process was nerve-wracking, and not only because I couldn't tell whether we were giving the right answers. I had downplayed the more problematic aspects of the truth. Demi had outright bent it. Sloane . . . Sloane had been Sloane, which was both the best and the worst we could have hoped for.

Now it was down to Jeff, and I wanted nothing more than to stick my head between my knees and hyperventilate until someone told me the review process was over.

"I'm going to call for pizza," said Andy. "We can't survive on donuts alone."

"Great," I said. "It should get here right about the same time as my pink slip."

"Don't be silly, Princess," said Sloane. "You're not gonna get a pink slip. You're gonna get an all-expenses-paid trip to rehab, and find out firsthand why I've always been so resistant to going back there. Won't that be fun?"

"Not funny," I said tightly.

"I wasn't joking," said Sloane. There was genuine regret in her voice.

What we all called "rehab" was a prison slash counseling center for people afflicted by spectrum-related complications. We called it Childe. Sloane had been sent there repeatedly over the years, after her Wicked Stepsister nature attempted to rear its ugly head and make her start spiking everybody's drinks with strychnine. She had managed to avoid rehab during her most recent bad patch only because I had vouched for her, and I hadn't been fully active yet. She seemed to be under control, but how certain was that? What would happen if I was replaced by somebody who didn't understand that her constant threats and back talk were how she blew off steam and kept herself from doing something that couldn't be undone?

Sloane smiled sadly as she saw the realization march across my face. "Now she joins the party," she said. "You've been pretty focused on what happens to you if this shit goes south. What happens to the rest of us, Henry? Demi's barely trained. I'm on a short list to be shipped to Siberia. Jeff's had one flare too many."

"I'll be fine," said Andy, putting a hand over his phone. "Everybody needs a big guy who can smile for the media."

"Thanks Andy," I said.

"Anytime," he replied, and went back to ordering pizza.

"We're the best field team this office has had in a hundred years. We close more cases and avert more stories than anybody, because we're *close* to those stories," said Sloane. "That also makes us dangerous. The records will bear that out."

"How would you know that we're the best field team in a hundred years?" I asked.

Sloane smiled. Technically. She showed me all her teeth, at least. "Because I was on the last best field team."

"Um, wow." The voice was Demi's. We all turned to see her standing in the doorway. "I didn't think you'd be here."

"We watched your interview," I said. "You did good. And we saved you some coffee."

"Thank God." Demi made a direct line for the pot. "You really think I did good?"

"I really do."

"Did you notice that the lady from HR has blue hair?" Demi waved her hand at the level of her hairline, just to make sure I understood what she was saying. "It was weird."

"She's a Bluebeard's Wife," I said.

Sloane jerked. "No shit?"

"No shit."

"I *knew* I got narrative off of her." Sloane shook her head. "I didn't want to dig too deep. She could've been a princess, and then I would've had to spend too much energy on not strangling her."

"On behalf of the ATI Management Bureau, we appreciate your restraint," I said.

Demi was frowning. "I thought Bluebeard always murdered his wife."

"Yes, but there can be a long window between activation and spousal homicide," I said. "Dr. Bloomfield understands the risks, and she seems to have found a good balance. I'm not going to criticize her life choices."

"Not until after she's out of our hair, anyway," added Sloane.

We arrayed ourselves around the glass and waited. Seconds ticked by; Ciara rearranged her notes. The door to the interview room opened, and Jeff stepped inside, adjusting his glasses with one hand, the way he always did when he was nervous. It seemed suddenly difficult to breathe.

The main thrust of this review might have been determining whether I was still competent to stand as leader of a field team, but I wasn't the only one in danger. Sloane and Jeff risked rehab for their recent narrative flares. Demi risked rehab, and worse, imprisonment: she *had* gone over to the dark side of the story, after all, even if we'd been able to lure her back. There were so many possible bad endings to this tale, and it was all riding on Jeff, who looked nervous enough to throw up on the table as he sat.

Andy leaned over without prompting and pressed the button to let us hear what was going on in the other room. I didn't know whether to thank him or curse his name.

"—Bloomfield," Ciara was saying, introducing herself one last time. "I'm going to be conducting your review today. It's a pleasure to meet you. I know your narrative can manifest as a sort of nervous disorder, so I just wanted to reassure you that you are not in any trouble at all: this is a fact-finding visit."

"Jeffrey Davis," said Jeff, offering his hand across the table. "And bullshit, ma'am, if you don't mind my being so forward."

Ciara blinked. "I beg your pardon?"

"This isn't a fact-finding visit. The fact-finding visit happened weeks ago. It happened in the Archives, rather than in the bullpen, so I suppose I can understand why you think the field teams wouldn't have noticed, but you've accessed all our records." Jeff sounded perfectly calm, even a little bored, like he was reading from a book of essay questions. "You know when I went active, and when Sloane asked for help. You know when and why and how Henry manifested her narrative. You have the facts. You're here to get context on them, and to make yourself feel better about whatever it is that you've already pretty much decided."

"I see." Ciara made a note. "It's interesting that you'd mention the Archives. I've heard a great deal about your accomplishments there. Is there a particular reason you haven't accepted a position there? I know the archivists would be thrilled to have you with them full-time, rather than sharing you with a field team."

"I enjoy working with the field team," said Jeff. "It's an interesting challenge. It keeps me from getting bored. I don't know if you have to deal with boredom in Human Resources, but there's only so much filing I can do before I start feeling the urge to do something else with my hands."

"Is that an oblique reference to making shoes?"

Jeff shook his head. "No. There's nothing oblique about it. Being on the field team offers me constant challenges. It keeps me from sinking into my own head. I'm aware of the danger that my story represents. Since I'd rather not let it win, I manage myself through the best means I have available to me. That includes field work."

"Does your relationship with Agent Marchen influence your desire to stay in the field?"

"My relationship with Agent Henrietta Marchen is the only reason I would consider leaving the field." Jeff looked at her coolly. "If you say to me, right here, right now, that we can't both be out there, I will cede my position to her. She's more important to this work than I am."

"Because she's a princess?" asked Ciara, leaning forward, like a hawk getting ready to swoop in for the kill.

Jeff's expression turned disgusted. "Because she's a damn fine field agent," he said. "What else is required?"

# # #

Jeff appeared in the doorway of the observation room and blinked, taking in the edifying sight of the rest of us waiting for him. Sloane slid off the counter where she'd been sitting, and carried him a mug of tea without saying a word. Jeff blinked again, looking from her to the liquid, before he appeared to decide that the threat of poisoning was less important than his need for tea. He took a long drink.

"Well?" asked Demi.

"Well, what?" He lowered the mug. "I'm assuming you sat in here through my interview?" We all nodded. "Then you know as much as I do. She took notes. She asked questions. She didn't quite imply that I am completely ruled by my genitals, but she certainly edged around the subject."

"If I'd known Henry was such a great lay, I would've seduced her years ago," said Sloane.

"Hey!" I yelped. She smirked, and showed me her middle finger.

"You really do function well as a team." We turned to the doorway, where Ciara was standing, her notepad held against her chest. She smiled as we stared at her. "It seems like you shouldn't. Four disparate narratives and one man who's never been touched by the narrative at all? You should be at best a mess, and at worst completely dysfunctional. But you work. Why is that, do you think?"

"The whole 'ragtag bunch of misfits' trope came out of fairy tales a long time before it came out of movies," said Sloane. "Maybe we're something older and stronger than you know."

"Maybe so," said Ciara. She looked to each of us in turn. "If any of you want out, if any of you want a transfer, tell me right now. No one will think you're being disloyal. No black marks will go into your file. But if this team is not what you want, you need to say so."

None of us said anything.

"Very well. It was . . . pleasant, meeting all of you. You've managed to build something surprisingly coherent out of a bunch of pieces that shouldn't fit together, and I respect that. My recommendation will take everything you've told me today into account."

"Wait." I stepped forward. "Am I suspended?"

"Suspended? Why, Agent Marchen." She smiled. "You have work to do. I don't open doors that are better left closed. That sort of thing gets a girl in trouble. Good luck out there."

She turned, and walked away, leaving my team—shaken but intact—staring after her.

"Well, boss?" said Andy, once Ciara was out of sight. "Now what?"

"Now?" I turned and smiled at him. At all of them. "Now we get back to work."

Broken Glass

Memetic incursion in progress: tale type 315 ("The Treacherous Sister")
Status: ACTIVE

It was never quiet in Childe Prison.

Night and day, screams and laughter echoed from the walls. The more dangerous prisoners were kept sedated as much as possible, but they were surprisingly resilient and had a way of shaking off their restraints as soon as the guards weren't looking. The prison, built in an old sanitarium originally intended to house victims of tuberculosis, followed a ring system. The deeper you went, the farther you were from the sun, and the more dangerous the stories around you became.

There were Sleeping Beauties on an inner ring, going slowly out of their minds from the drugs that kept them from sleeping. There were men and women who had eaten of the flesh of the White Snake, clawing at their ears as the rats in the walls told them terrible lies. There were Pied Pipers and Rumplestiltskins and Thumbelinas and Clever Jacks, all of them weeping in their boxes. But they were not the innermost ring: no. They were the heroes and heroines of the stories that had shaped them, and while they might have been dangerous enough to warrant locking away in this terrible place, they were nowhere so terrible as their villains.

Evil Queens. Wicked Kings. Robber Bridegrooms and False Princes and Sea Witches and Untrue Loves. All the darkest faces of the fairy tales were there, locked away where no one could reach them, sealed behind iron bars and strong stone walls. The guards were on the spectrum but fully averted, narratively dead. Anything else was too much of a risk.

On the edge of the inner circle, in a cell without windows, a pale-skinned girl with a mass of frizzy, coppery hair lay on the floor, her cheek pressed to the stone. She was whispering, a low, constant stream of nonsense syllables that had attracted some attention from the guards during her first days in the prison. They had checked the behavior against her tale type—315, The Treacherous Sister—and against her records, which said that she'd been apprehended while trying to manifest a Cinderella scenario.

"She's out of her mind, but she's not doing anything wrong," had been the verdict of the warden, a big, burly man who had almost been cast as the leading role in a manifestation of Pinocchio when he was a boy. Blame Disney for that one: the story was a recent invention, as narratives went, but it was close enough to parts of the ATI that the narrative had been able to latch on to it and start turning flesh to wood. He still walked with a limp. "Leave her alone as long as she's not hurting anyone."

Elise had been muttering since then, muttering for months, reminding the walls what her story was supposed to be. Still, her eyes widened in surprise when the mouse skittered out of its hole, a brass key clutched in its jaws. She held out her hand. The mouse dropped the key into her palm before sitting back on its haunches and beginning to groom its whiskers.

Elise sat up. Elise looked at the key.

Slowly, Elise smiled.

# # #

We'd been on cleanup duty for most of the morning, picking up the pieces of a fairy-tale pyramid scheme, better known as a twenty-thirty-five—a House That Jack Built. Each element had chained onto the last until it formed an inevitable tower of ridiculous coincidences and unsustainable expense. Then it had started to crumble and had caught the attention of dispatch. Since my team was currently low man on the totem pole, on account of having barely survived our HR review, we were the ones called to corral the cow with the crooked horn, catch the horse and the hound, and recover the hammer our eponymous Jack had used to build his house in the first place. Once we had them all locked safely away, we'd be able to take care of any remaining narrative disturbance.

Sloane had managed to locate the cat that chased the rat, and was sitting on the back bumper of our van, petting the feline and making little cooing noises. It was weird as hell, and I was considering going over to ask her what she thought she was doing when Jeff walked up with a mopey-looking teenage girl.

"This is Agent Marchen," he said. "Tell her what you told me."

"Um," she said. "Jack? Like, the guy who built us this clubhouse? He went to my high school up until last year. He's pretty cool. He didn't do anything wrong."

"He didn't file proper building permits with the city," I said, giving Jeff a sidelong look.

'Wait for it,' mouthed Jeff.

"But he did," said the girl. My attention snapped back to her. "This lady, she showed up with a toolbox and a bunch of papers. She said her husband had filed everything before he died, and she just wanted to see his final project completed. Jack didn't do anything wrong. He had all the papers, everything. If you look in what used to be the living room, you'll find them."

"Did this woman have a name?" I asked.

The girl shook her head. "No. She was short though, if that helps. Way in need of a better hairdresser. She looked like she had a perm that melted."

"What color?"

"What? Uh, white lady. I think that's sort of, you know, racist? As a question?"

I forced a smile. The girl took a half step backward. Lips as red as blood and skin as white as snow do not make a friendly combination when viewed in the real world. "No, I didn't mean 'what color was her skin,' I meant 'what color was her hair?' That melted perm you were talking about, what did it look like?"

"Oh! Uh, it was blonde. She was blonde. I don't know what her eyes looked like, she was wearing really thick glasses."

There was only one person I knew who fit that description, and she was supposed to be locked up in Childe for the rest of her life. Trying not to sound as disturbed as I felt, I asked, "How long ago was this?"

"Like six months," said the girl.

"Excellent. Thank you for your help." So Birdie Hubbard had given this Jack his hammer and his building plans before she'd challenged the entire Bureau. The House must have been part of her attempt to overwhelm us with more stories than we could handle—a plan that had nearly worked and had left plenty of time bombs scattered around the city, waiting for the right set of circumstances to set them off.

"Goddammit, Birdie," I muttered, pinching the bridge of my nose. "If you weren't already in prison, I'd wring your neck and put you there myself."

"Henry?"

The voice was male, deep, and worried. I lowered my hand and turned. Andy was looming over me.

"What is it?" I asked. Out of my entire team, Andy was the only one not on the ATI spectrum. That meant he was less sensitive to the ripples and eddies in a site like this one. That was good. He might be slower to recognize certain dangers than the rest of us, but he was also immune to the little narrative needles that made us twitch out of our skins. If Andy looked this upset, something was genuinely wrong.

"Dispatch just called," he said. "They're sending Piotr and his team to this site to finish cleanup. We have a new assignment."

"What's that?" I asked.

Andy's anxious look didn't change. "There's been a breakout at Childe. Six prisoners are missing, including Elise Walton. Our self-made Cinderella."

"Oh, fuck," I breathed. Then I whirled, shouting as I marched toward the van, "Pull back, we're leaving!"

Sloane raised her head and blinked as the cat leapt out of her lap and dashed off to find a new rat. Demi and Jeff looked up from their own tasks. I kept walking. They'd move when they realized I was serious, or I'd leave them here. I didn't see any other choice.

"The fuck?" demanded Sloane, when I was close enough.

"Elise got out." It wasn't the gentlest way to tell her. There wasn't any way to tell her that would actually be *kind*. Elise and Sloane shared a story. No amount of trying to be kind was going to change that, and so there was no point.

Sloane jerked to her feet, cupped her hands around her mouth, and shouted, "We're leaving! Get in the fucking van or get out of the fucking way!" Dropping her hands, she stomped for the passenger-side door. I ran after her. If I didn't move fast enough, she'd hot-wire the van and leave without me. I couldn't blame her. I would have done the same if it had been someone who shared my story.

I started the engine as the side door slammed open and the rest of my team tumbled inside. "Andy, fill them in," I said, turning the flashers on. We weren't police in the traditional sense, but we were close enough to get away with breaking a few traffic laws when we had to.

I was planning to break them all.

"Hold tight," I said, and slammed my foot down on the gas.

Our van had been outfitted by the finest mechanics the ATI Management Bureau had to offer, and since some of them could bend metal with their bare hands, that *meant* something. If it hadn't been for the sirens giving people time to move out of our way, we would have been in multiple crashes before we reached the turnoff for the prison.

There's only one prison in North America rated for containing fairy tales. Maybe that sounds silly, but the wards alone took up half the attention of the Archives, and opening another would have required us to pull staff from elsewhere in the world. Having one prison for a continent was problematic enough before you started trying to transport prisoners. Sleeping Beauties couldn't be safely loaded onto airplanes; if the pilot passed out at the controls, a lot of innocent people would die. Bluebeards had a tendency to manifest on ships and trains, and we'd once had a full-on Big Candy Mountain incursion when trying to transport a Robber Bridegroom. The only answer was to set up a transit network that skipped over those risks.

When I said I was planning to break *all* the laws that governed motorized vehicles, I meant it. That included the laws of physics.

We came tearing around a bend in the road, at a spot the locals had helpfully started calling "Dead Man's Curve" some twenty years before. The needle was hovering at ninety-five, which was as fast as we could go without risking me losing control. The guardrail loomed up ahead of us, so close that I almost hauled on the wheel and followed the road. But that would have missed the point of this little exercise, wouldn't it? I slammed my foot down instead, and we broke through the rail and sailed off into the abyss, already falling.

# # #

Trips to Childe always did a number on our shocks. The van hit the prison parking lot like a load of bricks, all excess speed swallowed as payment for the transport. I jerked against my seatbelt. Demi swore. Sloane didn't say anything. She just kicked her door open and ran, heading for the prison. I unbuckled my belt and checked that my badge was clipped in place before I opened my own door and slid out—

—and staggered, almost falling over as a wave of peace, contentment, and absolute calm tried to hammer its way into my forebrain. My badge blocked some of the impact, but the rest was bad enough to make me want to vomit. I caught myself against the side of the van instead. My story, which had been relatively quiescent recently, reared at the back of my mind, stretching tendrils out like it was going to manifest in self-defense.

"Henry?" It was Jeff's voice. I realized I could feel his hands supporting me. That was when I realized something more alarming: I couldn't see.

He must have realized I was in distress, because he lowered his voice as he leaned in, and said, "It's all right. You closed your eyes. I forgot that you hadn't been here since you fully activated. Take a deep breath. Remember who you are."

I'm Snow White. The words popped into my mind, so compelling that I started to open my mouth and say them aloud. I snapped it shut again, alarmed. "I'm Henrietta Marchen," I said. There was no strength in my voice. I might as well have been whispering.

"Your full name."

"I am . . . I am Agent Henrietta Marchen, ATI Management Bureau." This time, I spoke loudly enough to be heard. I stood a little straighter. "I am Agent Henrietta Marchen, ATI Management Bureau." The story stirring inside my skull backed off and backed down, curling back into the place where it slept. The pressure radiating off the prison didn't go away, exactly, but it died down to manageable levels. I opened my eyes.

"I am Agent Henrietta Marchen, ATI Management Bureau," I said, for a third time. Three was always a good number to go for in fairy tales. Then I turned to look at my team.

Jeff was holding my free arm, keeping me from collapsing. He let go when I started to move, although the look of worry on his face didn't die. Demi and Andy were behind me. Demi was pale, and she was holding her flute, fingers clenched so tight that her knuckles were white.

"Sucks, don't it?" she asked, forcing herself to smile. It looked more like the grimace of a grinning skull. "It's supposed to keep us from freaking out and killing each other when we're all locked up together like a big box of stories. All it ever did for me was scramble my brains into pudding."

"You were *here*?" I stared at her. I knew Demi had been taken into custody after Birdie Hubbard subverted her—my team had made the arrest. But I'd seen her in the interrogation room, and she'd always been available when I called with questions. I suppose I'd believed, on some vague, hopeful level, that she'd been kept somewhere in our offices until she was cleared to return to field duty. Not Childe.

Never that.

Demi nodded fractionally, her hands never leaving her flute. "Yeah," she said, lowering her voice to something that was barely above a whisper.

"I didn't know," I said. I looked over my shoulder to the prison, which loomed, cold and foreboding, like something out of a Gothic romance. *Old sanitariums have their own story,* I thought. *Maybe they chose the wrong place to build.* "I didn't know you were here, and I didn't know it was like *this* once your story was active. Sweet Grimm, I'm so sorry."

"You're one of us now," said Jeff. I looked back in time to see him pushing his glasses up, a wry smile on his face. "Maybe management will listen when you say that this is inhumane. They're letting you lead a field team, after all."

Speaking of my field team . . . "Did Sloane run straight inside?" I asked. "We need to catch up with her before she does something we're all going to regret."

"Sloane has her 'free-story' charm," said Jeff. "We need to get you yours."

"You have one already?"

Jeff nodded and pulled his key ring out of his pocket. One of the charms dangling from the overloaded steel hoop—an oversized crystal spike that I had always assumed was plastic—was glowing with a serene blue light. "They gave it to me years ago, when they approved my access to the Archive. They use the same charm sets in the two locations."

It would've been nice if someone had mentioned any of this to me: if there had been an orientation packet of some sort, handed out when my story consumed the last chances I'd been holding for a normal life. But there was no point in getting upset about it now. Not when we had a job to do. "What about Demi?"

"I have to get a visitor's pass," said Demi. "I don't think I'm eligible for a permanent charm."

"This place is creepy as all fuck: I'm not contesting that," said Andy. "I don't see what's so upsetting about it. What's it doing to you that I can't feel?"

"It wants us to be calm and docile and obedient and not riot," I said. "It's like having a bunch of *really happy* maggots shoved into my brain, and it makes me want to burn the whole thing to the fucking ground."

Andy frowned. "That's probably not the result they were looking for."

"You think?" I started storming toward the prison doors. The happy maggots writhed and bit inside my brain. I did my best to ignore them. Let them bite and squirm. I knew who I was, and no charm or personality manipulation spell was going to change that.

I was fucking pissed, that was who I was.

A guard in the standard slate-gray uniform of Childe Prison was standing outside the doors when we arrived. He was alone. That wasn't normal: they usually insisted their guards travel in groups of at least two. Then I saw how he was fidgeting, and realized there was a reason for his solo status.

"Your friend is already inside," he said, as soon as we were close enough to speak without shouting. "She was quite insistent."

"How many guards did you send with her?"

"Three."

"That's not enough." Thirty might not have been enough. "I'm Agent Henrietta Marchen. This is my field team. I'm also an active seven-oh-nine, and your prison is trying to make my brains dribble out my skull. My agent, Demi Santos, is an active two-eighty. We need whatever protections you have to offer against your compulsion charms."

"I was told you'd be accompanying Agent Winters," said the guard, casting an uneasy glance at Demi, who was still holding her flute like a lifeline. "I've been cleared to provide you with a countercharm, but Agent Santos is on the watch list. I can't let her have one."

"Yes, you can," I said. "If you want us to go in there and fish Sloane out before she starts putting people through walls, you'll give Demi her own charm. If you don't think that's an important use of our time, we'll go wait in the van. I'm sure Agent Winters can do plenty of damage without our help."

The guard stared at me. "You wouldn't dare."

I looked calmly back. "We were summoned to Childe. We came to Childe. As the leader of this field team, it's up to me to decide how my people can be of the best use. If I say we're most useful sitting in the van and listening to the radio, then that's what's going to happen. Good luck getting Sloane back under control. She doesn't listen to most people."

The guard paled. "Please wait here. I'll be right back with two countercharms."

"Thanks," I said, and smiled so he could see all of my teeth. My naturally red lips did an excellent job of making them seem very white, and very sharp.

The guard turned and fled.

"You're feeling assertive today," said Andy, giving the prison walls another unhappy look. He couldn't feel the compulsions they radiated, but he didn't have to feel them to dislike the place. All he had to do was look at it. "This because you figure it'll take HR six months to put together another review?"

"It's because I refuse to let a member of my team be treated like a second-class citizen when we're the ones who failed to protect her," I said. My voice was tight with anger. "Birdie got to Demi because we didn't think to check the downsides of the Piper story. That was *our* fault. She doesn't get punished for it forever."

"Or I do, but I have people like you to keep it from sucking as much as it could," said Demi. I looked at her. She smiled a little. "I know I'm never going to be a deputy director or anything fancy like that. Even if I'd been the first Pied Piper with an impeccable record, that would always have been one step too far. But I like my team, and I trust you to take care of me. Because you do. You always have. Even when I couldn't see it."

"Demi—"

"Here." The guard came trotting back through the prison doors, moving so fast that the only thing between him and the word "run" was the stiff way he was holding his arms, like he was afraid they'd drop off if he let them bounce too much. He had a crystal spike in each hand. The crystals were glowing. Our charms.

He stopped in front of me. "Here," he said again, and thrust the crystals toward me.

I raised an eyebrow as I plucked the crystals from his hands. "Thanks." The effect was instantaneous. The pressure that had been rolling off the prison since we arrived faded like it had never been there in the first place. The maggots stopped chewing at my brain, and suddenly I could breathe again.

Wordless, I turned and offered one of the crystals to Demi. She took it, and an expression of profound, heartbreaking relief washed across her face. We shared a look. This was what the Bureau was doing to all the stories they had in custody. Innocent people whose only crime was being afflicted with an incurable narrative were being kept under the same spells that were used to control and contain real villains. It wasn't right. It needed to change.

For the moment, however, we had other things to worry about.

"Stay together; do not follow anything, no matter how tempting, unless it's Sloane," I said. "That goes for the guards too. Some of these stories may allow for shape-shifting, illusion-casting, or creating decoys. If you are unsure of what you are looking at, find a member of the team and ask them if they see the same thing. Any questions?"

"Yeah," said Andy. "Wasn't this girl trying to manifest as a Cinderella when we locked her up in here? How the hell did she become this dangerous?"

"Really, Andy?" I looked at him flatly. "If you think the princesses aren't dangerous, you haven't been paying attention. Now let's move."

# # #

Walking through the doors of Childe Prison was like forcing my way through a soap bubble that refused to pop. Instead, it clung and clutched until I had moved past its reach. Then it let me go, with a release that was almost as shocking as walking into it had been.

"I hate this place," I muttered.

"We all do," said Jeff. He probably meant for it to be reassuring. It just made me think of all the people we'd sent here over the years, the ones who were being kept inside these walls "for their own good," while the maggots of the compulsion charm crawled across their brains and erased everything they had ever been. It was no wonder Elise had tried to escape. If anything, it was a miracle that she was the first.

"Maybe we're going about this all wrong."

Andy shot me a sidelong look. "What was that?"

"Nothing." Andy was a good guy, but he wouldn't understand. I wasn't sure I understood yet, to be honest. But maybe there was a middle ground between quashing every manifestation of the narrative before someone got hurt and torturing the people who'd been caught up in that manifestation. Maybe it was on us to find it. "Jeff, any idea what part of the prison Elise was being kept in?"

"Third ring," he said. "Past the quiet wards, and before the really *bad* levels."

"There's worse than this?" asked Andy.

"Yes," said Demi. Her voice was scarcely louder than a whisper. "They said . . . they said a good Piper could make music from anything, so they put me on the fourth ring, with the villains who need constant supervision. They tied my hands and feet, and they shot me up with Novocain so I wouldn't be able to whistle or sing. Somebody had to hand-feed me."

"You sounded normal when we called you," I said, horrified.

Demi's smile was more like a grimace. "They have this stuff they can rub on your skin that wakes it up again. I don't know what it is. No dentist I've ever gone to has used it, probably because it stings like nettles, but it cancels the Novocain right out. I talked to you because they took the numbness away, and I didn't cry because I wanted you to think I was strong enough to be worth saving."

"Oh, Demi." I'd never been a physically demonstrative person, and this wouldn't have been the place anyway: not with cells to every side of us, each holding a prisoner just like Demi had been. I still wanted to hug her. "We would have saved you anyway. You're always going to be strong enough for us."

"I hope that's true," she said—but this time her smile seemed a little more sincere, and that was good enough for me.

"This way," said Jeff. We followed him.

The prison halls were wide and had originally been covered by white linoleum. They still were, toward the center and in front of some of the doors. But the presence of this much narrative energy couldn't help but warp the world around it. Patches of linoleum had transformed into cobblestone, or hard-packed dirt, or brick. One cell had piles of straw in front of it, and shrill giggles drifted from inside. We gave it a wide berth. The door to another cell had twisted into something that would have looked more appropriate in the belly of a pirate ship, and the floor in front of it was damp wood that smelled strongly of brine. The door seemed to rock from side to side, like it was rolling on the waves, unless I looked at it directly.

"I *really* don't like it here," said Andy, who looked faintly sickened by the piratical door.

Those of us who were tied to the narrative were vulnerable to the compulsion charms and spells used to make the prison large enough and secure enough for our needs, but Andy, who had no natural or borrowed magic to protect him, had to feel like the entire world was shifting under his feet. It was rare in the modern era for the narrative to gather enough momentum to actually transform things. Here in Childe, where narratives were penned up and given no means of escape, it was happening constantly, and Andy's modern mind had no real way of coping with it.

We stepped around a corner and found ourselves facing a door made of straw. "I got this," said Demi. She pulled out her flute and blew one long, resonant note. The door crumpled inward, revealing a stretch of identical hall. Demi lowered her flute and smiled. "I huffed and I puffed," she said, sounding pleased with herself.

"Good job," I said. We walked on.

The next door we encountered was made of sticks. "Mine," said Jeff, who leaned forward and began pulling sticks out of the door, slowly at first, then with increasing speed, until his hands were a blur of motion. When he was done, the door was gone, and he had sorted all the sticks into tidy piles, divided by size.

I blinked. "What?"

"Sorting the materials for the shoes is a part of my job," said Jeff. He shook his hands, looking unhappily at the grime blanketing his fingers. "You'd think they could wash the things before they used them as wards."

"Uh, forgive me for sounding like I don't understand that our job is about impossible crap, but what good are doors that come apart when you poke them?" asked Andy, as we resumed walking. "Straw and sticks—that's for pigs in nursery rhymes, not for building a prison that you actually want to hold prisoners."

"If we didn't have the countercharms, the doors would represent a compulsion to obey the story," said Jeff. "For someone like Demi, who has Big Bad Wolf tendencies but no natural ability to huff and puff and blow someone's house down, she would stand there blowing on the door until she collapsed from lack of air. For someone like me, who has Little Pig tendencies, I would wind up braiding and weaving and improving the door to make it stand up better to attackers. It's only the charms that allow us to cling to our actual narratives, instead of falling into a narrative that's just close enough."

"Is everyone a wolf or a pig?" asked Andy.

"Not everyone," I said, as we turned another corner and found ourselves facing a door made of thorns. I sighed. "Okay, isn't this supposed to be made of bricks? I was looking forward to getting my hands on a sledgehammer."

"Some pigs, some wolves, some princesses," said Jeff, almost apologetically.

"I don't even want to know how Sloane got past all three, although one assumes the guards have keys." I stepped forward and put my hands on my hips, giving the door of thorns a withering look—no pun intended. "Fuck off."

The door fucked off, the thorns unknotting and letting go of one another before they retracted into the walls, where they vanished without a trace. I looked back to my team. Andy and Jeff were staring at me. Demi was covering her mouth with one hand, but not quite managing to hide her smile.

"Come on," I said. "Sloane may have murdered a bunch of people by now, and I don't want to deal with the paperwork."

The feeling of compulsive calm closed around us again as we walked, stronger than before. I slipped my hand into my pocket and clutched the crystal spire so hard I could feel it bite into my skin. That made the pressure a little easier to bear. At least there weren't any maggots in my brain. Not yet, anyway. There was no telling what the prison was going to throw at us next.

The sound of shouting drifted down the hall. One of the voices—the loudest, angriest voice—was Sloane's. The others were unfamiliar, and I didn't know if they were fighting with her, or if she was the reason they were making so much noise.

"Move," I snapped, and broke into a run. My team ran with me.

We came around the final corner to find Sloane, now wearing a crystal-beaded ball gown and elbow-length gloves, slamming the face of a man in full livery against the prison wall. He was struggling, trying to grab hold of her as she battered him. He was also not completely human: large mouse ears topped his head, and a pink tail hung from the seat of his pants. Three more of the mouse-men were down, one with a hole in the middle of his chest that could probably be ascribed to the guard who was backed against the opposing wall, eyes wide and service weapon trembling in his hands. Several of the cell doors were open, making it impossible to tell whether we were dealing with more than one escapee.

"Mouse footmen," I said, voice somewhere between a whisper and a sigh. Cinderella's story wasn't mine, wasn't even a close cousin, but I knew the trappings, and a corner of my treacherous princess heart yearned for them every night when I closed my eyes. "Fuck. Watch out for pumpkins."

"What?" said Andy.

"Got it," said Jeff.

"I don't know what to do," said Demi. She looked from the fight to me, eyes wide. "What do I do?"

For once, I had an easy answer. "The narrative has them, and it's turning them into things it can use, but it didn't count on you, did it?" I leaned closer, like that could keep the looming story from guessing what was about to happen, and whispered, "They're still rodents."

Demi lit up like happy ever after. "Cover your ears," she said, and pulled out her flute.

"Sloane!" I shouted, clapping my hands over my ears as instructed. "Get some quiet!"

Sloane glanced my way, startled. Then she nodded and slammed her mouse-man against the wall harder than ever, so hard that he stopped fighting back and collapsed at her feet when she released his collar. She put the heels of her hands over her ears and took a step backward, skirts swishing.

It wasn't just her, I realized. All three guards were now wearing fancier versions of their uniforms, with gold brocade around the shoulders and cuffs, and diamond buttons in place of their previous brass. Somehow, whatever route Elise had used to escape, she had left her stolen story behind—and it was on the attack.

And I'd walked straight into it. The realization was almost sickening. This was a princess story, and like it or not, I was a princess. If Demi couldn't pipe it away, we might have a problem.

The first note of Demi's rat-charming song trilled through the air, high and pure and only slightly muffled by my hands. That little bit of protection was enough: I didn't feel any urge to start dancing. The mouse-men weren't so lucky. All the ones who weren't dead or unconscious started to waltz, first toward Demi, and then toward the door to an open cell. She took a step forward, upping the tempo, and their dance turned frantic, the mouse-men all but falling over one another in their hurry to get into the cell. More of them kept appearing, either from farther down the hall or out of the other open cells. She was gathering them all together. That was good.

A hand grabbed my arm. I looked back to see Jeff, who had uncovered one ear, holding me. I scowled at him. He let go.

"Your jacket!" he shouted.

I looked down.

I always wear black and white suits. Not because I have a *Men in Black* obsession, although tapping into the modern narrative of the faceless, interchangeable government agents had come in handy more than once. I do it because as a storybook princess, if I give the narrative anything to seize on, color-wise, it can get me into trouble. There are lots of stories about girls in green, or pretty red gowns that catch fire when the light hits them just right. Black and white are only princess colors when they're talking about skin and hair.

Apparently, when the narrative gets rolling strongly enough, color ceases to matter. The buttons on my blazer had been replaced by diamonds, and silver brocade was starting to creep up from the bottom, giving me the distinct appearance of having been frosted.

"Shit," I swore, and didn't take my hands off my ears.

The mouse-men had stopped appearing from the rooms around us. Demi kept playing as she advanced on the open cell door. With a final loud trill she sent the mouse-men crashing to the rear of the cell, and slammed the door, locking them inside. One of the guards hurried to lock the door, and she stopped playing, lowering her flute.

A fine sheen of sweat stood out on her forehead, and there was a light in her eyes that I didn't see very often, bright and wild and slightly disconnected from everything around her. She looked like a marathon runner at the end of a race, half-drunk on adrenaline and not quite processing her surroundings yet. "Did I get them all?"

"Yeah," said Sloane. "Didn't get the frog coachman, though. He hopped off that way." She hooked a thumb down the hall. "Not sure I give a fuck, as long as he doesn't come back with a bazooka or something."

"Nice dress," said Andy.

"Screw you," said Sloane. "At least the story didn't get my boots. These things are expensive."

Squinting at Sloane's ball gown, I could see the outlines of her original clothes. It wasn't a black dress, probably because the graphic on her T-shirt had included blue and purple, and had given the story something to work with. She looked like something out of a Broadway revival of *Cinderella*, all ruffles and lace and unlikely quantities of rhinestones—although given the strength of the narrative in question, they might just be diamonds. More than one fairy-tale princess had been able to fund her escape after she started spitting rubies or turning everything she touched into gold.

"Ever seen a three-fifteen go infectious like this?" I demanded. The guards, who had followed Sloane into the prison before I was even out of the car, turned to look at me. I flashed my badge at them. "Agent Henrietta Marchen, ATI Management Bureau. I'm Agent Winters's superior officer. Somebody want to answer my question?"

"We had her filed as a three-fifteen—that's why she was on the outside of the ring—but the narrative she's manifesting is a five-ten-a," said one of the guards. "That's why we didn't realize what was happening until someone saw a mouse run into her cell."

"Don't you have someone monitoring the mice in here?" I asked. The question sounded as bad outside my head as it had sounded inside. There was still a reason for it. So many stories depend on the movement of rats, mice, and other vermin that it's a miracle the ATI Management Bureau decided to become a government agency rather than an extermination firm. Kill all the rats and half a dozen stories will have to shift away, just because they won't have anything to latch on to.

"We had a resident five-four-five-b up until recently," said one of the guards. "She's been reassigned to a field team on the East Coast. They lost their active in an ogre incident, and started pulling from the prison staff."

"I see." A five-four-five-b was a Puss in Boots: ideal for keeping track of the vermin inside of the prison. But field teams needed their actives as much as the prison did—maybe even more. Actives were better equipped to spot a story as it was getting started, and before it could do any serious damage. Most of the time, HR tried to limit field teams to one, maybe two actives, but all had at least one.

My team had four, or maybe three and a half, depending on how you wanted to look at Sloane. Suddenly, I found myself worrying about what was going to happen when someone in HR decided that we'd be more valuable to the Bureau if we were all assisting different teams.

That was a concern for another day. "Okay, we have ball gowns and formal jackets growing like kudzu, we have mouse-men and a frog person who we're not worrying about right now; what else are we looking at?"

"Here," said one of the guards, and beckoned for me to follow him over to an open cell door. I did, poking my head through to see what he was trying to show me. Then I grimaced.

"All right, that's not good," I said.

Elise's cell—because only it could have been ground zero for this particular narrative outbreak; nothing else explained the density of changes inside—had been transformed into a virtual pumpkin patch. Vines snaked up the walls, clinging to the stone so tightly that they had started to break it down in places. Heavy orange, yellow, and necrotic-green gourds studded the floor, which had become heavy loam. One wall was missing, revealing a hole that ran through several rings of the prison to the distant outdoors.

In case that wasn't decisive enough, there was a single glass slipper in the middle of the room. It wasn't the classical "dancing shoe": it was a plain slip-on, with lines and ripples that showed its origin as a standard-issue canvas sneaker. No laces, of course, those were considered a suicide risk. Just impossible glass.

"She must have left this on purpose," said the guard, stepping into the room and reaching for the shoe. "Shoes like this don't fall off your feet. They're designed to be tight enough—"

The narrative tensed around me. I realized what was about to happen a split second too late. "Don't touch that!" I shouted, lunging forward to grab his arm.

Sloane grabbed mine instead, pulling me up short a few inches shy of the guard, who had just touched the glass slipper. He started screaming instantly. He stopped almost as quickly, when the transformation that had started with his fingertips finished racing up his body, leaving a solid glass statue in its place.

"Get back, get back, *get back*!" she howled, dragging me out of the cell and slamming the door. The sound of the guard's frozen body exploding echoed down the hall. I peeked cautiously up at the small viewport set in the cell door. Glass shards protruded from everything inside, and from the nearest walls of the hall on the other side of the hole.

"Nobody touches those," snapped Sloane. "Cinderella's mother was a cedar tree in a lot of variations, so cedar won't turn to glass; get some cedar tongs from Munitions and use them to collect the shards. If you touch them, you're fucked. So don't touch them."

The two surviving guards stared at her, clearly too shocked to fully understand what had just happened. The woman stepped forward and asked, "Is Carl . . . ?"

"He's dead," snapped Sloane. "Be glad. If he was still alive, he'd be a living mass of contagious glass shards, and that sort of thing never does anything good for anybody."

"I have never heard of a Cinderella story doing this," said Jeff.

Sloane looked at him tiredly. "That's because the modern Archives are all about a world where she," she pointed at me, "is the living embodiment of the most popular fairy tale in North America. Go back a century. Go back two. People used to be *way* more into Cinderella, because everybody wanted to believe that if they lived as the perfect Puritan princess, one day they'd get carried off to a castle. The Bureau was smaller then. More people lived in isolation, in little houses on the edge of the woods. Stories weaponized themselves a lot more frequently in those days, and five-ten-a was the most dangerous of a bad lot. Snow Whites will freeze your heart. Cinderellas will make sure you never make a mess again."

"So how do we stop her?" asked Demi.

Sloane fixed her with a weary look. "We find her. We shoot her. We bury her on unhallowed ground, and we never speak her name again, ever, for as long as we live."

The rest of us stared silently at Sloane, briefly unified in our shock. Sloane shook her head.

"Come on," she said. "If there's any chance she's still in this prison, we need to find her."

# # #

The prison's ring system worked against us as we tried to backtrack along Elise's path. We couldn't go straight through her cell due to the glass shards everywhere, but getting to the other side necessitated going back through the doors of thorns and sticks, making a hard left, and going through a door of bones. The guards had keys that would dispel any of the doors with a touch—convenient. They still slowed us down. Sloane was swearing steadily by the time we got to the second ring.

Her swearing increased in volume, speed, and variety when she saw the glass vines that had grown across the hallway into the next cell, making the area effectively impassable. "Fuck my life," she said, when the first flush of anger had passed. "They're still growing."

"How is that possible?" demanded a guard. "Carl exploded, and all he did was touch that damn shoe."

"He wasn't part of the story." Sloane bent to study a vine, careful not to touch it. "Until we get this out of here, we're not going to be able to follow her."

"I have an idea," said Jeff. We all turned to look at him. He had his phone out, and there was a piece of sheet music visible on the screen. "Demi, remember when we were looking at songs that could move liquid?"

"Yes," she said, sounding like she didn't much like where this was going. I couldn't blame her.

"You were managing it by the time we had to stop to work on something else," Jeff continued.

"I was managing to move a spill back into a glass of water," said Demi. "That's not earthshaking."

"It's better than we've got. Glass is an amorphous solid, not a liquid, but for a long, long time, people *thought* glass was a liquid. The narrative says glass is a liquid." Jeff's eyes sparkled. He was getting excited. "All you need to do is tell the glass that it's a liquid, and pipe it all back into Elise's cell."

"I don't think I can—"

"You can," I said, cutting off Demi's protests. "If Jeff says you can, and you have your flute, you can do it. Now come on. Clear this path before she gets away for good." Although that had almost certainly already happened. We'd been called when they realized she was gone: between the clearance issues, the mouse-men, and the exploding glass, Elise was probably nothing but a memory by now. I knew that. I also knew that if we could clean up the cursed glass, we had to do it. Otherwise, the whole prison could be contaminated, and we could lose a lot more than just one twisted Cinderella.

"Glass is a slow liquid, if it's a liquid at all," said Jeff, positioning his phone in front of Demi. "Play at half tempo, and you should be able to find a connection."

"Do we need to cover our ears?" asked Sloane.

"Not this time," said Jeff. "She's not playing for the living; she's playing for the inanimate. It's a different tune."

Demi, who still looked uncertain, pulled out her flute as she squinted at Jeff's phone. Then she nodded once, sharply, and began to play.

The song was sweet, haunting, and somehow elusive: I enjoyed it as I heard it, but as each note followed the next, the earlier parts of the piece seemed to vanish from my mind, wiped away by the progression. Demi kept her eyes on the phone screen for maybe eight bars. Then she closed them, playing from somewhere deep inside herself. It was beautiful. It was heartbreaking.

It was working.

Slowly—so slowly that if I looked directly at them, they didn't seem to be moving at all, even as I could see them shift and twist out of the corner of my eye—the glass vines began to turn back on themselves, retracting toward Elise's cell. The glass fragments embedded in the walls turned into fluid, rolling drops, moving like water until they came into contact with a larger drop or with a vine. Then they would merge together, continuing their motion all the while.

Sloane also closed her eyes. But she didn't look transported: she looked pained, like something about the song hurt her. She stayed where she was, not shifting positions at all as the glass flowed around her. The rest of us dodged the moving glass, avoiding any contact with our clothes or skin. Sloane just trusted that it wouldn't touch her, and it didn't. I wasn't sure whether that showed serenity or madness. I wasn't going to ask.

Demi played and the glass moved, and the world held its breath. Then, with one final descending trill, she stopped and lowered her flute, opening her eyes as she turned to look around the glass-free hall. Slowly, she blinked.

"It worked," said Demi.

"You're *terrifying*," breathed one of the guards.

Sloane's eyes snapped open. She turned on the speaker, a manic, almost feral smile on her face, and said, "We all are. Demi's just the one you've figured out that you need to be afraid of." Then she turned and stalked through the hole in the wall, following Elise's now glassless passage to the outside. The rest of us followed her.

There were no bodies in the halls we passed. There was no way to know for sure whether that was because no one had been killed, or whether it was because all of Elise's victims had been turned to glass. I glanced to one of the surviving guards. He shook his head.

"I can't raise half my men on the radio," he said. "Maybe they're alive and hiding, or maybe they exploded like Carl. It'll be hours before we know for sure." He looked like he'd been beaten, and I knew what he was expecting to find.

The final hole opened onto the grounds. Sloane was already there, stooping to examine the ground, looking awkward and regal at the same time in her transformed, jewel-encrusted ball gown. She looked around at the sound of our footsteps.

"Carriage tracks," she said. "Elise came through here. She found a coach waiting for her. It went that way." She straightened and pointed at the stone wall on the other side of the prison grounds. There were no breaks in the wall, no visible holes or other ways a carriage could have disappeared. The story the tracks told and the story the wall told were incompatible. That didn't mean either one of them wasn't true.

Sloane straightened and took off running without waiting for any of us to comment on what she'd found. She followed the tracks right to the wall, and we followed her, trying to stay close enough to help if she needed us. When I say "we," I mean my team: the guards who had accompanied us outside hung back, apparently feeling that whatever was going on was outside of their pay grade.

I felt bad for them, I really did. Most of their days were probably calm and predictable and didn't include exploding into glass shards. At the same time, I couldn't really feel *sorry* for them. They had chosen to take jobs at the only prison in North America built to contain living stories. What had they been expecting?

Sloane was beating her fists against the wall when we caught up with her. Andy looked at me. I nodded, and he stepped forward, closing his hands around hers when she pulled back to swing again. She looked at him, eyes wide and startled and surprisingly young in her pale, pale face.

"Let me go," she said, voice full of unspoken threats.

"Will you keep hitting the wall if I let you go?" he asked. "Because we sort of need you to keep having hands. It's important to the team that you not break them into little bits."

"She came through here," said Sloane—but she wasn't trying to pull away. That was reassuring. "She got into her carriage, and she came through here. Can't you smell the sap and pumpkin guts in the air? This is how she got away."

"It's a solid wall now, Sloane," said Andy.

Unsurprisingly, it was Jeff who realized what Sloane was trying to say first. "Dear Grimm," he breathed. "Doors, doors—who makes doors? Alice, of course, but that's such a recent story, it shouldn't have this sort of power yet. Or there's the Twelve Dancing Princesses. If one of them had come here to meet her . . ."

"They could have opened her a door straight through to the other side," I said. "Sloane. She's gone. We've lost her."

Sloane twisted to look at me, her hands still engulfed by Andy's. She wasn't struggling. That was something, anyway. "Don't you understand what this means?"

"Try me," I said.

"She changed her story. She went from one thing to another, and she did it so completely that her new story fought for her—you can let me go, Andy; I'm not going to run." Sloane tugged gently on her hands. Andy released them, and she settled back onto the flats of her feet, looking heartbroken. "She *changed* her *story*."

I finally caught her meaning. Sloane had been struggling with her narrative—sometimes violent, always angry—for longer than anyone knew. Elise had started out struggling, and then began to twist the peo-ple around her until they fit a world where she was Cinderella, not the wicked sister: where she was the princess. She had broken every rule, crossed every line . . . and her reward had been a new story, one where she had something Sloane would never have: the potential to live hap-pily ever after.

Sloane looked at me, and I could tell from her expression that she knew I understood. I shook my head, not saying anything, and we stood together as a team, each one of us waiting for someone else to figure out what we were supposed to do next. We'd never lost a prisoner on my watch before: Heads were going to roll over this one. Maybe figuratively, maybe literally.

Either way, I just needed to make sure they weren't ours.

Brotherly Love

Memetic incursion in progress: estimated tale type 327 ("Hansel and Gretel")
Status: ACTIVE

Gerry March, high school English teacher and ordinary guy, was aware that he was lucky to have a job, given that he'd abandoned his classroom after seeing a bunch of oddly behaving deer on campus. He had always made it a policy to refuse gifts from the ATI Management Bureau since the organization was rooted firmly in the fairy tales it purported to prevent, and taking gifts from people in fairy tales was always a bad idea. After some soul searching and some contemplation of his bank account, he'd agreed to make an exception when his sister, Henrietta Marchen, had offered to call the school and claim their mother had died.

It wasn't technically a lie: They *did* start their lives with a mother, and she *did* die. It was just that she'd done it shortly after they were born, and they'd never really mourned her.

Still. Gerry had been a responsible, reliable employee for years before "the incident," and having his sobbing sister on the phone begging for him to be given a second chance had convinced the administration that nothing like this would ever happen again. It had been incredibly kind of her, and as he looked out his classroom window at the menacing forest inexplicably looming beyond the football field, he had to wonder if it had all been for nothing.

His sophomore Creative Writing class was as silent as a room full of teenagers could be, only whispering and shuffling a little as they tried to complete their papers. This wasn't one of the "easy A" electives, and he usually got the kids who were serious about the idea of being better writers. Half of them just wanted to get better so they could improve their *Pacific Rim* hurt/comfort fanfic, but there was nothing wrong with that. Besides, one of them had let slip that a good portion of the class was posting on Archive of Our Own, and he'd spent a few nights with a beer in his hand, learning more about his students. He hadn't read the NC-17 pieces—there were professional limits—and yet he felt he respected them more as writers because he'd seen what they were capable of when they weren't being graded.

"Suzie, can you come over here please?" he asked.

One of his students—a gawky, bespectacled girl who was going to be gorgeous when she finished her awkward stage, and who wrote extremely involved coffee-shop AUs about everything she came into contact with—looked up from her paper. "Sure, Mr. March," she said, and rose, walking over to join him at the window. A few of the other students looked up as well, curious about what was going on.

Gerry pushed the window a little further open. "What do you smell?" he asked.

Suzie gave him a sidelong look and leaned forward. Then she blinked. "Gingerbread."

Gerry March, who had spent the better part of his life running away from fairy tales, and hence recognized them more readily than most, closed his eyes. "That's what I was afraid of."

"Mr. March?" asked Suzie. "Are you all right?"

"I'm great," he said, opening his eyes and turning to give her what he hoped would seem like a reassuring smile. "I just remembered that I need to call my sister tonight. That's all."

Call his sister, and tell her to get her bleached butt over here before the witch in the woods devoured them all.

# # #

Things I enjoy: driving.

Things I do not enjoy: driving for long periods with my entire field team in the van, because taking two vehicles would be fiscally irresponsible in these days of short staffing and expensive gas. Jeff was in the passenger seat, having claimed it by sheer dint of will, and by agreeing to let Sloane control the radio. Which meant, naturally, that we'd been listening to a band called "Five Finger Death Punch" since leaving the office, and I was starting to consider the virtues of earplugs.

Demi had already given in to temptation. She was wearing noise-canceling headphones and had stretched out across the van's rearmost seat, playing air flute as she listened to something light, classical, and less likely to make her eardrums bleed. Andy, caught in the middle as always, was sitting with his arms crossed, feigning sleep, while Sloane was methodically ripping the magazine she'd brought for the trip into confetti.

And we still had over an hour to go.

"You're riding in the back on the way home," I said, glancing to Jeff. "I can't handle another three and a half hours of screaming men telling me about carnage."

"I understand completely," said Jeff. He looked back to the book he was balancing on his knees. "Since we're almost there, are we ready to address the elephant in the room?"

"Which one? The one where this is the second narrative incursion my brother's been involved with in the last six months, or the one where this is potentially the second three-two-seven *Demi's* been involved with?" The first one had nearly led to us losing her for good.

We still didn't know whether that was solely due to Birdie's influence, or because Pipers were uniquely vulnerable to the witches who built gingerbread houses.

There was only one way to find out for sure. The places where stories rubbed against each other were hard to document without actual exposure, and the records were woefully incomplete when it came to questions like "are Pied Pipers always vulnerable to temptation, no matter how self-destructive it would be to give in?" That was why Demi had been allowed—more like "required"—to come with us, even with both me and Jeff saying it would be better to leave her behind.

Deputy Director Brewer could require me to take her into the field, but he couldn't force me to let Demi anywhere near the narrative taking root behind my brother's school. Demi wasn't going to meet another gingerbread witch if I had anything to say about it. I'd handcuff her to the van before I allowed that to happen . . . and judging by the way she'd gone pale and silent when she heard about this assignment, she'd let me. She had no more desire to be lost again than the rest of us had to lose her.

"That's it," I said, as the lead singer of Five Finger Death Punch went into a particularly loud tirade. I turned off the radio.

Jeff immediately relaxed, a look of blissful peace spreading across his face. Andy's shoulders dropped down from where they'd been trying to touch his ears. Sloane looked up from her magazine and scowled.

"Hey," she said. "I get to pick the music this trip. You promised, remember? I didn't stab your boyfriend for taking my seat, and you let me pick the music."

"I remember," I said. "If I turn the radio back on, it will definitely resume playing your music. But for the moment, I need my head to stop pounding, and we need to talk about what we're going to do when we get to the school. Can somebody get Demi's attention?"

"On it," said Andy, before Sloane could propose something unpleasant. He twisted in his seat, reaching back to set a hand gently on Demi's upper arm. "Hey, time to come back to the land of the living. Boss lady's going to start talking, and we're expected to pretend to listen."

Demi sat up, sliding her headphones down. The sound of something sweet and classical drifted through the van before she switched her MP3 player off. "Are we there already?" she asked, making no attempt to conceal her anxiety.

"About an hour out," I said. "I just wanted us to take a minute to talk about how this is going to go. All right?"

"We get there, we find the story, we punch the story until it stops kicking, and then we leave it for the cleanup team," said Sloane. "Case closed, let's go out for ice cream sundaes."

"Cute idea, but no," I said. "For one thing, this is a school day, and we don't have a good excuse to evacuate the campus."

"Yet," added Andy.

"Yet," I agreed. If the narrative gathered enough strength, we'd have to close the school or risk losing any student who could be said to have a sweet tooth. And any diabetics. They were uniquely susceptible to three-two-sevens, even when they didn't normally like candy. Something about the irony of using a gingerbread house to kill people who had issues with insulin seemed to appeal to the story. "Right now, however, there are kids there who don't know that anything's going on. For the sake of Gerry and his job, we're going to keep it that way for as long as we can."

"Does anyone there know what you look like?" asked Andy.

"No, thankfully," I said. "They've only spoken to me over the phone, and since Gerry and I have different last names these days, they may find it to be an odd similarity, but they shouldn't put anything together."

"It's not like you look alike," said Sloane.

I glared at her in the rearview mirror. "Yes, I'm aware that I look nothing like my twin brother. Thanks for the reminder. Looking at my reflection every morning just wasn't getting the point across."

For once, Sloane actually looked apologetic. "Sorry," she said. "I meant that we didn't have to worry about any additional similarities."

"Fair enough," I said. Gerry and I had been tapped by the narrative at birth to play Snow White and Rose Red. I got the white skin, black hair, and inborn lipstick. Gerry got the red hair, freckles, and rosy cheeks. We had a similar bone structure, but given the differences of gender and coloration, no one would see that. He was the only family I had in the world, and I didn't look a damn thing like him. That stung sometimes, when I was feeling particularly alone.

"Regardless, teenagers are more likely to have camera phones and to photograph their surroundings than any other demographic," said Jeff, taking up the explanation and giving me the break I needed. "That means that if we can't keep strange things from happening in their presence, those things are likely to wind up on the Internet. No one wants that."

"Why not?" asked Demi. "Before I knew all this was real, I would've just assumed somebody was having me on."

"Because it's not safe," said Sloane. She pushed her shredded magazine to the floor and began braiding her hair. "Fairy tales are attracted to fairy tales. That's why the first thing we do when there's an outbreak in a house with children is bag all their Disney videos. A teen walking around with a phone full of pictures of an active narrative is five times more likely to be targeted by an incursion than someone who owns a blue macaw."

"Blue . . . what?"

"Bluebirds show up in a lot of stories, and birds in stories can almost always talk," said Sloane, still braiding. "Blue macaws are like a big shiny 'come fuck with my life' flag."

"Fairy tales are weird," said Demi.

Andy chuckled. "Got that right, kid."

"Anyway, as I was saying," said Jeff. "We need to be as unobtrusive as possible, because we don't want to sow the seeds of a hundred second narratives while we're cleaning up this one."

"The official story is that we're from the EPA, and we're investigating a strange smell originating from the woods," I said, rejoining the conversation. "We aren't wearing moon suits because there's no current reason to believe the smell is related to any sort of toxic spill. If there *were* any reason to believe the smell was related to any sort of toxic spill, we would have alerted the authorities by now."

"Ergo, no toxic spill, got it," said Demi. "Aren't they going to think we're a little, um. Funny looking? To be federal agents?"

"I can do funny, but Henry's the one with the clown makeup," said Sloane. She tied off her braid and began winding it into a tight bun at the back of her neck. It was an impressive bit of stylistic chicanery: somehow the way she had it twisted managed to conceal the red and green streaks in her white-blonde locks, making her seem like a normal, if severe, federal agent.

Too bad I couldn't disguise my natural coloration as easily. "I have a badge, the badge has my picture; if they want to comment on my complexion, they can enjoy being threatened with an ADA lawsuit," I said. "Sloane already looks more respectable than she has for the last year."

"I brought a button-down shirt, and I'll change before I get out of the vehicle," added Sloane, plucking at the front of her "Bad Kitty" T-shirt. "I understand the game, Agent Santos. I've been playing it since before any of you were alive."

"That's sort of the problem," said Demi uncomfortably, and everything became clear.

"You're worried they're going to think you're too young, and that it's going to blow the whole thing," I said. Demi nodded, worrying her lower lip between her teeth. I tilted my head and asked, "Are you sure that's all you're worried about? Because you've never been concerned about your age before."

"We've never been going to a high school before," said Demi. "I'm barely *out* of high school."

"So we say you're on an internship program if anybody asks," said Sloane. "Shit, Demi, there was a time when you'd have been married with two kids and a household to run by now. Chill out and assert your womanhood. They'll fall in line, because they won't have any framework for *not* falling in line."

"Much as I hate to agree with Sloane, 'fake it until you make it' may be the best approach here," I said.

Demi sighed. "To dealing with the people maybe, but what do we do when the story decides that it wants to take me again?"

"We don't let it," I said firmly. "We're never going to let that happen again."

Demi met my eyes in the rearview mirror. She didn't say anything. She didn't have to. She knew that I was bluffing.

I drove on. We were almost there.

# # #

The school parking lot was surprisingly crowded when we pulled up at a quarter after four o'clock in the afternoon. Classes were done for the day, but it looked like every teacher who had been able to come up with an excuse had stuck around to see the federal agents. How did I know that they knew that we were coming?

Well, the news vans were a bit of a tip-off.

Andy sighed when he saw them, sitting up a little straighter and beginning to retie his tie. As our most charismatic member, he was always the one tapped when we needed to convince the bystanders and lookie-loos to move on. "What's our cover story this time, boss?"

"Same as we're giving the school: we're here to investigate reports of an unusual smell, we don't believe it's toxic, but in the interest of containment and public safety, we're going to have to ask the media to keep a wide berth. You may have to stay here and distract them. The last thing I need is some ace reporter following us into the woods and getting footage of a gingerbread house."

"Maybe she could get some footage of the inside of the oven," suggested Sloane. There was nothing kind about her tone. Then again, there so rarely was.

"Let's not make more of a mess for the cleanup squad than we have to, all right?" I pulled into a spot near the front of the school. The reporters who'd been standing outside the news vans immediately started pointing in our direction, and a few began moving our way. "Remember, a good incursion is an incursion that doesn't require any-one to accidentally burn down a news station."

"Spoilsport," said Sloane. She pulled her shirt over her head, fling-ing it unerringly at Jeff—who, as the only person in the car who was attracted to women, apart from Sloane herself, had turned bright cherry red as soon as he'd realized what she was doing. She pulled on her but-ton-down shirt without bothering to undo the buttons and grabbed her jacket. "We ready?"

"We're ready," I said, and opened my door.

My team may be odd at best and dysfunctional at worst, but we're good at what we do, and thanks to the number of narrative incursions we've dealt with and survived since Demi first joined us, we can pull ourselves together fast. The reporters on the scene didn't see our bicker-ing or our quick wardrobe changes. No, they saw a pale, severe-looking woman with black hair marching toward the front of the school, fol-lowed by a thin man who walked with the grim purpose of a morti-cian, a woman whose hair was virtually white and whose face was set in a seemingly permanent scowl, and a younger, darker-skinned woman who moved with the quick uncertainty of the trainee.

Then their view was blocked by Andy as he swooped in and took over. We were almost to the school doors when his voice boomed, "All right, settle down, and I'll be happy to answer all your questions—"

I smirked, and we were inside, and the first hurdle was behind us. Now the real work could begin.

High schools around the country tend to follow a similar floor plan: the office is almost always located near the front, where it's convenient for visiting parents or people from the school board. I spent a lot of time in the office back when Gerry and I were in high school. He was never big on kicking the crap out of people who called him a freak. I, on the other hand, was almost Sloane-like in my furious desire to see my fellow students bleed.

Oh, yeah. I was definitely thrilled to be back in high school.

The question of which of the doors lining the hall was the one we wanted was answered when one of them creaked open and a head popped out. A red-topped head, with familiar features, pulled into a familiar expression of mild distress. I perked up, trying not to let my delight at seeing my brother show. He was at work, after all, and we were trying to keep our relationship as quiet as possible. Still, I offered him a quick, private nod, and he returned it, making no effort to conceal his relief.

"I'm Agent Henrietta Marchen," I said, offering my hand. He pushed the door open further, revealing the people who were clustered in the office behind him. They were watching our interaction with the wary suspicion the general public tends to reserve for vague, black-clad government agencies. It wasn't a bad survival mechanism, all things considered. "My team and I are here about your possible chemical spill."

"Gerald March," he said, taking my hand and shaking it. There: we had established ourselves as strangers in the eyes of his colleagues. "I'm a teacher here. Principal Hanson is this way." He let go of my hand, gesturing for me to come into the office. I, and my team, did as we were told.

The office was actually a warren of smaller offices, all connected to a large hub that was dominated by a secretary's desk. The secretary was a woman who looked to be somewhere in her midfifties, sitting behind a computer that was four generations out of date and pretending to take notes as she eavesdropped on the people around her.

I decided not to call her on what she was doing. The more people we had backing up the official story about what had happened here, the better off we were going to be. I turned a politely bland look on the other inhabitants of the office, careful not to smile. Most people didn't like it when I smiled. "Hello. I'm Agent Henrietta Marchen, and this is my team. May I ask which of you is Principal Hanson?"

"I am," said a woman with ash blonde hair and a sensible lilac pantsuit. She took a step forward as she spoke, putting herself between us and the others. I decided I liked her. Any superior who didn't try to hide behind her people was okay by me. "I'm afraid I still don't understand exactly what's going on here. I called the police, and they didn't know anything about your organization, or what its connections are to the EPA."

Damn. "I was unaware that you'd spoken to local law enforcement. I'm going to have to call the office and ask them to send in a cleanup team."

"You'll be able to talk to them yourself; I called them when the reporters showed up outside," replied Principal Hanson. She looked at me coolly. "May I assume your office decided to contact them? Were you not going to get enough media attention without stepping in?"

Double damn. "I assure you, ma'am, my office operates under conditions of utmost secrecy, to avoid the possibility of triggering a public panic. The chemical spill we're here to investigate is almost certainly not toxic. Going on what was described by Mr. March, it's probably a form of rare but naturally occurring fungus. You think we want to spend the next few weeks fielding calls from panicked homeowners convinced that we're covering up an outbreak of flesh-eating black mold? I don't know about you, but my agency has better things to do."

"Well, we certainly didn't contact the press," said Principal Hanson, thawing only slightly. She might be willing to accept that I wasn't to blame, but that didn't mean she was letting go of her anger just yet.

By my elbow, Sloane cleared her throat. I glanced in her direction. "Agent Winters?"

"Pardon me for interrupting, ma'am, but I think if we're looking for the source of a media leak, and we're all policing each other, maybe we should be considering the only person in the room with an Internet connection." Sloane sounded almost bored. She probably was. There was punching to be done out there in those woods, and as long as we were standing here arguing with the locals, she wasn't getting the party started. The bloody, violent, unpleasant party.

As one, we all turned to look at the secretary. She reddened, hunching her shoulders defensively.

"I did not stay after hours so that I could be accused of wrongdoing by a stranger," she said. There was a shrill note in her voice that screamed "guilty" more loudly than anything shy of a confession could possibly have done.

"No one asked you to stay after hours in the first place, Natalie," said Principal Hanson. "Did you alert the media that we had a possible chemical spill on school property?"

Natalie sat up a little straighter and sniffed. "Well, I suppose that's a matter of opinion."

"She posted on the school's Facebook group," said Demi. Most of us turned to look at her. She shrugged, ears turning red as she lowered her phone. "There are two. One official one, for the school to make announcements, and one that's supposedly set private, for complaining about the administration. She posted about the chemical spill on the private page. Which—oh look—has three local reporters listed as 'friends.' Have you been having issues with the press lately? Because it looks like this lady has been making sure they heard about every little thing that happened on campus."

"That's private, you have no right without a warrant," snapped Natalie.

There were two ways this could go. Thankfully, Sloane went with the better option. She looked almost amused as she asked, "What do you think this is, lady, an episode of *Law & Order*? Facebook is a public resource. If logging into her account gives Agent Santos access to your 'private' group, then that's what she's going to do, and that's what we're going to act on. Since you're the one who spilled details of an ongoing EPA investigation, I think maybe you should be a little nicer to us right now."

That was my cue. "Natalie," I glanced at her nameplate, "Barrick, you are hereby under arrest for endangering a federal investigation, and for exposing government secrets on a public forum. You have the right to remain silent. Anything you say can and will be held against you in a secret court of law."

"I have the right to an attorney," she said, all traces of smugness or superiority gone as she jerked to her feet and took a step back, away from me, away from Principal Hanson, and most important, away from Sloane. "I want an attorney."

"Oh, actually, no," said Jeff. "That's just for civic authorities. We're the *government*. We don't have to give you an attorney. We're allowed to make you disappear, as long as we fill out all the appropriate paperwork."

"I just wanted people to realize there was corruption at this school!" protested Natalie, suddenly frantic. She took another step backward, and stopped as her shoulders hit the wall. "They're so busy chasing make-believe bullies that they don't look at the pay imbalances, at the people sneaking food out of the cafeteria, or the kids stealing from the supply cabinets—"

"We have a high population of low-income students," snapped Gerry. He sounded angrier than I was accustomed to hearing him. "What do you want them to do, flunk all their tests because you treat pencils like they're made of platinum? We're here to teach. Students don't learn with empty stomachs and second-hand notebooks. They learn with food, and paper, and *understanding adults*."

Natalie looked around the room, apparently seeking a friendly face. She didn't find one. She slouched a little. Then her eyes fell on Sloane.

Sloane didn't say anything. She just smiled. That was more than enough. The unfortunate Natalie fell over in a dead faint, hitting the floor with a loud, boneless thud. For a moment, everyone was silent, looking at the collapsed secretary.

Principal Hanson spoke first. "She's fired when she wakes up, of course. The union won't be able to protect her from this one," she said.

"Is there any way I can convince you not to arrest her? The reporters out there are going to be suspicious enough when it comes out that she's been dismissed from her position, especially if she's been feeding them information about the school. I'd rather not see what happens if she disappears completely."

"If we're given full cooperation with the rest of our investigation, I believe we can be lenient in this instance," I said blandly. "Please understand, however, that this is for your safety, and for the safety of your students. It's important we not encounter any further complications." The threat didn't need to be spoken to be heard. That's the nice thing about threats. Sometimes they can make themselves clear without any outside help.

"Of course," said Principal Hanson. "How can we help?"

"You called it in, right?" asked Sloane, turning on Gerry. "I remember your name from the report."

"Yes," he said, glancing toward Principal Hanson. She would probably interpret his discomfort as related to our jobs, since no one likes to be singled out by a government agency. That was fine. I knew that he was actually uncomfortable about the idea of being identified as my brother. The more wrong everyone's assumptions were, the better off we'd be.

"Good," I said. "We'll need you to show us the source of the smell. We have an extra face mask you can wear, in case we determine it to be dangerous. Principal Hanson, if you'd remain here in case the press causes any additional trouble, we'd be very appreciative. One of our agents, Andy Robinson, is outside speaking to them now. When he makes it in, please let him know we've gone on ahead. He'll determine for himself what the best course of action is."

"Certainly," said Principal Hanson. She didn't look thrilled about the fact that we were walking off with one of her people, but she didn't raise a fuss either. After her secretary calling down the local news on our heads, she didn't have a leg to stand on.

"Follow me," said Gerry, and started for the office door. We fell into step behind him.

The last thing I saw before the door closed was Principal Hanson staring after us, a disturbed look on her face. Her world was changing, and she didn't like it one bit. I understood the feeling, but I couldn't stick around to commiserate with her. I had work to do.

# # #

Gerry stayed quiet until we emerged at the rear of the school, and the rest of us followed his lead. He'd been working here long enough to know where the cameras and poorly designed vents were located, and the last thing any of us wanted was to be overheard while we were trying to get to the incursion.

The smell of freshly cut grass assaulted us as soon as we stepped out of the hallway and onto the blacktop behind the school. The smell of gingerbread followed, worming its way under the grass, seeming almost to whisper promises in my ears.

"Does anyone else hear that?" I asked.

"Mild synesthesia has been associated with the smell of gingerbread houses in the past," said Jeff. He didn't sound any happier about it than I felt. "It's a way to lure even those who are not necessarily vulnerable to the promise of sweets. Suddenly there's a whole second layer to the temptation, one that the conscious mind may or may not be able to process."

"You can make *anything* sound boring, did you know that?" asked Sloane. She seemed genuinely curious, at least until she punctuated her question by turning and punching Gerry in the arm.

He yelped. "What did you do that for?"

"You could have called and warned us that we were coming into a press situation," snapped Sloane. "We might have been able to park down the street, and keep Andy with the rest of the team."

"Look on the bright side: no one had a chance to notice how young Demi is," said Gerry. Then he stepped around Sloane, leaned over, and hugged me. "It's good to see you, Henry."

"Good to see you too," I said, returning the hug as quickly as I could before letting him go. The smell of gingerbread was starting to put my back up. "Are you sure no students have wandered into the woods?"

"No," said Gerry grimly.

We all turned to stare at him. He shook his head.

"The wood appeared before the smell, and they're teenagers. All the curiosity, none of the 'oh hey wait, I could die' self-awareness. Younger kids are pretty good about avoiding this sort of thing, because they've been so schooled on not trusting strangers that they know there's something about it that isn't right, but teenagers? We'll be lucky if there aren't already a dozen of them in there, being digested by the house."

"I love my job," said Sloane, and started stalking across the blacktop toward the distant, looming wood.

The rest of us followed. Demi had her flute out and was clutching it tightly, eyes darting here and there as she watched for attack. I didn't say anything, not even to reassure her. She needed to do this. This was the story that had been used to take her away from us once before. If she was ever going to feel like she could trust herself again, she needed to face it without someone holding her hand.

That wasn't going to stop me from ordering Sloane to smack her over the head and carry her back to the van if it proved necessary. I was all for my team experiencing personal growth and learning to deal with their demons, but my tolerance ended as soon as their lives were in danger. We had come here as a team. We were going to go home as a team, if I had to kill people to make it happen.

"The forest appeared sometime between the end of classes yesterday and second period this morning," said Gerry, falling into the easy, almost lecturing tone that had always come so naturally to him. It used to make me want to punch him in the stomach when we were kids and

I thought he was talking down to me. Distance and adulthood had made it clear that this was his way of distancing himself from the situation and coping with his fear. "Normally, you can see straight through into the neighboring housing developments. They keep the underbrush trimmed back to cut down on truancy and lunchtime drinking."

"Do high school students sneak out during lunch to drink?" asked Jeff, sounding appalled.

Sloane gave him an amused, not unkind look. "Nerd," she said.

"Proud of it," Jeff countered.

"I noticed the forest midway through second period," said Gerry, ignoring them. "I confirmed that my students could see it too, which is when I noticed the scent of gingerbread and contacted you."

"You did the right thing," I said.

His smile was thin and bitter. "Why did I have to? Have I been exposed to so much fairy-tale crazy that it's going to start following me around now? Because that was never what I wanted, and you know it."

"I know," I said. What I didn't say was that when he had run from the "fairy-tale crazy," he'd done it by leaving me behind: he'd broken free of his half of our shared story and condemned me to princesshood, whether I wanted it or not. Nothing was ever going to put color in my cheeks or keep the apple from my hand, and as soon as he'd realized that, my brother—the one person I'd always counted on, my twin, the other half of my soul, if not my story—had walked away from me.

I could understand why he'd done it. I could even forgive him. I might have done the same, if our positions had been reversed and I'd had the option. But that didn't mean I was ever going to forget the history behind the words "fairy-tale crazy," and that didn't mean they were ever going to stop hurting me, deep down, in the place where I wasn't an agent or a princess, but just a frazzled, frightened little girl.

Gerry sighed, looking at my suddenly tight jaw and the lines that had appeared below my eyes. "Sorry, Henry. You know I didn't mean it like that."

"You never do, Gerry," I said, and kept walking.

Sloane was ranging about six feet ahead of the group—far enough that if anything decided to attack us, it would go for her first, and close enough that we'd be able to step in and help whoever was attacking her before she ripped their heads from their bodies. Traveling with Sloane sometimes meant adjusting our idea of whose side we were supposed to be on. Yes, we'd come to her aid before we helped anyone who had happened to trigger her ire, but for the most part, we wanted to keep her from killing anyone. The paperwork when she did was a *nightmare*.

The smell of gingerbread grew stronger the closer we got to the trees. Sloane reached the tree line and stopped there, rigid, her hands balled into fists by her sides. I exchanged a glance with Jeff and sped up, leaving Demi and Gerry to trail behind us. Demi wasn't a physical combatant. Gerry was thin, but he was out of shape; he'd never needed to learn how to outrun an onrushing story. That was something I had that he didn't.

I wasn't sure it was a good thing.

When we reached Sloane, we both stopped, Jeff so fast that he nearly overbalanced and crossed into the wood. I grabbed his arm before he could fall, pulling him to a halt sharp enough that it was probably going to leave bruises. He cast me a thankful glance all the same. The consequences of falling would have been far worse than a few bruises.

The sound of children laughing drifted out of the trees, distant, ghostly, and thin. It was impossible to tell whether the gingerbread house had managed to attract supplicants already, or whether the laughter was a special effect generated by the story to lend veracity to its claims of joy and peace within the dark, dark woods. It didn't matter. The laughter, whatever its source might have been, was less important than the glimmering barrier that kept us from pursuing it. Had the sun been a little lower in the sky, or had Sloane not been so attuned to the presence of stories in the process of unfolding, we might have missed it. It was a subtle thing, after all, and we'd all been so busy moving toward the sound of laughter that we hadn't been looking down.

Glass shards glittered amongst the grass, rammed into the ground to form an unbroken line. I glanced to Sloane for confirmation. She nodded, her jaw set in a hard line. I could almost hear her teeth grinding.

"Elise was here," she said.

"Who's Elise?" asked Gerry, panting a little as he stopped. He squinted at the ground. "Is that broken glass? God, have those kids already started drinking out here? I swear, they think everything is an excuse to throw a kegger."

"So did we, when we were their age," I said. "Jeff?"

"On it," he said, and crouched, careful not to get any closer to the shards. After a moment of study, he said, "They're not actually touching anything but the grass."

"Grass has its own narrative weight," I said. "Demi, can you do that trick you pulled back at Childe? Pipe the glass out of here?"

"Step back," she said, trying to sound confident. I did as I was told. So did Jeff and Sloane, who grabbed Gerry's sleeve and dragged him with her as she moved.

Demi waited long enough for all four of us to be out of her potential line of fire before she lifted her flute and began to play. It was the song she'd used before, but sweeter somehow, like all the rough edges had been sanded off while the music was bouncing around inside her brain. The glass began to move almost immediately, flowing like water into a single solid sphere that then proceeded to roll to rest against one of the trees. I held my breath, waiting to see if the tree would turn to glass. Nothing happened.

Demi lowered her flute.

"There wasn't any other glass near here," she said. "Not even Jeff's glasses."

"Nope, they're more 'plastics,'" he said, tapping one lens while he chuckled unsteadily at his own joke. "We're going to have to come back for that. Even if it's inert right now, there's no guarantee that it won't wake up again later."

"This is why I became a high school teacher," said Gerry. "Nothing inanimate ever 'wakes up' around here."

"Yeah, well, lucky for you," I said. "Sloane, we good?"

"Nothing else seems out of the ordinary for a horrible haunted forest being inhabited by a child-eating witch," said Sloane, grabbing Gerry's arm again. He gave her a startled look. She smiled thinly. "You're with me now, handsome. I'm going to explain why your sister's going to murder you soon, and you're going to listen." She dragged him into the woods.

Demi looked alarmed. "Are you really going to murder your brother?"

"No," I said. "But I'm going to yell at him a lot if he doesn't cut this 'my life is so much better than yours because it's not under constant attack by stories' bullshit. Come on. We don't want to let them get too far ahead of us. I'm willing to bet that people get lost in this forest." I started walking.

As expected, Jeff paced me, glancing nervously in my direction several times before he said, "You know it can't be a coincidence that Elise is involved with this story, and that it's happening this close to your brother's school."

"I know," I said. "I think Gerry knows the story didn't land here by accident. It would explain why he keeps rubbing it in my face that he got out and I didn't."

"Henry . . ."

"We were doing so *well* for a while there, you know? I was almost starting to feel like my brother and I could have a relationship that wasn't about fighting with each other all the time." The sound of giggles drifted through the trees. I scowled. "And maybe this is not the right time to get upset because my brother got the good end of the stick."

"Did he really?" Jeff's voice was soft. "He didn't get caught in a story, because he was born part of a story that could never have been his. Maybe if he'd been given a Jack's role, or a second son's, or even a stableboy . . . but no, the narrative wanted him to be a princess, and the only way to get away from it was to leave everything behind. Was to leave *you* behind. I know he loves you. You're the most important person in his world, you're his *twin*, and the only way he's been able to wrest even the thinnest sliver of peace from the universe has been by cutting you out. At least you had the option of accepting yourself for what you were. At least you knew it wouldn't destroy you."

"Yeah." I sighed. "I don't want to forgive him for leaving me the way that he did. And I don't want to just shrug and let him insult my life's work because it makes him feel better. But I don't know how else to deal with this."

Jeff smiled, the expression barely visible through the gloom of the wood. "Ah, but you see, you've already made some great strides. A year ago, you would have suffered in silence, rather than saying anything to anyone. Now you're opening up to me. That means you're feeling much more confident in your place."

"A year ago we weren't dating and we didn't have Demi to help balance out the power levels on this team." A year ago, I hadn't been a Snow White: I'd been holding myself in permanent abeyance, praying I could get through the rest of my life without slipping up and letting my story take me over. A lot of things had changed in a year. My relationship with my brother wasn't even the biggest of them.

My relationship with . . . oh, shit. I stopped dead, my eyes going wide as I searched the trees ahead of us for any sign of Gerry or Sloane. Had I seen them since we stepped into the woods? It seemed like I must have, and yet I couldn't remember even catching a glimpse of Sloane's ice-white hair, which should have been standing out like a searchlight in the gloom.

"I just stepped into the dark woods where a gingerbread witch lives, in the company of my brother," I said, voice gone tight. "My *twin* brother, who broke his story and is at the center of an unassigned narrative. Where's Demi?"

"Right here," said a small voice. I turned. Demi was close behind me, clutching her flute to her chest. She forced a wan smile. "I wasn't letting you out of my sight. I'm not feeling like getting baked into gingerbread today."

"Good," I said. "Stay close." I looked down. There, as I had more than half expected, was a small white stone tangled in the grass. It was visible, despite the darkness and our shadows falling across it. Of course it was. Without it, how would we have known which way to go?

"This is a trap," I said, as quietly as I could. "The story isn't after you, Demi: it's after Gerry."

"The story is after Gerry and his sister," corrected Jeff. He sounded worried. "Elise proves stories can be changed. Recast you from Snow White to Gretel, and whatever threat you pose is reduced, or even nullified."

"I'm not a threat," I said.

"Someone thinks you are," said Jeff.

I hesitated before nodding. "All right then: We move. We go fast, and we go quiet, and we get our people back. Understand?"

"Yes," said Demi.

"Wish I didn't," said Jeff.

"Let's go," I said, and resumed walking.

Following the trail of little white stones through the trees was easier than it should have been. Every time I thought we'd missed one, another would appear, visible enough that there was no mistaking it for anything else. My fingers itched with the compulsion to start collecting them. I balled my hands into fists and kept walking. Touching them would mean accepting this story more than I already had.

"If the story wants you to be Gretel, and Gerry to be Hansel, what does it want with Sloane?" asked Demi.

I glanced at her. "What do you mean?"

"It took her too. Gerry didn't just vanish into the trees: they both did."

I froze. It all made perfect sense now. Perfect, terrible sense. "Jeff, do you have cell service in here?"

"What?" Jeff pulled out his phone. "Yes, four bars. Why?"

"I need you to call Andy. I need you to tell him to get down here. And I need you to tell him to swing through the cafeteria first."

Jeff blinked. "What for?"

I told him.

I just hoped it would be enough.

# # #

Standing still in the dark, creepy forest full of distant giggles and the smell of gingerbread was even harder than walking through it. At least when we'd been moving, we'd been *doing* something. Part of me hoped Gerry and Sloane would come walking back through the trees, pissed off because we'd fallen so far behind. The rest of me—the sensible part of me—knew that wasn't going to happen. They'd passed out of sight because the story had taken them, and it wasn't going to give them back without a fight.

The sound of branches breaking alerted us to the approach of someone, or something. I leaned up onto my toes as I tried to see. Demi clutched her flute a little tighter, ready to start calling ants out of their nests to attack whoever was coming.

Andy stepped into view, a basket slung over one arm. An actual, honest-to-God wicker basket, complete with the soft white cloth lining and looped handle. It was full of red apples. They were too far away for me to smell them from where I was, but my mouth began to water all the same. I *wanted* those apples.

I was going to have them. "Over here," I called, waving. Andy turned, orienting himself on my voice, and trotted over. "Have any trouble getting away from the reporters?"

"Nah," he said. "I explained how the chemicals we were checking for were nontoxic but could cause massive acne outbreaks in adults, and they all split for safer ground. We'll probably have complaints about pimples from the locals for a little while, but that's not so bad, considering what we could've been dealing with."

"You are a genius of public relations," I agreed, and reached for the basket.

Andy pulled it back, out of my reach. "Nuh-uh. I brought them because Jeff asked me to, and I generally trust him not to let you hurt yourself—much—but I'm not giving them to you until you tell me what you want them for. Where's Sloane? And your brother?"

"That's what I want them for," I said. "We found signs that Elise had been here. Maybe she still is. She managed to twist her own story into something that was more useful to her: well, Gerry and I are twins, and orphans, and we just walked together into a dark wood where a gingerbread witch is supposed to be lurking. I'm pretty sure she's trying to use Gerry's undefined narrative to warp *him* into a Hansel, which would allow the story to turn *me* into a Gretel."

"Dangerous if you're a witch, but nowhere near as dangerous for anyone else, when compared to the potential damage that an active Snow White can do," said Jeff, before Andy could ask why that was a bad thing. Andy nodded, accepting Jeff's explanation without question. Jeff was our expert, after all. "The apples will keep Henry grounded in her story. Gretel is hungry—that's what makes the gingerbread house so tempting—and Snow White always knows where the nearest apple tree is located."

"Before you say anything, none of us like this either," I added. "Now give me the basket before Sloane bakes my brother."

Andy gave me the basket. I smiled.

"Thank you," I said, and turned on my heel, and began stalking forward, following the trail of little white stones into the deep dark wood. The rest of my team walked behind me, not saying anything. The time for conversation was over. The time for action was upon us. As long as the action didn't get us all killed, that was for the better. We needed this to be done.

The smell of gingerbread got stronger with every step. My stomach rumbled. I lifted the basket and inhaled, letting the smell of apples wash away everything else. My stomach rumbled again, louder this time, demanding I give it the one fruit that could ever truly fulfill me. I kept walking. The time for eating apples would arrive eventually, but it wasn't here yet, and I wasn't going to push it.

Then we stepped out of the trees and into a clearing, and I forgot about the tempting smell of apples in favor of gaping at the towering, Addams-esque gingerbread house that was occupying the entire skyline. The giggling continued, seemingly without a source. That was a good thing: that meant the narrative probably hadn't snared any actual children.

Sloane was standing on the porch, blank faced and motionless, one hand resting on the twisted peppermint banister. Gerry was nowhere to be seen. Under the circumstances, I couldn't even begin to see that as a good thing.

"Hi, Sloane," I called, stopping about ten feet from the house and gesturing for the others to do the same. "What are you doing up there?"

"You should come inside," she said. "It's a nice house. I couldn't find the witch, but you should see the place. I didn't know you could do so much with fondant." Her voice sounded oddly distant, like she was disconnected from what she was saying.

"I think I may know why you couldn't find the witch," I said, as gently as possible. "Where's Gerry, Sloane?"

"He's in the kitchen." Her tone didn't change. It still sent shivers down my spine.

"You know he's not your Hansel, right, Sloane?" It felt strange to use her name so much, but it was necessary: I needed to ground her back in the story she had been born to live through. "He's my brother. He used to be my Rose Red, and now he's feeling his way through things, but this isn't his narrative. No matter how hard it's pressuring you to treat it like it is, it's not. It's not your narrative either."

"The line between witch in the woods and wicked stepsister is thin and academic," said Sloane. Her voice was sounding emptier with every word she spoke, like she was breathing out her own story and breathing a new one in. It was terrifying to watch. "This story has a shape and a structure, and it loves me. My story never loved me."

"Yeah, but Sloane, feeding kids? Fattening them up on delicious candy? That's not your gig." I reached into the basket with my free hand, choosing the largest, reddest apple I could find, and took a step forward. "Look at this apple."

Sloane looked at the apple. Her eyes lit up a little. I chose to see that as a good sign.

"Doesn't the apple look delicious?" I raised it to my nose and sniffed exaggeratedly. "Smells good too. I bet I could eat it without suffering any negative consequences. Too bad there's nobody around to poison it."

Sloane's right eye was starting to twitch.

I took that as my opening. "Catch," I said, and lobbed the apple at her.

Sloane snatched it out of the air with both hands, clutching it and staring down at its reflective red surface. Then, without saying anything, she spun around and hurled the apple through the candy-glass window of the house. Shards went flying everywhere. I ducked to avoid being hit. Demi wasn't fast enough; she yelped. I didn't turn to see if she was okay, because I had other things to worry about—namely Sloane, who ran through the open door without saying a word.

"Move," I snapped.

We moved.

The house was already beginning to break down as we stormed up the porch and into the gingerbread living room. Sloane hadn't been careful, and had kicked several holes in the floor. Maybe that was a new way of leaving us a trail. We followed the holes to the kitchen, where she was untying a stunned-looking Gerry.

She looked up, eyes widening. "Get out! All of you, get out! The house isn't—"

The house collapsed on our heads.

# # #

Gingerbread is a poor building material, in part because it's so light. We finished digging ourselves out and looked around the thinly wooded stretch of land behind the school, which resembled a deep dark wood only inasmuch as a toy poodle resembles a wolf.

"I think we broke the story," I commented.

"I hate you," said Sloane, and threw an apple at my head.

"Is someone going to tell me what just happened?" asked Gerry.

He looked utterly lost. Poor guy. He might have gotten away from the day-to-day adventures with the narrative, but he would always be on the ATI spectrum. All he'd done by breaking free was make sure he would never be quite prepared for what was coming. I couldn't blame him for running. I couldn't hate him because I'd stayed. But I could take pity on him, and I could love him.

"Let's go tell the school there's no chemical spill, and then grab dinner," I said. "It's a long story."

Demi snorted, looking amused. She wasn't clutching her flute as hard anymore. That was a good thing.

Together, the six of us brushed off the crumbs and turned to walk, side by side, back to the office.

Split Ends

Memetic incursion in progress: tale type 310 ("Rapunzel")
Status: IN PROGRESS

She didn't know her name. She hadn't known her name for a long time: not since the car crash that took her lover's eyes as they fled from her abusive mother, not since that same mother cast her out to wander the streets of the city, alone, starving, and pregnant. She didn't know how long ago that had been—past and present seemed to blend together these days, until sometimes she almost felt like none of it had happened at all, like her sweet boy might open the door to her windowless cell and sweep her away again, the way he had before.

It couldn't have been *too* long ago, could it? It couldn't have been, because her belly was flat, tight as a drumhead, and not swelling with new life. She knew she was pregnant, just as surely as she knew that her name was . . . her name was . . .

She didn't know her name. Somehow, she always circled back to that.

The nameless girl paced in her cell, and the long golden trail of her hair followed her, disregarded and virtually unseen as she chased her ghosts down the long and haunted hallways of her mind. She had been chasing them for a long time.

Maybe someday she would catch them, and they would show her the way home.

# # #

"I hate paperwork," announced Andy, looking up from his desk. "How is it that we have a form for 'you got a gingerbread house dropped on your head'? How do we have a job where that's something you'd need a form for?"

"There's a recession going on," said Demi, not looking up from her own report. "My *abuela* says we're lucky to have jobs at all, and we shouldn't be too upset when they ask us to do reasonable things."

"Paperwork is not a reasonable thing," said Andy.

I understood how he felt. As leader of the field team that had walked into a manifesting three-two-seven, I got *extra* paperwork, including a full report on all interactions with the staff of the high school where my brother worked. I also had to proofread and approve my brother's statement, which mostly consisted of "I smelled gingerbread, so I called my sister." If there was one thing we shared, thanks to our upbringing in an ATI-aware household, it was the knowledge that the sudden smell of mysterious baked goods never meant anything good for anybody.

Jeff snorted once and kept reading. He had already finished his paperwork and was working his way through an alternate translation of Grimm's collected fairy tales for reasons he hadn't bothered to share with any of us, but which probably had something to do with his unending need to know absolutely everything about the narrative. It didn't matter that stories had more "weight" when people thought about them regularly, which meant the more obscure stories almost never manifested in the physical world. Thank Grimm for that. Much as I hated the assortment of Little Mermaids, Donkeyskins, and Pusses in Boots that we dealt with on a regular basis, there were worse things lurking in the corners of the fairy-tale world. Much worse, and much harder to explain away as gas leaks, people in masks, or teenage pranks.

"Do what I do," suggested Sloane, trotting to the printer. She had been printing recipes for apple pie all morning. None of us were saying anything about it. She was still shaken from the gingerbread incident, and if collecting a large stack of what were, for her, potential murder weapons could help, then we were going to let her go ahead. We just weren't going to eat anything she baked.

"What's that?" asked Andy.

"Burn all your paperwork and pretend you have no idea what people are talking about if anyone asks you for it," she said, picking up her printout and walking more decorously back to her desk.

"No one is burning their paperwork today," I said. "We're all going to do our jobs, and no one is poisoning anyone else, and no one is setting anyone else on fire. Am I clear?"

"As ice," said Sloane, rolling her eyes.

"Agent Marchen?" The voice belonged to my boss, Deputy Director Brewer. I turned, and there he was at the mouth of the bullpen, a balding, uncomfortable looking man in a three-piece suit. There was an unusual tightness around his eyes.

"Sir?" I stood. Behind me, my team went quiet. They knew how odd it was for the deputy director to come to us: usually, he sent someone to fetch me when he wanted to talk, rather than roaming around the building without a handler. He wasn't on the ATI spectrum. He was a career agency man who had made a wrong turn somewhere, and wound up in storybook land instead of managing a bigger, better, less secret government office.

"I need to speak to you," he said. "Will you please come with me?"

My mind was already racing, reviewing everything I could have done wrong over the course of the past few weeks. It was a good-sized list, given our visit to Childe Prison and the whole thing with the gingerbread house. I stood. "Should I bring my team with me?"

"Not at this time, Agent Marchen," he said. "You'll be back with them soon enough." He turned and walked away, quickly, like he was afraid life in the bullpen was contagious and would infect him if he stayed near it for too long.

I looked back to my people. "You heard the man. I'll be back soon enough. How about you surprise me and have all your paperwork done by the time I get back here?"

"We'll try," said Demi.

Jeff looked disturbed. "Henry . . ."

"I know," I said, and followed our deputy director down the hall. It was time to find out what we'd done—and whether it was too late for it to be fixed.

# # #

Deputy Director Brewer didn't say anything until we were in his office with the door closed. He gestured for me to take a seat. I didn't want to, but I sat anyway. He was my superior officer. Listening to him was the best way to survive what might be turning into a bad situation.

"Agent Marchen, before I begin, I have to ask: has your team experienced anything unusual lately?"

I frowned. "Sir, forgive me if this sounds flippant, but unusual is what we do for a living. You'll have to be more specific."

"I reviewed your account of what happened at Childe. I also read your recommendation that all agents on the spectrum, whether active or not, be provided with access crystals to prevent the prison's protections from interfering with the performance of their duties. I assure you that I'm taking your request seriously and will be discussing it with prison management." He leaned forward, resting his elbows on his desk. "Your report said the story had become 'infectious.' What did you mean by this?"

"If you read my report, you're already aware of what I meant," I said. "Somehow, the glass generated when Elise changed her story was capable of transforming other living things into glass, which then exploded. It was very messy and could potentially have wiped out the population of the prison, had a large enough chain-reaction been allowed to form."

"And you say Agent Santos was able to extract all of this, ah, 'infectious glass' from the walls by playing the right song on her flute?"

"Agent Santos is a Pied Piper, sir. We're still not sure what the limits of her powers are, providing she has the correct sheet music. Yes, she was able to pipe all the dangerous glass into a single location, where it was left for the cleanup team." A sudden thought struck me, trailing dread in its wake. "Did the cleanup team not find the glass?"

"Oh, they found it, Agent Marchen, and they were able to test its properties in a narratively-sealed room. Even clumped together as you left it, it continues to transmute living flesh."

I stared at him, appalled. "*Please* tell me you didn't explode an agent to find out whether we were telling the truth about that stuff being dangerous."

"No. One of our agents who speaks in toads, snakes, and lizards agreed to read a prepared statement in the presence of the remaining glass. She's in counseling now, and is expected to make a full recovery."

I had met the agent in question. She was a good sort, spoke almost entirely in ASL, and would never have agreed to let one of her cold-blooded friends be sacrificed in that manner if she had been told what the Bureau intended ahead of time. I shook my head and didn't say anything. Deputy Director Brewer grimaced, taking the meaning from my silence.

"We had to be sure."

"You could have lobbed a watermelon at it," I said. "There were petrified vines on location. We knew the glass could affect plant matter." But it hadn't transformed the grass when we'd seen it again outside the gingerbread house. Maybe the rules weren't as static as we wanted them to be.

They never were.

Deputy Director Brewer shook his head, expression soothing back out to its normal grave neutrality. "Agent Marchen, have any of the members of your field team been behaving in an unusual manner recently?"

"You mean more unusual than normal?" I asked. "No. Demi's stressed about her place in the organization, Andy's in the middle of trying to get approved for adopting a kid, and Sloane keeps threatening to poison us all. The only one who's *not* being weird is Jeff, and that's because he's so busy reading and filling out all his paperwork that he doesn't have *time* to be weird. I'm sure he'll start once he's all caught up on things. Why do you ask?"

"You didn't mention yourself," he said.

"I think I'm the least qualified person to comment on whether or not I've been behaving oddly," I said. "I passed my HR review and my psych exam, and it no longer snows in my bedroom when I have a bad dream, so I'd like to think I'm doing pretty well. Why don't you tell me if I've been behaving oddly?"

"There's no need to get defensive, Agent Marchen."

"Begging your pardon, sir, but you've dragged me away from my team and started asking invasive questions that you don't want to explain. This is the perfect time for me to get defensive."

"There's been another incident at Childe Prison," said Deputy Director Brewer.

I went very still.

"I asked whether any members of your team had been behaving oddly because there's going to be an investigation. As we both know, coincidences are rare in this line of work." He looked at me gravely, and for the first time, I saw the sorrow, and the concern, behind his eyes. "We need to know for sure that no one here has been subverted."

"Sir? What happened? Was someone hurt?"

"Yes, but that's almost secondary to the fact that someone escaped. Two someones, in point of fact. A fully active three-ten who had been kept on the inner ring of the prison, to prevent her from performing the classic 'let down your hair' maneuver, and one of the newer prisoners, who had been moved to the inner ring following her narrative exam and sentencing." Deputy Director Brewer's gaze never wavered.

My stomach sank. There was only one person I could think of who fit that description and had ties to my team strong enough to justify these questions. "Birdie," I said, trying to keep the tremor from my voice. "She got out, didn't she?"

The deputy director nodded. "Yes," he said. "Agent Marchen, I'm sorry, but for your own safety, you're being restricted from the field until she is recovered and brought back into custody. As the woman who first activated your story, we don't know how connected she may be to your narrative, or whether she would be able to—"

"Wait," I said, cutting him off midsentence. Maybe it was rude to talk over my boss. At the moment, I didn't care. What was he going to do, restrict me to a desk? He'd already done that. "Why did you ask about Elise and the glass? There's something you're still not telling me."

"Agent Marchen, please—"

"I have a right to know!" My voice broke at the end, becoming higher and shriller than I was comfortable with. I shook my head, swallowing until my throat felt halfway normal, and continued: "My team has been in her crosshairs more than once. She targeted Sloane. She *stole* Demi. Now you're going to send me back to them, to say that our personal bogeyman is out of her box. You need to give me something to work with. You need to tell me everything you know."

Deputy Director Brewer fixed me with a stern look. "Do you understand that I might be withholding information for your own good?"

"Frankly, sir, if I thought you were in the habit of withholding information 'for my own good,' I would've sought employment elsewhere by now." The words were out before I could fully consider what they meant. Because there was no other employment for me now, was there? There was the ATI Management Bureau, and there was Childe Prison, where we kept the active stories and ongoing narratives. The moment Birdie had put me into a position where I had to eat the apple, she had trapped me. There was no escaping for me now. There was just enduring, until I reached whatever botched mission or poisoned fruit pie spelled the end of my happy ever after.

"It's snowing." The deputy director's gaze flicked toward the ceiling. I looked up. Fat white flakes were falling from the air, drifting down around me. The air was growing colder. Soon, we'd be in the middle of our own private blizzard. "Agent Marchen, I recommend you drop this line of inquiry at once."

"Tell me."

He looked at me for a moment. Then he sighed. "Our missing three-ten had been kept in a windowless room."

"Can't let your hair down if there's no window," I said, acknowledging the wisdom of this choice.

"Someone transmuted half the wall of her cell into glass, which shattered to create a window through which her hair could be lowered," said Deputy Director Brewer. "Somehow, the wall to former Agent Hubbard's cell was breached, and she was able to gain access to the three-ten. From there, they made their way to the outer wall of the prison, and the three-ten, ah, 'let down her hair.' Both of them disappeared without a trace."

Something had been bothering me about his calm, measured recitation. Finally, I realized what it was. "What was her name?"

"Excuse me?"

"The three-ten. What was her name before the story took her?"

He blinked at me, looking startled, like the question I had just asked had been in some incomprehensible foreign language. "I don't know."

"Yeah." It was still snowing. When the flakes struck my hair, they stuck, unmelting. "I didn't expect you would."

The deputy director shook his head, shaking away the confusion, and said, "One of the guards who responded to the disruption came into contact with the glass. He was transmuted almost instantly. Two more guards were struck by flying shards when he exploded. Their families have been notified. The rest of the prison is on high alert."

I stared at him, too horrified to speak for several seconds. The snow began falling harder. "We lost two prisoners, and three guards died, and your response is to bench my team? Look, we know Birdie better than anyone. Demi can play the glass away, Sloane can punch her way through narratives—you *need* us. We can't sit back and let other people risk their lives if it's this bad."

"Yes, you can." He turned to his desk, opening a folder, and produced a single sheet of photo paper. He held it out to me. Automatically, I took it.

It was a picture of an apple, one bite missing, sitting in the midst of a pile of glistening glass shards. One of them was a perfect replica of a human's eye and cheekbone, the terrified expression preserved forever, or at least until the glass was destroyed. The apple's skin was as red as blood, as red as my lips, and made my heart stutter in my chest with combined fear and longing.

It was a message. It was a message that could only be meant for me. And I had no idea what it meant.

# # #

My team was still in the bullpen when I returned. They were pretending to work on their paperwork, stealing anxious glances at the door—all save for Sloane, who was neither working nor looking for me. She was still focused on her pie recipes. I found it strangely reassuring. No matter how bad things got, Sloane would never let on that she gave a fuck about anybody but herself. That was the way the world was meant to be.

Jeff was the first to stand, his eyes fixed on my face, and on the small snowflakes studding my hair. "Henry?"

"I'm going to say this once, and I'm going to say it without any of you interrupting me, because we need to get to work, and we don't have time to screw around with a lot of questions," I said. "Sloane, that means you too. Look at me."

Sloane turned her chair around, frowning as she took in the snow on my hair. "How bad?"

"Bad enough that there's a mini snowstorm going in the deputy director's office, and didn't I say no questions? Shut up and listen."

Sloane shut up. I had to trust that she was going to listen.

I took a deep breath, tasting the lingering promise of snowfall in the air, and said, "An unnamed three-ten escaped from Childe Prison today, after the wall of her cell was transmuted into glass by an unknown individual who, let's face it, was probably Elise. The three-ten took another prisoner with her. Former Agent Birdie Hubbard."

"Birdie's loose?" squeaked Demi. I decided not to treat it as a question. She looked terrified enough without me getting mad at her.

"The transmuted wall possessed the infectious qualities of Elise's earlier glassworks. Three guards were killed before they realized that they couldn't recover the prisoners." I took a deep breath. "There was something else. An apple, with a single bite missing, was left in the wreckage of Birdie's cell."

"They don't serve apples in Childe Prison," said Jeff. "It's considered too dangerous. Figs, pomegranates, and honey are banned for similar reasons. That apple can't have come from inside the prison."

"Exactly," I said. "Elise, or whoever she sent to recover Birdie, was leaving a message. I don't think I'm being egotistical when I assume it was for me."

"It might not have been." Sloane's voice was soft enough that it took me a second to realize she was the one speaking. I turned to her. She looked at me, and her walls were down: I could see agony and longing in her face. "Elise made a big point of how she changed her story, back when we arrested her. She was going to be free, and she was going to be the heroine, not the villain. She's done it. She's done it fucked up and weird and wrong, but she's still *done* it. The apple could be for me as much as it's for you. A reminder that I don't have to end in poison, if I'm willing to give up on everyone who's ever given a damn about me and go to join her."

"That's not going to happen," I said. Then I paused. "Is it?"

Sloane shook her head. "No. I don't give up that easy. What's a terrible narrative that will eventually destroy everything I love compared to the sheer joy of a government pension? She can't have me. I'm too fucking stubborn to go to work for someone like her."

"Assuming she's even in charge," said Jeff. "I don't believe Elise has it in her to mastermind something this complex. Birdie, on the other hand . . ."

"Birdie fancies herself a Storyteller," I agreed. "She could have put this all together as a contingency plan. Which means we don't know what else she has in place, ready to be triggered."

"What did the deputy director tell you to do?" asked Jeff.

"He told me to come back out here and tell you we're all benched for the foreseeable future," I said. "There's too much risk that Birdie will try to take control of our stories. Frankly, Demi, I think he's right where you're concerned. You're too new, and you're too powerful. We can't risk her taking you."

Demi nodded. There was no masking the terror and relief in her voice as she said, "I don't want to be okay with this. I want to fight with you. But I don't want to be the girl she made me into ever again. I'm me. I'm not some story she gets to tell the way she wants to. I can't go near her. I . . . I'm sorry. I just can't."

"Hey," said Sloane. Her tone was harsh, and I braced myself for whatever terrible thing she was going to say next. "Don't be sorry, okay? This isn't your fault. Our narratives can make us do terrible things, and someone using them as weapons against us is the worst thing I can imagine. So you stay here where it's safe, and if that bitch comes anywhere near you, you scream your fool head off. We'll come running.

Me, especially." She cracked her knuckles. "I want another shot at her so bad that I can taste it."

"Does it taste like desk duty and paperwork?" asked Andy. "You heard Henry. We're grounded for the foreseeable, and I for one am not going to argue with that. Birdie's dangerous. She's already hurt Demi and activated Henry. You think I want to give her another shot at us?"

"I think if we don't, there's no telling how many people she may harm," said Jeff. "We can't sit back and let others risk themselves while we hide in the corner."

"I love how 'please don't ask any questions' has turned into 'argue with each other while not actually asking questions,'" I said. I folded my arms. "All right. Who has vacation time to burn?"

Every hand went up.

"Good. Who here wants to stop Birdie?"

Every hand stayed up.

"Even better. If you want to stay here and anchor a desk, I am completely supportive of your choice. Demi, you need to keep yourself safe. Andy, the same thing goes for you—and more, you need to keep *Demi* safe. We're not leaving her alone here."

"I'm with you," said Jeff.

"If you even ask, I will rip your earlobes off," said Sloane.

"So we're going after her. The three of us will file for vacation, and we will find Birdie before she hurts anyone else." I looked to Jeff. "Do you still have a cot in the Archives?"

He looked guilty, but nodded. "Yes," he said. "I haven't been using it since I've been staying at your place. I just haven't had the time to dismantle it. Why do you ask?"

"Because the first thing we need is information, and if there's one place where I can learn more about people rewriting their own stories, it's the place where my own story was born." I uncrossed my arms, reaching up to brush the snow from my hair. I'd have more snow than I knew what to do with soon enough. "I need to go to the whiteout wood."

There was a momentary silence. Then Sloane slid out of her chair, standing, unfolding to her full and imposing height. "Why?" she asked.

"Because when Gerry was on the verge of manifesting as a Rose Red, he saw a field filled with flowers," I said. "Because some of the women in the wood have said things that make me think it's not the only one—that every story has its equivalent. We've just been rounding up the fairy tales and locking them away so fast that no one gets to talk about where their monomyth comes from." If you dug deeply enough into the Snow White story, what you found was blood on the snow, and the sacrifice at the heart of winter. There had to be something similar in all the narratives, something dark and enduring and cruel. It gave them the strength to feed, generation upon generation, on the hearts and lives of children. It gave them the strength to create people like me. I'd been born with white skin and black hair and red lips. I'd never had a chance.

It gave them the strength to kill.

"Let me see if I follow you here," said Andy. "You want us to help you drop down into that really vivid dream where all the other Snow Whites who've ever lived teach you how to be a better fairy-tale princess, and once you get there, you're going to what, go looking for the giant fireplace where all the Cinderellas are?"

"Something like that," I said. But it wouldn't be a fireplace, would it? It would be a forest like mine, made entirely of hazel trees sprouting from the graves of dead women. Their roots would be ripe with bones, and every branch would be heavy with birds, their avian eyes watching everything that happened. I knew it, deep down, in the part of me that was no longer Henrietta Marchen, but was something much older and more terrifying.

"Why?"

"Because maybe someone there will be able to tell me how Elise is pulling off this trick with the glass—how she was able to shift her story in the first place. All the Snow Whites are connected by the whiteout. Maybe the Cinderellas are the same. If they can give me anything that would tell me what Elise is planning, or what Birdie needs her for . . ."

"I don't like this." Jeff's voice was small. I turned to face him. "Henry, I know you're mad at Birdie for betraying us. I'm mad at her too. But if you start going to the whiteout wood because you want information on other people's stories, you're going to be giving *your* story more power over you. I don't want to lose you in there just because you don't have time to go through normal channels."

He looked like he was scared out of his wits, and I realized, with a distant sort of despair, that I loved him—genuinely loved him, the way I was supposed to have fallen in love with my personal Prince Charming, and not with a nearsighted Archivist who liked to keep pre-sliced fruit in the fridge so he wouldn't resort to the old stereotypes about elves and cookies. That wasn't the part that caused the despair. No, the despair came from the fact that I loved him, and it wasn't going to be enough.

"Birdie is manipulating the narrative. She has to be behind what Elise has been able to do. I don't know what kind of wood the Mother Gooses have, but I know the Snow Whites and the Cinderellas are close enough to one another that I can find out what sort of ripples Elise is causing. I have to do this. It's not a lack of patience or a lack of time; it's necessity. If we don't stop Birdie before she creates another Elise, who knows what damage she could do?" So many people were already dead, and I had the sinking suspicion that this was only the beginning.

"How do you get to the wood?" asked Sloane. "Just go to sleep?"

"Sometimes that works, but there's a faster way—and I think I know how to make it absolutely guaranteed." I swallowed the pulses of fear that were clawing their way up my throat, sent by the princess who was curled, sleeping, around my heart. "You're going to give me an apple. And I'm going to eat it."

Silence fell.

Silence didn't last. "That's it, she's snapped," said Sloane. "Call the men in the white coats, the snow bitch has gone off to happy fairy la-la land."

"No, I haven't," I said.

"I don't believe they wear white coats anymore," said Jeff.

Sloane stared at him. "Way to miss the fucking point, Poindexter. Your girlfriend wants me to feed her an apple. *Me.* I never met a piece of fruit I didn't want to poison. You get that, right? Even if you watch me like a hawk, I could still kill her."

"That's why I know it'll work," I said. "If I eat an apple you hand me, I'll be in the wood before I can blink."

"What about us?" asked Andy.

"You're going to stay here. You're going to do your jobs and stay safe, because that's the way it needs to be," I said. "Jeff, can you get that vacation paperwork started?"

"I still don't like this," he said.

"I'm not going to ask you to," I replied. "I'm just going to ask you to help me stop Birdie. Will you give me the apple? Will you help me into the wood?"

Jeff looked at me for a long moment before he sighed and stood. "You know I will. Wait here, both of you. I'm going to go get the paperwork." Then he was gone, moving with the sort of speed he only accomplished when there was something to file.

Sloane looked at me. "You sure about this, Princess?"

For once, I didn't bristle at the title. "No," I said. "But I don't see any other way."

She took a deep breath. "Fine," she said, finally. "I'll do it—*after* you try going to sleep and getting into the wood the way you normally would. All right? We're not risking your life and my status as a non-villain just because you're in a hurry. Okay?"

"Okay," I said, relieved. We might not be taking the fast way, but that didn't matter. We were moving forward. We were going to fix this.

# # #

It had been years since I'd taken a vacation. The amount of time I had banked up was as depressing as it was substantial. According to HR,

I could have walked off the job for a year before I ran out of stored days—assuming anyone would let me. Even getting a month approved was difficult, and probably wouldn't have happened without Deputy Director Brewer stepping in and saying we were doing it on his orders.

He knew. He knew what we were planning: I could tell as soon as I saw his face. His lips were set in a thin line, but his eyes were sad, like he wanted to say no and knew that he couldn't afford to stop us. Instead, he signed the paperwork that made me, Jeff, and Sloane free agents for the next thirty days, handed the pen back to the woman from HR, and left the office without saying a word.

After that, there had been nothing to do but make our way to Jeff's hidey-hole, where the cot was waiting. Going back to the bullpen would have been a waste of time, and time was becoming a limited commodity. We had a month. A month without Bureau resources, but without Bureau rules either.

We had to make the best use of it that we possibly could.

Jeff's cot looked like it had been stolen from a summer camp. It was long and narrow and made to military specifications, with creases at the corners and a blanket drawn so tight that I could have bounced a quarter off of it. There was a single pillow at the head of the cot, thin and uninviting. Looking at it made my heart hurt. This was what he'd had before he followed me home and started sharing my bed, which was utilitarian, but was at least more comfortable and more personal than this. We'd both been running from our stories in our own ways, and we'd both done ourselves a great deal of damage.

I unbuckled my belt and set it on the nearest shelf, not bothering to unclip my badge or service weapon. Neither of them could come with me where I was going. Then I shrugged out of my jacket and stepped out of my shoes.

"Jeff has done this with me before," I said. "It usually takes me about five minutes to fall asleep. I should be in the wood immediately after that. Don't wake me up. No matter what, not even if I'm thrashing around or having a nightmare, unless I'm clawing my own skin off, don't wake me up. I need to stay in the wood long enough to learn whatever there is to learn."

"You make this sound more and more appealing," said Sloane.

"Yeah, well, I never said it would be easy." I handed my jacket to Jeff, who kissed my forehead. I smiled at him briefly, not quite meeting his eyes, before I turned and sat down on the edge of the bed. From there, it was just a matter of stretching out with my head on the pillow and my hands folded on my chest in classic "dead girl in her glass coffin" style.

I closed my eyes.

I didn't go to sleep.

Seconds ticked by, stretching into minutes, until I had to admit defeat. This wasn't going to happen. Whether it was stress or the fact that it was the middle of the day and I've never been a napper, I wasn't going to be able to fall asleep. I opened my eyes. Jeff and Sloane were standing by the cot, watching me—him with concern, her with a sort of academic curiosity, like she was waiting for me to perform a particularly unique magic trick.

"It's not working," I said, and sat up. "We have to go to plan B." The apple would guarantee I fell asleep. I wasn't worried about waking up. We already knew Jeff could kiss me back to consciousness, if it came down to it.

"Are you *sure*?" Jeff's eyes were wide and worried. "We could find another way."

"Unless your other way involves me either taking a sleeping pill or running a marathon and eating a lot of turkey, I think this is our best bet." I stood. "I don't have any other method of guaranteeing I fall asleep before someone else dies. Do you?"

He turned his face away.

"I didn't think so." I turned to Sloane, who was standing silently by, watching our interactions. "Do you have the apple?"

"There's a question I never thought you'd ask me. It's weird, but I don't think I wanted you to. I think I would have been happier if it had never come to this." She pulled her hand out of her pocket. Somehow, she was holding an apple.

It was perfect. Red and gold and pink-skinned, with a rounded shape asymmetrical enough to look real, and flawless enough to look like the promise of paradise. My mouth started watering instantly.

"Honeycrisp," I said. "Really?"

"Go big or go home," she said, and held it out toward me, balancing it in the center of her palm. Her face was grave and serene. She was doing what she was made to do, just like I was. "What's it going to be, snowflake? Are you going to eat the apple, or are you going to turn around and run for safety?"

"Did you poison it?" My fingers twitched, aching to snatch the apple from her hand no matter what her answer was. It was there, it was *right there*, and I could have it, because it was meant for me. All I had to do was reach out and take it, and all this stupid worrying would be over. I could continue my story. I could be free.

"Does it matter?"

No. "Yes," I said, and took the apple, and bit deep. The flesh crunched under my teeth like all the leaves of fall. Juice filled my mouth, sweet and sharp and bitter at the same time. I chewed. I swallowed.

I fell, and I didn't even feel myself hit the ground. I just kept falling.

# # #

The ground beneath me was soft and cold. I stayed where I was, trying to get my limbs to respond. They felt like they had been weighted down. So did my eyelids. I moved my head to the side and felt the weight shift. Snow. I was covered in snow. Since I didn't think my private snowstorms had ever produced more than a few inches, it couldn't be mine, and that meant I had reached my destination: the whiteout wood, the place where my story went to live when it wasn't playing out in the waking world.

I opened my eyes. Snowflakes stuck to my eyelashes, turning the world prismatic and blurry. I blinked them away before sitting up, dislodging the snowbank that had formed on top of me. It was snowing harder than I had ever seen it snow here before. It was always winter in the wood—we were seasonal creatures, we girls born to bleed out until we brought back the sun—but the sky was usually clear, allowing us to see the black trees that grew in leafless splendor all around us. Black, white, red. Those were the colors of our world.

Only now the world had been reduced to nothing but white. I sat up further, brushing the snow from my arms and chest. No, not quite nothing but white: I was wearing a blood-red silk gown, like something out of one of the Colored Fairy Books. The trim was black and white brocade, matching the braided leather belt that rode around my hips. The theme of our story was being continued in my clothing, it seemed.

Our. That was the other problem. Normally when I arrived in the wood, the other Snow Whites were eager to come and greet me. Tanya had been elected my teacher, and she was doing an excellent job, all things considered, but as one of the few who was still capable of leaving the wood, the others saw me as a connection to the outside world, a place beyond the monomyth, where things happened. Ayane was always asking me about television and had tried to convince me to attend something called "San Diego Comic Con" before Tanya had shushed her. Judi usually wanted to know about current events. All of them wanted something from me, and that meant all of them should have appeared when I collapsed into the snow. So where were they?

I pushed myself to my feet, fully on my guard now that the strangeness of the situation was sinking in. The trees—barely visible through the snow—stretched out in all directions, never thinning, giving me no clue as to where the wood's edges might be, or which way I should go. Somewhere out there was a field of roses, where the Rose Reds whispered their own version of the monomyth into the uncaring wind. Somewhere was a city built entirely of towers, ringed with windowsill gardens that rioted with rampion, a Rapunzel in every window, a wall of thorns in every alley. And somewhere there was a forest of hazel trees, as ash gray as this wood was white. All I had to do was find it.

My sensible work shoes were gone, replaced by dainty, princess-like slippers. I kicked the snow off them and started walking.

The whiteout wood could seem limitless, especially when it was snowing, and I didn't know where I was supposed to go. I kept trudging forward, trying not to listen to the whispers carried on the wind. The whiteout wood talked to all its girls, telling us how our stories were supposed to go, coaxing our inner fairy-tale princesses out of hiding and into the light. It wasn't a quick learner. One of the Snow Whites I interacted with on a regular basis was a Deaf woman named Judi. She couldn't hear the wood whispering, because it hadn't yet figured out how to speak her language. She fought it with everything she had, and in her fight, she kept the girls around her from succumbing.

So where the hell were they? I plodded onward, forcing my way through the howling snow. Snow Whites would sometimes retreat to their private clearings when they felt threatened, or like they needed to be alone. I squinted at the trees I could see through the blizzard. Most of them were close-set, allowing me to walk, but not making it easy. Every now and then, however, there would be a pair that had grown in such a way as to look like a natural doorway.

The wind picked up, pushing me back. I adjusted my angle, pointing my body toward the nearest of those doors. The storm howled. I dove forward, grabbing the trees and forcing myself through, not quite sure what I was hoping would happen, but knowing I needed to try *something*, anything to get out of this weather. This was a fairy-tale world. Logic didn't apply the way it would have when I was awake, in a reality where diving between two trees didn't change the weather. I let go of the trunks, falling forward—

—and found myself tumbling into a pair of strong arms. They held me up with ease. "What are you doing here?" asked a voice, heavy with a Nova Scotia accent and with concern.

I tilted my head back and met the kind, anxious eyes of my teacher, Tanya. "Falling," I said, pushing myself upright. "Did you know there was a massive storm going on out there?"

"I did," she said, cocking an eyebrow upward. "Did no one ever tell you that when you have to fight to get into the wood, that means you probably don't want to be here?" She sniffed. "Your breath smells like apples. You little goose, what have you done?"

"Drugged myself into the narrative, because it refused to drag me down," I said. "I needed to talk to you. It couldn't wait—wait." I paused. There was no snow falling here, not even the light powder that was a semi-constant trait of the wood. The ground beneath my feet was brown, actually *brown*, covered in dead grass and withered clover. "Where am I?"

"My clearing, and I'll thank you to mind your step," said Tanya. I realized she was frightened. It seemed appropriate, under the circumstances. "It's very irregular to come into another Snow White's clearing without an invitation. Most of us won't come even when invited. It smacks of impropriety, and we want to avoid that at all costs."

"I'm a little less concerned with impropriety than I am with saving the world," I said, looking around.

It was definitely a clearing, in the truest sense of the word: we were at the center of a patch of open ground that looked like it was nearly thirty feet across. I looked behind me. There was the "doorway" I had thrown myself through, two widely spaced black trees through which I could see a howling blizzard. There was no logical way for me to have gotten so far from that door in my short fall, but I had done it, and once again had to remind myself that the laws of rational reality didn't necessarily apply here.

The ground was blanketed with dead grass, showing no traces of green, but it was still odd when compared to the unrelenting white and black and red of the rest of the wood. There was a large tree stump off to one side, as black as the rest of the trees, and two short logs had been rolled up next to it, where they could serve as chairs.

"I used to have a bed," said Tanya, apparently in answer to my scrutiny. "It was a lovely thing, all black wood and lacy white linens. But I stopped needing to sleep after I'd been here for a while, and it went away one day, while I was out visiting with the others. The wood knows what we need to be comfortable, and it provides it."

"Humans have to sleep," I said, looking back to her. "People who don't sleep are considered clinically insane."

"I'm not a person anymore," she said. "I'm a story. I've been here long enough that some of the trappings of humanity are starting to seem like pointless wastes of a time that's limited enough already. Here in the wood, I have as long as I could want to stand and look at the snow and think about what's to come. I could exist forever, if that was what appealed. But I don't sleep, or eat unless I want to, or make use of any bathroom facilities. It seems like we got things backward, doesn't it? All the time wasters go to the ones who don't have much time."

I frowned. Tanya was a Snow White. The wood whispered to her, and she whispered back: she knew what it wanted, and all the training she'd given me was partially designed to guarantee that one day, the wood would get what it was hoping for. I was the only active Snow White ever to serve within the ATI Management Bureau. If anyone was going to be in the position to start making changes to our shared story, it was me. So why the hell was she being so cagey and weird?

"Look, Tanya, I'm sorry if I broke some unwritten rule by bursting into your clearing without permission. If I'd been aiming, I would have gone for Ayane, since she's usually pretty up on what's going on around here." I always tried to use the names of the individual Snow Whites when I was speaking to them. It kept them more anchored in the here and now, and in the idea that they had identities of their own. "I know the Rose Reds have their equivalent of this place. Do the Cinderellas? I need to go there. I need to talk to them."

Tanya frowned. "You don't know what you're proposing, child. This is an idea that will do no one any good and will do you a great world of ill."

"I just ate an apple handed to me by a Wicked Stepsister, because there's an evil Cinderella wreaking havoc in the waking world, and I need to stop her before she kills anybody else," I said. "I think I'm sort of the queen of bad ideas right now, and I don't feel like fighting about it. How do I get to the place where the Cinderella story started? How do I get to their wood?"

Tanya continued to look at me, dazed and a little disconnected. It was like she wasn't really processing my words. That worried me. She had been my mentor since I first tumbled into the wood: she was the woman who really understood what it was to be a Snow White, and was helping me to control myself. She had never seemed like this before, disconnected and half aware of the world around her. Something was wrong. Something bigger than a blizzard.

"Where does Ayane live?"

"Who?"

"Ayane. Japanese, beautiful, sarcastic as all hell?" She had skin as white as snow and lips as red as blood, just like the rest of us. Our shared story didn't care about ethnicity or heritage. It just cared about rewriting us until we fit within its narrow walls.

"There's no one here by that name, my dear," said Tanya. "We're all Snow White here. You're Snow White too. You know it all the way down to the roots of you."

I stopped dead. Finally, I said, "You're not Tanya, are you? You're the wood. I'm talking to the wood."

To my horror, she smiled. She looked relieved, like she'd been hoping she could drop the pretense. "Yes, my dear," she said, and her accent was gone, replaced by a sweet neutrality that could have come from anywhere, from any*when*. "You didn't listen to the snow, so I had to find another way to reach you. This is a bad path you're setting yourself upon. You're not Little Red Riding Hood, to stray from your story, or seeking something East of the Sun and West of the Moon. You should stay here, in the trees, until the time comes for you to wake back into your own sinew and skin. To do anything else is to risk yourself, and I can't have that. I need you too much to allow it."

"You're not in charge of what I do with my life," I said, taking a step backward.

The wood continued to look at me, a soft, alien compassion reflecting through Tanya's eyes. "But I am, my darling. I've been in charge of your life since before you left your mother's womb. We can work together, when we need to. So many Sleeping Beautys birth my snow girls, my rose daughters. You've always been mine. I am your true mother, the only mother to matter, and I am telling you to set this quest aside. Let the little Cinderella do as she will. All the damage she can cause is not worth the loss of you."

"Wow," I said. I took another step back. "You know, I've always suspected stories weren't that smart. They can't be, because they have to leave so many of the details to the storyteller. You know what, lady? Or . . . deciduous forest, or whatever you are? I believe you when you say that you're responsible for my existence. My life is too fucked up to have been an accident. What I don't believe is that you're so unaware of who I am that you think this sort of approach will work on me."

The wood blinked Tanya's eyes. "You would defy me?"

"Lady, I'd defy the Brothers Grimm if it would save the world." I let my face go slack, eyes focusing on a spot just behind her. This was a lot to risk on the sort of thing that most second graders wouldn't fall for, but I didn't see another way. "What the hell is that?"

The wood turned.

I bolted.

Tanya's doorway might have regressed after I came through it, but it was still a pair of trees, rooted in the earth, and the woman who controlled them was trying to figure out what I'd been looking at. I dove through them, back into the blizzard, where the howling wind buffeted me and the snow struggled to whisper sweet lies in my ears. I wasn't safe, but I was away from one threat, and that was worth the difficulty of dealing with another. I started wading forward, into the white.

A pair of hands shot out from between two trees and grabbed my arm, yanking me to the side. I stumbled into another clearing. This one contained two women, and was carpeted in leaves the color of blood. That was less jarring than Tanya's dead grass. At least it fit the color scheme.

"What the hell are you doing here?" demanded Ayane, letting go of my arm. Behind her, Judi was signing violently. My ASL was still bad enough that I couldn't tell what she was saying, but she looked as angry as Ayane. I had never been so glad to see either one of them.

"We have an infectious Cinderella back in the real world, and I need to find the Cinderella equivalent of the whiteout wood so I can figure out how to stop her," I said. "Did you know the wood could take over people's bodies?"

"Uh, duh," said Ayane. "We're all doorways here. The wood does what it wants." Judi signed something; Ayane smiled. "All of us except for Judi. The wood can't tell her what to do. Every time it tries to take me, she shakes me out of it. You shouldn't be here. This place isn't safe for you right now."

"I'm picking up on that," I said. "Call me paranoid, but I *really* don't like the fact that the whiteout wood is having a temper tantrum at the same time that someone's using the Cinderella story to kill people. It's too big to be a coincidence."

"It's not," said Ayane flatly. "The Cinderella story is testing our borders, and the whiteout wood is reacting out of self-defense. You need to get out of here. Wake up."

"I can't," I said. "I ate an apple to get here."

Ayane stared at me. Then she turned to Judi and signed something—presumably a summary of our conversation. Judi stared at me before starting to sign back. Ayane nodded.

"Judi says you're a fool," said Ayane.

"I think she said a little more than that," I said.

"Yeah, but there are things I won't repeat unless I'm serving as a formal translator," said Ayane. "Do you have someone staying with your body? Someone who'll wake you up when necessary?"

"I do," I said. "My body's safe. Now tell me how to get to the Cinderellas."

Ayane sighed. "You're incredibly stubborn, you know that?"

"I do," I said again. "Which way do I go?"

"East," she said. "That's where the Cinderella girls go. To the east, and be careful. Bad things are coming."

"Bad things are here," I said grimly, and stepped back out into the blizzard.

The snow was howling past me, the wind struggling to push me backward, but I knew where I was going now; I had a direction, and that lent me the strength I needed to keep moving. The air blowing from the east tasted like cinders and empty rooms. That told me I was going the right way. I fought through the snow, hoping time wasn't distorting, and that I'd be able to reach my destination and ask my questions before Jeff decided I'd been sleeping long enough and kissed me awake.

"Hello again, little doorway," purred a voice behind me.

Something slammed into the back of my head, pitching me forward into the snow. Blood dripped past my open eye, painting the world red for an instant before everything went black, and my story slipped into silence.

Sleeping Beauty

Memetic incursion in progress: tale type 709 ("Snow White")
Status: IN PROGRESS

Henrietta Marchen was a perfect exemplar of her kind. Her skin was white as snow, and never tanned or freckled; the best she'd ever been able to accomplish was a violent burn that turned her entire body as red as her lips, which were the color of fresh-drawn blood. Once, in the third grade, she had gotten in a fight with another student who insisted on calling her a clown. She had blackened both his eyes, and he had mashed her red lips back against her white teeth, until real blood appeared to make the contrast in her coloration even more glaring. She had smiled, bloody toothed and feral, until he started crying for his mommy, and he'd never called her clown again, and her classmates had stopped looking her in the eye.

Her hair was the deep, unforgiving black of a raven's wing, and when she stood in the sunlight it threw back hints of other colors, buried gleams of blue and purple and green. But she wasn't standing in the sunlight now, and her eyes—normally so blue, like a morning sky, or a robin's egg—were closed. She wasn't moving. She wasn't visibly breathing. Henrietta lay on the narrow cot like one dead, her hands folded over her chest, and somehow, it seemed to be her coffin; it seemed to be the last bed she would ever know.

Like all Snow Whites before her, and all Snow Whites to come, Henrietta Marchen enjoyed the silent, blameless sleep of the departed. The air around her was cold, and smelled of apples, and nothing stirred.

# # #

This was inevitable.

I leaned against the wall, the half-eaten apple in my hand, and watched as Jeffrey mashed his lips to Henry's again and again, kissing her in a way that said less about love than it did about despair. I could have told him this was always going to be the ending. He wasn't a prince, and only princes can wake the dumb bitches when they fall fully into their glass coffins. They'd been able to play at happy ever after for longer than I'd expected. I didn't think he was going to be grateful about that.

I lifted the apple, turned it to the side without tooth marks, and took a bite. It was firm and crisp and a little too floral for my taste. I've never understood the way Snow Whites yearn for apples, but then, they've never understood the way I long to kill them all, so I figure it balances out in the end.

The sound of my teeth breaking through the skin of the apple was loud in the tight, confined space that we'd packed ourselves into for this little doomed experiment. Jeffrey raised his head. Salt spots glittered on the inside of his glasses, ghosts of the tears he'd been shedding for the past hour.

"Why won't she wake up?" he demanded. His voice was low and harsh from crying. "I've been kissing her. True love's kiss always worked before."

"I am not the expert here, and before you ask, no, I didn't poison her." I pushed away from the wall. "But I am the one who's seen this shit happen before. Henry's not the first snowflake to fall into the Bureau's clutches, just the first one to do this voluntarily. You know what happens next."

"No." Jeffrey gathered her into his arms, shaking his head violently. Henry hung limply in his arms, as unresponsive as the corpse she so closely resembled. "We can't."

"Uh, does this look like an enchanted forest to you? Have you been watching that show on ABC again? Just because she's a fairy-tale princess, that doesn't mean the laws of reality don't apply to her." I took a step toward him and another bite of the apple at the same time, chewing and swallowing before I said, "She's in a coma. The apple put her there. We need to move her to the modern equivalent of a glass coffin, or she's going to die."

"No," said Jeffrey.

"The Bureau has doctors who understand this sort of shit. They'll take care of her, okay? They'll hook her up to all sorts of tubes and wires and machines that make beeping noises whenever she pisses, and they'll keep her breathing until they can figure out how to wake her up." I didn't mention the fact that waking her up would probably involve taking a prince out of Childe on work release, or that receiving a prince's kiss would almost certainly cause Henry to be wiped away forever, replaced by the simpering Snow White the narrative had always wanted her to be. I didn't need to say those things. Jeffrey was a Bureau lifer, and he knew the score, no matter how much he wanted to deny it.

"Did you poison the apple, Sloane?" His voice was still low, but now it was dangerous too, filled with the kind of threat that only comes from a good man who's been pushed too far.

Normally, I would have applauded Jeffrey growing some balls. But Henry was barely breathing, and Snow Whites who sank too deep into their comas didn't always wake up again even *after* a prince got involved. For her sake, I couldn't fight with him.

"Having friends is *awful*," I muttered before saying more loudly, "No, I didn't. I wanted to. I always want to. But I also wanted her to wake up, because unlike some people I could name, I'm not a psycho who wants to wipe out the whole fucking human race and replace it with a giant ensemble production of *Into the Woods*. Okay? Now pick up your damn girlfriend and help me find someone who can get her to a hospital."

Jeffrey stared at me, looking like a startled rabbit. Then he sniffled, nodded, and stood, lifting Henry easily in his arms. The little Shoemaker was stronger than he looked, and she was lighter, at least right now. She was supposed to be someone who could be lifted by dwarves, and that meant the laws of physics had to bend, just a little, in her presence.

"Good," I said. "Now move your ass."

He moved his ass. I followed.

It was a damn shame it was all going to be for nothing.

# # #

"Please state your name."

The man from Human Resources looked at me like I was less than the dirt beneath his heels. I could feel the shadows of a story swirling around him, intangible but undeniable. I just couldn't get a fix on them, couldn't figure out what the narrative had wanted him to be. He was either averted or in abeyance: either free or waiting for the axe that hung over his head to come crashing down and split him in two. HR had a nasty tendency to hire those people, thinking they would "better understand" the plight of people like Jeffrey and Henry, who were fully on the spectrum.

What they forgot was that people who were waiting for their stories to activate tended to hate and resent the people who were living the tales that they were always meant to embody, and that people who'd been averted were afraid of the narrative coming back for a second pass. Basically, the Bureau stacked the deck against anyone who was on the spectrum, and they did it in the interests of keeping us all a little safer. The Bureau meant well, but sometimes I suspected that if the modern government were a fairy tale, the Bureau would have been the villain.

"I didn't ask you to make sure I remembered my name, I asked you to tell me where you'd taken Henrietta Marchen." I crossed my arms and glared at him. He was pretty short, and I'm five foot eleven. I barely even had to tilt my head back. "Where is she?"

"Please state your name," he repeated.

I narrowed my eyes. "Agent Sloane Winters, ATI Management Bureau, official designation five-eleven, Wicked Stepsister, verified as in abeyance. Where is Henrietta Marchen?"

"You're lying."

"And you're a Boy Who Cried Wolf," I snapped, his impending story suddenly coming into perfect focus. No one knows how to spot a liar better than someone who lives to lie. "Since we're both stuck here, how about you tell me where my boss is and then go fuck yourself?"

"Please state your name."

I stared at him.

The way I saw it, I had two choices. I could murder the shit out of this asshole, stuff his body in the nearest recycle bin, and try to find Henry on my own, or I could play along with him and see where it led us. He was with HR. It wasn't like he couldn't pull my records. "My name is Amity Green. I'm an agent with the ATI Management Bureau. My name change paperwork is on file with HR, along with the written records explaining why my birth name was no longer safe for me to use. Now where, you incredible asshole, did you take Henrietta Marchen?"

"Stand down, Tom." The voice was familiar. I turned. Ciara Bloom-field was behind me, her pirate shirt covered by a tailored jacket and her hair hanging loose around her face. The blue streaks were more pronounced than they'd been when she'd come to perform our review. Instead of being confined to her roots, they twisted all through her hair, extending to the tips.

She smiled when she saw me eyeing her hair. "It gets excited when it thinks we're going to start opening doors that we're supposed to leave alone. And no, I don't usually refer to myself in the plural, nor does my hair really have a mind of its own. No more than anyone else's."

"Okay, one, go fuck yourself," I said. "Two, go fuck yourself twice. Three, where the fuck is Henry and what the fuck are you doing here?"

"I've always found profanity to be a lot like bacon," said Ciara. "It works wonders on the flavor of your speech, but it lacks impact when used excessively."

"I'll use my foot right up your—"

She cut me off. "I apologize for Tom. He *was* sent here to stall you, while your boss scrambled to reach me at home. Fortunately for the organization, my husband and I hadn't left for our cruise yet." She produced a piece of paper from inside her jacket. "I regret to inform you that your vacation has been canceled." She produced a second piece of paper, holding both out toward me. "I also regret to inform you that you're not allowed to kill me, as I am your new temporary field leader."

"The fuck?" I took the papers from her hand and skimmed them. They seemed to support what she was saying to me. I looked up, eyes narrowed. "What is this shit? Field teams promote from within. You barely know us."

"Agent Santos is too new, you're too you, Agent Robinson is ineligible due to his lack of connection to the ATI spectrum, and Agent Davis is taking a medical leave of absence while he cares for his domestic partner." Ciara's smile was quick and thin, a razorblade of an expression. "He doesn't know that part yet. We'll be explaining it to him when we get to the hospital. Sorry about your vacation. I hope you weren't planning on heading for Disney World or anything."

"I have no idea what's going on right now, but I'm pretty sure I don't like it." I swung around to glare at Tom. He flinched. Good. If he could flinch when I looked at him, he could scream when I started hitting him. "Did you know about this? Is that why you kept asking for my name and not telling me where my teammate was? Think carefully before you answer. There will be penalties for answering wrong."

Tom looked uncomfortable and didn't say a word.

Jeffrey and I had left the storeroom together, him holding Henry in his arms, me following at what felt like a polite distance, still munching on the apple that had essentially killed her. It wasn't evidence, not in the strictest sense of the word, and I'd been hungry. Can't blame a girl for that.

Only it seemed that some people can. Andrew had started shouting as soon as we stepped into the bullpen, and then the deputy director had appeared as if by magic, and Jeffrey and Henry had been whisked away to an emergency vehicle, for transport to the nearest Bureau-approved medical facility. Andrew and Demi had followed in the team's van, leaving me alone.

No, not totally alone: the man from HR had appeared while I was throwing away the apple core and grabbing my jacket, and our little game of truth or dare had commenced.

"Please don't blame Tom, Sloane," said Ciara. "The procedures for handling transfer of authority during an emergency situation were established more than a century ago, and they didn't leave him much wiggle room. He needed to hold you here, and he needed to prevent you from becoming upset enough that your story would flare."

I rolled my eyes. "Oh my Grimm, you people. Ciara. You read my file before you came to interview us, right? I'm assuming that when they called you and said the shit had hit the fan, they supplied you with another set of files. A *thicker* set of files, with fewer things redacted. Did you read those?"

"I haven't had the chance," she said, somewhat apologetically. "I just got this assignment, and my clearance didn't allow me to look at the unexpurgated personnel records until I was already on my way over here."

"Gotcha." I took a step toward her. "I know the protocol you're talking about. I *wrote* the protocol you're talking about. See, for a long time, there was only one 'villain' working for any branch of the Bureau. It's funny, but they don't tend to hire much from the darker side of the narrative. Something about the body count being bad for morale."

"I don't understand what this has to do with anything," said Ciara.

"It means I know the protocol inside and out, and it says that in the event that a transfer of power has to occur following the injury or incapacitation of an active team member, all functional members of the team should be given the opportunity to go to the side of their injured colleague." I crossed my arms. "I wrote it that way when I first drafted the proposal, in 1884. So don't stand there pretending you followed the rules. It's not going to win you any points."

"I didn't follow the rules," said Ciara. "I followed orders. That's what I *do*, Sloane. Because if I start breaking orders, even the ones that sound pointless, I'm going to find myself in front of a door with a key in my hand, and then I'm going to be parted from my head."

I narrowed my eyes. "Who the fuck told you to stall me getting to Henry?"

"I did." Deputy Director Brewer stepped through the door behind Ciara. He looked tired. I remembered when he'd been a bright young thing, so enthralled by the idea that fairy tales were real—that his beloved girlfriend was a *legend*—that he hadn't considered the dangers.

He'd left the Bureau for thirty years after what happened to her. Most people thought the narrative had never laid a finger on him. I knew that wasn't true, but I also knew he'd been more than punished for what he'd done. He'd loved a happy ever after. He'd lost it all to once upon a time.

"Henry thinks you're a norm," I snapped. It was the nastiest thing I could think of to say.

His cheeks reddened. Reminders of Mary always did that to him. Pretty, sweet, guileless Mary, who could still be seen if you stood in front of the right mirror, and if you called her name three times. "Henrietta is occasionally blind to what's in front of her. She's spent too much time focused on her own story. That's part of what makes her an effective team leader: she doesn't get distracted. But it can mean that if you're not threatening to destroy the world, she won't realize there's anything unusual."

I transferred my glare fully to him. "Yeah, well. If you don't tell me why you're keeping me away from my team, you're going to find out how threatening I can be."

"Agent Winters, did you poison the apple you gave to Henrietta Marchen?" Deputy Director Brewer's face was long and sad, and I could barely see the echoes of the boy I'd known behind his tired eyes. Time is a bitch. Nothing good has ever come of it.

"No," I said.

"Are you working with Elise?"

"I'm sorry, did you mean to say 'are you intending to rip Elise's spine out through her mouth and show it to her before she chokes to death on her own blood'? Because that would be a much more reasonable question under the circumstances." I narrowed my eyes. "No, I am not working with Elise. I have every intention of *murdering* Elise as soon as I get the opportunity. You know what murder is, don't you? Do you need a demonstration?"

"She's telling the truth," said Tom. He sounded unsettled. I have that effect on people, especially ones who didn't know what they were walking into.

I used to feel bad about that sort of thing, a long time ago, back when I believed that one day the world would realize its mistakes and start playing fair. I stopped waiting for that sort of cosmic correction a long time ago. These days, I just try to make sure the people I unsettle deserve it, at least a little.

I narrowed my eyes further. It was getting hard to see through my heavily mascaraed lashes, but what I *could* see told me the effort was worth it. Both Ciara and the deputy director were squirming, refusing to risk meeting my gaze. "You did this—you kept me away from my team—because you wanted to be sure I hadn't switched teams. Really.

After all this time, you still don't trust me, Dan? I thought we understood each other better than this."

"No one understands you, Sloane; you least of all," said Deputy Director Brewer. Now he just sounded tired. "Birdie managed to subvert several other dispatchers and workers in the Archives before she was arrested. I had to be sure."

His words were like an electric shock. I stood up a little straighter. "Are you serious?"

"I don't tell your team everything that happens in this building; the word 'field' means you're supposed to be handling external threats, while the word 'director' means I'm handling the internal ones," he said. "I didn't tell Henrietta. I knew it would only upset her, and wouldn't change anything. Birdie was in prison. We didn't anticipate her escape. That was an error on my part. It won't happen again."

"But you weren't sure about me," I said. "How could you leave me in position if you weren't sure about me?"

Now the faintest hint of a smile touched his lips, and I saw my old teammate and rival in his face. Only for a moment, but still. That was long enough. "Because I knew that if you did anything, it would be huge and showy, and that if you *were* working for Birdie, leaving you in place might give us a bit of a heads-up when she was ready to move. Poisoning Henrietta would have qualified as huge and showy, but if you say you didn't do it, and Tom says you're telling the truth, then you're telling the truth."

"Why is it that I haven't murdered you all yet?" I asked, dropping my arms. "You would make beautiful corpses, and you would be way less irritating. More smelly, but less annoying."

"You'd miss us and you know it," said the deputy director. "I need you to accept Ciara as your temporary team leader. More importantly, I need you to convince your teammates that she's in charge. Henrietta is . . . we don't know when she's going to wake up. There are medical options. We're going to explore them all."

"And then you're going to go looking for a prince," I said grimly. "And what you wake up isn't going to be Henry anymore. You've got that, right? When you kiss a snowflake out of a storm, what you get is the princess at the center of the story, not the shell she wore. I've seen it before. I'll see it again." I was seeing the start of it now. There was a reason I'd always held Henry at arm's length, even when she was struggling to get closer to me: even when I wanted, more than anything, to be her friend. Because I'd always known that this would be the end.

Someone like me doesn't get to be friends with the princesses. We always wind up getting left behind.

"We'll be exploring all options," said the deputy director. "In the meantime, as you have been informed, your vacation has been canceled. You will report to Agent Bloomfield. You will follow her directions as you would follow Agent Marchen's."

"So when they're convenient and I don't think they're stupid, got it," I said.

"Convince your team. Agent Bloomfield will take you to Agent Marchen now." He turned and began walking away.

I should have stayed quiet. I knew it was the wiser course of action—but sometimes my better nature can't win out over my demons. "You know this is your fault," I said. "If you hadn't made it clear to her that she needed to find a way without using Bureau resources, she might not have gone for the apple."

He stopped, stiffening, but didn't turn around. Finally, he said, "I think about these things every night," and resumed walking.

# # #

Henry hadn't been moved to the nearest Bureau-operated facility, since it specialized in transformations and physical changes, people who had become trees or giant cockroaches or started aging in reverse. She was still in her own body, still the black and white bitch she'd always been, and so the ambulance had taken her to the coma ward above the local hospital, where we kept the sleepers whose naps weren't contagious. She was the only current patient, her hair making a splash of almost garish-seeming black against the white sheets of her bed.

Jeffrey was in the chair next to her, balancing a laptop on his knees, with half a dozen books resting on the edge of her mattress. In a pinch, he had been happy to turn his girlfriend into a desk. Considering the pair of them, that was almost romantic.

Andrew and Demi hovered around the edge of the scene, clearly unsure of what they should be doing. When they heard approaching footsteps they both turned, so unintentionally synchronized that I had to bite back a laugh. They wouldn't have appreciated it, and I didn't feel like picking a fight if I didn't have to. I was sure I'd find a reason to have to soon enough. That's the thing about being me: I can always find something to fight over. Call it my superpower.

"Sloane," said Andrew. "We didn't think you were coming." There was a challenge lurking in his tone, and the black, bitter imp that dwelt in my soul yearned to rise up and answer it. He'd thought I didn't care enough to come to Henry's aid when she fell, that much was plain.

With many of the Snow Whites I'd known, he would have been right. It had always been an insipid little milksop of a story, birthing pallid princesses whose idea of rebellion was doing someone else's laundry. Disney hadn't helped when he chose her as his crown princess, his template for a new generation of little girls to dream of. All he'd done was spread what used to be a relatively obscure fairy tale back into the public consciousness, undoing centuries of hard work, waking the sleeping blizzard in children around the world. Snow White was meant to run and bleed, a frozen hart in the body of a girl. How I had hated her, every time I'd met her, decade upon decade, century upon century.

But Henry was different. When my own story had started to struggle for freedom, Henry had been there, ready to put a hand on my shoulder and anchor me in my own body. When Henry had gone into the whiteout wood, she had come back as an avenging goddess of the living winter, with brambles for hands and frostbite in her eyes. Henry was *Henry*, and of course I cared. I would never have risked myself by giving her the apple if I hadn't.

Our relationship was complicated and painful and wonderful and one of the closest things I'd had to a true friendship since Mary. I wanted to tell Andrew that. I wanted to make him *understand*. I opened my mouth, and what came out was a genial, "Go fuck yourself with the nearest available vorpal blade. Maybe we'll get lucky, and the snicker-snack will leave you gelded."

"Can you not?" whispered Demi. "Just this once, can you not? Henry won't wake up."

"I know." I managed, somehow, not to insult her or tell her to go jump off the nearest bridge. Maybe it was her eyes. She looked so miserable, like she was the one in the coma, and not Henry. "I gave her the apple."

"And she thanked you for it, as do I," said Jeffrey, finally looking up. "What took you so long, Sloane? I know you wouldn't have dawdled without a good reason."

"Well, my vacation has been canceled, and as the senior member of this field team who *isn't* in a coma, I needed to officially greet our new team leader," I said. Ignoring the gasps from Andrew and Demi, I continued, "She's filling out the last of the paperwork needed to transfer control of the team to her. Once that's done, I figure she'll be joining us. That, or she'll realize this is a terrible fucking team and we're going to get her killed, and she'll be running for the hills."

"They can't give us to some stranger!" gasped Demi, sounding scandalized. For the moment, Henry's enchanted sleep had been superseded as the most offensive thing in the room. It was always fascinating to see where people's priorities lay. "We can't . . . I mean, I won't . . . I'm not going to take orders from somebody I don't know!"

"Demi, you work for the government," said Jeffrey, removing his glasses and pinching the bridge of his nose. He looked worn out, like Henry's nap had been going on for years instead of hours. Illness, whether enchanted or natural, had a way of doing that to people. It used them up, like my father's death had used my mother up, all those years and names and narratives ago. "You're always going to be taking orders from people you don't know. Even when you get them from someone familiar, they're probably originating with someone you don't know. Please don't make this harder than it has to be."

"But they can't replace Henry! She's our leader, not some stranger!" Demi's fingers curled, like she was trying to summon her flute from its case through the sheer force of her indignance. "They can't do this!"

"I know why you're angry." Jeffrey and Demi both turned toward me, her eyes widening, his mouth narrowing, like they'd forgotten who started the discussion. I shook my head. "Henry's a fairy-tale princess in an enchanted coma, and now they're bringing in a ringer. It pretty much says, 'she's never coming back' to me. Even if she wakes up, she's looking at a short ride to Childe and a long lockup in a room with no doors. But that's not going to happen, because she's *our* fairy-tale princess, and I'll be fucked before I'll let them have her. Our temporary leader isn't a stranger either. It's that Bluebeard-fetishist bitch from HR."

"Ciara Bloomfield?" asked Jeffrey.

"That's the one. She doesn't want to stay here. I mean, sure, she works for the Bureau, but look at how she's been controlling her own story. She married her villain and she's staying with him because she wants to." I'd never heard of a Bluebeard's Wife who'd been so changed by her narrative before meeting Ciara. The blue hair, the pirate blouses . . . she was turning into something new, because she was wrestling her story to a standstill. "She's going to keep us from getting killed while we figure out how to wake up the snowflake here, and then it's going to be back to normal. You'll see."

They kept staring at me. Finally, Andrew spoke. "You're not normally the encouraging one," he said. "Are you sure she didn't put some sort of a spell on you? An HR spell, that makes you play nicely with others for a change?"

"Believe me, if HR was developing that sort of spell, we would have used it on Agent Winters long ago," said Ciara, stepping through the door and walking toward the five of us. She had taken the clips out of her hair, emphasizing the blue streaks. Either she was trying to look like part of the team, or she had been playing respectable for the deputy director. Time would tell which was true.

"I'd slit your throat before your pet witch could say more than a sentence and you know it," I said.

"It's good to see you too, Agent Winters," said Ciara, with a hint of a smile. Then she turned to the others. "Greetings. While we've met before, it seems appropriate to introduce myself again at this juncture. I'm Ciara Bloomfield, and I'll be your field team supervisor until Agent Marchen recovers from her current situation. Once she wakes up and is judged fit for duty, I will be glad to step aside. We want to preserve the continuity of your team, and HR understands that Agent Marchen's leadership is a large part of that continuity."

Demi's fingers were still twitching, marching through unseen lines of notes as she played some destructive melody in her mind. Aloud, she asked, "Who gets to judge her fit for duty?"

"Among others, I do," said Ciara. "I know we don't know each other as people yet, and that you have no concrete reason to believe me, but please try to trust me when I say I don't want this job. I wouldn't even be taking it if we weren't in a Bureau-wide state of emergency right now."

"Birdie?" asked Jeffrey.

Ciara nodded. "All vacation has been canceled. All non-critical medical leave has been canceled. Agent Davis will be allowed to remain here to monitor Agent Marchen, in part because former Agent Hubbard has already targeted this team several times. Leaving one of its members unguarded and defenseless would be foolish."

"So we're leaving two of them unguarded and defenseless; much better," I said. "How many hearts were you in the mood to scrape off the ceiling? Ballpark number, so I can start shopping for funeral gear."

"There will be guards stationed at the door at all times, and Agent Davis will be expected to keep up his research duties while he remains here," said Ciara, ignoring me like a pro. It occurred to me that she could have read *all* my files. She'd said she hadn't, but if she was a liar, most of my tricks would be familiar to her. Damn. "We'll be in constant radio contact, if nothing else. No hearts will be scraped off the ceiling on my watch if I have anything to say about it."

"How bad are things out there?" asked Jeffrey.

For the first time, Ciara sobered. "Bad enough that I canceled a cruise with my husband to come here and take over this team. Bad enough that Childe is calling inactive guards back to duty. There have never been this many breakouts in a short period of time. They're turning up the calming charms, and the inmates are still on the verge of riot. They can taste change on the air, and they want a part of it."

"Do we have any idea what Birdie *wants*?" asked Andrew. "I know she was going for the Index before—at least that's what Henry said; I was asleep at the time—but it's just a book. It doesn't control anything."

Now it was my turn to stare at someone. All of us gaped at Andrew, even Demi, who had only been part of the Bureau for a short time. I had seen the organization born, and the urge to claw his eyes out for saying that was stronger than I cared to consider. I took a deep breath, trying to calm the murderous impulses that were suddenly thrumming in my veins.

Be better than this, you have to be better than this, I thought, scolding myself the way my mother had always scolded me, before the narrative started taking root in our innocent little family. *You are a wicked, wicked child, and I will never ask you to be a good girl, but I will always ask you to be better.*

It didn't help as much as it used to, back when I could still remember what my mother's voice had actually sounded like, instead of what I had turned it into, one century at a time. It helped enough that I could trust myself to speak without screaming. "The Index links every story in the world to their monomyth," I said. "It says 'Snow Whites have skin as white as snow, and hair as black as coal, and lips as red as blood,' and it says 'they will always eat the apple, except when the apple is a pomegranate, or a wine-red grape, or a slice of cake.' It says 'this is how they live, this is how they love, this is how they *lose*,' and we protect it because when you change it, you change the stories it connects to."

"That doesn't make any sense," said Andrew.

"Snow Whites used to wear a poisoned girdle," I said. "Disney left that out. It got less common, because people didn't think about it. But the Index remembers, because the Index was written by people who wanted to know *every* angle, *every* aspect. They codified legends, and they turned them doubly dangerous."

"The original, mundane ATI only covered European and some Middle Eastern stories," said Jeffrey, sparing me the rest of the explanation. "We've expanded it since then, because we've had no choice. There are more stories in the world than just the ones that emerged from Germany or the British Isles."

"You don't say," said Andy, tone turning sarcastic. "I still don't understand how writing them down made them worse, or why we kept doing it if it was such a bad thing."

"Writing them down made them easier to identify and prevent," said Jeffrey. "When a baby is born with Henry's skin tone, or with hair that grows unnaturally fast and strong, it's easy to figure out what story the narrative is trying to shape them into. The trouble was, increased iconography came with increased awareness. The more we write the stories down, the more they anchor themselves in the public consciousness, and the less they change."

"Stories are like the sea," said Ciara, jumping in. "They naturally ebb and flow and change. They're tidal things, mercurial and wild. We put them in cages when we started the Index, and they're angry. They grow stronger the longer they stay caged, which makes them harder to contain. They also grow more rigid, less capable of adapting to new situations and circumstances."

"So like when this little girl in my first grade class got angry because I was cast to be Cinderella in my school play?" asked Demi hesitantly. We all turned to look at her. She reddened and ducked her head, but kept talking. "She said you couldn't have a Mexican Cinderella. Our teacher said *anybody* could be Cinderella, but this girl just kept shouting how that wasn't the story."

"First grade racists," said Andrew. "I hope you knocked that kid down on the playground."

"Somewhat like that, although the narrative is less strict about race and gender than some children can be," said Ciara. "The stories don't change as much, because they've been written down, and the versions people tell one another come from those transcriptions. But when they do change, they have teeth."

"None of this explains why we're still keeping the Index," said Andrew.

"Because we'd rather have a bunch of really nasty monsters that we know how to identify and fight than uncounted invisible monsters that can strike at any time," I said wearily. "The mundane ATI covers Europe. Ours covers everything, because there was a period where only the European stories could be averted." A Woman with Two Skins had stalked the streets of Boston once, when I was younger and less willing to ask for help; she had killed more than fifty people trying to enact her story, and would have killed more if one of the Archivists hadn't convinced someone to tell him her story and let him write it down. The Index was our greatest weapon and our greatest burden, all at the same time.

"If Birdie gets the Index, she could rewrite any story to end in any manner she wanted," said Ciara. "She could make it so that Snow

Whites all died a true death upon eating the apple. She could make the Sleeping Beautys put entire continents to sleep. Her potential for mayhem would be unlimited."

"It's worse than you think," said Jeffrey. He turned back to Henry as he spoke, like telling her would somehow hurt less than telling the rest of us. "She could write her *own* stories. The Index . . . it started off as a way for people to keep track of the narrative. We told each other about it. We taught each other to trust it. We gave it narrative weight, and there's no way we can take that away again."

There was a moment of stunned, horrified silence. Finally, Ciara asked, "Are you sure?"

"No." Jeffrey looked up again. "I'm not sure of anything anymore. But am I right? I'm terribly afraid I am. If you want to save the story you call the world, you need to move, because you don't have as much time as you need."

We moved.

# # #

Birdie's house had been roped off by the Bureau since the explosion that had taken out the living room, half the yard, and most of the back hallway. It helped that there weren't any neighbors: she had been a loner, living on the edge of the forest in her own little fairy-tale cottage. That probably should have been a warning sign. It was definitely a sign that the Bureau had gotten too big to police itself safely. Back when I'd joined up—first as a prisoner, then as a curiosity, and later as an agent, when all the people who remembered my origins were safely in their graves—we'd been in one another's business constantly. No one would have been able to hide a plan like hers.

"The modern world sucks sometimes," I muttered, turning over a piece of charred drywall with the toe of my boot. That was one place where the modern world *didn't* suck: The ready and affordable availability of sturdy footwear. I firmly believed that no one really understood the value of a good pair of boots anymore.

"What was that?" asked Andrew.

"Nothing," I said. I kicked the piece of drywall across the room for emphasis. It hit the far wall with a thud; somewhere deeper in the house, Demi squeaked with surprise. "She's not coming back here. There's nothing in the Mother Goose framework that says she has to have a single nest, and this place is trashed. It's not fit for human habitation."

"So where's she gonna go?" asked Andrew. "She has no job, no known associates, no credit cards. Her bank accounts were frozen after she was locked up in Childe. Face it, the lady's out of options."

"She has a Cinderella who can transform people into glass with a single shard, and a Rapunzel we still haven't identified," I said. "She doesn't need anything else. Between the two of them, she can take over whatever she wants."

"So where do *you* think she is?"

I paused, narrowing my eyes. "That's not my job."

"I know," said Andrew. "You're the lazy one. You go where you're sent, and you do what you're told. I've watched you for years, and I've never understood it. You don't seem like the type who likes to follow orders."

"I hate it." I flipped another piece of drywall with my toe. "It makes me want to scream and slit throats. That's why I do it. Sometimes you have to act against character if you want to have any freedom at all. Why are you talking to me, anyway? You don't talk to me."

"Henry talks to you."

That was true. Henry talked to me, which was something hundreds of people had decided not to do since the day I became the Bureau's problem. I would never have been as nice to her as I was if she hadn't talked to me. I wouldn't have been as mean to her either. She was a target because she'd made herself an ally, and if there was one thing I knew for sure, it was that I wasn't allowed to have allies. The narrative wouldn't stand for it.

"Henry doesn't have the sense Grimm gave the seven dwarves," I said. "Fuck off."

"Nope." Andrew crossed his arms. "Not going to do that, because we're down two people for as long as Henry's in the hospital, and I don't know this Ciara lady well enough to trust her with my life. I've got a husband. I'm starting a family. Demi's still just a kid. It's time for you to step up, pull your head out of your ass, and do your damn job like the rest of us."

I blinked at him slowly, trying to process his words. Finally, almost gently, I asked, "Do you know how long it's been since somebody spoke to me like that?"

"Too damn long, apparently," he said. "What do we do, Sloane? If Birdie isn't coming here, where is she?"

I took a deep breath, forcing down the rage that struggled to rise up and overwhelm me. Anger was my constant companion, more faithful than my sister's memory, more familiar than my mother's faded voice. Finally, I said, "Rapunzels are only comfortable in towers. Cinderellas are drawn to glass. And Birdie's going to want something that fits her whole 'bird' theme. Look for a skyscraper or hotel with an avian name."

"Like the Swan?" Demi's voice was hesitant. I turned. So did Andrew. She was standing in the hallway door, her flute clutched tightly in her hands. It occurred to me that she was holding it more and more these days. It was becoming her security blanket, and maybe that wasn't such a good thing, considering what she was.

Then again, maybe we weren't going to live long enough for her to turn on us. "Where's the Swan?" I asked.

"It's a tourist trap hotel outside of town, near the wineries," said Demi. "My mom used to work there, before she quit to stay at home with me and the brats. It's four stories tall, and the whole front of the building is glass, so the tourists can see the grapes growing while they're sitting inside, drinking their wine. It's really expensive."

"Bird name, glass wall, near something that has vines?" I said. "That's it. That's where Birdie's going to be hiding, at least for right now."

"Don't you think it's a little on the nose?" asked Andrew.

I looked at him flatly. "Haven't you learned anything from your time with the Bureau? The narrative is all about 'on the nose.' That's what gives it the power it needs to do the things it does. The more 'on the nose' something is, the better position it's in to serve the story. This place exists, so it's where they're going to be."

"Then we need to be there too," said Andrew. "Good work, Sloane." He turned and walked away, presumably to find Ciara. I stared after him, unable to shake the feeling that he'd tricked me somehow, and that bad things were inevitably going to follow.

# # #

We pulled up in front of the Swan barely forty-five minutes later. Ciara wasn't as aggressive a driver as Henry sometimes was, but let's face it: neither was Mr. Toad from *The Wind in the Willows*. Henry never met a stop sign she didn't feel needed to be run, or an unprotected left turn she didn't want to take at top speed. Ciara obeyed traffic laws and brought the vehicle to a complete stop whenever necessary. It was just that somehow the car handled better for her, and the lights seemed to stay green just that fraction of a second longer than she needed to blow through every intersection that we came to.

She caught me looking at her speculatively as we pulled up in front of the hotel. Her grin was a cutlass slash across her face. "The narrative doesn't know what to do with me. I'm a Bluebeard's Wife. My story ends in either decapitation or widowhood. So it's trying to fit me into something else. I think it's hybridizing me a bit with Sweet Polly Oliver and a little bit with Anne the Pirate Queen. Any ship I sail finds calm seas and safe harbor, and that includes the cars I drive."

"You should join NASCAR," said Andrew.

Ciara laughed. "Believe me, I've considered it."

The hotel looked normal, save for one thing: It was perfectly still. Nothing moved. Sunlight glittered off the glass front of the building, and a bird chirped somewhere in the distance, but apart from that, everything was still. Ciara stopped laughing. Slowly, the four of us got out of the SUV. Demi was clutching her flute again. I didn't say anything about it.

The Bureau has used me as a story detector for years. I'm wound tight in the narrative without quite belonging to it—quite—and so I can tell, sometimes, when things are about to start happening. As I closed the door behind me, the sticky-sweet feeling of being wrapped in a hundred yards of cotton candy began to muffle my limbs, trying to tangle them and hold them fast. There was a story unwinding here. I just didn't know which one it was.

"We were right," I said. I projected irritation and outright anger at the cotton candy shackles, and they loosened enough to let me move. The madder I was, the more the narrative recognized me for what I was, and the less it would try to restrict me. It wasn't fair. The Bureau only kept me fed and free because I was useful to them, and being useful meant embracing the parts of myself that played most into my story. I would lose myself someday, and all for the sake of serving them a little better in the time I was allotted.

I'd already had a fuck-lot more time than anybody else got. I snorted once, pawing at the ground with one foot as I shook off the last of the cotton candy. And then I ran.

I've always been good at running. Sometimes I wish the narrative could have found a story about a girl who ran around the world and shoved me into *that*, instead of into the role it chose for me. I could have run forever in the service of the story, and counted myself lucky when my heart burst in my chest and my body fell lifeless to lie on unhallowed ground. But that was not to be, and instead of becoming the Girl Who Runs, I became a girl who was always running, running from herself, running toward the story, running for the things that would destroy me. I just wished they'd hurry up and get on with it.

The door wasn't locked. It slammed open when I hit it, swinging back until it struck the wall and rattled in its frame. I stumbled to a stop, gazing in horror at the lobby. My feet seemed to have been nailed to the floor. I looked down, and saw that I was standing in something black, viscous, and sticky. Pitch. There was pitch on the floor.

In some versions of Cinderella, her shoes fit fine, and the ball went on for three long, glorious nights. But the Prince got tired of his beautiful girl running away from him, and so on the third night he ordered pitch spread on the palace steps. She ran, because that was what Cinderellas were built to *do*, and she lost a shoe when her feet got stuck.

"You were taunting *me* all along, weren't you?" I felt strangely serene all of a sudden. I didn't have any knives on me, and the thing about good stompy boots was that they tended to come with sturdy laces. I was tied into my shoes from ankle to knee, and there was no way I was going to get out of them before the glass statues surrounding me started to explode.

Elise must have entered the lobby without anyone noticing that something was wrong. That was good information, in its way: she still looked more human than storybook, she could still move easily through crowds. Some of them had turned to look at her. I knew that, because they hadn't moved since. There were only eight of them, two behind the front desk, the other six scattered throughout the room. Eight was more than sufficient. When they fractured, they would spray shards everywhere, and there would be nowhere for me to hide. Not with the pitch gluing my feet firmly to the floor.

"Agent Winters?" Ciara sounded more concerned than distressed. My body must have been blocking all direct view of the lobby. With the sunlight glinting off the glass, the statues inside would look like ordinary people. By the time anyone realized they weren't moving, it would be too late.

"Don't come in here!" I twisted as far as I could with my feet glued to the ground, putting out one hand in a warding gesture. Ciara stopped. Demi and Andrew stopped behind her. "It's a trap. You can't come any closer."

"Why are you still standing there?" demanded Andrew.

"Because she spread pitch on the floor, you ass," I snapped. "I'm stuck. Trapped. Finished. Fucked. Back off before she gets you too." I was in the doorway. The door wouldn't close enough to save me, and that meant I couldn't keep the shards that would be flung when my body exploded from getting the rest of my team.

"I can fix this," said Demi, raising her flute.

Suddenly it all came clear. The glass statues, standing frozen rather than exploding into contagious fragments, were a trap for more than just me. "If you play one note, I swear to Grimm I will find a way to return from the grave and rip your fucking arms off," I snarled. Demi froze again, this time looking hurt. "You play, the statues go boom, we all die a horrible death, instead of just me dying a horrible death. Get out of here, all of you."

"Why are you not trying to get loose?" asked Andrew.

"Too many shoelaces, not enough knives," I said. "I'm not allowed to carry anything sharp. Something about the Bureau liking the rest of you without any holes."

"How much can you lift, Agent Winters?" asked Ciara.

I blinked. "I don't know. A hundred pounds?"

"Good. Catch." With no more warning than that, she flung herself at me, traveling on an arc that would have carried her past my position and into the pitch if she wasn't stopped. Instinct kicked in. I grabbed her around the waist, stopping her in midair.

Ciara turned her head so that she could grin at me. Then, in a surprisingly fluid gesture, she pulled a rapier from her side—which didn't make any *sense*, I would have *seen* it if she'd been carrying it before—and sliced cleanly through my shoelaces.

"All better," she said, which was when the statues began to vibrate.

"Fucking *run!*" I shouted, leaping out of my shoes with Ciara still tucked under one arm. I ignored the pain of the stones and thorns under my feet as I hauled ass toward the SUV. After a moment of stunned surprise, Demi and Andrew followed.

Ciara might be an excellent driver, but she wasn't much for vehicle security, and she hadn't locked the doors. I jerked the driver's side door open, flung her through, and then jumped in on top of her, slamming the door as I did. There was a matching slam from the back as Andrew and Demi took cover.

The sound of the front of the Swan shattering was like the world's biggest Christmas ornament being dropped. The glass shards hit the side of our vehicle a moment later, the shock wave setting the whole thing to rocking. Miraculously, the windows held.

Silence fell. Ciara pushed weakly at me; I shifted to let her crawl out from under me.

"They're not playing fair," said Demi.

"No shit." I looked out at the shattered Swan. The trees and bushes in the formerly manicured yard were transforming into glass—more slowly than flesh would have changed, but just as irrevocably. There was no telling whether anyone in the hotel was still alive, not until the cleanup crew got here and we were able to start sifting through the shards.

"So here's a question for you," I said. "What are we going to do about it?"

No one said a word.

Frostbite

Memetic incursion in progress: tale type 709 ("Snow White")
Status: ARCHIVED

Her name was Adrianna. It had been something else once, something longer, but that no longer mattered. Her family had forsaken her, and she was happy to forsake them in return. Here and now, within the walls of Childe Prison, her name was Adrianna. She had skin as white as snow, lips as red as blood, and hair as black as coal. She was young and beautiful, tired of being a captive.

It had taken the better part of nine months to earn the trust of the Miller's Daughter in the cell next to hers. She'd accomplished it, because she'd had no other choice. It grated on her nerves to play the victim, to put hurt and hopelessness in her voice, where only anger and resentment belonged. But that was done with: like her name, like her family, it was in the past. What mattered now was the thin golden rope she held in her hands. It was long enough to loop around her cell's single light fixture. It was strong enough to hold.

Oh, yes. She was sure of that.

Adrianna had been locked up in 1972, after her rampage left more than a dozen people dead across the heartland of America. It wasn't the Bureau that stopped her, amusingly enough: they'd still been chasing their tails around her hometown when she'd been picked up by the local police. One of the taillights in her stolen car had been out. Just her luck. They might still have let her go, if she hadn't been covered in so *very* much blood.

She'd been carted off to a mundane prison, surrounded by mundane prisoners who had no idea what kind of monster had been dropped into their midst. She'd killed eight of them before the Bureau managed to tote her away to Childe Prison, where the whispers in the walls were crueler than the whispers on the wind in the whiteout wood.

Shame, shame, whispered the forest. *You shame your story.*

Bad little girl, whispered the prison. *Learn your place and be grateful that you have it.*

Adrianna dragged her low wooden chair into position under the light fixture. They had been more than happy to lock her up, those mundane policemen with their eyes full of confused fear, those Bureau bastards who never thought to ask what had set her off and left her to be consumed by rage. They had never once asked how she had grown to adulthood without losing herself to either her temper or her story.

She could have told them, oh yes, she could have told them. She could have told them about redheaded sisters who decided they didn't like their stories anymore, who dyed their hair and went looking for a different life. She could have told them about accidents, and comas, and princes who never came. It was surprisingly easy for a Rose Red to become a Sleeping Beauty, if the situation was orchestrated carefully enough and if that Rose Red's Snow White wasn't around. The narrative will have its due.

No matter how hard you fight, no matter how cunningly you rewrite the world around you, the narrative will have its due. Adrianna had learned that the hard way when it cut her sister down, and if she had reacted poorly, well. It was no more than could have been expected of her.

The wood might shame and disdain her for what she'd done, but it couldn't keep her out. She was a Snow White, just like all the pretty porcelain princesses who'd chosen to live and die within the structure of their story, and the whiteout wood would always be open to her. She knew how much it hated her presence. It treated her like a disease, blackening the ground under her feet, sweeping the sky free of clouds and replacing them with plumes of smoke, like all the world was burning. Snow White could come in ash and ember as well as in ice and apples.

Let it do its worst. She was still its child; she belonged within its borders, and it couldn't keep her from knowing when another sister in story was born. The latest was just a baby, barely a day in the world, unaware of what destiny awaited her. She'd have plenty of time to learn to hate the narrative before she was old enough and strong enough to serve Adrianna's purposes.

Really, it wasn't theft, no more than it was suicide. The girl would grow and learn what a terrible hand she'd been dealt. By the time Adrianna came along, she would be pathetically glad to get out of her life and into the whiteout wood, which would love and welcome her as one of its own.

"I'm coming for you, little doorway," whispered Adrianna, slipping the golden noose around her neck. "Just be patient, and I'll open you wide."

The guards didn't find her body until morning. While no one said it, they all secretly agreed that it was a good thing that they wouldn't have to deal with her anymore. She upset the other prisoners.

In the whiteout wood, the clouds began to change.

# # #

Adrianna's first blow had managed to catch me from behind, sending me sprawling and helpless into the snow. I'd even blacked out for a few seconds—which, ironically, was probably what saved me. She couldn't use me as a door into the waking world if I wasn't awake.

I awoke to find her shaking me viciously back and forth, slamming my head down so hard that I would probably have suffered a concussion if not for the snow that covered everything. "Wake *up*!" she snarled, princess-pretty features distorted with rage. "I did *not* bring you this far just to have you slip away from me now!"

I responded with a fist to her jaw, followed by a shove that sent her reeling backward, away from me. I scrambled to my feet. There was a black branch on the ground nearby, its thicker end red with blood. My blood. I grabbed the branch with one hand as I reached back to feel the base of my skull. My fingers came away sticky. I narrowed my eyes.

"You are a piece of work, you know that?" The branch was a good weight, almost like a baseball bat. It would serve me well. It had already served her.

Adrianna was standing slightly hunched over, her permanently bloody mouth twisted into a cruel line. She glared at me. I glared back.

"You have no idea what you're doing when you fight me, little doorway," she snapped.

"That's not my name."

"Neither is 'Henrietta.'" She spat it out, letting the wind whip away the syllables that defined me. "Your mother would never have given you such an ugly name. You should have been a Nieve or a Bronwyn or something else elegant and lovely. But they named you 'Henry,' and you tried to grow into your name rather than making your name grow into you."

Both the names she'd suggested meant "white." I remembered when some of the girls I'd gone to school with had looked up the same names in the library, bringing them to me on a sheet of paper along with a dozen others, all sharing the same insipid, predictable meaning. We were eight at the time. They'd been making fun of my corpse-like complexion. "Did you never mature past second grade?" I asked. "Mocking my name doesn't make me like you."

"Reject me all you like: deep down, you know I'm right. They've been trying to limit you since you were *born*. You should have been more than what you are. They took that away from you." Adrianna's smile was sudden and feral. "All I want to take are the scraps they left behind."

She had no weapons. She had no superior ground. Something about the look on her face told me it didn't matter. Still clutching the branch she'd used to ambush me, I turned and fled deeper into the wood.

# # #

The whiteout wood had boundaries. It had to: without them, it could never have touched the other narrative preserves, the hazel wood of the Cinderellas or the rose briars of the Rose Reds. As I ran through the trees, skirts billowing behind me, hair snapping in the wind, it felt like those borders were the real fiction. Every other lie I'd ever been told had just been preparing me for the big lie, the lie that claimed the wood had limits. I would run forever, and I would never be free.

Worse, my dress—my warm, wine-red silk dress—stood out against the black trees and white snow like a flag, betraying my presence to anyone with eyes. I looked back. Adrianna was nowhere in sight. That didn't necessarily mean anything. Unlike me, she was dressed in sensible black and white. I didn't know what inspired the wood to dress us in specific colors, but in that moment, I hated it for not foreseeing that I might need to get away from a serial killer who looked just like me.

There was a thick copse of trees up ahead. I put on an extra burst of speed and threw myself into their shadow.

"She's *your* problem, not mine," I whispered. My voice sounded too loud to my own ears. "If you have any control over what's happening here, you need to help me now. You *owe* me."

The wind whistled around me, but if the wood gave any answer beyond that, I couldn't hear it. I dropped my branch into the snow and hauled my dress off over my head, revealing a white silk slip that was distinct from my skin only in that it had a faint, translucent sheen to it that I lacked.

"Thank you," I whispered, kicking off my red slippers. I wrapped my dress around the nearest tree, where it would hopefully snap and dance in the breeze and attract Adrianna's attention. Then I grabbed my branch, turned, and ran in a new direction, seeking to lose myself in the wood. It was funny: my coloring had always marked me as a freak, something to be gaped at and avoided in public places, like a lack of melanin was catching. Here and now, that same lack of color might be the only thing that saved me.

Too bad I shared it with Adrianna. If my black and white nature concealed me from her eyes, her nature did the same from mine. She could have been anywhere, hiding between any two trees, and I wouldn't have known. I might have run past her a dozen times in that initial headlong flight. I didn't stop to find out.

I just kept running, barefoot and half naked, through the snow.

# # #

Time didn't work the same way in the whiteout wood. Neither did bodies: most of the girls here were either dead or sleeping in the waking world, and they didn't have the physical needs they once had. Even so, I was still among the living, and I was beginning to tire. I stopped in the middle of a clearing, panting as I bent to rest my hands on my knees. My feet were numb, and while I knew intellectually that I should have been dealing with severe frostbite by this point, even that small and creeping numbness was terrifying. If I didn't keep running, she was going to catch me. If she caught me . . .

She'd called me "little doorway" since the moment we met. If she caught me, she was going to do whatever it took to open that door. I wasn't certain what the consequences would be, but I could make an educated guess, and I didn't like what I kept coming back to.

All Snow Whites were connected. The whiteout wood was proof of that. It was the physical manifestation of our monomyth, the place where blood on the snow meant something bigger and more important than death. We were the heralds of spring and this was our frozen fastness, where the sun never warmed but flesh never chilled all the way down to the bone. Every magic mirror was a Snow White who had "gone bad," turning her back on the story that shaped her. The wood protected itself. Adrianna hadn't become a mirror yet, but that time was coming. She had to see her future in every reflection, every skittering bolt of color cast through ice. She wanted a way out.

She wanted a doorway.

Some Snow Whites didn't want their lives back after their inevitable stay in the glass coffin, whatever shape it took. When the story had been young and princesses had been expected to marry the princes who kissed them awake with no questions asked, it wouldn't have mattered if the girls who fell asleep and the girls who woke up were the same person. There would have been no basis for comparison. Once your black and white girl was in your arms, smiling up at you with her bloody lips, what did it matter whose body she was wearing?

There were always girls who didn't want to go back into the waking world, who didn't want to wear the shape the story had created for them. And there were always girls whose bodies didn't survive their personal versions of the apple—girls like Ayane, who died on an airplane, too far from land for any glass coffin to have saved her—who wanted nothing more than to be alive. To be a citizen of the whiteout wood was to be involved in a great square dance of bodies and birthrights.

I was here. My body was empty. Adrianna was here. She wanted to fill it. I didn't know why, and frankly, I didn't care. She wasn't going to take me. She wasn't going to steal my life. I was going home.

I put a hand over my mouth to block the red slash of my lips as I straightened and backed up, squeezing into a gap between two trees. Branches tangled in my hair, claiming it as their own. The wood was silent. The blizzard had died down while I was running, and I had to interpret that as the wood trying, in its curious, narrative way, to help me. The snow had allowed me to escape from Adrianna more easily, covering my footprints and obscuring her vision. Now that I needed to see her coming, it was tapering off.

My heart was a steady drumbeat against my ribs, beating almost hard enough to hurt. I forced myself to breathe slowly, watching the trees for any signs of movement. I was black and white and perfectly still against a landscape that mirrored me in all but form.

Adrianna stepped out from between two trees on the other side of the clearing. I hadn't seen her approaching; I didn't know if she had seen me move. She had another branch. This time she'd gone to the effort of sharpening it, creating a vicious-looking spear. I didn't know whether Snow Whites could die in the whiteout wood, but I knew—from both past and recent experience—that we could be hurt. It seemed unfair, that we should have to hurt to bleed in a place that was all about emptying us out onto the white page of winter, but it was how the world was made, and I didn't have the authority to revise it on my own.

"I know you're nearby, because the wood keeps telling me you're far away," she said, her eyes scanning the clearing. For a moment, they paused on me, almost as if she'd picked my silk-clad form out of the landscape. I held my breath. Her gaze moved on. "It doesn't have to be this hard, little doorway. Come to me. Let me stroke your hair and kiss your brow and slit your throat and steal your skin. It can be pleasant for both of us." Her voice never changed, not even as she talked about effectively murdering me.

My stomach lurched. The urge to charge her was strong. But I had a single blunt branch, and she had a spear. I had everything to lose, and she had everything to gain. I stayed where I was.

"Come on, little doorway, little princess with the terrible name. Your mother would have come to me by now. She loved me better than you can imagine, and she left me anyway. They always leave. You know that, don't you? Your sister left you too."

It was only the presence of my hand over my mouth that kept me from gasping.

"My sister is the reason we know stories can be changed. She couldn't escape hers, but she could massage it into something new. Trade the thorn for the spindle; it's still a prick, and she still gets away from the bear." Adrianna stalked forward. "It's not her fault she forgot how that story went when it was new. The narrative is a vengeful god. It didn't like her changing the rules it had decided she would live by. So it made her pay for what she'd done, and I made everyone else pay for what it had done to *her*!"

On the last word she whirled and hurled her spear into the space between two trees, a space shaped vaguely like a woman, all curves and soft angles. Had that space been shaped that way when I took shelter here, or was the wood doing what it could to protect me? I couldn't be sure one way or the other . . . but I suspected the latter. The whiteout wood didn't want Adrianna to win any more than I did, even if we had different reasons.

Adrianna glared at the trees as she stalked forward to retrieve her spear. "You can't hide from me forever, little doorway. You're only making things worse for yourself. You know that, don't you? Give up, give in, and let me open you, before you make me *mad*."

She kept going after she had her spear back, vanishing into the black and white distance. I stayed where I was, not moving, and began counting silently down from five hundred.

I had just reached three-fifty when she appeared again, leaping from between two trees and looking wildly around the clearing. I didn't move. She muttered something and left again, slipping out of sight as easily as a shadow.

This time, I moved immediately, taking two steps backward and whirling around before I ran for the other side of the whiteout wood. I didn't look back. I didn't dare.

# # #

It was some indefinable amount of time later, and I was digging a pit with my bare hands, scything through layer after layer of snow as I sought the earth beneath, when I realized I hadn't seen a single Snow White, apart from Adrianna, since she had appeared. I hadn't even seen the oddly-spaced trees that signaled the presence of another Snow's clearing, where I might have been able to find temporary shelter, if not an ally.

"Is this because they don't want to get involved, or because you won't let them?" I murmured, keeping my voice low. I didn't want to attract Adrianna by talking to myself, but the stress and fear were getting to me. I needed something to anchor me to the world.

The wind gusted around me, caressing my cheek as it blew. There was a whisper there, like the faint voice of the wood trying to answer my question, but I couldn't tell what it was saying. I was still enough of an outsider that the wood couldn't speak to me directly. That was a good thing—a *very* good thing, considering I wanted to go home more than I wanted almost anything else.

Home. It was already starting to feel like a foreign concept, like the life I had lived was the fairy-tale dream, and this frozen, virtually monochrome wood was the reality. I couldn't tell if exhaustion was wearing me down or if my memories were actually changing, twisting to suit a more storybook narrative. Either way, I didn't like it.

So I was digging holes.

This was my fifth. Dig deep enough that a leg could get stuck, then cover the opening with a thin sheet of ice pried up from a frozen snowbank, and cover the ice with more snow. If Adrianna tried to follow me, she'd risk breaking a leg. Maybe the wood would heal her and maybe it wouldn't. Either way, the injury would slow her down.

Something snapped in the trees up ahead: the sound of a small branch breaking. I froze. I was out in the open, too far from the trees for their bark to camouflage my hair. There was only one thing I could think of, and so I dropped onto my back on the snow, hastily shoveling armfuls of the stuff above my head. My eyebrows and eyelashes were also a risk. I slathered a fistful of snow over my forehead and eyes, clapped a hand over my mouth, and waited.

Anywhere else, this solution would have been useless. Lying on my back in the snow, trusting the villain to pass me by? It was so simple as to be completely impossible. But this was the whiteout wood, and fairy-tale logic reigned supreme. I was a black and white girl, and I had covered my hair with snow the exact color of my skin. I may as well have been invisible.

I heard Adrianna walk past me, her feet crunching in the snow. When silence fell again, I opened my eyes and looked warily around, waiting for an ambush, looking for Adrianna. It didn't come. I didn't see her. But I saw something else: flecks of red beneath the snow, uncovered by my frantic shoveling. How they'd appeared after something so simple, when they hadn't been uncovered by the wind or by my frantic running, I didn't know and wasn't going to ask. If I was going to use fairy-tale logic to survive, I had to trust fairy-tale logic to steer me truly toward safe harbor—if such a place even existed anymore.

I reached for one of the red specks, digging my fingers into the snow until I could grip it and pull. It came away easily. A strawberry. The flesh wasn't frozen; it was as soft and pliant as anything from a grocery store. I placed it on my tongue, where it melted into sweetness and the taste of frost. Winter strawberries weren't usually a part of this story, but I recognized them from other places in the narrative, other stories of girls and snow and isolation. I swept more of the snow away with the palm of my hand, uncovering a riot of strawberry plants with leaves sculpted from delicate glacial ice and berries as red as my bloody mouth.

"Okay," I said, and started picking.

When I had a handful of berries I stood, placing a second in my mouth as I began to walk. I didn't watch for Adrianna. I didn't look to the left or right. I just ate strawberries and walked through the wood, letting it guide me, trusting it, for this little while, to take me where I needed to go.

The maze appeared when I placed the final strawberry in my mouth. One moment the way ahead of me was clear, the snowy ground spattered with black-branched trees, and then there was a labyrinth stretching all the way to the horizon, walls made of blue-white glacial ice. I knew salvation when I saw it. I broke into a run, heading for the safety of the maze.

For Adrianna to win, she had to catch me and do whatever was necessary to "open" me. Given our previous encounters, I was more than reasonably sure that "opening" was a painful process. It might not be fatal in the wood, but that didn't mean I would enjoy it. I definitely wouldn't enjoy being trapped in this snowy, story-clad wonderland, knowing Adrianna was somewhere in the waking world, wreaking havoc with my hands. So I couldn't let it happen.

For me to win, all I had to do was stay away from her until Jeff got tired of waiting and kissed me awake. I didn't know why he hadn't done it already, but as I kept reminding myself, time was funny in the wood. Maybe I'd only been under for a few minutes, and this was all happening with the speed of a particularly vicious lucid dream.

The wind blew past my ears, carrying the ghost of Adrianna's voice. I couldn't tell what she was saying, but the warning was clear: she was getting close. I dove forward, losing my footing on the snowy ground, and belly-flopped through the entry to the maze. There was no snow inside, just hard-packed, icy ground. I landed hard enough to knock the wind out of myself, and quickly found myself presented with another problem as I began sliding forward like a kid at a water park. The ground wasn't slanted, but still I slid, skidding around a corner and impacting with a dead end wall. I lay there in a heap, trying not to wheeze.

There was no mud on my nightgown, despite my inglorious arrival. Black, white, red: those were the only colors allowed to me. Anything else would have contradicted my story.

The wind wasn't blowing inside the maze. For the first time, I could hear everything. I heard footsteps. I heard an exasperated sigh. And worst of all, I heard Adrianna say, "You'd favor her over me this much? We're both your children. You ruined the both of us. What makes her so special, that you would try to help her get away?"

If the wind answered her, I didn't hear it. But I heard Adrianna snort.

"Fine, then," she said. "You can change the world to suit yourself, but you can't save her. All you've done is push her one step closer to the mirror." Then came the footsteps, stalking into the maze, prowling slow and easy as a jungle cat.

The dead end where I was so inelegantly sprawled didn't leave me anywhere to hide. I looked frantically around before compacting myself into the corner, pressing my head back against the icy walls in an effort to hide as much of my hair as possible. I clapped one strawberry-sticky hand over my mouth, hiding my lips. There was nothing I could do about my eyebrows and lashes, and I didn't dare close my eyes. If I couldn't see her coming, I thought I might go mad.

The footsteps paced by, accompanied by rippling reflections on the glacial walls. Adrianna either hadn't seen the cul-de-sac I'd fallen down, or had assumed I was too smart to hide this close to the entrance. Either way, I heard her walk away and started to relax. I could run the other way now. Maybe I could make it to the hazel wood, or to the rose fields of the Rose Reds, and hide among a different story. She'd never think to look for me there. I could wait out the rest of my nap in peace.

I got carefully to my feet and crept back along the way I'd slid. There were no marks on the ground. The icy floor of the maze didn't take footprints or, apparently, bellyprints. That was a good thing when it came to not being followed. It was a bad thing when it came to being sure I was going in the right direction.

Then I came to where I was *sure* the entrance to the maze had been, absolutely *sure*, and it wasn't there. Instead, a blank ice wall stood across the path, barring me from escape. I stopped where I was and stared.

"Please tell me this is a joke," I said.

The wall of ice didn't disappear. Either I'd gone the wrong way, or—but no. There was something on the ground, a little speck of red that didn't fit in with the monochrome world around it. I knelt, picking it up.

It was a strawberry top, white as snow, but with a few faint traces of strawberry pulp still clinging to it. This was where I had entered the maze, and where the whiteout wood had—for whatever reason—closed the door behind me.

"Thanks a lot," I muttered, and turned to face the labyrinth.

If I was going to escape, I was going to need to find another way out.

# # #

The walls weren't all identical. I realized that fast, when my eyes adjusted to their new, frozen world and started picking out the subtle details. Some of the walls had a wave pattern worked into their bases. Those were the ones that led north to south. Others had a faint series of cracks running along their centers, like they had been hit lightly but repeatedly with a small hammer. Those were the walls that led east to west.

It should probably have been difficult to tell the cardinal directions here, in this virtually featureless maze, but somehow it was easier than ever, like the wood was trying to provide what guidance it could. The hazel wood was to the east, and when I faced that direction, I could smell floor polish and glass cleaner and char—the distant shadows of a place built around soot and cleanliness. If I could find the eastern edge of the maze, I could scale the wall and tumble to safety, like a black and white Alice falling down the rabbit hole.

Don't mix your stories here, I scolded myself silently, as I crept along one of the north-south walls. I hadn't seen any sign of Adrianna since she'd walked past my hiding place, but that didn't mean she wasn't lurking. The sealed door kept us both inside the maze. *There's no telling what you could change.*

It couldn't be as simple as a thought. If it were, every reimagining that made Snow White a vampire would have left me anemic and yearning for a rare steak. But I was a living incarnation of the narrative trapped in the sleeping heart of my own story, and I didn't want to find out the hard way how much I could revise. Skin as white as snow was inconvenient. I burned too easily, and was probably putting my dermatologist's kids through school. I was also used to it. It was the story I knew.

Something tapped against the ice up ahead. It was a faint sound, almost not there. In a louder world, I would have missed it entirely. In the silence of the maze, it echoed like a bell. I froze, looking around me for a moment before ducking through the nearest opening and pressing myself against the wall, becoming still and silent.

The footsteps began barely a second later.

"You can't run from me forever, little doorway," said Adrianna. She sounded annoyed now. I was running harder than she had expected, and she didn't like it. "You should stop while you can, while there's still a chance that I'll have some mercy on those fools you call friends. They don't all have to die. Their lives are in your hands."

I said nothing. I didn't move.

"Where's the gratitude? Where's the 'thank you, Aunt Adrianna, for letting me grow up in my own body, instead of here in the wood'? I could have taken you the day you were born, you know, and no one would have known the difference. I would have grown up in your place. Instead, I let you have your life, at least long enough to learn how much you didn't want it. The world isn't easy on the fairy-tale girls."

Was it my imagination, or were her steps slowing?

You couldn't have taken me, I thought, like yelling at her in my mind could somehow make her back away. *My story wasn't active. I didn't come to the wood. I wasn't yours.*

I was in the wood now. Carefully, I began inching away from the sound of her footsteps, staying up against the wall. My bare feet made no sound on the icy ground. I barely noticed the cold anymore; it was just one more feature of my environment, of no more or less importance than the ground beneath my feet or the wall against my back. That probably wasn't a good thing. I was sinking deeper into my story with every step I took, and unless I could find a way out, I was going to be trapped here.

Jeff, I'm sorry; I should never have asked you to help me eat the apple. I'd thought I could handle it. Snow White's crimes were supposed to be beauty and innocence, not hubris. I guess everyone gets to interpret the story in their own way.

"Don't you want to talk to me, little doorway?" Adrianna's tone was cajoling. She sounded almost reasonable, which was the most terrifying part of all. "I could tell you about your mother, what she was like when she was my Rose Red, and she loved me. We're not so different, you and I. We were meant to be sister-stories, and we both lost the girls we loved when they walked away from us. My sister left me to be a Sleeping Beauty. Yours left you to be a man. I wonder, which was the greater betrayal? At least mine remembered she was meant to be my twin. She remembered that the face in her mirror was mine too, and she didn't change it to get away from me. How much did you hurt your sister, that she changed her *face* to stop seeing you in the mirror?"

The desire to turn around, run back to her, and scratch her eyes out was almost unbearable. I forced myself to keep moving. *Gerry isn't here: he doesn't hear the things she's saying about him, and none of them are true, you know none of them are true. He didn't transition to get away from you, he did it so he could be who he was always supposed to be. You know that, you know that.*

I'd always known that, but hearing her say those things still made my heart ice over. *This* cold, I could feel. *This* cold had been with me ever since the person I thought was my sister and the other half of my unwanted story had explained to me, haltingly, that he was my brother, and whatever story he was going to live through, he was going to do it on his own. I loved him. I respected who he was. I had supported him every step of the way. I just wished that so much of who he was hadn't depended on leaving me behind.

"I'll make her pay, if you give me what I need," said Adrianna. Her voice was closer now, even though I still couldn't see her, even though I still seemed to be alone in my corridor of ice. "I'll make her understand that the worst thing a sister can do is leave you behind."

Every time she misgendered Gerry my jaw clenched a little harder. I kept inching away, wishing I had a weapon, wishing I had something I could use to make her *stop*.

"You're not going to get away, little doorway. No matter how hard you try to run from me, you're not going to get away. It would be better for both of us if you'd just stop trying."

If I stayed here any longer, I was going to start screaming. I wouldn't be able to help myself. Knowing that the sound might give me away, I turned and ran down the icy corridor, fleeing from the sound of her voice. I kept running long past the time when her laughter had dropped away behind me, replaced by the familiar silence. I wasn't getting tired or winded, at least not yet, and the more distance I could put between the two of us, the better. I didn't know whether it was our shared story or her bitter understanding of human nature, but Adrianna was pressing my buttons with remarkable skill. I couldn't let her catch me. I couldn't let her get anywhere *near* me. So I ran.

The farther I went, the more I resented the maze. It had seemed like a safe haven when it first appeared, but I'd been safer out in the white-out wood, where at least there had been black trees to disguise my hair, and soft snow for me to dig traps in. Here, everything was frozen solid, and I had no weapons, and I had no options apart from continuing to flee. I couldn't fight back. There was nothing for me to fight back *with*.

I thought wistfully of all the fallen branches out there in the whiteout wood, wishing I had thought to carry one—or hell, an armful—with me into the maze. And I kept running, right up until an arm jutted out from behind a wall and clotheslined me across the throat.

I collapsed in a heap, choking and wheezing. Even here, at the heart of my story, I needed to breathe. I was still retching and trying to get my feet back under me when Adrianna stepped into view, a smug smile on her pretty face.

"Hello, darling," she said. "Did you miss me? I can see from the way you're glaring that you must have. No one feels that neglected by an absence they didn't feel. Well, don't worry. We're going to be together from now on, at least until we're never together again—although in a small way, I suppose we'll *always* be together."

She reached down and grabbed my hair, hauling me up. I struggled as best as I could, still wheezing, trying to grab for her hand. Adrianna sighed.

"If you're going to be like that about it," she said, and hauled back her free hand and punched me in the throat. Everything went red as my air supply was cut off, and then everything went black, and I went away for a while.

I didn't dream. Dreaming was apparently not a priority in the whiteout wood, which was already half dream in and of itself. Instead, I simply ceased to be aware of my surroundings until some unknown, unknowable time later, when I came back to my senses just as abruptly as I had left them.

The first thing I noticed was the ground, which was passing underneath me. The second thing was my position. I was slung over Adrianna's shoulder in a fireman's carry, my wrists and ankles tied with strips of fabric. I could see my hands if I tilted my chin down at the right angle. They were bound with what looked like a piece of my shift.

It was a good use of the materials she had available. It still made me want to punch her in the eye. Maybe both eyes, just so she wouldn't start looking asymmetrical.

"Oh, good: you're awake." Adrianna sounded perfectly pleased with herself, and why shouldn't she have been pleased with herself? She had won. She'd knocked me out, and now she was carting me off to Grimm-knows-where, to have her way with me.

There had to be a way out of this. "Put me down," I said.

"No."

So much for the easy way. "Adrianna, you don't want to do this." We were still in the maze: When I twisted, I could see the icy walls to either side. That struck me as both a good thing and a bad thing. We hadn't gone far, but if I managed to get loose, it wasn't like I would have anyplace to run. We'd just wind up right back here again.

"See, that's where you're wrong," she said calmly. "I most certainly *do* want to do this. I've been thinking of nothing else for years. I've missed the real world. This place has no character. Or rather, it has just one character, and I'm tired of her. There's only so much Snow White I can take before I start wanting to claw everybody's eyes out. Don't you find the same, little doorway?"

I said nothing.

"You can hate me if you like—I won't deny you that right—but you know I'm telling the truth, just like I know that twenty years from now, you're going to do the same thing I'm doing now. Some dumb little doorway is going to come along, holding herself closed as tightly as she can, and you're going to blow her open and take her for your own."

"You're getting disturbingly close to using rape metaphors here, lady, and I'd appreciate it if you'd cut it the fuck out." Swearing at her felt good, like it was allowing the smallest fragment of my hatred and anger to find a target. Suddenly, I understood Sloane a little bit better. "I'm never going to be like you."

"Why, because you've always been such a good princess?" The walls dropped away around us as Adrianna stepped into a clearing. There was no warning before she shifted me off her shoulder and dropped me ignominiously to the ground. At least there was snow here, instead of hard-packed mud: I hit hard, but not hard enough to knock the wind out of me.

Adrianna moved before I could react, kicking a clot of snow into my face. I coughed, trying to blink it out of my eyelashes.

"You've *never* lived up to our story," she said. "At least I was a good princess, before my stupid sister decided she didn't want me anymore. What have you ever done but try to press the once upon a time out of yourself?" She kicked another clot of snow in my face.

I pushed myself up onto my elbow, glaring at her through the haze of white. "Pick a narrative, will you? You're tormenting me because you're my aunt and you feel like my mother abandoned you—which I'm still not sure I believe, by the way." Except I did believe it, because Adrianna looked like me. It wasn't just coloring. I shared my coloring with everyone in the whiteout wood. It was the shape of her face and the angle of her smile, the way she moved her hands and the slope of her shoulders. We were family, she and I. No matter how much I wanted her to be a liar, I couldn't deny that we were related. "Or you're tormenting me because you think it's fun. Or you're doing it because you don't think I do a good enough job of living up to our story. Just *pick* one!"

Adrianna stared at me. Then her eyes narrowed, and her stare became a look of raw, unfiltered hatred. "You still think you're better than I am, don't you? Just because you fought the story for longer than I did."

"That's the fourth reason you've given for doing what you're doing," I snapped.

Adrianna paused, a confused expression flitting across her face. Pressing the palm of one hand against her temple, she said, "No, that can't be right. I only have one reason. I gave up on being good because my sister gave up on being with me. I want your skin because I want my life back, and leaving you here is the kindest thing I can do. That's my reason. Those other things . . . I don't know where those other things came from."

I looked at her silently, and was afraid that I might know.

Tanya had said—or the wood had said, speaking through her—that she no longer dreamt. When Adrianna had knocked me out before, I hadn't dreamt either. I'd just gone away. Dreams were necessary for humans to stay sane. The wood was a dream all by itself, and maybe that could sustain us for a while . . . but for how long?

Adrianna talked like someone else's reasons were creeping into hers. Maybe they were. She wasn't the first Snow White to have gone bad, just the first I'd met. The others had been consigned to magic mirrors, locked away where they couldn't hurt anyone else. The wood was capable of communicating with its "children." Were the mirrors?

"I don't think you want to hurt me," I said, trying to keep my voice low and reasonable. It wasn't easy, lying on the ground with my hands tied and my face full of snow. Still, I tried. I tried like I'd never tried before. "Adrianna, the mirrors are messing with your head. This isn't you."

She froze, eyes going wide. "Who told you about the mirrors? I never showed you the mirrors. How do you know about the mirrors?"

Well, crap. Score one for good guessing, immediately lose one for forgetting that sometimes it's a bad idea to reveal information the bad guys don't expect you to have. "Tanya. She's my teacher. She told me about the mirrors."

"She's a good girl. The wood loves her. She knows *nothing* about the mirrors." Adrianna stepped forward, grabbing my wrists and using them to haul me off the ground. I made a wordless sound of protest as she wrenched my shoulders. Adrianna ignored it. "She never had to learn about the mirrors, that spineless, gutless little princess. No one ever took anything away from *her*. How can she teach you about something that she doesn't understand?"

The pain was intense enough that it took me most of her little speech to realize what she was doing. She was untying my hands.

"She understands them enough to know that the mirrors lie," I said. "I don't think you're quite yourself. You keep changing your story. I think . . . I think the mirrors are bleeding over into you."

"So what?" She pulled the cloth loose and dropped me back into the snow. This time, I was able to catch myself, and I didn't hit the ground as hard. That was a relief. Adrianna paced away. "I know who I was when I was still in my own body. Who cares if I've picked up the shards of a few new narratives? I'm going to open you, little doorway, and there's nothing you can do to stop me. We've come too far for that."

"You tried to open me once before, and that didn't work out too well for you." I strained toward the cloth that tied my feet. My shift was almost a foot shorter than it had originally been, and the smooth hem had become a ragged tear. "Maybe we should talk about this."

"I stabbed you; you bled," said Adrianna. "It seemed to work out just fine to me."

I undid the knot and began unwinding Adrianna's makeshift rope. "Yeah, thanks for that."

"You can't win, little doorway. You can't run from me. You can't escape from me. Your body isn't waking up, because I'm not going to allow that to happen until I'm ready. You've lost. You're still fighting me, because fighting is what you people *do*, but you've already lost."

"I don't even understand why we have to fight!" The last of the fabric binding my ankles came loose. I scrambled to my feet, swaying as my head tried to adjust to one change in altitude too many. The places where Adrianna had hit me ached and throbbed. The whiteout wood wasn't real the way the waking world was, but it was real enough for me to suffer here. "You keep saying you're my aunt. Fine. Tell me about my mother."

Hearing the words said aloud—said in my own voice—woke a deep, almost submerged longing in my chest, like I'd just invoked the thing I wanted most in the entire world. Adrianna had known my *mother*.

She had known her as a living, breathing human, not as a shell, scraped clean and used up by the story that had consumed her. She had known my mother before she became a Sleeping Beauty, before she found the spindle and dropped into the dark.

The questions were endless. Every time I tried to formulate one, two more appeared, shoving it aside and making themselves the center of my attention. I felt like a Little Mermaid, rendered voiceless by my own yearning.

"She was headstrong, arrogant, wild," said Adrianna. Her voice was softer, like I'd distracted her into telling me the truth. "She never listened to anyone she hadn't already decided to pay attention to. Sometimes that included me. I was older than her by five whole minutes, and she used to say that only mattered because it meant I got the snow-story, and left her with the roses."

Rose Red was a much less common manifestation, because her story was harder to tell in isolation. Snow White got seven dwarves and a happy ending, regardless of whether she had a sister. Rose Red only ever had the bear, and the forest, and her sister's hand, holding her close and terrified of ever letting go.

"She left me." The softness was leaching out of Adrianna's voice. "She saw the opportunity to do something different with her life, and she *left* me."

"Wait!" I put my hands up. "What was her name?"

Adrianna blinked at me. "What?"

"What was my mother's name?" I tried to look unobtrusively around myself as I spoke, searching for an exit. Adrianna was sounding more and more ragged. I didn't know why. I didn't want to stick around here long enough to find out.

We were at the center of the maze. We must have been: There was no other reason for such a large, empty circle of space to have been cut into a place that was, after all, supposed to keep people lost and wandering for as long as possible. There should have been openings every few feet along the walls, allowing weary maze-goers to seek another way out. Instead, there was only unbroken ice, extending in a gentle curve in all directions. There was no escape. Not unless I was able to get enough of a head start that I could boost myself over a wall.

"Angele," said Adrianna. Her voice broke a little at the end of the word. "Her name was Angele, and she was my angel, and she *left* me. She left me for another story. She left me for you, little doorway. You, and your brother, and the chance you'd get out. She never wanted you to be story-touched like we were. All I'm doing here is what she would have wanted."

"I don't think my mother would have wanted you to do this." I took a step back. My mother had never wanted anything for me that I'd been aware of. She'd been a Sleeping Beauty. She got pregnant while she was asleep; she gave birth the same way. Any plans she'd made for her future children had been made in the abstract, and I had to wonder if she would have kept us, my brother and me, when she realized we were echoing the story she'd already run from once.

Not that I'd ever know. My mother was dead and gone, and whatever wood or tower housed her monomyth was a place I had no interest in visiting.

"She would have wanted me to do anything that would spare you," said Adrianna. She pulled her hand from behind her back, and there was a shard of ice the length of her forearm clutched in her fingers, gleaming bright and deadly. She lunged. I braced myself.

Adrianna was evil, or at least twisted, but she wasn't the most skilled hand-to-hand fighter I'd ever encountered. I, on the other hand, had been dealing with Sloane on a daily basis for years. My elbow caught Adrianna in the solar plexus as she was pulling back her ice blade to strike. She staggered back, and I kicked her in the stomach, sending her sprawling into the snow.

That seemed like my opening. I went in for a stomp, and she stabbed me in the calf, sending freezing pain lashing through my leg.

I jerked away, kicking her in the chin in the process, and she stabbed me again, this time in the belly. The cold that spread outward from the wound was intense, almost enough to make me black out again.

I jerked away, grabbing for her hair, intending to introduce her face to my fist. She responded by stabbing me in the stomach for a second time, twisting the ice blade inside my body. I felt something snap, and looked down to see blood pouring from the wound, turning the snow at my feet red, red, apple red, poisoned kisses red, wine red, death red. Blood on the snow: it always comes back to blood on the snow.

"I told you there was no point in fighting me," hissed Adrianna. The vagueness was gone from her voice, replaced by nothing but cold. She pulled the blade out of my stomach.

I dropped to my knees.

"Ugh," I said.

"But this was how it had to be. Don't you see? You had to think you could win. It makes the opening easier. Now rest, little doorway. Your part in this story is done."

She brought the glass blade down one last time, slashing it across my throat in a hard, unforgiving arc. Blood poured down like a torrential rain, hot and thick and salty as my tears. I collapsed, eyes open, into the snow. I couldn't move. I was bleeding out, and I couldn't move.

Adrianna walked to the wall of the maze and dropped her blade before she ran her bloody hands along the ice, inscribing a rough archway. Then she stepped through it, through the solid wall, through the doorway she had crafted from my body, and she was gone.

The blood kept flowing, slower now, like I was running out. I closed my eyes, and all the world was black and white and red as blood, and I was gone too.

False Love's Kiss

Memetic incursion in progress: tale type 332 ("Godfather Death")
Status: IN PROGRESS

Dr. Mortimer Pierson had been practicing medicine long enough that he'd heard all the jokes. "Ha-ha, here comes Doctor Death," and "did your mother hope you were going to grow up to run a funeral home?" He tried not to tell patients his first name if he could help it. It wasn't bad enough that it was old-fashioned; it had to be old-fashioned and carry connotations of the grave. It just wasn't fair.

That feeling of unfairness had been haunting him all morning, making the world seem vaguely out of focus, like he was viewing it through a long, distorting lens. He'd managed to go through his morning rounds without betraying the fact that anything was wrong, but by the time he reached his last appointment before lunch, he wasn't sure how much longer he'd be able to keep it together. The world was just . . . it was just *wrong*.

"Physician, heal thyself," he muttered, and opened the exam room door. The patient was an adult female, height and weight normal, who had checked herself in complaining of stomach pains, headache, and generalized flu-like symptoms. Perfectly normal, and a perfectly reasonable way to finish the first half of the day.

"Ms. Thomas, I'm Dr. Pierson," he began, looking up from his clipboard. Then he froze, words dying in his mouth, and stared at the woman sitting on his examining table. She frowned, clearly unsure how to react to his expression.

She just as clearly couldn't see the hooded, skeletal figure standing behind her, the oh so traditional scythe clutched tightly in its bony hands.

Dr. Pierson began screaming.

It seemed like the only reasonable thing to do, and once he'd started, it was surprisingly difficult to stop.

# # #

Some people shouldn't be allowed to go into medicine. People with names that mean "death," for example. Back in my day, anyone named "Mortimer" would have been discouraged from coming into contact with the ailing, since everybody would have recognized it for the ill omen it was. These days, it's equal opportunity for everybody, even the people who don't have the common sense to change their names when they decide to become doctors.

The doctor in question was currently holed up in a supply cupboard. He'd slashed two nurses and a patient with scalpels before security had gotten off their asses and gotten involved. Dispatch had sent us over right after, saying we had a three-three-two on our hands. Because it wasn't bad enough that the poor guy's parents had named him after his own mortality: they'd somehow managed to go and invite the Big D to become his godfather at the same time.

It was all symbolic, of course. His parents probably just made too many skeleton jokes when the guy was a baby. But the narrative thrives on symbolism, and now our healer was seeing Death everywhere he looked. Literal, bony, "I am going to cut your head off with my big farming implement" Death.

"You people have the worst relationship with your own mortality," I muttered, before pressing my ear against the closet door. I could hear him shifting around in there. He didn't put a scalpel through the wood. I decided that meant he liked me. Raising my voice, I called, "Hey, Doc, why don't you open the door so we can talk about this like rational people?"

"You're not a rational person! You're a demon from Hell, sent to trick me into surrendering my immortal soul!"

"He's got you there, Sloane," said Andrew. He was staying well back, out of our violent physician's potential strike zone. Of the two of us, he was definitely the more breakable.

I scowled at him anyway. "I'm not a demon, I'm just a bitch." I turned back to the door. "Dr. Pierson, I'm with the government. I know what you're seeing, and I need you to understand that it's not real. There was a gas leak in the hospital. You're under the influence of a highly potent mix of psychotropic drugs. Please come out of the closet and let us help you through this."

"I *killed* people!" He sounded offended. I couldn't tell whether it was because I wasn't threatening to arrest him, or because I didn't seem to be afraid of him. Quite honestly, I didn't care either way. Offended was something I could work with.

"You sure did," I said cheerfully. "You killed a coat rack, and a balloon bouquet, and an IV stand. Very good killing of things that the drugs made you see as people. A-plus murderousness. Now please come out of there, before we have to come *in* there."

There was a pause. I was not following whatever script he'd written for his inevitable arrest. I wasn't following the script, period. I was tired, I was cranky, and I didn't appreciate the fact that my field team was operating at half strength, thanks to Henry being unconscious and Jeffrey having been ordered not to leave her bedside. Ciara was a decent enough team leader, but nothing I did seemed to get under her skin, and that was a big problem for me. I *needed* to piss her off. Until I did, I was just going to get more frustrated.

And now poor Dr. Pierson was getting it all dumped on his head. Poor, homicidal Dr. Pierson. I didn't have much sympathy. He wasn't the first Death's Godson I'd met, but he was the first who'd reacted to the looming specter of his honorary godfather by starting to cut throats.

The door opened a crack. An eye appeared. I forced a tight smile. If he was going to come out on his own, I should be as encouraging as possible. The eye widened. Then the opening widened, and Dr. Pierson appeared.

"He's . . . he's not with you," he said, sounding amazed. "How is he not with you?" His gaze flickered to where Andrew and Demi were waiting for me to deal with the dangerous, hallucinating target. "He's with *them*. He hasn't deserted this place. So how is it that he's not with y—"

He stopped mid-word as my fist slammed into his nose, sending him toppling backward against the closet wall. He stayed there for a few seconds, looking profoundly confused. Then he sank down to the floor, eyes closing, and was still.

"Me and Death have an agreement, asshole," I said. "He doesn't mess with me, and I don't tear his skeleton nuts off."

I turned. Demi and Andrew were staring at me.

"Sloane, I know this is sort of what you do, but could you try, I don't know, *not punching doctors in front of security cameras?*" Andrew gestured toward the camera in question as he spoke, in case I'd missed the urgency in his tone. "See that? That is a security camera! You just assaulted a doctor! On camera!"

"I protected myself from a man who'd already killed three people under orders from a hallucination, and who directly referenced seeing that same hallucination immediately before I struck him. He had a knife when he went into the closet. I had valid reason to believe he had a knife when he came out of it." I produced my badge from my pocket and held it up for the camera to see. "Agent Sloane Winters, ATI Management Bureau. We're with the United States Government; we're allowed to punch people if we want to."

"Please tell me that's not going to be our new motto," said Demi. "I think my grandmother will disown me if I come home with a T-shirt that has that written on the front. Even if it's in Latin."

"Does your grandmother read Latin?" asked Andrew.

"Doesn't everyone's grandmother read Latin?" I tucked my badge back into my pocket. "Go find some rope. We need to get this asshole restrained before he wakes up and starts trying to play guess-the-future with our guts."

"What about you?" asked Demi.

I flashed a toothy smile. "I'm going to stay here, and hope that he wakes up."

The two of them exchanged a glance and fled.

# # #

It was reasonably easy to scavenge a chair for myself. That's one thing I'll say about modern hospitals: they always have plenty of seats. Seats for patients, seats for physicians, seats for the people who inevitably accompany patients out of the darkness of ignorance and into the darkness of knowledge. My first doctor hadn't even kept a practice. He would come to your house if you had money, or you could come and see him in his parlor if you didn't. Mama used to pay him with vegetables from the garden, or with whole chickens, plucked and ready for the fire. He hadn't been married by the time I was near to coming of age, and I knew she'd been considering paying him with my hand.

It wouldn't have been a bad match, all things considered. He'd been a kind man, and he'd always smiled for me. I could have made him happy. He could have made me happy. Too bad we'd never been given the chance to find out.

Dr. Pierson stirred, groaning. I kicked him in the head. He stopped stirring.

"You're boring, and I don't want to listen to you talk, so stay down," I snapped. "Where the fuck are those guys with the rope? I'm getting old here, I'd like to leave."

My phone rang.

I pulled it out of my pocket, warily eyeing the display screen—"unknown number"—before sliding my thumb along the screen to answer the call. I raised it to my ear. "Hello?"

"Sloane? What's your status?" Ciara sounded slightly out of breath, like she hadn't been expecting me to answer. She didn't sound worried, though. If anything, she sounded relieved.

It was the relief that did it for me. "When did she wake up?" I asked.

There was a long pause before Ciara said, "About fifteen minutes ago. It's taken this long for us to get her cleared by the doctors. They say she's transitioned into normal sleep, and is breathing fine."

"Wait—I thought she was awake."

"She's not in a coma anymore. That's basically the same thing."

But it wasn't, not for a Snow White. Henry should have gone from deepest coma to perfect wakefulness in an instant, with no pause for recovery in between. Hell, the shock of waking up sometimes caused the sleeping princess archetypes to get the narrative equivalent of the bends, becoming disoriented and time-displaced while they readjusted to having a body.

I didn't say any of that. Something was wrong, and until I knew what it was, I was going to take things slow and careful. Instead, I said, "Our man's down. Andrew and Demi are fetching rope, and we should be ready to leave here in less than twenty."

"That's a negative, Agent Winters. I want you to remain where you are until the cleanup crew arrives to take Dr. Pierson to Childe. He's already displayed violent tendencies, and if this is going to get out of control again, it's not going to happen on my watch."

I opened my mouth to reply. Then I stopped and counted backward from ten, in Greek, before saying, "Excuse me, *ma'am*, but if I'm not allowed to see my teammate as soon as possible, Dr. Pierson's violent tendencies are going to be the least of your concerns."

"Are you threatening me, Agent Winters?"

"No, ma'am." Dr. Pierson groaned again. I kicked him again. He was probably going to need some dental work when he got to Childe. "I'm simply stating a fact. My story doesn't give me a lot of cause for patience."

Ciara sighed. "I'll see what I can do to speed up the cleanup crew, all right? Please don't murder anyone. I can see the light at the end of the tunnel on this assignment, and I'd rather not be called up before a review board before I can head out with my husband."

"I'll do what I can to keep my temper under control, but if you want to see the Caribbean this year, you should hurry it up." I disconnected the call before she could say anything else. Something was wrong. I knew it, and if she talked to me long enough, she would know it too: She wouldn't be able to help herself. She'd hear it in my voice. So I needed to be quiet, and think, and keep an eye on our prisoner.

He stirred again. I kicked him in the head again. It took the edge off of my nerves.

"You're going to give him a concussion," said Demi. I turned to see her walking down the hall toward me. She wasn't holding her flute for once, but her right hand was sketching out pantomime chords in the air. I narrowed my eyes, studying her face. She didn't even seem to realize she was doing it.

Our little Piper might become a danger again, sooner than anyone thought. "Why should I care if I give him a concussion?" I asked. "People are *dead*. Innocent people, who never expected to find an active narrative incursion at the hospital."

"People die every time a fairy tale goes live, don't they? I thought the people who got touched by the stories were victims too." Demi's phantom chording became more aggressive. She was probably trying to pipe me away from her.

She could have done it too, if she'd been holding an instrument. "This guy's caught in a three-thirty-two, a Godfather Death. The kid in that story isn't usually a villain, and he doesn't kill people, he just stops saving them when he sees the reaper's shadow. It makes him an incredibly famous and wealthy doctor. We don't catch most three-thirty-twos, because they follow that pattern. When they start seeing Death appear next to their patients, they stop taking the ones who come with their spectral godparent, and their survival rates spike. Dr. Pierson didn't have to be a villain. He could have been the hero. Once he chose the darker path, he signed himself up for a few concussions."

"What's going to happen to him?" Demi looked at Dr. Pierson, her fingers stilling.

"Ciara just called. We're waiting for the cleanup crew, and he'll be transferred to Childe, where he'll probably wind up assigned to the medical staff. Not the happiest ending, but he'll have some freedom of movement and protection from the compulsion charms. Which is more than he deserves, seeing as how he *killed people*." I kicked him in the head again. Childish? Maybe, but it made me feel better. I like things that make me feel better. They can be so rare in this world.

Demi frowned. "Doesn't him seeing Death mean those people were going to die anyway?"

"Not before he'd made up his mind to kill them. None of the stories are as precise as we want them to be. If they were, you'd still be in musical school, and I'd be dust on the wind." Footsteps echoed down the hall. I turned to see Andrew come around the corner. "There you are. Is the cleanup crew here yet?"

"No," he said. He looked exhausted. His tie was loose, and the top button of his shirt was undone: sure signs that whatever battle he'd been fighting, it had taken more out of him than usual. "I've pacified the media and calmed hospital security. Official story is that Dr. Pierson was mugged by some kids who dosed him with a synthetic hallucinogen that has a long lead time. I've probably just triggered half a dozen panicky 'do you know what your kids are doing?' news reports and a bunch of inappropriate budget upgrades to the local police, so you'll forgive me if I'm not thrilled about it, okay?"

"Okay," I said. I looked from him to Demi, and sighed internally. Neither of them was in a good place to hear my suspicions: they were tense and unhappy and dismayed by the day's events, and I couldn't blame them.

Ah, well. Either I was borrowing trouble and everything was going to be fine, or I was right, and they'd figure out that something was wrong when we got to the hospital and Henry was still asleep.

"Ciara called; Henry's awake," I said. "We're supposed to stay here until the cleanup crew arrives, but she's going to hurry them along as much as she can."

Demi's eyes were so wide and round that they looked like they were about to fall out of her head and roll away across the floor. Andrew's reaction was more subdued. He blinked once, slowly, before he nodded.

"All right," he said. "It'll be a relief to get back to normal." And to find out what Henry had learned during her time in the whiteout wood—what had kept her away from us for so long. Whatever it was, it had to be important. There was no other way she would have borne it.

"Yes," I said. "It will."

# # #

The cleanup crew arrived forty-five minutes later and took control of the scene. They barely had time to claim their paperwork before we were heading for the door. Andrew had parked the car in one of the spaces supposedly reserved for doctors. A parking ticket jutted from under the windshield wiper, fluttering in the breeze. Andrew yanked it off, wadded it up, and threw it to the pavement.

"People need to learn to read the damn permits on this thing," he muttered, and dropped himself into the driver's seat.

"We'll be back in the SUV in no time," said Demi, climbing into the back. "We just didn't need such a big car when we weren't at full staff, that's all."

"See? A few more of us drop into unbreakable enchanted slumbers and you'll be able to get that motorcycle you've always wanted." I slammed the door as I got into the front-passenger seat. "Now drive like Henry's grading you."

He drove.

On his best day, he didn't drive with Henry's lawless mania or Ciara's easy grace, but he knew how to operate a motor vehicle, which was more than could be said for me. He was eager enough to see Henry that he violated a few traffic laws, coasting through stop signs and roaring through intersections as the light turned yellow. Every so often, he would flash the lights, signaling any nearby police that we were government officials on business, and didn't have time to deal with being pulled over and ticketed.

I maintained my usual position in the passenger seat for the entire drive, languid and boneless and flicking through the radio like I believed it was some sort of oracular power that would direct our coming actions. Andrew kept his hands tight on the wheel, and Demi hummed along with every song. It all seemed so *normal*, like we'd never been touched by tragedy, like we weren't racing even now toward an uncertain future.

My relationship with my own story has made me more attuned than most to the narrative at work. It wants me badly, has wanted me for centuries; it murmurs to me in the night, sometimes in my mother's voice, and oh, I love it because it sounds like my memory of her, who is so long in the ground and would otherwise be a hundred years forgotten. But I hate it for taking me from her, and from the doctor who might have been my husband, and from all the others I once loved. So I've learnt to watch for it, when it opens its eyes upon the world.

Henry had always seemed to me to walk in a perpetual winter. Flowers grew in the carpet of her apartment, but they should never have been able to blossom in the cold. Everything about her would have screamed "Snow White" to me, even if she had dyed her hair and buried her complexion under a showgirl's share of pancake makeup. That was just the way she was, and she had no more choice in being it than I had in seeing it writ across the world.

Compared to what radiated from the hospital as we pulled up in front of it, she might as well have been narratively dead. I shivered as the wave of cold washed over me, suddenly wishing I had a coat of some sort. The air tasted like apples, fresh-cut, so sharp they burnt the back of my tongue. I glanced toward Andrew, who was parking the car, expression grim but not disturbed. He didn't feel anything. Demi's reflection in the rearview mirror revealed the same sort of casual concern. They were worried about Henry, but they didn't know how worried they were meant to be.

Something was very wrong.

The hospital door opened and Ciara came striding out, incongruous as ever in her mix of piratical blouse and businesslike black suit. The blue streaks in her hair had spread since I had seen her last, and that had been less than half a day before. She didn't appear to have noticed, and I wondered how surprised she'd be when she next glimpsed herself in the mirror. The narrative swirled around her, smelling of saltwater and the sea. Her own story might not be up in arms, but it was active, and it was hungry. We all needed to tread carefully for the next little while—and I had no idea how to warn them.

"Sorry it took so long for us to get the cleanup crew to you," she said, once we were out of the car and she was close enough to talk without shouting. "We had a Girl Who Couldn't Smile and a Clever Jack manifest on opposite sides of the city. The support teams have been running themselves ragged all day."

"That's an awful lot of narrative activity," said Andrew.

"Given the reports of what happened the last time former Agent Hubbard was loose, this is no more than we expected, and frankly less than we've been braced for," said Ciara. "I'm concerned that it's only the beginning. That's why it's a good thing you're here. We've been waiting for you."

"Is Henry actually awake?" I asked, earning myself startled looks from Andrew and Demi. I hadn't bothered telling them about her transition from coma to seemingly ordinary sleep. Without more information, it would have done no good, and would have moved me into the position of needing to explain things I couldn't yet put into words.

Ciara nodded. "She woke completely about fifteen minutes ago. She was disoriented at first, but she recovered quickly, and she's been asking for you. She said she wanted her entire team here when she explained what she had been able to learn."

"Then why are we standing around here?" demanded Demi. "Let's go!" She hurried forward, and Ciara turned to lead her inside. Andrew followed them, leaving me to bring up the rear.

The air was cold, and the wind tasted of apples, and something was very, very wrong.

# # #

Henry was sitting up in her bed when we entered the room. Jeffrey had moved his chair away from her bedside, and was sitting about four feet away, nervously cleaning his glasses on the tail of his shirt. He didn't look as happy as I would have expected for a man whose lover had just awakened from an enchanted sleep. Maybe it was the fact that his kiss hadn't been able to call her back to us this time. That's the trouble with "true love's kiss" as a concept: when it doesn't work, you know there's a problem.

Or maybe it was the fact that he also knew that something was wrong. He just didn't want to admit it.

Henry's eyes found the four of us as we appeared in the doorway. She looked from one face to another, measuring, assessing. She didn't pause when she got to Ciara; she didn't show any sign she thought our temporary leader didn't belong. That didn't necessarily mean anything. Ciara had been at the hospital this whole time. She could have filled Henry in on the changes that had occurred in her absence. But still, that failure to hesitate made me even more uneasy.

The taste of apples was heavy in the quiet air of the hospital room. It was underscored by a faint, floral smell I didn't recognize, sweet and cloying at the back of my throat. I tried to take shallow breaths.

"I wondered when you were going to get here," said Henry. "What, a lady takes a nap, and you all decide to get on with your lives? I'm *sure* there's something in the employee handbook that says that's not cool."

"Henry!" Demi's delighted cry twisted itself into a wail as she ran across the room and flung herself into our erstwhile leader's arms. Henry hugged her back with barely a pause.

Andrew stepped forward, leaving me to stand alone with Ciara in the doorway. "We were worried sick about you. What the hell kind of stunt was that? If the whiteout wood is that dangerous, I don't think you should be going there anymore."

"I can't help it, Andy. The wood is connected to my story, and it pulls me in whether I want to go or not." Henry grimaced at him around the slope of Demi's shoulder. "On the plus side, I got what I was looking for. I know where Birdie and Elise are hiding."

"*What?*" Ciara stepped forward. I didn't make any motion to enter the room. I was still trying to sort through the conflicting fairy-tale signals I was getting from the air around Henry, and until I knew what I was walking into, the safest thing seemed to be holding as still as I possibly could. "Agent Marchen, I know you were hoping to have your whole team present before your debriefing, but if you had information of this much tactical significance, you should have shared it as soon as you awoke."

"Why, so you could have seized control of the situation and rushed off to guarantee you got the credit for solving the problem? My team paid for this knowledge." Henry grimaced, her permanently bloody lips making the expression seem exaggerated. "They paid more than *you* could ever know. They deserve to be the ones who see this through."

Ciara frowned slowly. "I'm sorry. I never thought of it that way. I was just concerned about putting an end to a clear and present danger." Her words were light, chosen with obvious care. At the end, she glanced back at me, and I knew that she shared at least a part of my concern. Something was wrong with Henry. Whatever had happened to her in the wood . . .

"I'm just glad you're feeling as well as you are," said Jeffrey, replacing his glasses on his nose and shooting Henry a look that was equal parts confusion and longing. "Disorientation and mood swings are common side effects of magical coma. I wasn't sure you'd be able to explain what you'd found for at least an hour."

"No, you wouldn't have been sure, would you?" The look Henry shot at Jeffrey was pure malice. "You were supposed to wake me up."

Jeffrey flinched. "I tried," he said.

"You failed." Henry turned back to the rest of us. "I know where they are. I know what they're planning. We need to get moving, and we need to get moving *fast*."

"Why?" asked Demi. "You need to get better."

"Not as much as I need to stop Elise," said Henry. "They have a Dorothy. They're going to use her to summon a poppy field, and then they're going to use the pollen to spread the glass through the city. Thousands—maybe millions—of people will die. Sorry, but my recovery doesn't matter nearly as much as preventing that. Now get off me. I need to get out of bed."

Demi let her go. Henry promptly cast her blankets aside, pausing to blink at the nightgown and socks she was wearing.

"Huh," she said finally. "All right: somebody get me some clothes, and then we'll go save the world."

# # #

Having Henry back meant we were once more traveling in the SUV: big, black, and built like a tank. Jeffrey was in the front seat. Andrew and Demi were seated in the middle, while Ciara and I sat in the far back, away from the tension that radiated from the front like some terrible cold. The winter had followed Henry into the vehicle; it seemed to radiate from her skin now, like she was a woman in the process of freezing from the inside out.

"I guess you can go on that cruise now," I said, slanting a glance at Ciara as I tried to read her expression.

"I suppose that's so," she said. Her fingers were folded over the key she wore around her neck, stroking the metal in quick, anxious gestures. She looked unhappy and confused, like there was something about the situation that didn't make sense. "That's . . . that's a good thing."

"Is the Bureau going to let you? Last I checked, all vacation had been canceled. Pretty sure they're even pulling people off of sick leave."

"My story is so unstable that they approve any requests for leisure time involving the ocean," said Ciara. "Being on the water stabilizes my husband, which in turn stabilizes me. It works out." She was still frowning, her fingers moving constantly. Uncomfortable as it no doubt was for her, it was hard to read that as anything but positive. I needed *someone* on my side.

Jeffrey looked miserable with this newly awakened Henry; he kept stealing glances at her, cringing like he was afraid he'd done something wrong. He'd been in love with her for ages before she'd shown signs of reciprocating. There'd been a time when I'd believed he'd carry that torch all the way to his grave, and never the chance to set it to a forest fire. But for one brief and shining moment, he had been in possession of everything he'd ever wanted, and now—because of one kiss that had somehow been judged not quite true enough—he could see it slipping through his fingers.

I wondered, and not for the first time, how the narrative judged a love to be true, rather than any of the other things a love could be. I'd kissed my fair share of lips during my lifetime. Maybe more than my fair share, given how many years I'd spent among the living. But I couldn't say that any of those kisses had been "true love's kiss," or anything close to it. They had been pleasant, and sometimes there had been love behind them. In any rational world, that would have been enough. True love, whatever quality it was, had always eluded me.

If he hadn't loved her . . . ah, if he hadn't loved her, he might have been able to see what I saw. The stiff, uneasy way she held her shoulders; the faint leftward cant of her head, like she was listening to something the rest of us couldn't hear. Henry was awake, yes, but she had woken up somehow subtly *wrong*. I couldn't put words to what had changed. I knew only that she moved in frost and the scent of apples, and that none of the people I depended on to have my back seemed to sense the change.

We were driving fast, heading down a series of back roads toward a destination that only Henry knew. One thing hadn't changed: She still drove like she was afraid her license was about to be revoked, taking corners as if they had personally offended her. We were all so accustomed to it by this point that no one batted an eye.

No one seemed to consider how far we'd driven from the hospital until Henry turned a corner and started driving down a narrow, winding road surrounded on all sides by trees. Demi shifted in her seat, hands tightening around her flute. Ciara cleared her throat.

"Agent Marchen, what, precisely, is our destination?" she asked. "I need to notify our backup units before we arrive."

Bless you, I thought, and said nothing. Ciara was enough of a challenge to Henry's authority. She didn't need me wading in and making things worse.

The idea was amusing. *Why, Sloane Winters, are you finally learning restraint?* I thought, and had to swallow my laughter. There was nothing restrained about me. There was just the natural predator's urge to go still in the presence of danger, at least until that danger could be understood and—if necessary—devoured.

"The old glassworks," said Henry, her voice tight. "It doesn't show up on any city maps. It was supposed to have been destroyed a decade ago. The contractors who took the money for the job knew no one was going to check their work for years—the site was too remote—so they just took off for the Bahamas with their pockets full and their consciences clear."

"Nothing in the records we saw mentioned anything about an old glassworks," said Ciara suspiciously. "I would have expected that to be the first thing the Archives tagged, given Elise's newfound predilections."

"Birdie had access to the Archives for years," said Jeffrey. He sounded tired. "She could have pulled dozens of site flags without anyone realizing anything was going on. We don't download the city records on a regular basis. If she deleted the plans, deleted anything that indicated it was an area of interest, and didn't create such a large hole that someone would notice, it's entirely possible she could have effectively hidden the place."

"But how did she *know?*" asked Andrew. "There's no way she could have just waved her hand and said 'hey, someday I'm gonna have a crazy bitch who controls glass on my side, better make sure I have the right supervillain hideout all ready to go."

"Why couldn't she have?" I asked. His casual slurs irked me. I like profanity—it's practically my mother tongue—but I try to use words that insult without demeaning, when I can. Anything else risks losing the point, and if I insult someone, I want them to understand that I mean every word. "Elise is not insane, no matter what you want to imply. She's just a mean fucker, and we ran into her for the first time before we locked Birdie up. We know Birdie likes a long game. This could all be part of whatever scam she was running the first time."

"Who gets themselves locked in Childe on purpose?" asked Demi.

"Someone who really, really wants access to a bunch of broken stories," I said. "A bunch of stories *we* broke. The Bureau locked those people up together. Birdie—who sort of *is* a crazy bitch, because all Storytellers are—knew that they'd be mashed together like a big story-cake. All she'd have to do to build herself a new army would be to get thrown in there."

"She didn't have an old army," said Andrew darkly.

"Yes, she did," said Henry. I jumped in my seat, trying to cover the motion by crossing my arms. I wasn't supposed to be afraid of my own team leader. That was the sort of fear that led to nothing good.

I looked toward the front of the vehicle. Her eyes were locked on the rearview mirror, watching us. Watching *me*. My discomfort intensified.

"We were her old army," said Henry. "A Stepsister, a Snow White, a Piper, and a Shoemaker? She could have taken on virtually anything if she'd been able to get our stories to manifest the way she wanted them to. We didn't follow the rules she'd put in place, and so she had to try something else. Sloane's right. Childe Prison would have seemed like a giant grocery store full of options, and we're the ones who made it possible for her to go shopping."

I frowned. Something about that metaphor didn't feel right to me. But then again, nothing about this felt right. "So she never actually had an army. She just had the idea of one."

"For a Storyteller, that's enough," said Henry.

That was where the conversation ended. We came around a bend in the road, and there it was: The old glassworks, rising out of the trees like a ruined monument. It was brick-faced and blind-eyed, dotted with the ghosts of broken windows. There wasn't even any graffiti on the walls. That was how completely the place had been forgotten, after the people who were supposed to have destroyed it decided to walk away with the walls still standing.

It was easy to see how they could have gotten away with it. There was no line of sight between here and any road, and I had to wonder, just a little, who would have built a major factory this far out in the middle of nowhere. Maybe that was part of what had caused the factory to fail in the first place.

Or maybe someone had been rewriting the woods and roads around here, to better suit the idea of glassworks as ancient castle, to better prepare for their new role as fairy-tale antagonist.

"I hate magic," muttered Andrew, whose thoughts had apparently mirrored mine.

"Don't worry: magic hates you too," said Ciara.

I fixed her with a baleful stare. "That is, like, the *opposite* of encouraging," I said.

"It's not my job to be encouraging," she said.

"It's not your job to do anything relating to this team," said Henry, steering the SUV to a stop in front of the building. "You're here as an observer, nothing more."

"And nothing less," said Ciara. Her eyes were narrowed, her face set in an expression I could only describe as predatory. She was a pirate's wife with an untamed narrative behind her. I found myself wondering what sort of advantage that would be in the hours to come. "You still haven't been medically cleared to return to duty, Agent Marchen. If I say you're not stable, this team remains mine, and you get to have some time off. So I suggest you learn how to smile and pretend you really, really want me here, because the alternative is that one of us leaves—and right now, it wouldn't be me."

"See, this is why I hate HR," snarled Henry, and kicked open her door.

It slammed behind her. For one glorious moment, we were alone.

"Anybody else feel like she woke up scrambled?" I asked.

Silence answered me.

So we were going to do this the hard way. Fine. I'm Sloane Winters: I *invented* the hard way. "You want to ignore what's right in front of your faces, that's okay by me. I'll just laugh even harder when it turns around and bites you. Assholes."

"Thanks for the motivational speech, Sloane," said Andrew, wrinkling his nose. "Any time I start to feel like things are going well, all I have to do is remember your contributions to this team."

"That's my job," I said. "Now open the goddamn door before Henry starts to suspect something's going on in here."

He opened the door.

When we were all out of the SUV and standing on the cracked remains of the old parking lot, Henry pointed toward the factory, and said, "This place used to supply most of the glass for the local area. If someone built a house or repaired a shop, they got their supplies here. There are probably still hundreds, if not thousands, of their windows scattered around the city."

"The glass Elise creates is all sympathetically connected," said Demi. We turned to look at her. She reddened but continued: "When I pipe one piece, I can feel the rest trying to respond. All the pieces of glass that have been made here would be attuned to each other in the same way, all over the city."

The idea of someone seizing control of a bunch of glass as part of an evil plan should have seemed silly. Too bad we lived our lives according to fairy-tale logic. I opened my mouth to say something snide, and froze—which may have been a bad choice of words, given what had just occurred to me.

"Fuck," I breathed. "Fuck *fuck* fuck, they're going to pull a Snow Queen."

Jeffrey might have been upset by his failure to rescue Henry on his own, but he was an Archivist: His training had been complicated and had taken years. He knew his fairy tales. Slowly, he turned to face me, mouth hanging slightly open.

"Dear Grimm, I think you're right," he said.

Henry looked annoyed, like our realizations about the dangers at hand were nothing more than an unwanted distraction. Andrew put up his hand.

"Someone want to tell the rest of the class what that's supposed to mean, *before* we go charging in there with our guns half-cocked? Because anything that makes the two of you look like you're going to barf is something I think I'd like to know about now, not later."

"The Snow Queen narrative was codified by Hans Christian Andersen, as part of his work with an organization much like the Bureau," said Jeffrey, reaching up to adjust his glasses. "At the time, the world's scholars were working under the mistaken belief that knowing stories weakened them, since it tended to lower their flexibility. We didn't have the data that would show the dangers of memetic repetition."

"What Poindexter here is trying to say is that before old Hans wrote down the whole 'scary lady lives in the mountains and will freeze all your shit' story, there were still women in the wind," I said. "Snow Queens use magic mirrors to watch the world—sort of like Ladies of Shalott or Wicked Stepmothers. But unlike Ladies or Stepmothers, their mirrors are contagious. Who do we know who has control over infectious glass?"

"If Elise could attune herself to the glass that was made here, she could seize control of all the windows it became, and blow them out," said Ciara, with understanding and dawning horror. "She could kill hundreds of people."

"So it's important we move fast, and we hit hard," said Henry. She looked impatient. I couldn't blame her for that. My feet itched; I wanted to move, to *run*, and to cut these bastards off at the knees for what they had already done to us, and for what they were potentially about to do. Henry might be cold and smell of apples, but she was behaving reasonably, for once. "Under the circumstances, I think it's fair to say that if you have the shot, you should take it."

"Agent Marchen, are you sure—" began Ciara, only to cut herself off mid-sentence. "Never mind. These people have already caused civilian casualties. I apologize for questioning you."

"Apology accepted. Let's move." Henry stalked toward the factory. Andrew and Jeffrey were close behind her, and Demi hurried at their heels.

Only Ciara lingered. "You're right," she said tightly, once she was sure she wouldn't be overheard. "Something's wrong with her. She makes my locked door fingers itch."

I didn't know which fingers those were, and I didn't care to ask. "So what are we going to do about it?"

"Watch her. Try not to let her get herself killed. Try not to let her get anyone *else* killed." Ciara shook her head. "I don't have enough familiarity with Snow White stories. This may be normal."

"Or it may not," I said, and started walking. Wrong or not, Henry was my team leader, and my friend. I didn't have very many of those— I'd never been able to get the knack. If there was a way for me to protect her from herself, I was going to find it. No matter what that took.

# # #

The front door was padlocked shut, and an imposing sign warning of penalties for trespassers had been nailed to the wood above it, presumably to discourage non-existent vandals. Ciara looked at the lock for a moment, her fingers twitching and a small smile on her face.

"I know this isn't my team, Agent Marchen, but would you mind if I took this one?"

Henry looked over her shoulder at Ciara. Then she smiled. "Be my guest," she said, stepping to the side.

Ciara didn't so much walk to the door as float: her feet barely seemed to touch the ground. She leaned forward, putting herself on eye-level with the lock, and studied it until I began shifting my weight from foot to foot, eager to be moving. I didn't like the idea of rushing into a death trap, but neither did I appreciate the notion of standing perfectly still in plain view of whomever might be watching from the inside.

"You're a handsome one, aren't you?" she cooed. "So strong and sturdy. What a good hasp you must have; what a firm sense of your purpose. But you've been holding your place for so long. You can't be expected to stay closed forever. Why, that simply isn't fair! The people who put you here don't appreciate you the way that I do. They don't *understand* how difficult it is to be a lock, and to do the things you do. I would appreciate you always. I would never leave you alone in the rain to rust."

"Are we watching a woman try to seduce a lock?" asked Andrew. "I'm not objecting if we are—your kink is okay and all—but I just want to confirm that everyone else is seeing what I'm seeing, here."

The lock clicked as it released, popping open.

"No, we're watching a woman *successfully* seduce a lock," said Jeffrey. "Fascinating."

"Her love life must involve a lot of handcuffs," I said, earning myself a snort from Ciara as she reached out and removed the padlock from its place on the door.

"Don't ask about mine and I won't ask about yours," she said, making the lock disappear into her pocket. She straightened, tugging her jacket back into place. "We should be able to go right on in, and make no noise to warn them that we're coming."

"Nice parlor trick," said Henry, and began pulling the chains off the door. Andrew and Jeffrey hurried to help her. Demi stayed close. She was holding her flute now, fingers wrapped tight and ready to play.

Ciara walked back to stand beside me, patting the pocket where she had placed the lock with one hand. She looked smug. "It's not a parlor trick," she said, voice low, like she was confessing something incredibly important. "It's the world."

"Not going to argue," I said. The door was open now, Andrew slinging the length of chain over his shoulder like he anticipated finding a use for it later. Maybe he did. The stuff was pure iron, and while fairy tales didn't usually have any problem with iron, pure *anything* could have its uses.

"Wise choice," said Ciara, and followed the others into the dark, leaving me once more to bring up the rear.

Henry was at the front of the group. That was normal—the woman never met a threat she wasn't willing to face head-on, especially when she had the rest of us with her. It was like she felt like she couldn't endanger us unless she was endangering herself as well, and if that was the case, who was I to judge? I, who had been throwing myself at the face of the world for centuries, and wondering always whether this would be the day when the world failed to blink, and I could return to the earth that had borne me?

I was happy to judge Henry for the things that she did wrong. In this case, more than any other, she was simply demonstrating common sense. I couldn't fault her for that. But I could follow her into the dark, and hope that whatever was wrong with her was not so wrong that it was going to get her—or the rest of us—killed.

The glassworks had been abandoned for decades. The windows were dark with dust, and the smell of it hung in the air, thick enough to obscure the scent of apples. The chill rolling off of Henry was nothing compared to the cold of unused halls and empty rooms. We were walking into a tomb, or might as well have been, and the only question was whether it was going to be our burial mound.

"Stay together," said Henry, voice low. "We don't know how many of them are in here."

"Oh, this just gets better and better," muttered Andrew. He had drawn his service weapon at some point, and was holding it in both hands, aimed low, but ready to rise.

Each of us was holding our weapon, such as they were. Jeffrey and Henry had their guns. Demi had her flute. Ciara had the key at her throat, which she touched almost continually as we walked, while her other hand rested on the pocket where she'd concealed the padlock. I had my fists and my anger. They wouldn't do much against a hail of bullets, I supposed, but I'd had more than time enough to see that sometimes, hitting the enemy until they went away was an excellent approach.

"Shh," said Henry, and pushed onward, deeper into the glassworks.

The rust in the air made it hard to focus on what the narrative was trying to tell me—or perhaps trying to avoid telling me if Birdie had somehow been able to reshape it in this limited area. She said she was a Storyteller. What did that *mean*? I had only met a few people who claimed that title, and they'd all been working for the Bureau, dedicated to the idea that the human race deserved to tell its own stories, craft its own future, not be shaped by echoes from a distant past that had never really been. They'd been odd people, one and all, but none of them had done what Birdie had done: none of them had awakened sleeping stories and aimed them like arrows at me or the people that I cared about.

There were traces of narrative here, yes, and not just the narratives that wafted from my companions like the smoke from a candle. When I narrowed my eyes, the walls glittered like glass. When I inhaled sharply, I could taste rampion on the back of my tongue. No matter what Henry might have experienced while she was trapped in the whiteout wood, she had done at least one thing correctly. She had brought us to the place where Birdie was hiding.

The hall ended at a junction, continuing off in three different directions. We stopped, considering our options.

"This is not an episode of *Scooby Doo*," said Andrew, before Henry could speak. "We are *not* splitting the party."

"We don't need to." I paused for a moment, realizing I was the one who'd spoken. Lovely. Everyone was looking at me now. Even better. I pointed down the left fork. "The narrative energy's coming from that direction. I can't tell you exactly what the story is, but we'll find it that way."

"Better than a hunting hound," said Henry. "Andy, you're with me; Jeff, keep Demi safe. Demi—"

"If I see her, I'll pipe her back into the Stone Age," said Demi.

Henry smiled. "Good girl," she said, and began walking.

Apparently, Ciara and I didn't need instructions. That was unsettling. We were useful tools in whatever plan Henry was enacting, that much was clear, but thus far, she had acknowledged our presence as little as possible. We exchanged a look and followed her. My shoulders were tight with worry, and from what I could see of Ciara's posture, hers were much the same. Good. Whatever we were walking into, we weren't doing it while off our guard.

Henry and the others had managed to get a lead on us while we were hesitating. I was about to turn a corner when there was a strangling sound, and the soft clang of something hitting the floor—something the size and shape of a concert flute.

"Demi!" I shouted, and whipped around the corner, only to find myself facing one of those scenes that make me question the reality in which I live.

Ropes of dingy golden hair hung from the ceiling, and had lashed themselves tight around the throats of my teammates, hoisting them off the ground. Demi, as the smallest and lightest of the four, had been lifted the highest; she clawed at the hair around her throat, feet kicking helplessly at the air.

Andrew and Jeffrey were kicking as much as she was, but Henry wasn't moving: she hung still as the grave, like she had retreated back into her coma. The sight of her motionless body sent rage singing along my every nerve, hot and uncontrollable.

I turned to Ciara. "A knot is a kind of lock, *get them down*," I spat, before grabbing the nearest hank of dangling hair and beginning to pull myself up it, hand over hand, like a pirate scaling the rigging, or a little girl in Massachusetts climbing a tree. She was never far from me, that girl I had once been, all anger and action, an arrow in quest of a bow.

She never did find her bow, but a story found her, and tried to make her into a better weapon. It failed, or maybe it succeeded: it made her into *me*, and I wanted nothing more than to strike at the heart of every story that had ever harmed a child.

The hair pulsed under my hands like the umbilical cord of some terrible living thing. I squeezed tighter as I climbed, hoping I would do some injury to its owner. Something above me moaned, although whether it was from the pressure or from the weight of all the bodies tangled in its hair, I couldn't have said.

"Drop them and I might not knock out all your teeth," I called into the dark at the rafters. "If you enjoy chewing, you'll back down."

The hair pulsed, but did not retract.

"Suit yourself," I said, and kept climbing.

The hair of a Rapunzel is stronger than a normal person's: it has to be, to allow for use as an impromptu ladder. It also distorts space in small, subtle ways, allowing the climber to reach the top before their strength gives out. In half the time I should have needed, I had reached the top of the hair and pulled myself up onto the rafters, where a wild-eyed blonde woman in an ill-fitting floral dress crouched.

She smiled when she saw me. "Are you my prince?" she asked.

I hesitated. The fact of her narrative washed off her like a wave, but her smile was vacant and innocent. "How long were you at Childe?" I asked.

She looked at me blankly.

Right: she was a Rapunzel. "How long were you in the tower?"

"Long time, long, long time," she said. "So long Mother forgot where to find me, and had to send her friends to bring me here. They said to watch the hall while they went for my prince." Her smile became a pout. "They've been gone a long time. People keep pulling on my hair."

The compulsion charms at Childe were virtually narcotics. If they hadn't disconnected her from reality, the withdrawal after her summary removal would have done it. "My friends are caught in your hair," I said. "Let them go."

"But Mother's friends said—"

"They lied to you. They don't know where your prince is. But I do."
I spread my hands, showing that they were empty. God above, I hate
non-violent solutions. "Let them go, and we'll cut your hair and take
you to him."

She looked at me suspiciously for a while. Then she nodded.

There were several crashes from below, followed by a scream.

"Oh, for fuck's sake—stay *here*!" I snapped, and grabbed a loop of
her hair, and jumped.

# # #

Descending from a height on a ladder of human hair is not to be recom-
mended; descending from a height on a rope of same, less so. I reached
the floor in a matter of moments. Demi, Jeffrey, and Andrew were on
hands and knees, wheezing and clutching at their throats. Ciara was stroking a lock of hair, teasing the knots away, leaving it straight and shining.

And Henry was gone.

Jeffrey saw me and pointed, still wheezing, to a hole in the floor. I
dropped the hair I was holding and rushed to drop to my knees beside
the pit, looking down.

Henry dangled some three feet down, her hands locked on a broken
bit of flooring. She frowned when she saw me.

"Took you long enough," she said.

"I was busy," I replied. The cold still came off of her in waves. She
was helpless. Whatever was wrong with her, she couldn't use it against
me now. "How are you feeling, Henry?"

"Like I'm about to fall into the basement. Help me up."

I didn't want to. I wanted nothing more. "You've been acting weird
since you woke up."

The look she gave me was pure disbelief. "You want to talk about
this *now*?"

"You got a better time?"

"Yes. When I'm not *hanging on for dear life*."

She sounded like herself on that last phrase: annoyed and anxious and barely holding on to her temper. I wrestled with my conscience for a moment. If she had come back wrong, I was risking my team by saving her. If she was just disoriented . . .

Either way, she was still my friend. I thrust my hand down into the hole, and she grabbed it, grinning briefly.

"Thanks," she said, and pulled herself to safety.

# # #

Birdie and Elise were long gone by the time we coaxed their abandoned Rapunzel down from the rafters and went searching for them. We waited for the cleanup crew out on the lawn. Ciara continued to comb out the Rapunzel's hair with her fingers, cooing sweetly to keep the girl calm. Henry stood off to one side, talking quietly with Andrew and Jeffrey, while Demi played her flute for a murder of crows that had collected. I looked that way and smiled.

Then I paused, feeling a chill work its way through me.

The grass around Henry's feet was dead and brown. The grass everywhere else was still growing green.

Whatever was wrong, it wasn't over yet.

Holly Tree

Memetic incursion in progress: tale type 709 ("Snow White")
Status: INCURSION STATUS UNCLEAR

Summer is an impossibility in the whiteout wood, the liminal space set aside between the story and the sigh for the use of the snow girls, the apple girls, the blood and ice girls walking through the steps of their ancient, unkind tale. They blend into the trees, black and white and red, colored to match the world around them. Theirs is a perfect camouflage, and it has always served them well when they stepped out of the palace and into the pines. No one can find them in the wood if they don't want to be found. No one can hurt them there.

No one, except for one another.

She lay where she had fallen, a bloodless body on the bloody snow, and the only motion was the wind running its fingers through her bark-black hair, ruffling it like an anxious mother. *Get up get up get up,* whispered the wind, and the goosedown girl, the ruby girl, the coal girl remained as she was: unmoving, unaware, as much a part of the wood as any rock or tree. She hovered in a space between living and dying, and it was anyone's guess which way she would go, for she had eaten the apple; she had fulfilled her part of the compact, and once the apple has been eaten, it becomes both very hard and very easy to kill the princesses of garnet and char and bone. She had no glass coffin, but she had the ice in her hair and the snow all around her, and every snowflake that fell was clear as a whisper.

She had no true love to kiss her, but she had the favor of the wood, and it was the wood that sent the wind to run its fingers through her hair, whispering *Get up get up get up*. It wasn't the same thing. It wasn't the right thing at all.

It was close enough. Henrietta Marchen opened her eyes, and the world moved on.

# # #

I woke with frost on my eyelashes and a pounding in my ears that felt loud enough to shake the foundations of the Earth. The wind howled around me, smelling of apples and blood. Everything was white, and everything hurt.

Piece by aching piece, I pulled myself out of the snowdrift that had formed around me. It was deep enough that I struggled to sit up, the snow crumbling under my hands like it was trying to keep me pinned. I should have frozen to death. Lying in the snow for that long, with no protection but a torn and bloody silk slip? I should have *died*.

But I hadn't. With dawning horror, I realized I wasn't even cold. I might as well have been taking a nap in a sun-warmed, grassy meadow somewhere, and not in the middle of the worst blizzard I had ever seen.

The maze was gone. Adrianna was gone. I was alone with the snow. The last thing I remembered was—

My hand flew to my throat and found only unbroken skin, all marks of Adrianna's icy blade washed away by whatever magic had put the blood back in my body and kept me from freezing. I was weak—magic isn't a real solution for blood loss and a severed carotid artery—but I was alive, and that was considerably more than I'd been expecting when Adrianna walked away from me.

I stiffened, something more chilling than the howling winter wind washing over me. Adrianna had called me "little doorway" because she'd been a part of this story long enough to understand one of the hidden sides of the Snow White narrative. We were supposed to be orphans. We were supposed to meet our princes *after* we fell into a sleep like death, *after* we ate the apple and were sealed under glass. No one would know if our personalities changed, because there wasn't supposed to be anyone who really knew us as people. We were cyphers, black and white checkerboard girls, completely interchangeable.

Adrianna had slit my throat and used my blood to open the way for her to enter my body. She was me now. She was standing with my legs and breathing with my lungs, and I was here, and I had no way of waking up.

"Oh, sweet Grimm, what do I do now?" I whispered.

The wind whipped my words away. I had never been more alone.

# # #

Time had always been difficult in the wood, maybe because I'd always been dreaming when I went there. Dreams stretch things out, turning minutes into hours, taking advantage of the brief periods of REM sleep that the human mind is heir to. They also skip over what doesn't seem important. I trudged through the whiteout wood, fully a part of it for the first time—I was stuck here, after all, just as much a part of the narrative as the others—and realized that I'd never thought about how *big* it was. It had always been dream distance before, meant to be skipped past. Now that I was walking through every awful inch of it, I wanted nothing more than to go back to sleep and be able to cover miles of snow-covered ground in a second, the way I'd always done before.

Or I could wake up. That would also be nice. If I were asleep, the walk would be tolerable, and waking up would be an option. But I wasn't asleep anymore.

I stepped between two trees and the wood changed. The wind died; the snow stopped falling, although the ground was still white. It was like it had gone from the worst part of winter to the best in a single heartbeat. Even the air tasted sweeter, like apples and pine instead of apples and blood. This was a winter where snowmen could be built and children could go sledding before fleeing inside for cocoa and cookies.

It still wasn't a winter I wanted to belong to. I never asked for this.

The clearing ahead of me was ringed with trees, spaced so that each pair formed a rough doorway, with enough space between them that it would be easier to go around than to go through. I took another step forward, and the doorways filled with white-skinned, black-haired, red-lipped women. I knew them, and they knew me. I'd been here before, after all.

The nearest was a tall, thin woman with ashy freckles spattered across the bridge of her nose, sharing her doorway with a shorter, rounder-faced woman whose eyes were a startlingly deep brown. Brown was rare here, rendered fascinating by the monochrome world around it.

The tall woman's hands moved in silent speech. Her companion translated, "You got away, but you didn't get away. Is that true?"

"She cut me." I touched my throat and stomach involuntarily. My flesh had healed, but the tear in my nightgown hadn't. I was afraid to look down and see how much blood was soaked into the fabric. "She took my blood. I think she took my body too."

"She did," said a new voice, rich with a Nova Scotia accent. I turned. Tanya was stepping out from between two trees, leaving her private clearing for the communal one. "We felt her go. The Cinderella story had been attacking our own, testing the borders of the wood."

"Ayane told me," I said, gesturing toward Judi and the woman who was her best friend and translator. "She said it was why the snow was coming down so hard before."

"That's true," said Tanya. Her voice was clear and filled with sorrow.

The last time I'd seen her, the whiteout wood had been using her as a puppet, speaking through her lips because I wasn't listening to the whispers embedded in the snow. I frowned as I studied her, looking for signs that she remembered our conversation. I didn't find them. She looked worried, sure, but not embarrassed or angry, either of which would have made sense, given the way our last encounter ended. Who knew that something as ageless and inhuman as the whiteout wood could be tricked with a simple "hey, what's over there"?

"Adrianna took my body." Tanya had already acknowledged that, but it felt like I couldn't stop saying it. It was the most important thing that had ever happened, to anyone. I needed everyone to know, because maybe then, I could start figuring out what I was going to do about it. "She cut me, and she took my body."

"It happens to the best of us," said Ayane, and the bitterness in her voice would have been impossible to miss even if I hadn't come to know her so well. Tanya was my official mentor in the wood, but I liked all the Snow Whites I'd met so far, with the glaring exception of Adrianna. I just wasn't ready to become their permanent roommate.

"I'm sorry," said Tanya. She looked to her left. I followed her gaze.

There was a pair of trees there, with no one standing between them. I could see the clearing on the other side, white snow on the ground broken by a scattering of tiny red flowers, like drops of blood. It spoke to me in a way that nothing in the wood ever had, and the word it said was "home."

I wrenched my eyes away. "No," I said. "I'm sorry, but no. I can't. I have to find a way back. Adrianna—she's going to go after my team, if she hasn't already started." Sloane could hold her own, but Andy had no actual connection to the narrative; he'd be a sitting duck. Demi was too untrained to take on someone like Adrianna, who had been honing her story for decades. And Jeff . . .

I didn't think Jeff could attack someone who was wearing my face, even if he knew it wasn't actually me. He was a good guy and a loyal friend. He would have had trouble fighting back before we'd gone and fallen in love with each other. Now that we had, I couldn't risk him sitting back and letting her do her worst. I knew all too well how bad her worst could be.

"Henry, I don't think you understand," said Tanya. "You can take another body, but yours is not there to reclaim. You won't be yourself anymore. It's not the sort of thing you can do lightly."

"Neither is standing here and letting Adrianna kill everyone I care about," I protested. "If there's a way, I want it."

"You can't control where you go," said Tanya. "You could wake up anywhere in the world."

"That's not true." The voice was Ayane's. I turned to face her, but not before I saw the shock and anger in Tanya's eyes.

Ayane had her shoulders locked and her chin lifted, glaring defiance across the clearing at the other Snow White. "There's a way to control it," she said. "It's not easy, and it's not fun, but it's possible. You owe her that."

"I owe her nothing," said Tanya. "She lost."

"I'm right here," I said. "Tell me."

Tanya looked at me, and while there was no mercy in her eyes, there was sorrow there. Maybe she'd been trying to spare me, not punish me.

I didn't care either way. If it would get me back to my team, I would take whatever punishment my story wanted to dish out. I wasn't giving up. This was *not* going to be the way my story ended.

"If you go to the mirrors, they may be willing to make a trade," she said, finally.

I frowned. "Define 'trade.' Becoming somebody's enchanted looking glass isn't my idea of making progress."

"You might," said Tanya. "I won't lie to you about that. Our story is . . . hungry. All stories are hungry. They eat all the history they can find, because it can be used to create variations on the theme. We didn't have poisoned combs before a Snow White came to the wood with tales of mermaids in her heart. If you go to the mirrors and show them a story they don't know yet, they might be willing to show you something in return."

This sounded too good to be true, which meant it almost certainly was. Warily, I asked, "Which stories do the mirrors know?"

"That's the problem," said one of the other Snow Whites, our Midwestern dairy princess. She had died on a parade float, something she reminded us all bitterly of whenever she had the opportunity. "Nobody has a list. And if you don't have anything they want . . ."

"I know how it goes in fairy tales. Don't make deals with the devil unless you're sure you can pay them off." I turned to look at Tanya. "Is there *any* other way for me to find a body that isn't being used, that's close enough to my team for me to help them?"

Silent, she shook her head.

My decision was made—if it had ever really been a decision. Maybe this was all part of my story. I took a breath, and asked, "Will you take me to the mirrors?"

Again, she shook her head.

"I will," said Ayane. I turned. The Japanese Snow White was watching me with bright hope in her eyes. "I know the way."

I smiled, a small, bitter thing, like a poisoned apple in my mouth. "Then lead the way."

# # #

If the walk from where I had awoken to the clearing had been long, the walk from the clearing to the place where the mirrors waited to seal my future was unbearable. We trudged through snow, Ayane and Judi in the lead, me bringing up the rear in my bloody shift, and the wind wailed around us, making promises I couldn't understand. I would, though. If I stayed here long enough, I would, and then I would never find the way home.

"Almost there," called Ayane.

"Oh, yay," I muttered—and then, between one step and the next, the world changed. Gone was the snow and the forest and the whispering wind, replaced by a hall that stretched out toward forever, part of some great and unseen palace. I would have thought I'd stepped into a different story altogether, if not for two things: mirrors covered the walls so completely that the original wallpaper was all but obscured, and the air still tasted of apples.

"How can there be so many?" I asked, and my voice echoed in the silent hall like I had shouted. Ayane flinched. Judi didn't. And nothing, thankfully, stirred in the black and silent depths of the mirrors.

"Every Snow White who isn't in the wood somewhere is here," said Ayane. She reached out to touch a frame, brushing her fingers across the carved black wood. "Some of them are the ones who went bad, but not all. I have friends in this hall. They said going into the mirrors was like going back to sleep, only this time there's no true love's kiss to wake you. Just darkness and dreams and peace. Except when people like us come along and mess it all up for them."

"So what do I do?"

Turn and run, whispered the part of me that was always going to be a frightened fairy-tale princess, tied to the things other people said about my story. I pushed her aside with all the strength I could muster, and waited.

"Put your hand on the glass and say what you want," said Ayane. "That's all."

"Okay . . ." The nearest mirror was almost as tall as I was, with a white ash-wood frame. I pressed my palm against the glass. It was as cold as ice. Closing my eyes, I said, "My name is Henrietta Marchen. I'm a Snow White. Another Snow White stole my body, and I need to warn my team. Please, will you help me find a way back to them?"

The cold began to race up my arm. I tried to pull away, and found I couldn't: my palm was fixed to the glass. I tried to open my eyes. I couldn't do that either, and then the unpleasant sensation of someone rifling through my memories distracted me from the physical discomfort.

We are mirror; we see what is reflected, whispered a voice, and while it was cold as glass, I could hear the ghost of the woman it had once been. Somehow, that was the worst part of all. *Do you grant consent for all the stories you have touched?*

"Yes!"

Good, said the voice, sounding so pleased with itself that I instantly knew I'd made a mistake. But there wasn't time to take it back; I was falling, and somehow, even with my eyes closed, I knew the mirror was there, waiting to take me in and take me down, down into the cold darkness where all Snow Whites eventually went to die and dream forever. Down, down, down, and everything was black, and then even the darkness was gone.

# # #

I was standing in a farmyard that looked like something out of a BBC production of *The Crucible*. Chickens clucked and scratched at the dirt; a black and white cat prowled by, tail low, intent on some feline errand. I looked down at myself, relieved to see that I was properly dressed for the first time since I'd eaten the apple: black suit, white shirt, black shoes. Even my badge was there, clipped to my belt. The only problem was, I didn't know where the hell *I* was.

A woman—a girl, really, no more than sixteen—stepped out of the house, a basket over her arm and a kerchief tied over her neatly braided, wheat-colored hair. She was wearing a homespun brown dress, with an apron around her waist. Oddly, that wasn't what kept me from recognizing her at first. It was her face. She was smiling, utterly serene. She looked like someone who had never been anything but at peace with herself, and with the world around her.

Then she moved out of the sun and into the shadow cast by the elm at the edge of the yard. It added just a little darkness to her hair, and dimmed just a fraction of the sparkle from her eye. I gasped. I couldn't stop myself.

Sloane Winters was in front of me, and she didn't even seem to know I was there.

"But I don't know this story," I said, half protest and half plea. Sloane had shared enough about her past for me to know that she considered it something painful and private, something she didn't want to discuss with anyone, least of all me. And yet here I was, about to watch it all unfold in front of me. This wasn't right. This was a violation.

"You are a mirror," whispered the voice I'd heard from the glass. It sounded like it was coming from right next to me, but mine was the only shadow on the ground. "She passed before you and was reflected. You may not know her story, but your mirror's heart does. If you want us to give you what you asked, you'll keep your part of the bargain. You'll give us her tale."

It was an invasion of privacy at best, and a human rights violation that could see me losing my badge and maybe getting myself killed at worst. If Sloane ever found out about this, I was a dead woman.

And I had no other way of getting back to the people I cared about . . . Sloane included. I swallowed, hard, and forced myself to keep watching.

Sloane crossed the yard with quick, light steps, her basket hanging easy from her arm as she approached the henhouse. The chickens clucked and strutted, but didn't flee from her. One particularly large brown hen hopped onto her foot, making a soft clucking noise. Sloane laughed. I gasped again. It was a beautiful sound, as light as her footsteps, filled with an absolute certainty that when given the choice, the world would choose to be kind. I'd never heard her laugh like that. Whatever bright thing she had once contained, the world and her story had long since beaten it out of her.

"What do you think you'll have by doing that, hmm?" she asked, shaking the chicken off her foot. Her accent was like nothing I had ever heard before, caught somewhere between British and Southern. I still had no idea what year it was.

"Amity!" called a woman's voice, from the other side of the yard. Sloane—Amity, she must have been Amity when this was really happening, before the silence and the story descended on her—straightened and turned, the smile still resting easy on her lips.

"Yes, Mama?" she called.

"There's no need to fetch the eggs in," said the woman in the farmhouse door. She was tall and plump, with features that were an older echo of Amity's own. They were lined with worry, and there was an odd brightness in her eyes, one I'd seen too many times before. There was a story working on her, rewriting her heart's desires to suit what it wanted her to be.

Amity frowned. "But the chickens are my responsibility. I need to collect their eggs if we don't want them to spoil in the nest."

"No," said the woman. "Gabrielle will do it. You'll come inside, out of the sun, and rest yourself. You mustn't exert yourself if you're to find a handsome husband."

The look Amity gave her mother was pure confusion, mixed with a thin thread of fear. "Gabrielle does for the pigs, and brings in the cattle. The chickens—"

"Are her responsibility now. Come. Your sister is already inside." Her mother turned and walked back into the house. After a moment's confused staring, Amity followed.

"It's the start of her story," I whispered. I took a step toward the farmhouse. This was a new Sloane, but she was hurting, and she was my friend; I wanted to help her.

My foot rose in spring and came down in the fall, the world transforming around me to suit its change of season. The leaves on the trees exploded into reds and golds, and the chickens now scratched more sluggishly. There was an unfamiliar girl there, spreading corn on the ground while glancing anxiously back over her shoulder. Her hair was darker than Sloane's, and the shape of her face was different enough that I identified her as this story's Cinderella without a second thought. She was the stepsister, if you were standing in Sloane's position, and the heroine, if you were standing where the narrative wanted the story to be.

Amity stepped out of the farmhouse. She was thinner than she'd been the last time I'd seen her, and the light in her eyes was dim, almost extinguished. I could *see* Sloane in the bones of this girl, who had been so innocent only a few months before. The girl—Gabrielle, it must have been—flinched and shied away.

"I'm sorry, Amity, I meant to come in and see to your hair, I truly did, but the bread refused to rise, and I—"

"Hush, Gabby, hush." It was Amity's turn to glance anxiously back at the house, before returning her attention to her trembling stepsister. "I'm not here to yell at you. I fixed my hair myself, same as I've done every morning since I was nine years of age. I'm not some fine lady, to need a maid to do for me."

"That's not what Mother says," said Gabrielle. Her voice shook. I wondered how long it had been since she'd slept, or been allowed to eat a full meal. "That's not what you said either, last night."

"I wasn't myself last night." Amity's voice shook too, but hers was weak with uncertainty and confusion rather than hunger. I wondered what it felt like to have a story undermining everything she'd ever known herself to be. My story had been with me from the beginning; I was born with skin as white as snow and hair as black as coal. For Sloane . . . if she had had any natural connection to the narrative, it had been subverted when her mother took a new husband and brought a potential Cinderella into the house.

How the forces that control our lives love their princess stories! I've never understood why. They don't do the most damage, or have the highest body counts, but the narrative will almost always abandon its original intent to go after a princess. To be born a Cinderella is to have a target painted on your forehead in colors only the story can see.

Gabrielle looked at her stepsister with wariness and hope painted in equal parts across her face. "Mother says if I finish all my chores on time tomorrow, I might be able to go with you to the ball at the Mayor's house this weekend. She says I could wear one of my mother's gowns, and not be so dreadfully out of style as to embarrass you."

Amity's jaw tightened, not with anger, but with regret. I'd seen that look on Sloane's face a hundred times, usually when she thought no one was looking. "I left some rolls and cheese for you in the barn, behind the hay. If you eat quickly, she'll never know you've had it."

"You're a good sister, Amity. I only wish I deserved you." The raw longing in Gabrielle's voice made me close my eyes for a moment. It hurt to hear.

When I opened them again, the world had changed. I was standing in a church, rough hewn and lightly ornamented, but no less holy for all of that. Amity knelt alone in one of the pews, her clasped hands pressed against her forehead.

"I have these *thoughts*, I can't *stop* them, and I am truly afraid, Father, I am terrified of what I might do. Is it the Devil? I hear stories from travelers who have seen Salem, and they tell me the Devil gets into young women, twists them against their families. I've not signed his book, nor have I seen him waiting in the woods, but there must be some explanation for the malaise infecting my family. Mother has taken leave of her senses. She never scolds me anymore, even when I do wrong. She orders me and Isabelle to be idle, to sit upon our hands and stay in shadowed rooms for the sake of our complexions, while she heaps all manner of abuse upon poor Gabrielle. And I . . . I . . ." Amity stopped, seeming to choke on her own words before she continued,

"I have started to do the same. I don't *mean* to! If I allow my guard to drop, even the slightest bit, it begins, and Gabby *endures* it, like she has somehow earned it. Belle abuses her without cease. My youngest sister laughs while she causes our sister in all but blood the greatest of pain."

Amity took a shaky breath. Finally, she whispered, "I fear for the souls of my family if this does not stop. I fear for Gabrielle's life. I do not know what to do."

She stood, crossing herself, and turned to walk toward the church door. I watched her go, eyes wide and heart aching. I'd never seen Sloane like this: Young, vulnerable, and worst of all, *brittle*. This girl was on the verge of breaking. Maybe that was what had to happen to her. Maybe that was how you took Amity and turned her into Sloane. But that didn't mean I wanted to watch it.

Amity opened the church door. The sunlight flooded in, making me squint, and when the brightness faded, the scene had changed again. I was standing in a small, wooden-walled room, with a threadbare carpet on the floor. Some efforts had been made, probably recently, to gussy up the handmade furniture: there were more pillows than were strictly necessary, and a jumble of decorative knick-knacks had been piled on every available surface. There were a few books—the family Bible, a Farmer's Almanac, and a battered red volume of fairy tales.

My heart sank. This was when it happened, then; this was when she understood.

Amity slipped into the room, shoulders slumped. From behind her, her mother called, "See to it that you sit still! Sitting develops grace!"

"Yes, Mother," said Amity. Her heart wasn't in it; I could tell that much. Sadly, there seemed to be no fight left in her.

She paced back and forth like a captive animal, her hands twisting her skirts into knots around them. Finally, she grabbed the first book off the mantle and collapsed into the nearest chair. She glared at the cover for a moment. Then she opened it.

I didn't know enough about the time period to know how common it was for a woman to be able to read, but it was obvious that Amity could. The color drained from her face as her eyes grew wider and wider. She raised a hand to cover her mouth. That didn't stop me from seeing the slow tears that filled her eyes before running, unchecked, down her cheeks. Finally, she threw the book at the wall. It hit with a thump.

By the time it fell to the floor, Amity had already run out of the room.

"We shouldn't be watching this," I said.

"You promised," said the mirror's voice. "Now go after her."

There was too much at stake to give up now. *Sloane, forgive me*, I thought, and followed her through the doorway—

—into the farmyard, which had, through the strange logic of this trawl through her origins, replaced the hallway. Night had fallen. Amity stepped out the front door, easing it closed behind her, before turning to look back at her home. There were tears running down her cheeks.

"Forgive me," she whispered. "Forgive me and pray that I am right, for if I am, breaking this cycle before the dance begins will save you all." She kissed her fingers and pressed them against the wood before she turned and walked across the yard and into the waiting woods beyond. I followed. I had faith that whatever force was motivating my journey would keep me from losing track of her, even if I stayed exactly where I was, but I didn't want her walking into those woods alone. It was silly. This had all happened centuries ago, if the clothing and accents were anything to go by. And I didn't care. She was my friend, or she would eventually become my friend, and she deserved better than to walk into a forest alone at night while a fairy tale was trying to dig its thorns into her.

She walked for a long time. It was impossible to tell how long; I had the distinct feeling that I was skipping hours, if not entire days. She stopped a few times, to remove the bundle from her back and eat a bit of meat or cheese. Then she would resume, moving doggedly onward as she sought some undetermined goal.

It was dawn on the third day when the riders appeared. Three of them on horseback: one white horse, one black horse, and one brown horse. It would have been impossible to ignore the fairy-tale symbolism even if the sole female rider hadn't been pale as cream, with hair the color of arterial spray. Rose Reds might not be as easy to spot in a crowd as Snow Whites, but they had their distinguishing characteristics, and my own brother had been one. I knew her, even though we'd never met, and never would in the real world.

Her companions were men, one with golden hair, the other with a nasty-looking scar cutting down the side of his face. All three pulled their horses to a stop when they saw Amity. They exchanged a glance amongst themselves. Then their Rose Red leaned forward on her horse and called, "Excuse me, girl? Are we near your village?"

"I have walked for three days," said Amity wearily. "If I am still near my village then I am damned, and nothing in this world can save me."

The two men exchanged a look. The Rose Red frowned. "That may be so," she said. "Tell me, have you heard anything of a family with three lovely daughters, two born to the woman of the house, the third brought to her table by marriage? We're looking for them, you see. We have a gift for their youngest."

"She wasn't the youngest," said Amity. "Gabrielle was second of the three of us, if you reckon by years, and not by the day she arrived at the house." She chuckled mirthlessly. "I suppose she's the eldest now, with me gone and Isabelle remaining. I hope she will stand up to Mother, now that I am gone."

The Rose Red's eyes widened. "I'm sorry. Are you saying *you* come from such a family?"

"I've left them. They're safe now." Amity squared her shoulders and looked up at her interrogator. Her name didn't fit her as well now as it had when I first saw her coming out to tend the chickens. She was sliding further toward Sloane with every moment. "I'll not be a wicked stepsister for anyone. I will not let the Devil make a Cinderella of my beloved Gabrielle."

The silence that fell then was absolute and all-consuming. I realized I was holding my breath, waiting to see what would happen next.

The gold-haired man slid off his horse, trying to make the motion unobtrusive. The Rose Red didn't take her eyes off Amity.

"I don't think you know what you're saying, girl," she said. "Cinderella is a fairy tale."

"My father died not six months ago, when the robin was building in the holly tree. My mother loved all her daughters then, and I would never have raised a hand against my sisters, either of them. Isabelle was the gentlest creature in the wood. Even rabbits seemed like foul murderers compared to her! But the snow came, and everything changed." Amity shook her head. "We are good women. We work hard, and we trouble none. Yet Mother calls Gabrielle foul names and makes her sleep in the barn, and I caught Isabelle pulling her hair, while I dream of poisoned soup and ground glass in the well. I could not stay. Don't you see? There is a story older than my family, and somehow we stumbled into it, my sisters and I. But you cannot have a Cinderella without her wicked stepsisters, and I refuse that role. I will not be their destruction."

The man with the golden hair pulled a knife from his belt. "So you admit to being story- struck?" he asked, and his voice was low and dangerous.

Amity didn't seem frightened. She stood a little taller, lifted her chin a little higher like she was intentionally exposing her throat. "I admit to nothing but saving my family. If that is a sin, strike me down, I beg you. Keep them safe from me by removing me from this world." She cast a narrow-eyed look at the Rose Red. "You smell of roses. I wonder if the smell of blood will dull them."

The man with the scar raised his hand—the first motion he'd made since the riders stopped. Both of his companions froze. Leaning forward on his horse, he fixed his eye on Amity. For her part, she didn't flinch away. She simply looked back at him, cool and calm and resigned to her fate. She had given up, and in this girl, in this place and time, giving up seemed to have unlocked some great wellspring of anger in her soul.

How dare *you?* her gaze asked, and *Because someone must,* answered the eyes of the man with the scar.

"You smell roses on our Electa? How fascinating. There are no roses in this wood." His voice was mild, even pleasant, but there were teeth lurking in its depths.

Amity stood her ground. "Then the lady favors perfumes from France. She's *your* companion, not mine. Grill *her* as to why she smells of roses."

"But you see, I know she wears no perfume, and more, I know why she smells so. You are an enigma, child. Story-struck, yes, but only from the side; the story you stepped through was never meant for you. You should be a husk by now, devoid of will or want to do anything beyond what the tale commanded. So how are you here, in the middle of this forest, so many miles from your family? How is it that you smell the roses?" The man with the scar leaned even further forward. "You've done the impossible. I want to know how."

"Then you'll not kill me?" I would have needed to be deaf to miss the pain in Amity's voice, or the way it cracked on the final word. She sounded like a child who had just been denied her heart's one true desire.

"Not unless you force us to." The scarred man offered her his hand. After a moment's hesitation, Amity took it.

"Do you promise me I'll never be able to harm my family? That they'll be all right without me?"

"My companions will ride ahead and see that they are well," said the man. "As for you, I promise you'll harm none, lest we put an end to your time in this world. Will you trust me?"

Amity hesitated. I could see the confusion and trepidation in her eyes, the fear as she compared the danger of riding away with a stranger in the woods to the danger of walking those woods alone. Finally, she nodded. "I will try."

The man swung her up onto his horse like she weighed nothing at all. Looking to his companions, he said, "Go. You have your orders."

"We'll see you at home," said the golden haired man. He climbed back onto his horse. Then he and the Rose Red—Electa—were away, pounding off in the direction Amity had run from.

"Where are we going?" asked Amity. Her voice was very small.

"To explore your glorious mystery," said the man. He wheeled his horse around, urging it into a gallop. In only a few seconds, the road was empty.

I knew what was expected of me by now. I closed my eyes, and when I opened them again, I was standing in a large room lined with books and studded with oak furniture. Whoever owned this building had money to spare, something supported by the cut glass decanter of brandy on the table. The gold-haired man was sitting there, a glass of the stuff in his hand, while Electa paced. The black-haired man leaned against the wall, watching both of them. Amity was nowhere to be seen.

"I'm telling you, Jack, it was like nothing I've ever seen before," said Electa. She raked a hand through her cherry-colored hair. "The mother met us in the yard, asking if we'd seen her daughter, and *both* girls were with her. There was no sign of the story. The youngest was holding the Cinderella's hand and weeping. That girl we found, she broke a Cinderella in formation by *walking away*. How is that even possible?"

"I don't know," said the black-haired man, whose name must have been Jack. "It may have happened before. We have no way of knowing how many stories fail to happen, only the ones which occur and destroy and fade away. Perhaps this is how most Cinderella stories wither on the vine."

"And the angry young woman now sleeping in the garret?" asked the still-nameless man. "I'm amazed you managed to feed her so much laudanum without her noticing. She must have been very tired."

"Or had simply never tasted the stuff before," said Electa. "Look at her clothing. She's lived a simple, pious life. She probably has no idea what's going on. She's going to be a burden. We can't keep pets."

"She was strong enough to walk away from a Cinderella that had already started to revise the world," said Jack. "That bears some careful observation. I've already written to London—you remember London, don't you Electa? The Council of Librarians? They gave us permission to keep you alive, when most were baying for your blood as a dangerous, story-struck individual. This girl deserves the same chance, and besides, she smelled roses on you. That's unusual. I want to know more, and we have no one here with skill at learning secrets from the dead."

"How are we seeing this?" I asked. "I never met any of these people."

"Look at the stairs," murmured the mirror's voice. I turned my head. There was Amity, crouched low and hiding in the shadows of the bannister. She must have been there this whole time, watching, listening, as these three strangers debated her fate.

Electa glared at Jack. "She's a liability. She's story-struck, but she's not the Cinderella of the piece. Can we afford the risk of a Wicked Stepsister here, in our home? The work is great and there are too few of us as it is."

"You cut straight to the heart of the matter," said Jack. "The work is great. There are too few of us. She's been touched by a story; that makes her eligible to join us. And she smelled *roses* on you, Electa. Do you know what that could mean?"

"There hasn't been a hound for decades," said the unnamed man. "You're chasing, if you'll forgive the implication, a fairy tale. Cut the girl loose or kill her, but don't make her out to be the impossible."

"Impossible is a matter of perspective, Hiram," said Jack. "We keep her, for now. We expose her to a few more stories and see what she makes of them. If she can spot them like she spotted Electa, we tell her everything, and we convince her to serve with us."

Electa looked alarmed. Hiram emptied his glass in one convulsive swallow.

"This is madness," he said. "You'll doom us all."

"Or we'll save the Colonies from becoming nothing but a breeding ground for superstition and fable," said Jack. "The only way to know is to continue on."

Amity, still mostly in shadow, rose and crept back up the stairs. She made no sound as I watched her go, and it was no surprise when I turned back to the room and she was already there.

Her clothes had changed. They were still modest, but they were cut from a finer cloth, and better tailored to the shape of her body. I wondered which of her new "friends" had overseen that. If she was uncomfortable having her figure revealed, she didn't show it: she was sitting still as a snake preparing to strike, a blindfold tied over her eyes.

"This is your final test, Amity," said Jack. "If you pass, you'll be given a new name and a new place here, with us, to hold for as long as you like. If you fail . . ."

"If I fail, you kill me," she said. There was a sharp edge in her voice that hadn't been there before. She was wearing away the soft parts of herself, leaving nothing but a weapon in their wake. "Test me, then, and tell me whether I'm to live or die."

"Very well." Jack walked to the door and opened it, offering his hand to the woman who was waiting on the other side. She had long white hair, and she didn't say a word as Jack led her across the room toward Amity. Jack settled her in the chair across from the waiting, motionless girl.

"All right," he said. "Begin."

Amity sniffed the air, frowning. Then she said, "I hear waves, and I smell dead fish on the beach. Did you bring me a fisherman?"

The white-haired woman clapped a hand over her mouth, but didn't make a sound as she turned wide, wounded eyes on Jack.

"Not quite," he said to Amity, and "You may go," to the Little Mermaid he had brought before her. The white-haired woman fled through the door she had entered by. Electa led a man into the room.

He was wearing a flat cap and had a pleasantly vague expression, like the world was a new delight that was unfolding with every moment.

"Amity?" prompted Jack.

"Empty halls, and too many cobwebs, and graveyard dirt. Why—did you bring me a gravedigger? Why would you do such a thing?"

"Not quite," said Jack again. He nodded to Electa, who led the Boy Who Didn't Know Fear away. "We have one more test for you, Amity. Are you prepared?"

"As ever I have been," she said. "Test me or leave me be, but don't prattle on so. My ears ache to hear it."

"As you say," he said. He reached down and removed the heavy torque he wore around his left wrist. Instantly, he seemed to stand a little taller, and have a little more anger in his eyes. He looked like he could huff and puff and blow the whole world down.

Amity wrinkled her nose. "It smells of wet dog in here," she said. "Did you bring me a huntsman?"

"Not quite," said Jack, and his voice was full of gravel, and his mouth was full of teeth. Then he slid the torque back over his wrist, and he was a man once more. "You may uncover your eyes now, Amity. You've passed."

"How fortunate," said Amity dryly. She reached up to remove her blindfold, looking at Jack. "Now will you tell me what I've committed myself to?"

"Your sister," said Jack, taking the seat across from her while Hiram and Electa walked in from opposite sides of the room. They moved to stand behind Jack, flanking him. "She was a Cinderella in the making. Do you believe this?"

"I said it, and I meant it," said Amity. "I still dream of her—of doing terrible, unforgiveable things to her. Boiling and burning and poisons in her food. I don't know why. But the jealousy threatens to consume me whenever I think on her face, which I loved so well, and now wish so truly to destroy."

"That's because she was becoming a fairy tale, and she was taking you with her," said Jack. He began to talk. Amity listened, dubiously at first, but with increasing understanding and increasing horror as he explained the ways stories could and would parasitize the real world. This was before the Aarne-Thompson Index had been published, before the ATI Management Bureau was founded; this was an older, wilder form of controlling the fairy tales that would otherwise have run rough-shod over humanity.

Sloane predated the Index. My eyes widened at the realization. I'd never really considered that before, or wondered how much of what we thought we knew was only this year's wisdom. I'd always known she was older than she looked, but Colonial times? *This* much older? How much change had she seen? How much change was yet to come?

The things we thought of as constants were just ripples in the water to her. The only thing that had ever remained, century after century, was the story, and the poison it had planted in her heart.

When Jack stopped talking, Amity looked at him and asked, in a very small voice, "Is there any way this can be taken from me? I don't want this. I miss the girl I was. I dream of broken glass and poisoned pies. It burns me."

"The story that touched you was never *meant* for you," said Jack. He sounded almost gentle, like he understood how hard this had to be for her. I started to like him a little bit. He was doing his best in a world that didn't have the comforting framework of bureaucracy to fall back on. "Electa is what we call 'a Rose Red.' She was tied to an ancient Germanic story about sisters and gold and bears. I . . . come from a different tale. Both of us were meant to be the subjects of our stories, warping the people around us. You were not the spider, to sit at the middle of your web. You were a fly, caught by something too great for you to understand. You aren't a Cinderella in your own right. You are . . . something new. Something different. We'd like you to stay here, with us, if you would. Your skills could come in handy."

Amity looked at him. Something was dying in her eyes: some indefinable blend of hope and longing. "Am I a prisoner?"

Jack nodded. "Yes. You can't be one of us. You're too new, and too unpredictable. But we'll be kind, and we'll keep you as best we can."

"So you'd ask for my freedom, then," said Amity bitterly.

"We already have your freedom. You've been our captive since I lifted you onto my horse." Jack's expression hardened. "You'll pay three things in exchange for your life—because mark me, the other option is the blade. You'll pay with your freedom, because we'll never let you go. You'll pay with your future, because we will craft you into the weapon we want, and not the woman you would have been. And you'll pay with your name."

"My name?"

"Amity Green is a part of the world outside these walls. She has a family. They may miss her, someday. We can conceal you, keep any who might have known you once from recognizing you if they happen to catch a glimpse. What's more, we can protect your family. You can't be drawn back into the story if you're not one of them anymore. But you must give us your name, and you can never have it back again."

Amity sat up a little straighter.

"Take it," she said. "Save them from me. It's all I have left to give."

Jack turned to Hiram and nodded. Hiram stepped forward, pulling a small box out of his pocket. He opened it, holding it toward Amity. There was an odd pulling feeling, one that reached even me, despite my phantom presence at the scene. When it faded, he closed the box, and all three of them looked impassively at the nameless girl sitting in front of them. I couldn't think of her as Amity anymore; whenever I tried, my mind skittered away from the word, avoiding it as fiercely as it could.

"What shall we call you?" asked Jack.

"Sloane," said the girl, and Sloane she was, finally: my teammate, who would walk untouched through centuries to come to me. "Sloane Winters."

Jack smiled. "Let me show you to your cell."

The scene twisted around them, becoming a different room, a different time. Hiram was there, but older by at least forty years, a gnarled, weary-looking man sitting behind a heavy desk. He glared at Sloane, who stood unrepentantly before him.

"You must stop trying to escape," he said. "Your safety depends on these walls."

"You walk me like a hound when you're hunting a story, and then you lock me away again," she snapped. "How can you blame me for struggling toward freedom?"

"The last time you were free, someone poisoned the well," said Hiram.

Sloane looked away. "I would never do that," she said. "Children drink there."

"I know, Sloane. Jack was very clear in his notes on what you were and weren't capable of. But we answer to more than just ourselves, and the Council of Librarians doesn't know you as I do. I won't be here much longer. Whoever comes after me won't remember how young and confused you were. They'll only see a girl who doesn't age, whose story is unclear, who could kill us all one day. I'm your last friend here. Please. Be good for a little longer."

"Don't talk like that," said Sloane. "You'll be here a long, long time."

Hiram smiled. There was bitterness in his expression, but there was fondness too, and I found myself wishing the story hadn't skipped so far ahead. Who had they been to each other? Friends, uneasy allies, lovers? Sloane deserved some happiness. I hated that her memories seemed intent on skipping it.

"Mayhap," he said. "But you, I think, will be here a great deal longer."

The story shifted again, to Sloane standing stone-faced and silent by an open grave, while two men in broad-brimmed black hats held her arms, preventing her from running away. She didn't cry, but I knew her well enough to see the sorrow in her eyes, and in the hard line of her jaw. The men who held her took a step backward, forcing her to go with them.

She looked back once, long enough to see the tombstone. *Hiram Rogers—He Fought For All*, it read. His date of birth was given as 1678; his date of death was 1740. A long life, by the standards of the day. And Sloane still had so many years to get through before she'd reach the day we met.

I closed my eyes. When I opened them again, everything had changed.

Sloane was standing in front of a large oak desk, her back ramrod straight and her hands at her sides. She was wearing a tailored dress and a feathered hat. I couldn't place the year—fashion has never been my strong suit—but I guessed that we'd jumped forward a century, maybe more. The man behind the desk supported my guess. He was wearing a suit, and his mustache was groomed in a fat handlebar.

"Miss Winters, you have been the responsibility of this agency since its schism from the outdated Council of Librarians," he said. "I am offering you a choice. Be a part of our new Bureau, answering to the United States Government, or be one of the first occupants of our new prison. Childe is supposed to be a very pleasant facility for individuals like you. You could be happy there."

"No, thank you," said Sloane crisply. Her accent had faded; she sounded almost like the Sloane I knew. "I prefer my current living conditions."

"Then you must accept processing according to our new guidelines. The story structures as described in Aarne's *Verzeichnis der Märchentypen* will allow us to better detect and eliminate these foul acts of witchcraft."

"With all due respect, sir, none of those stories is mine," said Sloane. "I am not a Cinderella. You cannot hang my sister's story on my shoulders."

"Ah, but you see, we've found the story for you!" The man sounded smugly pleased with himself. "Number three-fifteen, 'The Treacherous Sister.'"

Sloane frowned. "Sir, I've read every book of fairy tale and folklore I could find, from all around the world. I have sponsored translations. The story you reference has nothing to do with me. It's about sisters who are untrue to their brothers, usually through the crime of falling in love inappropriately. I want to poison people. I want to feel murder on my fingertips. You can't give me a label that doesn't fit. It serves as no true warning."

"The stories will be what we say they are," said the man. "That's the point of this exercise. We'll remake them in the image that suits us best. Accept your designation and become an agent in our new bureau, or submit to imprisonment."

Sloane's frown became a glare. "Live a lie, or live no life at all? Is this to be the foundation of your brave new world? Lies are a form of story. Will you give them this much strength?"

"Choose," said the man.

Sloane glared for a moment more before she turned away. "I will serve you," she said.

The man smiled, triumphant. "Welcome to the Aarne Management Bureau, Agent Winters," he said.

The scene turned cold, freezing in place. Then it shattered, and I was falling through the dark, bits of broken glass spinning all around me.

"The fee is paid," whispered the voice of the mirror.

A piece of glass caught me in the heart.

Everything stopped.

# # #

I jerked awake in a hospital bed, machines screaming on every side of me. The hands I raised in front of my face were long-fingered and too small, with skin as white as snow. I had done it. But where *was* I?

Removing the catheter from my new body felt like an invasion—even more than stealing it, since I didn't intend to be here for long. I stumbled out of the bed, ripping IV tubes and monitoring wires away with every step. My legs were weak, like they hadn't been used in years.

It was a private room, with a private bathroom. I fumbled until I found the switch, and turned it on, revealing a face framed by straight, bed-rumpled hair as black as coal, with lips as red as blood. The eyes were green. Our story doesn't dictate our eyes. My new body looked to be in its early twenties. I let out a short breath of relief.

I was back in the world, and I didn't recognize her from the wood. She must have been one of the mirrors, or one of the girls who never wanted to go back, and so hid to prevent people like Adrianna from taking her over.

"I will give it back as soon as I can," I said, and walked away from the mirror.

I had to find my friends.

I had to warn them.

Feline Cobbling

Memetic incursion in progress: tale type 545B ("Puss in Boots")
Status: ACTIVE

The cat had promised him such wonderful things. Such magical, magnificent, wonderful things, and in the end, the cat had been able to deliver. That was the most incredible part. The cat had said "do this, and you will have a beautiful home," and he'd done it, and suddenly he'd been in his very own mansion. The cat had said "do this, and you will have a beautiful wife," and he'd done it, and suddenly the most beautiful woman he'd ever seen had been telling him she was his, that he could do whatever he wanted to her. It was a miracle from top to bottom, from beginning to end, and he never wanted it to stop.

But he couldn't find the cat.

His wife had been missing since morning. He'd found her robe in the hall, and the ropes he'd used to tie her to the bed—not to hurt her, no, he'd never hurt her, and besides, the cat assured him she was here willingly, the ropes were for her own protection, because she was a restless sleeper, that was all—the ropes had been lying in the foyer. He'd made it as far as the front yard before the sunlight had driven him back inside. That was when he'd thought to ask the cat. The cat could tell him where his wife was; the cat could tell him how to find her and bring her home, hopefully without leaving the house.

He'd searched the whole place, from top to bottom, and he couldn't find the cat. His wife must have taken it with her when she went out, no doubt to buy some trinket that had caught her eye. He reached for his hat and his sword. He was the Marquis de Carabas, after all. The cat had told him so. Now all he had to do was find it, and everything would be all right again.

# # #

If I were to make a list of "shit that is so clearly a terrible idea that I shouldn't even have to explain to people why I'm not going to do it," walking into the hedge maze behind a mansion full of dead bodies would have been right up there. Not top five, maybe, but high enough that I wouldn't have expected people to make me do it.

Ciara stopped at the mouth of the maze, giving me an expectant look. "Well?"

"Well, what?" I shook my head. "I don't want to go in there. I can go help Andy and Demi question the woman who escaped, how about that? That's a much nicer, less murder-y way for me to spend the afternoon."

"Henry and Jeff are already inside," said Ciara, like that was going to make some sort of difference.

I looked at her flatly. "Something is seriously wrong with Henry. You know it, I know it, Andrew and Demi know it—everyone knows it *except* for Jeffrey, and the only reason he's so far behind the rest of the pack is because he's still all fucked up about the whole 'true love's kiss didn't work this time' bullshit. He's going to snap out of his mopey fugue soon and realize that he's following a wrong thing into dark, creepy places."

Ciara opened her mouth. Then she caught herself and stepped closer to me, lowering her voice as she said, "Then it's all the more important that you come into the hedge maze with me."

"Come again?" I raised an eyebrow. "I realize you think of me as a villain, but I promise, I'm not interested in following wrong things into dark, creepy places. That's part of how I've managed to stay alive as long as I have."

"I've seen your records, Sloane. You've followed plenty of wrong things into plenty of bad situations."

I glanced away, uncomfortable. She was right, of course—my career was practically one long succession of wrong things, creepy places, and dark alleys where a sensible person would never go—but I'd always done what I'd done because someone I had trusted had asked me to. Henry, and Dan before her, and Marian before him, going all the way back to Hiram and Jack. I was fully capable of risking my own neck for someone who I actually gave a damn about.

Henry hadn't asked me to come with her this time. She had just started walking, trusting I would follow, and something about her was so wrong that it set my teeth on edge. Standing too close to her was like biting into frozen tin foil. The smell of apples was getting stronger every day. Even Jeff had started noticing it. He was sneezing and blowing his nose more, a look of perpetual confusion in his eyes. He was going to realize how wrong she was soon.

"If you really thought there was something wrong with Henry, you could have let her fall back in the factory. You didn't. You must have seen something in her that didn't seem off-kilter. Jeff and Demi, they're both active in their stories, and they've both accepted her."

"But you haven't, have you, Ciara?" I turned back to her, making no effort to conceal my frustration. If anyone was going to understand how I felt, it was going to be her. "You know something's wrong. You've been hanging back."

"She's your leader. I was only temporary."

"And yet they haven't reassigned you. It's almost like someone sent a report to the higher ups telling them that Henry couldn't be trusted with her own team."

This time, it was Ciara who looked away. She didn't say anything.

I snorted. "Oh, like you're fooling me. You *know* she came back wrong, and you *know* following her into that maze would be pure stupidity on my part. So give me one good reason why I should do what you're suggesting."

"Jeff's in there." Ciara turned back to me. "He's your friend, right? I mean, I've heard you describe him in friendly terms, and you only threaten dismemberment when you're talking to him. That seems to be a sign of affection, coming from you. Jeff's in there, and he thinks there's nothing wrong with Henry. He won't see it coming. If what you're afraid of happens, he'll just stand there and take it, because he loves her."

I glared at her for a moment before I started striding toward the entrance to the maze. "I hate you," I said.

"I know," said Ciara, following me.

"I'm going to play jump rope with your intestines."

"Won't that be fun for both of us."

"Don't make fun of me."

"I wouldn't dream of it."

On that last, smug rejoinder, we both stepped out of the sunlight and into the shadows of the hedge maze.

# # #

It had started as a fairly normal call. A half-naked woman had been found stumbling down a residential street in a wealthy neighborhood, wearing nothing but the torn remains of what had once been a fairly nice peignoir, screaming for help and telling anyone who came in range that a madman had killed her parents and tied her up in the guest bedroom. It would have been a matter for the police, under normal circumstances, except for the part where she called him a madman because he kept taking orders from an invisible talking cat. Even that might have been thin enough to keep the case out of our jurisdiction, had she not given his name.

According to the woman, she had been kept captive by the Marquis de Carabas, and she was terrified he was going to come and take her back again.

Dispatch had picked up the call when the police had reported the man's name, and the Bureau had taken the whole thing over before anyone knew what had happened. It was always awkward when we had to sweep in and claim custody of a case like this, and Henry, who was normally our main source of diplomacy and tact when it came to liaising with the mundane cops, was no help. The officer in charge was an old acquaintance of hers, Marcus Troy, and she'd swept past him like he was nothing, leaving Ciara to make awkward apologies. I'd considered getting involved, and decided it was a bad idea. Officer Troy didn't like me. I couldn't imagine *why*, but well, there it was.

Henry had sent the police packing, and we'd secured the site. She hadn't been herself lately, but at least she still had a modicum of common sense: she'd assigned Andrew and Demi to interview the woman, who was too upset to give a linear accounting of what had been done to her, before starting the search for the missing "marquis." Which had really meant telling me to go find him, since tracking down the missing stories was my job.

I had gone. I had tracked. I had followed his trail and the vague but unpleasant smell of wet cat all the way to the mouth of the hedge maze, where I had—quite sensibly, I felt—balked at the idea of going any further. Who the hell kept a hedge maze on their property, anyway? It wasn't just extravagance, it was virtually an invitation to the evil spirits of the world. "Come possess my property and rend me limb from limb during my next garden party, it'll be a good time for all concerned." Rich people were fucking weird. And there were crows all over the lawn. A full murder never meant anything good.

Henry hadn't seemed to care about how weird this all was. She had just gone in, Jeffrey sticking close to her heels, leaving Ciara to convince me to follow.

Now that I'd been convinced—now that the walls of the hedge maze were actually rising around me, green and silent and too tall to see over—I was even more certain that I'd made the right decision in the first place. We shouldn't be in here.

"This is a bad idea," I said. "Let's go somewhere else. Somewhere that isn't actively preparing to swallow us both alive."

"Not an option," said Ciara. "We need to find the others."

"See, this is what gets you killed," I said. "It's not splitting the party. It's trying to reunite the cursed thing."

Ciara didn't say anything. She just kept walking, and so I followed, trusting her to have some vague idea of where we were supposed to be going.

My trust was misplaced. Our corridor ended at a T-junction, with paths stretching off to the left and right, and no way to continue straight ahead. Ciara stopped briefly before she turned to me and said, "We're going to have to split up."

"No."

"It's necessary."

"No."

"It's the fastest way to find our people. If we head straight down our respective paths, we can't get lost, and—"

"Are you hard of hearing, or is this a Bluebeard's Wife thing I didn't know about? I said no. I'm not going to leave you alone in here just so we can find some assholes I don't like all that much five minutes faster." I shook my head. "Not going to happen."

"I thought you said splitting the party wasn't the problem," said Ciara.

I shot her a baleful look. "There's a limit."

"Yes. Let's limit how long we're in here without the rest of our people. I'll come back for you if I find them first." Ciara turned and started briskly down the left fork. I stared after her, scarcely believing what I was seeing.

"This has to be a side effect of this asshole's story," I said. "Because if it's not, we're dividing and subdividing ourselves into a slaughter. You can come back now."

Ciara didn't come back. I considered going after her, and maybe shaking her until she recovered a small fraction of the common sense she must have possessed. If she'd been this foolish the whole time she'd been associated with the Bureau, she would have been dead by now. In the end, I decided the candle wasn't worth the chase and turned to walk deeper into the maze.

There are those who would use me as a form of narrative bloodhound, and they're not entirely wrong in that: I'm a dowsing rod for active stories, shaking them out of the fabric of the world one sentence at a time, until they're pinned to the page before me. The trouble is, any dog can be confounded by a strong enough smell, and any dowsing rod can turn its holder in circles when there's too much water to be found. The entire maze reeked of damp cat and freezing winter snow, thanks to the combined presence of Henry and our wayward marquis. I was running as blind as anyone who had never been touched by the narrative.

I hated it. My life has been a long series of surrenders disguised as open doors. I ran from the story that was trying to claim my stepsister, surrendering my place in the narrative in order to save us both. That should have worked—*did* work, in its way, since my dear Gabrielle had been allowed to live and die as a member of her own family, and not a prize for some rich man to win. Belle had recovered from the narrative's hands upon her heart. She'd taken a pig farmer to husband, and had borne eleven children before she died peacefully in her own bed at the ripe age of sixty-three. Seven of those children had lived, and I kept tabs on her descendants. It was hard, sometimes, keeping myself from seeking them out, pretending I was a distant cousin who'd tracked them down through some genealogical site. It wouldn't even have been such a stretch, but it would have been a risk. The trouble with open doors is that they can be walked through in either direction. I was a bomb waiting to go off, and I needed to stay away.

The narrative had done its best to destroy everything I'd ever cared about, and the one consolation I'd been allowed to keep was that I could root it out in others, crush it under my heel and laugh as it squirmed, looking for an outlet I wasn't going to offer. Those few moments, like this one, where I got to feel like a normal person? They weren't a relief. They were just one more surrender pretending to be an open door. *See, you could still be normal,* whispered the narrative, in the small place at the back of my mind where it was always lurking, looking for a way to turn me into the weapon it had wanted me to be for so very, very long.

I narrowed my eyes and kept walking, scanning the path around me for signs that either Henry or the marquis had come this way. It was difficult; the walls were high enough to block most of the light, which meant I couldn't see footprints. They were also thick enough to keep the air from circulating, which meant the two almost diametrically opposed stories were at war all around me, curdling each other and twisting into new, unpleasant shapes.

"Who the hell has a hedge maze on their property, anyway?" I muttered. "Have these people never seen *Labyrinth*? Or read *The Shining*?"

"Those are both much more recent popular culture references than I expected from you," said Henry, stepping out of a cul-de-sac and falling in beside me, matching her stride to mine. I flinched instinctively away. She either ignored it or didn't feel the need to mention it—it was hard to say—as she continued, "I would have thought you'd go for the classics. Something about a minotaur lurking in here, all horns and bloodlust."

"There hasn't been a minotaur manifest in North America for almost a hundred years," I said, and hated myself for going along with her. I slanted a sidelong look in her direction. "Where's Jeffrey?"

"We split up to cover ground faster when we realized you and Ciara weren't joining us as quickly as you were supposed to. Did something go wrong?" Henry looked concerned. There was something off about the expression, like she'd practiced it too many times in the mirror and worn all the believability away. It didn't help my nerves any. It didn't help my burning desire to punch her in the mouth, either.

There are times when reacting to everything with violence is not just inconvenient, it's annoying, especially since I rarely actually allow myself to *hit* anybody. My life is a web of unfulfilled desires and unscratched itches. "Yes, something went wrong," I said. "You decided we should chase a dude who's already killed two people and kidnapped a third into a dark creepy hedge maze that has absolutely no business existing. If you don't consider that 'wrong,' there's something seriously wrong with *you*."

There *was* something wrong with her. I was surer of it now than ever. The air couldn't circulate, and so the cold radiating from her body was trapped, swirling around us until it felt like snow should start falling at any moment. I resisted the urge to move away. I would have been more comfortable, but it would have given her another opportunity to ask me why I was so upset, and I didn't want that. Everything about this situation seemed designed to set my teeth on edge.

To my surprise, Henry smiled. It was easy to forget how disturbing she looked, seeing her day to day as I did, but here and now, in the shadows of the maze, she looked like some sort of twisted murder clown grinning at me before she devoured my soul.

"Wow, I am not going to sleep this week," I muttered.

"You're right: this situation is disturbing," she said. "I'm glad you feel that way about it. I was afraid you wouldn't notice. Deputy Director Brewer has come to me with a few concerns about your behavior since I woke up."

"Is that so." It wasn't a question. It didn't need to be. I knew Dan Brewer better than she'd ever bothered to try, and I knew he wasn't having concerns about my behavior: I was well within the normal limits that the Bureau would put up with. As long as I wasn't putting arsenic in the communal coffee pot or smashing the mirrors where his story-struck girlfriend pined for the real world, he wasn't going to go to Henry with concerns about me.

She was lying. The only question left was why.

"He said the last time you'd rejected a team leader, the team you were on fell apart. We're effective as a unit, Sloane. We do good work. That doesn't mean the Bureau won't reassign us all if they think that we could do better work somewhere else."

"Maybe it's time for that," I said. "I mean, fuck. Demi's active now. *You're* active now. Your whole thing with Jeffrey is screwing up his ability to be an effective researcher. Andrew wants to be a father, and that probably means he isn't going to want to be in the field forever. Everything runs its course. Let it go."

"Maybe you're right," said Henry. "Maybe there's a time for everything. But Sloane, if that's true, don't you think it's time for you to think about letting go too?"

I gave her a sidelong look. "What do you mean?"

"You've been hating everyone, and everything, for a lot longer than you like to let on," said Henry. "Your story isn't done because it never really started. You're part of something bigger, and not something independent. Like being a part of this team. As long as you're doing this sort of work, your solo career can't stop."

"I don't follow."

The shadows in the maze were deep, but Henry's skin was pale enough that I could read her cool, calculating expression as she looked at me and said, "Maybe you're so stuck because you're still playing a supporting role in someone else's story, instead of starting up a story of your own."

I stumbled.

Recovering my balance took me a few seconds, and gave me the time I needed to get my breath back. Finally, I said, "You're high. You found whatever that Marquis de Carabas asshole was smoking when he started seeing imaginary cats, and you decided to try it for yourself."

"I'm serious, Sloane. You're stuck because you're a minor player in a Cinderella story that never really got started. You don't qualify to be a Cinderella in your own right—even if your family was alive, you lost your father and not your mother, which is the wrong direction for most versions of the story. There was probably a time when you could have washed the bitterness off and gone to a different ball, but that ship has sailed by now, don't you think? You need to find another story. Unless you really feel like being sixteen and angry about it forever. How did you wind up so *tall*? You shouldn't have had time to get so tall."

"There was a beanstalk incident." It had happened in the early 1800s, which made it worse. These days, I was a woman of above average height, but I wasn't out of the ordinary for, say, a supermodel. Back then, there had been a few carnivals willing to give me a job, had I ever decided to leave the Bureau. "You don't normally ask me these sorts of questions, Henry. Are you sure you're feeling all right?"

"You don't normally behave so poorly that my job is at risk," said Henry. "The kid gloves are off."

"Oh, are they? I hadn't noticed." I stopped walking, planting my feet firmly in the loamy ground. Henry continued for a few more steps before she turned to look at me, one eyebrow raised in silent question.

I said nothing. I wanted to see what she would do.

Seconds ticked by. Finally, looking frustrated, Henry demanded, "Oh, what *now*? Did I hurt your precious feelings?"

"Nope," I said. "I mean, one, that assumes I have feelings to hurt, and two, it assumes I'd ever give you the chance. You did tip your hand a little, though. You're not Henry. She might want to know those things, but she'd never just *ask* them like that. She'd give a fuck about how I might react. Because see, she cares about my feelings."

"Which don't exist," she said.

"Not for you," I replied. "Who are you? How do you have Henry's face? Are you a broken mirror, or some sort of doppelganger? Are you a Death on the Road? Can you die?" *Can I kill you?* Surely it wouldn't tip me over any edges to take care of someone who'd hurt my friend.

Heroes killed all the time, they just did it for the right reasons. I couldn't think of a better reason than "impersonated Henry, hurt Jeffrey, led us all into danger at least once."

I was going to enjoy feeling her nose break under my knuckles.

The woman who wasn't Henry smiled. Her posture shifted, becoming more relaxed, less formal—and more predatory. She didn't stand like a Bureau agent. She didn't stand like a fairy-tale princess, either. She stood like me.

She stood like a villain.

"Tell me, have you known the *whole* time, or did I actually tip you off just now? I'm trying to figure out how stupid you are." Her voice dropped as she spoke, acquiring a mild buzz that set my teeth on edge. "I've never thought your story gave you much reason for genius. It would be wasted on someone who only needs to know how much arsenic to pour into the evening tea."

"So you're really not Henry, then." I relaxed a little. Suddenly, all the dark and dangerous thoughts I'd been having about a woman who was supposed to be my friend seemed just a little less dark, a little less dangerous, and a lot more justified. I wasn't turning on the hand that fed me. I was behaving like a good soldier and watching for danger, no matter what form it took. "Who the fuck are you, lady, and what did you do with our boss? She's obnoxious and wound too tight, but we're used to her. I'd like her back, if you don't mind."

"Not happening," said not-Henry. She ran her hands down the front of her body in a way that was so disturbingly sexual that I wanted to avert my eyes. I knew Henry was no virgin. Jeffrey's silly grin after he'd moved in with her would have confirmed that, even if I hadn't dated her brother for the better part of a year. Twins, as it turned out, told each other everything. Gerry had been a deep wellspring of shit I didn't want to know about the woman I called boss.

None of that justified this stranger touching Henry's body that way—and it *was* Henry's body. I was sure of that. Henry had eaten the apple in my sight. Jeffrey had been by her side near-constantly from then until the moment when she'd woken up. Whoever this parasite was, she was wearing Henry's skin like a suit. It made me want to hurt her. It made it impossible for me to raise a hand.

"It's a relief, actually; I was hoping someone would figure it out, and more, I was hoping it would be you." The woman who wasn't Henry smiled. "You don't belong here any more than I do. The Bureau's had you captive for far too long, Sloane—or would you rather I called you 'Amity'? It's such a pretty name. I don't really understand why you walked away from it the way you did."

"I'm going to scratch your eyes out of your head and feed them to the first crow I see," I snarled.

"No you won't." She ran her hand down Henry's chest again. Technically, the hand was Henry's too, but it didn't seem that way, not with this woman moving it. "You miss her. You wouldn't be calling me out if you didn't. That means you won't do anything that might damage your precious Henrietta's perfect storybook of a body. You want her back too badly, at least right now."

"What, are you planning to force me into a situation where it's Henry's body or a whole bus full of orphans? Because lady, I don't think you'll enjoy the choice I make."

"No. Because I'm going to make you see that really, what you want is me. I'm so much better for you than she could ever have been. Oh, maybe the rest of your straitlaced little team will think this is some sort of a corruption, but you, Sloane, you're open-minded and ready to see the possibilities inherent in something new. Something *better* than you've been given up until this point." She lowered her hand, leaned a little closer, and said sweetly, "Aren't you tired of being the villain of the piece? Don't you want something more?"

Yes. Yes, I did. That was all I'd ever wanted: to be something more than a prop in someone else's story, condemned to fill my mouth with poison and my hands with knives. That was why I couldn't accept it—or anything—from her. I knew without asking that any apple she offered me would be a death sentence, and any mirror she showed me would already be burnt black from the inside. This was not the way to change my story.

"I'm listening," I said.

"The Bureau has made a lot of mistakes since its inception. You know that. You were there." Her smile spread. If I hadn't known better, I would have marked her for a Cheshire Cat. I would have been wrong. Cats could be cruel, but even they didn't toy with their prey this much. "It's sort of a marvel they were able to go as far off the rails as they have without you showing them the error of their ways. I kept expecting to find some massacre in your files, some bloodbath of a bureaucratic adjust-ment, and it was never there. It was just yes ma'am and no sir all the way down. Did they promise you a better story if you played along? They were lying if they did. Following the rules never bought anyone a fairy tale."

"They were my friends," I said. How many of my files had this woman read before she did whatever she'd done that had allowed her to seize control of my friend's body? She'd already called me "Amity." That meant she had access to Jack's files, and those were usually buried so deep that sometimes even I forgot that they were there.

Maybe if she'd called me by that name two hundred years ago, it would have hurt as much as she had clearly intended it to. Back then, I'd still held out hope for Amity, some small prayer that one day, I'd find a way to save the girl I'd been. But those days were far in the past, and Amity Green was buried with her sisters, in spirit if not in flesh. I was Sloane Winters. Changing my story wouldn't change my past, no matter how much I might wish it.

"Your friends used you and set you aside like a doll they no longer had time to play with," said the woman. "They never loved you. They never wanted to love you. It would have been too much of a risk, and they were long since done with risk-taking by the time they got to this palace of lost potential and doomed idealism. You were a tool to them, and they were the world to you. Don't you think it's time for that to be turned around?"

"What's your name?" It was a struggle to keep my voice level, but not as great a struggle as it was to keep my hands open and my arms by my sides. I couldn't kill her while she wore Henry's face. The thought of making her sorry she'd ever stolen it was becoming more appealing by the second. There are a *lot* of ways to make a person suffer without breaking the skin.

"We have two names between us: Sloane and Amity," said the woman. "We have a third, if you insist on cleaving to 'Henrietta' as a reasonable thing for this body to be called. It's a plodding, disgraceful name. As far from a proper address for a princess as you can get, and believe me, I've heard many names used for the princesses of this world. It's like they were trying to crush her spirit before she even got started, don't you think? Poor thing never stood a chance."

"Look, lady, fuck your math, okay?" I finally allowed my hand to move, dipping it into my pocket and pulling out my phone. "I'm calling Ciara. She's going to be thrilled to learn that I was right about you all along."

"I don't think so," said the woman. She didn't move, but the smell of snow and apples grew stronger.

That wasn't all that was growing stronger. I remained very still, only cocking an eyebrow upward as I asked, "No? Why wouldn't I call her?"

"Because we've been watching you, and I'm the lucky one who gets to make you the offer. Join us. We can change your story. We can make you anything you want to be. A hero, a villain in your own right, even a princess worthy of the crown—it can all be yours if you agree." She held her hand out toward me, a small smile on her bloody lips. She clearly thought she had already won, and that it was all over save for convincing me to go along with her.

She'd forgotten one essential fact of our situation. Sure, she'd managed to ditch Jeffrey, and sure, Ciara had gone in the opposite direction to look for her, but those weren't the only other people in this maze. Red-faced and sweating, the erstwhile Marquis de Carabas leapt from the shadows behind her, shouted, "*Villain*!" and swung his weapon—a groundskeeper's machete—at her head.

The woman who wasn't Henry yelped and hit the ground, rolling away from her attacker as quickly as she could. He made a wordless noise of frustration and raised the machete to swing again, only to stop when he saw me.

I had one clear path out of this. It all depended on how convincing I could be as a selfish, amoral, manipulative creature—which was to say, a cat. "Took you long enough," I said, injecting as much of a sneer as I dared into my voice. "I had time to kill six rats, three birds, and a frog before you found me." I raised one hand, studying my nails as I had so often seen the barnyard cat back in Salem studying its claws.

The Marquis's eyes widened. "Puss?" he said, in a half hopeful, half bewildered tone.

"Are you slow now, or just a fool?" I dropped my hand and glared. "You let the girl get away. She's your wife. You're responsible for her. Why are you running around this maze instead of finding her and bringing her back?"

"You didn't tell me you could be a woman," he said, like that was more important than anything else I could have to say. He looked me up and down and added, "You're beautiful."

"Yeah, well, my last owner had me spayed," I said. The woman who wasn't Henry was picking herself up from the ground. I pointed to her. "The ogre's back. You couldn't do that part of your job either."

Technically, it was supposed to be the cat's job to get rid of the ogre: after the Marquis tricked it into transforming into a mouse, Puss in Boots would leap upon it and gobble it down, resolving the situation in a quick, fatal fashion. Thankfully for me, this particular Marquis was seeing things rather than actually traveling with a talking cat, and so when I said "ogre," he reacted without hesitation. Not-Henry yelped and rolled away when he brought the machete down again, narrowly missing her head.

"Call him off!" she shouted.

I crossed my arms. "It's an interesting philosophical question, really. *I* can't hurt you because you're wearing Henry's face. *He*, on the other hand, has no such restrictions, and probably thinks you look like an alien invader. Don't you think it's time to tell me who the fuck you are, in case that gets me to stop the story?"

The machete came down. Not-Henry rolled away once more. It was a narrower miss this time. She wasn't going to be able to keep this up for much longer.

I wanted to feel bad. This was Henry's body I was endangering. But either Henry didn't live here anymore or the woman who had taken it over would leave the same way she had come. As soon as I had the slightest indication that Henry was back, I'd save her.

The gunshot was a surprise.

It echoed through the hedge maze. The Marquis staggered backward, blood spreading through the fabric of his shirt. The machete fell from his hands, and he shot me a pleading look before he fell, crumpling motionless to the grassy ground.

"See, they've broken you in ways that I'm just—well, I'm not entirely sure that we can fix." The woman who wasn't Henry picked herself up, holding the gun on me with one hand while she brushed herself off with the other. Some of the blood from our ill-fated Marquis had spattered on her front. She didn't seem to care. It smeared when she touched it. She didn't seem to care about that either. "You think like a hero. You think like the story will limit itself to the weapons it used traditionally. You think the good guys will always have the upper hand. I'm sorry, sweetie, but it doesn't work like that in the real world—and if there's one thing the narrative is good at, it's adapting to the real world. Little girls don't carry baskets into the deep, dark woods anymore. But there will always be alleys. There will always be places for the story to spread. And it *learns*. It *revises*."

"You definitely think like a villain," I said, putting my hands up. I didn't have the power to ward off bullets, but I could stand still with the best of them. "Stop monologuing at me and make your pitch. I'm bored, and I don't know how much more of this crap I can take."

"You've already changed your story once, Sloane, when you shed your name and your narrative and became a hunting dog for the people who want to keep us down in the mud with the rest of them," said the woman. "You know it can be done. If you're not doing it, it's only because you're afraid of what the cost might be. I'm here to tell you that the cost is everything you are, but the profit, oh, the *profit*. The profit is the world."

"You can't be Birdie, because you don't talk like her," I said. "You're not Elise, because there aren't any mice, and she's a little erratic sometimes. Pretty sure if you were Elise, you would have already gone for my eyes. So who the fuck are you?"

"I'm sorry?"

"I don't make deals with people who steal the bodies of my friends and then don't tell me their names. Call me old fashioned, but hey." I shrugged. "You've read my file. You know how old I am. I've earned a little resistance to change. What's your name?"

She rolled her eyes toward the sky, like it was going to explain my mulishness—although she didn't lower her gun or shift her position enough to lose sight of me for even a moment. "You are genuinely insufferable, did you know that? How did Henry put up with you for so long? And don't say 'Prozac,' we both know my niece was too strait-laced for that. No drugs or drinking for her. That would have seemed too much like actually having fun. You keep looking at me like I stole this body, but I assure you, the body sees it differently. I'm finally going to take the reins off and see what this baby can *do*."

"Pretty sure that's rape," I said.

"Not when the body's original owner isn't coming back. Manifest destiny was the term they used when you were young, wasn't it? God gave this country to you. Well, Grimm gave my niece to me. She left, and now everything I see belongs to me." The woman's lips tipped upward. "Stupid cow never should have eaten the apple."

Some stories were more primed toward going wrong than others. A surprising number of Rapunzels ended with strangulations. A slightly less surprising number of Frog Princes ended with blunt force trauma. Snow Whites, however, rarely heard the siren song of the dark side. They were too busy freezing from the inside out to worry about burning things alive. A lot of modern reimaginings have cast them as vampires, creatures that don't feel the cold, but suck the life out of everything around them. That's truer than those authors probably realize. It still doesn't make the Snow Whites *evil*.

When a Snow goes bad, it makes a mark. When a Snow goes bad, it draws attention. And when a Snow has gone bad within the last few hundred years, it's usually been something I would notice.

"Adrianna," I said. "Seriously? Why is it always you? I'd rather gargle glass than deal with you again."

She blinked slowly, looking faintly unsettled for the first time. "You weren't one of the ones who put me away."

"I didn't need to be. You keep talking about the power of stories. Well, you became one as soon as you started killing people who'd never even been story-struck." It was such an old phrase, but it was so much more accurate than any of the thin, puerile ones we used today. There was no blood in them. When the narrative grabbed you, it was like an assault.

We should never have moved away from the words that actually meant what we were trying to say. I glanced toward the Marquis. He was gone now, but his story endured; the air still smelled of wet cat, and of the promises of power. I had been his Puss in Boots, when he died. He'd believed in me. Adrianna said I could change my story.

Maybe I could use that.

"That may be so, but you're not in a position to criticize." Adrianna adjusted her grip on the gun. She was standing less like Henry by the second. It must have been a relief for her, to finally let her real self out to play the way she'd always wanted to. "They've made a story out of you, you know. You're whispered through the halls of Childe Prison.

The villain who somehow got away and managed to become one of the good guys. You're a legend and a traitor."

"Sometimes those words mean the same thing." Cats were quick, cats were clever, cats could disappear whenever they wanted to, sometimes while they were lounging in plain sight. I had been a Cheshire Cat for a while, when I needed to put on stripes in order to save my team. I knew how to be a cat, if I could find my way through the tangled strands of the story surrounding me to the place where the shit hit the scratching post.

"I'm offering you another way. Come on, Sloane. Join us. You know we're your destiny. We always have been."

"Elise is a Cinderella now, isn't she?" Tooth and claw and stripy fur, that's what little cats are made of. I reached for the smell of wet fur, trying to wrap it around myself without moving a muscle. It was harder than I expected it to be. It would be worth it if it worked. "You can't recruit me. She'd be dead long before her body hit the ground, and you need her. I can't control glass."

"We could leave you with the Bureau as a sleeper agent. Blow my cover, chase me away before I can hurt anyone. Console that little puppy dog who keeps pawing at me about losing his one true love." Adrianna grimaced. "I can't believe my niece ever touched him. What did she see in him?"

"A man who loved her even though she looked like a creepy clown out of a children's book? As a guess." Henry and Jeff were good together. I might not care about their relationship that much, but even I could see that they bolstered each other instead of tearing each other down. More relationships should work that way.

Maybe if more of mine had, I wouldn't have been rejoining the ranks of the single every time I turned around.

"He's weak. She's weak. Neither of them deserves their stories. So I took hers away from her. Really, she should be thanking me right now. She never wanted to be Snow White."

"You stole her body. How—how did you even *do* that? There's nothing about body snatching in the Snow White story."

Adrianna smirked. The expression was entirely hers. Seeing it on Henry's face made me want to mop the floor with her. Since that wasn't an option right now, I just dug deeper into the story around me, looking for the seams.

He called me Puss before he died, I thought. *He recognized me as belonging to you. That means I am you, and you need to let me in. Give me what I'm asking for. Let me have this.*

"Every story has its mysteries. You've never touched them, because you've never settled. Come with us. Let us show you how to settle."

"Thanks, but I'll pass," I said, and dove for the ground, praying as I fell that I had timed this right: that the story was welcoming me the way my heart and gut told me that it was.

There wasn't enough narrative energy here for a physical transformation, and I didn't want to be a cat anyway. I just wanted to be fleet and clever and hard to see; all the things the stories gave to felines when it wanted them to sneak around the edges, leaving claw marks in the margins and hair on all the tapestries. Adrianna jumped back, swinging her gun along to track me, and then stopped, a puzzled look flashing across her face. It was followed quickly by confusion, which faded even more quickly into fury.

"Where did you go?" she demanded. "Where did you *go*? You don't get to run away from me! This isn't how the story goes!" She shot the hedge at roughly head-height, face distorted into a rictus of fury.

I held perfectly still by the base of the hedge, barely daring even to breathe. There was a thin runnel of apple-scented air down there, warmer than the air that surrounded her. Sweeter too, like I was smelling a different version of the same story. *Something I am doing is echoing Henry,* I thought, almost dazedly, and the thought was so right that I didn't try to argue with it. I just let it roll.

There had been a maze, then, and Adrianna and Henry had been inside it. Adrianna had threatened her, and Henry had . . . had what? Had tried to hide? I was effectively invisible because I had stolen part of someone else's story. She was white in the truest sense of the word; she stood out against anything but a blizzard. So how the hell had *she* managed to disappear?

"I don't believe this," Adrianna snarled. "I *will* find you, Sloane, and you'll be sorry you passed on this opportunity. You should have joined me when you had the chance."

She turned and started walking deeper into the maze. I remained pressed against the ground, waiting. You don't spend centuries stalking fairy-tale villains through their own stories without learning a thing or two about the way they tend to think—and sure enough, after she had gone about ten feet she whirled around, raking her eyes across the corridor behind her. I didn't move. After a moment, she scowled and turned again.

This time, she didn't double back. I picked myself carefully up, pausing only to retrieve the machete from the felled Marquis. An unexpected pang of sympathy for the man struck me as I was prying the hilt out of his hand. Maybe it was the fact that I'd willingly enrolled myself in his fading narrative, or maybe it was just that he hadn't asked for any of this. He could have been anyone before the story grabbed him and turned him into a killer. He could have been me.

"Sorry, sire," I murmured. The word choice was more Puss in Boots than my own, but I didn't try to take it back. The Marquis, whatever his real name might have been, was dead. That couldn't be changed. If he could take any peace in believing that his story endured after he was gone, then I was happy to give it to him. He deserved that much, even if he didn't deserve anything more.

Holding the machete loosely against my hip, I turned and prowled, balanced on my tiptoes, deeper into the maze.

# # #

Adrianna moved surprisingly fast for someone who was wearing a body that didn't belong to her. Had she *ever* suffered a period of disorientation? I thought she might have, but that could easily have been hindsight, which was always twenty-twenty, trying to make me second-guess myself. I had known from the beginning that *something* was wrong. I was just trying to make it bigger than it had really been.

Sometimes the subtle signs are the truest. The switch of a story from apples to snow, for example. Or the brush of a thorn against my skin as I pressed myself hard against the hedge wall, sticking to the shadows. Adrianna was nowhere to be seen, but that didn't mean she wasn't still out there, or make her any less dangerous.

Would she kill me? That was the real question. She had seemed determined to recruit me to her cause, but that could have been a matter of convenience. When you had access to a potential ally who had in some cases literally written the book on Bureau response, why wouldn't you try to lure them over to your side? I had been an asset until I had shown her, conclusively, that I was no such thing. Now I was an enemy, and if she let me find my way out of this maze, I could blow her cover with everyone else.

Where *was* everyone else? A chill ran down my spine as I considered the all-too-plausible fact that she could have tried the same recruitment pitch with Jeffrey, only to be shot down even harder. I, at least, had been prepared to play along until I knew what I needed. Jeffrey loved Henry. Jeffrey had been by this woman's side since she woke up in his lover's stolen body—and if he had never realized that anything was wrong, he was going to hate himself. That was one more crime to lay at Adrianna's feet. True love's kiss hadn't worked on Henry's body because Henry hadn't been there. Now it might not work because Adrianna had slipped in and slit love's throat.

I'd just have to kill her extra slow.

Footsteps echoed softly through the maze. Adrianna was coming my way. I crouched further, tightening my grip on my borrowed machete. The smell of wet cat still clung to the air around me, although it was fading; the Marquis de Carabas was dead, poor story-struck soul that he had been, and while I was enough for the story to batten on to for a little while, I couldn't sustain it. I wasn't equipped to step into his role.

But what if I *was*? The thought was startling. Adrianna had been talking about changing my story, and I knew Elise had managed it—that was what had made her so damn dangerous. What if the answer was doing exactly what I was doing now, but forcing myself into the lead role, instead of taking up the sidekick's part? Kill a princess to become a princess, in other words.

It was a terrible thing to contemplate. It might well be the only thing that would let me out of the maze of endless years in which I had been so long marooned.

Thorns prickled against my back as I plastered myself more firmly against the hedge wall, waiting for Adrianna to come around the corner. Maybe I couldn't kill her while she was in Henry's body, but that didn't mean I couldn't hurt her a little. All I needed was to get the drop on her. She might be evil, while the jury was still out on me. She might be cunning.

I was a pissed-off wicked stepsister with a machete, and I would stack that up against anything else the story had to sling at me.

Adrianna stepped into view. I lunged for her, machete raised, moving with feline speed. She smirked and stepped to the side, as casual as anything. I tried to adjust and discovered that I couldn't; my legs were slow and felt too thick, like they had been standing in cold water for hours. Momentum carried me right past her and sent me crashing to the ground.

"We have so many things to talk about, you and I," she said, crouching to take the machete from my hands. I struggled to hold it, but she plucked it away from me as easily as pulling an apple from a tree. "That little stunt of yours—I don't know how you did it, and I want to. If you can share stories, instead of changing them, that will change everything. *Everything*. I'm sorry, dear, but you don't have a choice anymore about whether you come with me."

I tried to speak. I couldn't. I glared daggers at her instead, hoping that her ego would force her to keep talking. Her ego, and the story, which so often demanded that the villains explain their plans for the hidden heroes to hear.

But there were no heroes hiding here. Any member of my team would have stepped in to save me by now, even Ciara. We were alone, me and her, in the maze, and I couldn't move.

"Don't worry, Amity. The poison Elise put on those thorns will wear off soon, and you'll be fine." She tossed the machete aside and stooped, trying to scoop me off the ground. She stopped trying a moment later and straightened, grimacing. "Did my niece never lift anything heavier than her badge? This weak, useless body is going to need some serious improvement. No matter. Wait here."

She walked away. I struggled to move.

I was still struggling to move when she returned, pulling a wagon shaped from a giant pumpkin and accompanied by four of Elise's mouse-men. Together, they loaded me into the wagon and pulled me away. I couldn't fight them. I couldn't even sit up by myself. All I could do was stare at the crows perching atop the hedge maze, and wonder what was going to happen when my team learned that I was gone.

Adrianna had changed my story after all. She had made me a prisoner.

It was up to me to find a way to escape.

Untold Truths

Memetic incursion in progress: tale type 709 ("Snow White")
Status: ACTIVE

No one had come rushing in to see what was going on: My new body must have been here for a while. Long enough for the nurses to stop watching for changes in her condition and resign her to long-term care. It was good care, at least. The body had sufficient muscle tone for me to move around on my own, even if my legs were weak and shaky, and when I pulled the hair back from my face and secured it with a twist tie I'd found on the floor, my fingers responded without complaint. I could function. I might not be happy about it, but I could do it. That was what mattered right now.

I finished peeling the sensors off my skin, probably triggering a bunch of alarms somewhere, and left the room with the quick, furtive steps of a fugitive. I didn't want the hospital staff to find me, shove me back into the bed, and start contacting the family of the body I was wearing. This was a temporary stop on my way back to getting myself back. I would be as careful with her as I could. Even if the original owner didn't want it back, this body wasn't mine, and it deserved to be returned in mint condition, or as close to it as was possible.

Every step seemed to highlight another difference between this body and my own. My vision was crisper than I expected it to be, sharper around the edges, until it felt like everything had been magnified. Maybe it was time to look into getting contact lenses when I was myself again. Being several inches shorter than I expected to be was a lot more disorienting, as was the fact that I was substantially curvier than I'd ever been in my life. I needed to find a bra, and soon, or this was going to be a painful adventure.

Breaking out of a hospital turned out to be easier than it sounded, especially when breaking out of the coma ward. The staff was no doubt dedicated, committed to their jobs, and genuinely invested in the well-being of their patients. They were also accustomed to those patients remaining perfectly still for months, if not years, at a time. "She got up and walked away" wasn't a normal concern. I found a locker room, no doubt reserved for use by the nurses, and rummaged through the open lockers until I had assembled something that almost resembled a reasonable outfit: sweatpants, a loose hoodie, socks, and heavy-soled brown shoes that almost fit. I probably looked like a college student on laundry day. I didn't particularly care.

One of the nurses had left her wallet in her locker. I felt bad about taking the eighty dollars in cash that she had on her, but not bad enough to leave it behind. At the moment, I needed it more than she did.

"Sorry," I murmured, making the money disappear into my pocket. "The Bureau will reimburse you."

I closed the locker, turned, and walked away. There would probably be a taxi stand outside the hospital, somewhere. I should get moving. I didn't have a choice.

# # #

My feet were aching and the sweatshirt was starting to chafe in places I didn't like to think about by the time the cab dropped me off in front of the unlabeled, unremarkable building that served as Bureau headquarters. My new body had been sleeping off her story in my own hometown, which was a blessing, and also a terrifying reminder that we'd never known as much as we thought we did. How many stories like her were scattered around like little narrative grenades, waiting for the moment when their pins would be pulled and their fairy tales would explode into terrible life?

The fare was a little over sixty dollars. I told the driver to keep the change. Maybe tipping well would keep him from telling the hospital he'd seen me if they asked—and since I'd jumped into a body with coloring identical to my own, it wasn't like he was going to forget me any time soon. The skin as white as snow alone would be pretty memorable.

It had been years since I'd approached the Bureau via the front door. That was for visitors and people from other branches of the government, not for agents. Right now, my status was unclear. Did oaths of service travel with the mind, or with the flesh? Was I a part of the organization, or was I one more target?

We'd find out. I stepped inside, inhaling the stale, faintly artificial lobby air, and proceeded toward the desk. The receptionist on duty didn't look up from whatever game she was playing on her phone. Her hair was long, dark, and wet-looking, like she'd just dredged herself up from the bottom of a forgotten pond in the middle of an isolated moor.

I cleared my throat. She didn't look up.

Right: we were going to have to do this the direct way. "Agent Henrietta Marchen to see Deputy Director Brewer," I said. My voice was too high; I sounded chirpy and bright, even when I was trying to be serious and dour. Just my luck. I had to jump into a soprano.

The receptionist looked up, thick eyebrows raised under the damp fringe of her hair. "Bullshit," she said, in a voice that sounded like it was being forced through layer upon layer of thick, waterlogged peat. "I don't know what you want, kid, but impersonating an agent isn't the way to get it."

I took a deep breath and stood up straighter, trying to look imposing despite my perky collegiate form. I had the feeling things were going to get harder from here. "You're wet, despite having no obvious source of moisture. Your eyes are the color of riverbank mud. They'd be blue or green if you were drawn from a Grecian story. Also, you've been playing Candy Crush since I walked in here. Matching obsessions tend to come with the Slavic variations. You're either a Rusalka, which doesn't make sense with your hair, or a Berehyni. Did you not like drowning people and existing in an uncertain story? I'm not sure why the narrative keeps manifesting you, since it never knows what to do with you once you're here."

The receptionist stared at me, the only sound the water dripping from her long, unbound hair. Finally, warily, she said, "I'm calling the deputy director. Don't go anywhere."

"You do that," I said, with an agreeable nod. "I need to talk to him. It's important."

The receptionist didn't look reassured by that. She picked up her phone and turned half away, using her body to block whatever she was saying. After a few seconds she hung up and looked back to me, saying, "You can have a seat if you want one. The deputy director will be right with you."

"I'll stand," I said. "This body's been in a coma for a while, and I need to work on my muscle tone if I'm going to be of any use to anyone."

The receptionist stared at me. Then, shoulders still hunched, she returned her attention to her phone.

Bothering her further wouldn't have been productive, and more, it would have been cruel. I tucked my hands into my pockets and turned to face the door, waiting for what I knew was about to come. Deputy Director Brewer was a smart man, and he hadn't managed to stay in charge of the Bureau for as long as he had by walking blindly into bad situations. He wasn't going to come alone. The only question was who he was going to bring with him.

The door opened. A whipcord-thin man in a black suit that hung around his skeletal frame like an undertaker's rags stepped through. His hair was bone-blond, slicked back with pomade that smelled of lilies and ashes. I relaxed a little. Agent Piotr Remus might not be my biggest fan at the Bureau, but he was trustworthy and surprisingly open-minded for someone who presented himself as having died twenty or so years before the present day.

Another man followed him through the door, and I tensed again. This guy was built like a walking brick wall, broad-shouldered and straining the seams of his government-issue suit. He was dark-haired and tan skinned, and wearing mirror shades. No one who wears mirror shades has ever intended anything good. It's just a fact.

Deputy Director Brewer was the third one through the door. He moved into position between the two men, looking me slowly up and down. My coloring couldn't fail to make an impression, but there are a lot of Snow White stories in the world. More than I've ever been happy with.

"Miss, why are you here?" he asked.

"Because I belong here," I said. His voice even *sounded* different to my new ears, a little softer and with fewer hard edges. Maybe this body had some minor hearing loss. This wasn't the time to worry about it. I pushed on. "My name is Henrietta Marchen. I am an Agent of the ATI Management Bureau. My body has been taken by a hostile seven-oh-nine, better known as 'Adrianna.' My team is in danger. I want my body back. It would really help me out if you gave me a badge, a gun, and directions to where my people are."

There was a moment of silence, during which Piotr and the deputy director stared at me and the larger man stood silently by. Then the large man reached out, putting a hand on Deputy Director Brewer's shoulder, and said, "She's telling the truth."

"What?" The deputy director turned to look at him. "Agent Névé, I don't think we can be sure of that. She may believe what she's saying. That doesn't make it the truth."

"I know the difference between someone being mistaken about their situation but believing what they say and someone telling the actual, subjective truth," said Agent Névé. He sounded bewildered. Given the circumstances, I couldn't blame him. "This woman either is or completely knows herself to be Agent Henrietta Marchen."

All three of them turned their attention back to me.

"What did you get me for last year's Secret Santa?" asked Piotr.

"A bottle of good vodka and a stuffed wolf," I said. "Also, we don't call it a 'Secret Santa.' There's no point in borrowing trouble just because we're feeling the need for a little holiday cheer."

"What was your gift?" asked Deputy Director Brewer.

I sighed. "I drew Sloane, who gave me a subscription to the 'apple of the month' club. I've been donating apples to the local food bank all year. I think she's planning to do it again, regardless of whether she's supposed to be getting me anything. This is because Sloane is sometimes horrible. Look, are we going to stand out here and play twenty questions to prove I am who I say I am? Because honestly, I don't have time for that." I spread my arms. "I'm wearing a borrowed body, and my team is in danger. I need a gun, I need a badge, I need a *bra*, and I need someone to drive me to their last known location."

Deputy Director Brewer frowned. "How do you know they're not in this building?"

"If they were, there's no way you wouldn't have brought Andy with you, and even less of a chance that you'd have made it out here without Sloane shoving her way into the mix. She'd have picked up a seven-oh-nine entering the building, and she'd want to know what was going on." I shook my head. "They aren't with you. That means they're not *here*. I need to find them." I needed to warn them about what they were harboring in their midst, assuming it wasn't already too late. Time worked differently in the whiteout wood. Maybe Adrianna was just now waking up, and I could still step in and keep her from doing any damage. Or maybe she'd been here for years, and everything was already lost.

Deputy Director Brewer's frown deepened as he looked me up and down, searching my strange new frame for a sign, however small, that I was telling the truth. He was an ordinary man in a building full of fables, fairy tales, and urban myths, all of them wearing human skins and trying to get through their days with a minimum of trouble. That meant he'd needed to develop a better-than-average awareness of his surroundings, because anything else would have gotten him killed.

"How did your story become active?" he asked.

"I ate an apple to keep Birdie Hubbard from blowing my team to kingdom come. You nearly suspended me from field work over that. You said I should have found a different way. I told you there wasn't one. To be honest, sir, I still don't think I could have done anything differently. It was my story or my team, and I chose my team."

"Your team consisting of . . . ?"

"Sloane Winters, Jeffrey Davis, Andrew Robinson, and Demi Santos. That's in order of seniority, not in order of value to either the team or the organization."

"You didn't mention your sister."

"Because I don't have one, *sir*." I glared at him. I knew what he was doing, and I understood how important it was to establish my identity. That didn't make me happy about hearing him misgender my brother, even for something like this. "My brother, Gerald March, is a high school teacher and isn't involved with the Bureau in any capacity that he can possibly avoid. I can do this all day. My team needs me. Please don't make me do this all day."

Deputy Director Brewer looked at me. Then, without turning, he asked, "Agent Névé?"

"She's telling the truth as she knows it," said the bulky agent. "She's told no lies at all."

I turned my attention on the agent. "I don't know you," I said. "Why don't I know you?"

"I recently transferred to the field office from Human Resources," he said. "I was tired of pushing paper all the time. Thought I could do more good here."

"What's your story?"

"Agent Marchen—if that's who you are—we're getting off the topic," said Deputy Director Brewer. I turned my attention back to him. He was starting to look shaken. I was getting through to him, no matter how much he didn't want to believe me. "It's clear that whatever your situation is, it falls within the bailiwick of this organization. I'll get you clothing that fits, and then we will discuss our next steps. If you don't like this proposal, I'll be forced to conclude that you're not who you claim to be."

"If I *did* like your proposal, that would be a sign that I wasn't who I claimed to be," I said. "But I won't object to it. I need clothes. I need my team to believe me too." And it was going to be harder for them. They would have Adrianna *right there*, wearing my skin and my smile, while I was going to be the stranger.

I had to try. I had to save them. The deputy director motioned for me to follow him, and I did, even though the sound of the door swinging shut behind me was like a latch closing on a trap.

This was the only way out.

# # #

Piotr and the new guy from HR stood outside the women's locker room while I changed into the clothing provided for me. It was standard-issue Bureau attire, which meant it was the most comforting thing in the world: I hadn't voluntarily worn anything but black and white since they'd given me my badge. What's more, due to the range of standard heights and weights within an organization that included giants and leprechauns, everything fit. I didn't have to think about dressing for my new body. All I had to do was put things on.

My hair was too long. I didn't feel comfortable cutting it, not when it was growing out of someone else's head, and so I grabbed a scrunchie from the bin by the door and moved to stand in front of the full-length mirror, tying it back. Then I jumped.

I wasn't alone in the locker room.

The woman standing behind my reflection was skinny and disheveled, dressed in a paisley-print sundress that looked like it had come straight out of the late seventies. Her hair was dirty blonde and stick-straight, hanging to almost cover her face.

I spun around. There was no one there. I was alone. But when I looked back to the mirror, the woman was closer, standing so near to me that I should have been able to reach out and touch her.

"Uh," I said. "Hello?"

The woman responded by lifting her head and pushing her hair aside, revealing her eyes. They were light brown, the color of dust on glass, and utterly lovely, if I ignored the rings of blood around them. Streaks of it ran down her cheeks, like she had been crying the stuff. It was utterly chilling. I didn't dare allow myself to look away.

"You're in the mirror," I said.

The woman nodded.

"You're not a Snow White."

She shook her head. Then she pointed to me and nodded.

"That's right," I said. "I'm a Snow White. I had to pass through a mirror to get here. Is that why I can see you now? I've never seen you before."

She nodded again.

"Have you always been here?"

She paused before making a "sort of" gesture with her right hand, wobbling it from side to side like a small child trying to get a point across.

Right. "Does the deputy director know about you?"

A single bloody tear rolled down her cheek as she nodded, mouthing the word 'yes' this time, just in case I missed the point. I found myself wishing for Judi. Maybe she could have found a less binary way of communicating with this strange mirror-girl, one that didn't make her cry. I couldn't even turn to face her, or she would disappear.

"I'm Henry Marchen," I said, and the mirror-girl nodded again, agreeing that this was true. That was . . . something of a relief, actually, even if it wasn't much of a surprise. This woman lived *inside* the mirror. If anyone would be able to see the reality in my reflection, it was her.

Wait. That meant . . . I took a deep breath, and said, "This isn't my usual body. I'm supposed to be taller, and thinner, and a little older. Have you seen my body recently?"

She nodded.

Now for the ten thousand dollar question: "Was someone else wearing it?"

She nodded again.

I bit the inside of my cheek hard enough to draw blood. It had been long enough that Adrianna was up and out of the hospital. I had no way of knowing how much damage she'd done, and I still needed to convince Deputy Director Brewer that I was the real deal. "Thanks for letting me know. She's dangerous, that lady. It's probably best if you don't show yourself to her, if you have a choice in the matter."

The woman nodded.

"Look, I need to get going. I need to help my friends. Is there anything I can do for you before I leave?"

The woman hesitated. Then she reached into the pocket of her dress and withdrew a folded piece of paper. It was marked with bloody fingerprints. I guess that was unavoidable. She unfolded it and held it up for me to see.

Her handwriting was large and unsteady, more the handwriting of a child than an adult—but then I realized I could *read* it. It was mirror writing, designed to be read in a reflection. No wonder it looked so childish. She'd been drawing the letters, not printing them.

TELL DAN MARY SAYS HI, said the note.

"Deputy Director Brewer?" I asked.

She nodded, lowering the piece of paper.

"All right," I said, and turned, and she was gone.

Dressed once more in black and white, with shoes that fit and a bra that kept my breasts from being quite so much of a distraction every time I moved, I started toward the door. It was time to save my team and get my life back, hopefully in that order.

Piotr turned his head when I stepped out into the hall, giving me an appraising up-and-down look before he said, "You look more like Marchen now. I guess the clothes really do make the woman."

"I hope that next time, the wolf eats you," I said, earning a snort of laughter from Agent Névé. Piotr shot a glare at the taller man, who shrugged. Funny was funny, even when it was coming from the mouth of the woman who might or might not be who she said she was. I sighed. "Look, fun as it is to stand out here and banter with the two of you—or the one of you, since tall, dark, and quiet doesn't know me well enough to engage—I need to get back into the field, which means I need to convince the deputy director I'm the real deal. Can we get moving?"

"If you were really Henrietta Marchen, you'd know he hates it when people treat stories as interchangeable just because they have the same tale type," said Piotr. "Not all Snow White archetypes are created equal."

"True," I said. "For example, this one is running out of patience. Please. Take me to the man who can actually help me. You can snark at me later. You and Sloane can tag-team me for all that I care. I need to get to my people."

Piotr's usual expression of vague superiority wavered, replaced by uncertainty. "I'm not saying I believe you just yet. But I might be starting to."

"Good enough for me." If I could convince Piotr, who lived his life by the book, that I was who I said I was, I could convince anybody.

We walked down the hall toward the deputy director's office. Heads poked out of doors as we passed. News travels fast in an office like ours, and everyone wants to see the latest twist in the tale. A stranger with Snow White coloration showing up and claiming to be an established agent was definitely new. I tried not to glare at them. It wasn't their fault they were hungry for novelty.

Deputy Director Brewer's door was open. Piotr leaned past me to knock on the doorframe. "Sir, she's here."

The deputy director looked up. Like Piotr, he looked me up and down before he spoke. "Agent Remus, Agent Névé, thank you both. You are excused. Miss, please come in."

"I have a name, you know," I said, pulling the door shut behind me as I stepped into the office. The doorknob felt too high in relation to my hand, when really, it was exactly where it needed to be for someone of my new height. The world was out of kilter, and I didn't like it.

Deputy Director Brewer looked at me calmly. "Not until you've proven that you deserve it. Unless you have something else you'd like to be called?"

I knew him. He already had people calling the local hospitals and checking for missing coma patients who fit my description. Either he hadn't called the right one or they hadn't noticed my absence yet. It didn't matter. Eventually, he'd find someone who knew this body's name, a family member or friend, and they would have questions I couldn't answer.

"I don't know this body's name, and even if I did, it would be describing the flesh, not the person inside it," I said. "My name is Henrietta. Most people call me Henry. I need help. I need to find my team."

"I've been working with the Bureau for a long time, miss. I've seen a lot of things that people might consider unlikely, even impossible. Lots of white-skinned girls with red lips and wild stories have passed through those doors. But I have to say, this is a first for me." He still looked so *calm*. I hated him for that, even as I admired his restraint. "Assuming for a moment that I was willing to believe you might be Henrietta Marchen, and that I was willing to take my belief a step further, and say that someone else was currently occupying your original body . . . how? This strains credulity, even for me."

"Mirrors," I said. He seemed to flinch. I narrowed my eyes. Interesting.

When he didn't say anything, I continued.

"The Snow White story involves a lot of glass, and a lot of reflective surfaces. When a seven-oh-nine goes into her coma, she winds up inside the mirrors." That wasn't strictly true, but it was close enough to cover the basics, and I didn't want to tell him about the whiteout wood. The Snow Whites who lived there had kept their slice of the monomyth secret for centuries. I was a loyal agent of the ATI Management Bureau. I was also a Snow White, and I owed it to my involuntary sisters to protect what little peace they had left. "It turns out some of those past stories are still active. When I lost consciousness, I was ambushed by a Snow White who'd been looking for an opportunity to get out of the glass. By the time I recovered, my body was gone."

"So what, you did the same to another woman? You stole a body? Two wrongs don't make a right, miss. If you were truly a Bureau agent, you would know that."

"Two wrongs don't make a right, but not all Snow White figures want to wake up," I said. "The mirrors led me to this body because its owner wasn't interested in regaining consciousness. We should be looking at our location protocols, sir. I woke up at a private hospital, inside city limits." Inwardly, I winced at giving him any information he could use to identify my current form. I had to do it. I had to give him whatever he needed to believe that I was really myself, and not some imposter.

"Why didn't the woman you claim stole your body take one of the unused ones, if it was that simple? It seems like stealing a body is a lot of trouble to go to, if there are bodies just lying around, waiting to be claimed."

I frowned. "I already told you who took my body. Adrianna. You have files on her, I know you do, because I've seen them. She's a mass-murderer. She can't be trusted. And right now, she's wearing my face and targeting my team. Every minute I spend trying to convince you who I am is a minute where I'm not tracking her down and *stopping* her. You're my boss, sir, whether you're currently acknowledging my identity or not. That isn't going to earn you a scrap of forgiveness from me if she hurts my people because you kept me here longer than you should have."

"You're not answering my question."

"She took my body because this," I gestured around me, "is what she wanted! She wanted to be inside the Bureau, she wanted access to my *team*. Demi is powerful as all hell. Jeff is more important than even he realizes. Andy may not be connected to the narrative, but losing him would hurt us incalculably. And Sloane . . ." I trailed off, unsure how to continue without revealing secrets that it wasn't my place to share. Secrets even Sloane didn't know I knew.

Sloane had been with the Bureau since its inception—since *before* its inception. She had seen the stories shift and change for centuries. She was a good agent. She was a good friend. She could be an amazing weapon, if she was aimed correctly.

"You know a great deal about this team, miss," said the deputy director.

I glared at him. "I'd better. I've been leading them for quite some time."

"So you seriously expect me to believe you passed through a mirror, and as a consequence, Adrianna—who has been dead for a long time; not in a glass coffin, not sleeping, deceased—was able to seize your body, which she is now using to infiltrate the Bureau." Deputy

Director Brewer settled in his seat. "I'm sorry, but this story is a little difficult to believe."

I sat up a little straighter. "The mirror," I said.

Deputy Director Brewer frowned. "Excuse me?"

"This whole story hinges on my having passed through a mirror," I said. "If you believed that, would you believe I am who I say I am?"

His frown deepened. "I make no promises, but I might be more inclined to grant credence to your words."

"Did you know we have a woman inside the mirror in the women's locker room?"

The change in him was immediate. His face went white as his shoulders sank, eyes widening to almost comic proportions. His mouth moved for a moment, silently, before he managed to say, "What?"

"A woman. Inside the mirror. Maybe she's in more than just the one—I don't know, I never saw her before today, maybe because I'd never traveled through a mirror before. She said to tell you Mary says hello."

The deputy director paled further. "What did she look like?" he asked.

"Pale. Dark blonde hair, brown eyes. Pretty. She was dressed like a flashback to the nineteen seventies. If you asked me to identify her story, I'd need more information, but I'd be willing to wager a guess that it started sometime between seventy-seven and eighty-two."

"Why such a precise range?" His voice was virtually a whisper. This seemed to be hurting him. I just didn't know why.

"Her shoes," I said. "The rest of the outfit looked like she'd been wearing it for a few years—worn seams, a little mending. The sort of thing you wear because you love it. But she was wearing sturdy-looking sneakers, and they were newer than the rest of it. Means she can't have had them for that long."

"Was there anything else that stood out about her? Anything at all?"

Given how upset he seemed to be by her existence, I didn't want to tell him about the blood. But my team needed me, and I owed nothing to the strange woman in the mirror. "She was sad. She was crying when I saw her, but not tears. Blood. She was crying blood."

He slumped, staring at me. Then he asked, in a rough voice, "Did Sloane tell you about Mary? Is that what this is? Did she say 'if you ever need to get something out of him, just bring up the girl in the mirror'?"

"No, sir." I shook my head. "Sloane doesn't like to talk about her past. Or her present. Or much of anything that's not available on eBay. She's careful that way. I'd never even heard a rumor." But that wasn't quite true, was it? There were always rumors. I just hadn't given them any credence or seen any value in trying to follow up on them. They'd seemed harmless, the sort of thing that would inevitably spring up around a building filled with people who fought fairy tales for a living.

Deputy Director Brewer must have read that afterthought on my face. He actually laughed, dropping his forehead into his hand. "Dear God," he said. "You know, when they told me the Bureau was going into the business of foster care, I thought they'd lost their minds. We're not equipped to raise children, I said. We're barely equipped to keep adults among the living. And look at you, you and your brother. You're both so comfortable living in stories that it never occurs to you that something doesn't make sense. You never investigated because it was never dangerous."

"Sir?" I said.

"Her name is Mary. She used to be an agent in this same Bureau. She was the one who brought me here, thirty years ago." The deputy director sat up straight, looking at me. "She was a new tale type, they said. Something to research and learn how to use. And then one day the mirror swallowed her whole, and I haven't seen her since."

"I'm sorry to hear that, sir," I said.

"If you passed through a mirror to get here, as you keep insisting, it makes sense that you would have seen Mary." He looked at me assessingly. "You have my attention."

"I don't want your attention. I want your authorization to go back into the field and save my people from a mass-murderess who stole my body." I scowled. "All this 'prove yourself' bullshit is getting old, *sir*. I can tell you anything you want to know about my past, which should prove I'm myself. I can go out on the back lawn and trade secrets with the squirrels, which should prove I'm a Snow White. But if you don't want to believe me, you're not going to. I don't see where there's anything I can do about that."

"So what are you going to do?" asked Deputy Director Brewer.

I pushed my chair back and stood. "If you're not going to help me, I'm going to help myself. Thanks for the shoes. They'll make marching into hell a lot easier." I turned and started for the door.

The deputy director was silent as I crossed the room. When I reached for the doorknob, he said, "Agent Marchen, do you think you can drive in your current condition?"

It took me an instant to realize that by my "current condition," he meant the fact that I was dealing with the cognitive dissonance of being in a body that wasn't my own. "I'm not sure," I said, turning back to him. "I was going to give it a try."

"I'd rather you not get yourself killed when we don't even know the name of that body you're in," he said. "I'm sending Agents Remus and Névé with you to your team's last known location. They left this morning to respond to a five-four-five-B, and they haven't checked in recently."

I wanted to yell at him for wasting my time when my team was radio silent with a murderess in their midst. All I did was nod tightly and say, "Yes, sir. Thank you. My badge and gun . . . ?"

"Your badge is with your body; I don't have it to give," he said. "I'll issue you a provisional shield for now. As for your gun, I feel like the same difficulties you would have with driving will apply to marksmanship. I'll give you a Taser. You can still incapacitate your body if you catch up to it, but you're less likely to kill someone by mistake."

Meaning I was less likely to kill myself and strand my consciousness in another Snow White's skin. "Fine," I said. "Anything that gets me back into the field."

"Understood. And Agent Marchen?"

Here came the catch. There was always a catch. "Yes, sir?"

"I'm going to want to talk to you about Mary when this is all over."

Naturally. "Yes, sir," I said, and opened the door. I had my identity, if not my body, back. Now it was time to get down to business.

# # #

Piotr drove, leaving Agent Névé to pack himself into the back seat and look nervously at anything but the rearview mirror. Interesting. I had no such limitations. I watched him for a few blocks before I said, "So what's your story?"

He jumped, eyes darting instinctively toward the mirror before he flinched away and went back to looking out the window. "Ma'am?"

"HR usually keeps their people, since training you is a nightmare. What made them release you to the field?"

"My story was useful for personnel evaluations, but when Agent Bloomfield was put on assignment to the field office, she asked if I could come with her for logistical support," he said. "There was no room on her team. I got assigned to Agent Remus."

"And Agent Remus is smart enough to recognize someone whose story has been pushed to the point of breaking," said Piotr. "They were using mirrors to have Carlos evaluate their people without making direct eye contact. That's not healthy for him. When I threatened to call HR *on* HR, they said I could keep him for as long as he was needed."

Unhealthy mirrors . . . "Are you from a Snow Queen scenario?" I asked.

Agent Névé's big head nodded. "Yes, ma'am," he said. "I can tell truth from lies when I hear them spoken, but if you give me a mirror, I can see all your worst secrets in your reflection. It hurts. I don't like it."

"If he does it long enough, he stops seeing anything *but* your worst secrets," said Piotr grimly. He sounded personally offended, as if the things that had been done to Carlos before he was a part of Piotr's team had been an affront to Piotr himself. That sort of loyalty wasn't uncommon within the Bureau. It was still refreshing after what I'd been through. "He lived in a world peopled with rotting corpses pretending to be his friends, and then they had the gall to pretend not to know why he was unhappy."

"It wasn't that bad, Piotr," protested Agent Névé.

"If I could tell truth from lies, would I believe you?" asked Piotr. "They have other human lie-detectors. They were *torturing* you."

Agent Névé was silent.

I settled deeper in my seat. Snow Queens were nasty, destructive things, and they left long-term effects that most people didn't really think about. The Kay in the story—the child the Snow Queen inexplicably abducted, driven by the narrative even if she'd never wanted to have children—would be saved from the fragment of mirror caught in his eye. That was the role of the Gerda in the story, the little girl who got the chance to play heroine and go up against a villain who was more natural disaster than actual antagonist. But all the other children who had fragments of the Snow Queen's mirror in their eyes, they just had to live with it. No one ever came to save them; they were outside the scope of the central narrative.

Sometimes the mirror was an experimental drug, or a foster parent who enjoyed practicing a twisted form of home lobotomy. But none of those children ever got to put the past behind them.

We rode in silence for a while before Piotr asked, "So Henry, what's the plan here? Are you just going to charge in and hope they believe you when you start telling them you're the real deal?"

"You're pretty well accepted as unimpeachably honest, and you're backing me," I said. "Agent Névé is from HR, which means Ciara will know he's trustworthy. That should give me enough of a platform to start casting doubt on Adrianna's story. I don't care how long she's been watching me. They have to know that *something's* wrong."

Didn't they? There was no possible way she could be a better version of me than I was. I was the real thing, and she was just a ghost who refused to stay dead. Andy and Sloane would believe me. *Jeff* would believe me.

He had to.

"What if they don't want to listen to you?" asked Piotr. "I've seen this woman in the office since 'you' woke up, and she's believable. I didn't realize anything was different about her."

"Nothing, really?" I gave him a sidelong look. "Nothing at all?"

He paused before admitting, in a slightly embarrassed tone, "She seemed a little more relaxed than I remembered you being, like she'd finally pulled the stick out of her ass. I thought maybe being in a coma and being woken up by true love's kiss had left you in a better position to deal with your own shit."

"But she wasn't woken up by true love's kiss," said Agent Névé, before I could squawk. "I was talking to Ciara about it. Agent Marchen's boyfriend kissed her, and she didn't wake up. Not for quite some time. A lot of people have been waiting for the breakup, honestly."

"That's stupid," I said. "I don't know whether what Jeff and I have is true love, and I don't care. I like him. He likes me. He makes me feel safe. Why should I require 'true love' on top of all that?"

"We live in a fairy-tale world, Marchen. If we're going to suffer the downsides, we might as well hold out for the good parts." Piotr turned down a broad, tree lined street. It was the sort of idyllic-looking place where nothing ever seemed to go wrong, until it went wrong to a catastrophic degree.

That hint of catastrophe was borne out by the police cars parked on the street in front of a large, white-fronted McMansion. My team's SUV was in the driveway, nestled in next to an ambulance—and two of the people I was looking for. Andy and Demi were standing a few feet from the SUV, their heads close together in the way of people who didn't want to be overheard.

"This was a Puss in Boots scenario, correct?"

Piotr pulled to a stop, blocking the driveway and—not accidentally—cutting off all exits for my team. Even if they thought I was a liar or under an evil spell, they wouldn't be able to leave. He killed the engine. "Correct. A young woman who'd been held for several days by a home invader managed to break loose, and a team—your team—was dispatched to investigate. The young man, who we believe to be a Marquis de Carabas at this point, fled into the hedge maze behind the house."

I stared at him as I undid my belt. "There's a *hedge maze* behind the house?"

"Yes."

"Who the fuck has a *hedge maze* in a residential neighborhood?"

"This woman's parents," said Piotr. "Aside from that . . . serial killers, presumably. People who enjoy Stephen King novels a bit too much. And people who are hoping that one night, they'll wake up to find David Bowie standing at their window."

"Right," I said, and opened the door, sliding out of the car. I didn't wait to see whether Piotr or Carlos were following me, because waiting hadn't ever been something I did. I walked straight into danger, no matter how likely it was to get me killed. Loitering around and waiting for backup now would just make me seem weak, and more, it would make me seem like someone *else*, someone I had never been before.

The part of me that was tethered most strongly to the Snow White story had always been there, lurking at the back of every decision I made, trying to pull me into passivity. I could feel it now, as much a part of this body as it was a part of my own. I shoved it aside, marching straight up to the little conversational huddle that Demi and Andy had created. They were positioned to discourage strangers from trying to interrupt. That was fine. I wasn't a stranger.

"So we have a problem," I said, skipping the preamble in favor of getting straight to the part I knew they weren't going to like. They turned to look at me. Andy seemed amused; Demi looked disbelieving, like she couldn't understand how I'd found the nerve to interrupt them.

"Really?" asked Andy. His eyes skimmed across me, taking note of my coloration and the cut of my suit and filing me—correctly, if incompletely—as a Snow White employed by the Bureau. "Is your team here to take custody of the scene? Who are you working for?"

"My team already has custody of the scene, and I answer directly to Deputy Director Brewer," I said. I lowered my hands, letting him see that they were empty. "Andy, it's me. Henry. We have a problem."

Andy blinked. Demi looked confused. Then, to my surprise and annoyance, Andy broke out laughing.

"Oh, man, what field office did they dig you out of?" he asked. "I know we don't have any other seven-oh-nines working in this time zone. Henry would have introduced us by now."

"Your name is Andrew Robinson, you got married to Mike Dawson four years ago. I thought having your wedding at an amusement park was a little weird, but since it meant I got to give my best man speech while I was on an inverted roller coaster, I was cool with it in the end. Jeff threw up twice. Sloane laughed at him twice. The wedding cake was supposed to be the color of cotton candy, but it turns out that cotton candy doesn't translate into frosting, so it was the color of Pepto Bismol instead. Am I getting through to you yet? Do I need to get embarrassing? Because I am too short and my tits are too big and I *will* get personal."

Andy stared at me. Then his expression turned grim, and he took a step forward. It was all I could do not to take a step back. Was it just that I was smaller than I remembered being, or had he always been so damned *big*?

"I don't know what you're playing at, lady, but this isn't funny. Henry was hurt recently. Hurt bad. Showing up here pretending—"

"I wasn't *hurt*, I ate an apple, and I should have known better, but I was cutting corners because I was *afraid*, and I thought Jeff could wake me up. Only he couldn't, because Adrianna was already in the way." I glared at Andy, daring him to accept the truth in my words, to see the undeniable reality of my situation. Whether I was getting through, I didn't know.

But I was getting through to Demi. She shifted positions, ever so slightly, before putting a hand on Andy's arm. "When I was with Birdie, she talked about Adrianna," she said, voice barely above a murmur. "She said Adrianna was her get out of jail free card. Maybe . . . ?"

"Lady, I don't know what your problem is, but this isn't funny," said Andy.

"Henry's been weird since she woke up. Sloane feels it most. That doesn't mean I don't feel it too," said Demi. She turned to look at me. "Say something only Henry would know."

I smiled a little. "You still watch Saturday morning cartoons. You got so mad when they stopped being on broadcast television that you asked me whether the Bureau had any pull with the FCC. I'm still sort of sorry that we don't."

"Anyone who has access to your Facebook would know you were angry about the cartoons," said Andy.

"But would they know that she wanted me to call the FBI and claim that free cartoons for children of low-income households were a matter of national security?" I asked. Then I stopped, tensing. Someone was emerging from the maze. If it was Adrianna . . .

The figure was lithe, shorter than my body, with brown hair streaked in seemingly natural blue. Ciara Bloomfield. I relaxed a little; not completely. According to Deputy Director Brewer, Ciara had been assigned to my team as a temporary field leader while I was in my coma, and had remained as an observer after "I" woke up. She might believe me. She might put the nails into my coffin. There was no way for me to know, not here, not until she reached us.

Andy frowned when he realized I wasn't paying attention to him anymore. He turned and snorted at the sight of Ciara walking across the grass toward us. "Good. Someone else to help me convince you to stop messing around when we're on an active case. The last thing we need is for you to trigger some sort of body-swapping story."

"I'm not messing around," I said.

Ciara walked up to us, taking in me—and presumably, Piotr; I hadn't turned, but I was reasonably sure he was standing behind me—with a quick glance before she said, "We have a problem. I lost track of Agent Winters, and I can't raise Agent Marchen on the phone. Agent Remus, hello. Who's your friend?"

So Piotr *was* behind me. Good. He took a step forward, putting us level with one another, and said, "Good afternoon, Agent Bloomfield. Agent Névé is in the car, in case we need to make a quick exit. As for my friend, this is Agent Marchen."

Ciara looked at him like he'd just claimed that I was a swarm of wasps in a tailored suit. "Excuse me?"

"This," he indicated me with a sweep of his hand, "is Agent Marchen."

I gave him a sidelong look. "You could have stepped in a few minutes ago, you know."

"I was waiting to see if you could talk your team into accepting your identity," he said. "Since you clearly couldn't, I thought it was time for me to get involved."

"Thanks," I said flatly. I turned back to Ciara. "As I was just explaining to Andy, hi. I'm Henry. A dead woman stole my body, and I want it back."

A muscle at the corner of Ciara's mouth twitched. "What?"

"Agent Marchen arrived at the Bureau a little while ago, telling this fascinating story," said Piotr. "I'll be honest, I thought she was making it up, but she somehow convinced Deputy Director Brewer, and Agent Névé believes her. At this point, I believe her too. Pretending to be Agent Marchen gets her nothing but a life no sensible person would want. Only the real thing would be this insistent."

"What?" Ciara lifted her right hand as she moved toward me, wrapping her fingers around the key she wore at her throat. There was something almost predatory about the way she was focusing on my eyes, like she wanted to swing them open and pull out whatever was on the other side. I stood my ground. Backing down now would only cast everything I'd said into doubt, and I couldn't afford that. Not here, not now.

Ciara stopped with her nose barely an inch from mine. She narrowed her eyes, expression going blank for a count of five. Then, with no warning or shift in her stance, she smiled, wonder transforming her face into something beautiful.

"Henry!" she said. "I mean, Agent Marchen—we're not well-acquainted enough for me to be that informal, my apologies. It *is* you!"

"Wait, what?" said Andy.

Ciara's smile died as quickly as it had come. She turned to Andy and Demi. "This is the real Agent Marchen. The real Henry. She has the right eyes. They're the mirrors of the soul, you know. She hasn't been letting me get close enough to look since she woke up."

"I thought it was 'windows,'" said Demi. She had produced her flute from somewhere and was clutching it tight, elbows drawn in against her body like she was trying to make herself smaller and brace herself to start playing at the same time.

"Depends on who you're talking to," said Ciara. Her lips twisted downward, her mercurial mood shifting further into dismay. "Wait, if this is Henry, who have we been—?"

"Adrianna," I said.

Ciara's eyes widened. "What?"

"Finally, someone who reacts to that name like it's a *bad* thing." I threw my hands up. "She knocked me out and stole my body." She'd done more than knock me out, but I didn't feel like explaining the mechanics of the whiteout wood just now. That could come later, when the questions got harder and we were figuring out how to recover my original face. "She came here because she wanted access to the Bureau's records. This was always her long game."

"But why?" asked Andy. "The Archives are good. They're not worth killing over."

The Archives. I went still, feeling the cold wash over me like water, chilling and killing my sense of equilibrium. "Where's Jeff?"

"What?"

"You said you lost Sloane and that Adrianna isn't answering my phone," I said. It was a struggle to keep my voice smooth and level. "Three of you are here. That leaves one member of the team unaccounted for. Where's Jeff?"

Ciara's horrified expression was all the answer I needed. I took off for the hedge maze at a run, and I didn't look back.

# # #

It was too much to hope that Adrianna had simply taken my boyfriend with her, recognizing how useful he could be and carting him off to whatever Grimm-knows-where secret lair she was planning to hole up in. She'd been able to incapacitate Sloane somehow, and Sloane wasn't *small*. I knew the limitations of my own body. There was no way she had carried them both out of the maze. That didn't leave very many options for what she had done with Jeff.

Please don't be dead, I thought inanely as I ran. *I never got to say good bye.* Shoemaker's Elves had to have their equivalent of the whiteout wood, but I could sink back into dreaming and walk a thousand years before I'd find it. Our tales were too far apart for his story's homeland to touch on mine. All I could do was run, spinning worst-case scenarios for the audience of my own heart and feeling each of them strike truer than I wanted it to.

It was still a shock when I came racing around a corner and found him crumpled on the ground, a bloodstain covering the left side of his jacket. I kept moving, more out of inertia than anything else, until my knees hit the grass and my ear hit his chest.

He had a heartbeat. He wasn't gone yet.

"Medic!" I shouted, and the running footsteps closing from behind me told me the help he needed wasn't far away: He'd have it soon. We'd have it soon. I stayed where I was, my ear pressed against his bloody jacket, and listened to the beating of his heart. I needed to know that he wasn't leaving me. Not when I'd just gotten back from leaving him.

"She's going to pay for this," I whispered, and Jeff—whose breathing was shallow and whose eyes were closed—didn't contradict me.

She was going to pay.

Mirror's Face

Memetic incursion in progress: estimated tale type 503
  ("The Shoemaker and the Elves")
Status: ACTIVE

Dying, as it turned out, was quite a pleasant thing. The world went soft around the edges, taking all the pain and confusion and betrayal with it. They had seemed so important not long ago, when time had been measured in years, not in seconds. Now, it was finally clear that they'd never really mattered at all. This final descent into softness, into story, was what it was all about.

In the distance Jeff could hear the sound of tiny hammers tapping even tinier nails into hardened leather, driving them home. His hands were numb, but he felt sure that they'd be ready to hold the hammer when he opened his eyes again. Yes; it was time. He had frittered away his life on paperwork and pining after a princess who could never truly love him, and now he could let all that go. Now he could begin doing what he'd always been meant to do.

But she *had* loved him, hadn't she? The question was hot and sharp against the warm softness dissolving the edges of his consciousness. Jeff had never been one to shy away from a question just because it wasn't easy. He gripped it as tightly as his fading thoughts would allow, spinning it like a jewel as he studied every facet, every angle. Yes. Yes, she had loved him: he was sure of that. Her kiss had called him out of his story, once, when it had tried to take him before his time, and his kiss had pulled her out of the sleep that was supposed to last until the stars went cold. It wasn't her fault that true love's kiss hadn't worked a second time. He must have *done* something to erode her love for him, damaged it in some way, because his love for her hadn't changed in the slightest. He still loved her more than he'd ever loved anyone else. It was the kind of love that followed its owner to the grave.

Henry had loved him once. She had trusted him to wake her up when she ate the apple. She had *believed* in him. So why hadn't it worked? It should have worked.

Unless the woman who'd shot him wasn't Henry.

Everything began falling into place, suddenly making sense in the pause between darkness and death. She had been so *different* after waking up, and he'd been so consumed by guilt that he hadn't seen it. He was the fairy-tale lover whose kiss had lost its potency, after all; how could he have been anything but distracted? And yet. Henry had sounded different, acted different, even stood differently after she woke up, which she had done entirely on her own—something Snow Whites weren't supposed to be able to do. So what if the person moving Henry's body wasn't Henry? Things made so much more sense if that wasn't Henry.

He could die without feeling like she'd blamed him for failing her if that wasn't Henry. And maybe, just maybe, he would see her again, in the silence on the other side of the story.

Jeff's eyes were already closed, but still, it felt as if he was closing them and letting go.

He had so far left to fall.

# # #

"Where the fuck is the medic?!" I screamed, my head still resting against Jeff's chest, where the thready beat of his pulse told me he wasn't gone yet, but he was going; he was going fast, and once he'd gone, he wasn't coming back. His skin was starting to cool under mine. I didn't know how much blood he'd lost. All I was sure of was that it had been too much, and that he couldn't afford to lose any more.

Ciara, Andy, and Demi came pounding around the corner, scrambling to a stop when they saw me. Demi's eyes widened, her hands tightening around her flute. She was staring more at me than at Jeff. I looked down at my hands. The blood stood out remarkably well against the bone-white of my skin. Everything always came back to those colors, to black feathers against the sky and red blood on the snow.

"He's dying," I said, lifting my head. "She shot him, and he's dying and *where is that medic?!*" My last words came out in a piercing wail, higher and shriller than my own throat could ever have managed. For the first time, I was glad of my borrowed body. It seemed only right that I should be capable of keening.

"Piotr is getting the EMTs," said Ciara. She took a half-step forward, her voice dropping, turning soothing. "Henry, what happened?"

I narrowed my eyes. I knew what she was thinking, and I needed to stop it here and now, before it could spread to the other members of my team. "Look at the blood. Feel how cold he is. He was shot before I got here—long before I got here. That *bitch* who stole my body did this to him, because . . . I don't know. Maybe he figured out who she was. Maybe she got tired of him. He's bleeding out. Do you understand what I'm saying? He's *dying*. Where is that medic?"

"Blood is a liquid," said Demi abruptly. We both turned to look at her. She didn't shy back. If anything, she relaxed, her fingers beginning to sketch a phantom melody on the body of her flute. She was playing the song even before she had breath to put behind it. "Liquid moves. Do you trust me?"

"What?" I sat up straighter, trying to figure out what she was saying.

"Do you trust me?" she repeated.

The answer was easy. "Yes," I said. "I always have."

"Then don't move." Demi raised her flute to her lips and began to play.

There are no words to describe the tune that poured from her flute. It hung in the air for a moment, crystalline and demanding my full attention. Ciara and Andy were equally rapt, barely blinking as they listened. The music rose, peaking in a series of high, jagged points that seemed to climb to an impossible height, passing outside of the range of ordinary hearing. Something slithered over my hands. I looked down.

The blood on my hands was moving, turning liquid and rolling together to form larger and larger drops, until they pooled into a single ruby pool between my outspread fingers. It sat there for a moment, glistening and impossible, before rolling down Jeff's neck and vanishing under the collar of his shirt, which was looking less bloodstained with every second that passed. The blood was pulling itself out of the fabric and rolling back toward his wound—and then inside, every drop of it returning to the veins from which it had fallen.

I barely dared to breathe. I kept pressing down, feeling Jeff's pulse strengthen under my fingers. This went against all medical logic and modern understanding of how blood and the body worked, but neither of those things mattered here or now, in the shadow of the hedge maze: what mattered was that in a fairy tale, this would have worked, and when you brought people like us together in a place like this, a fairy tale was essentially what you had.

Demi pulled her mouth from her flute, catching a whooping breath before she said, "I'm going to pipe the bullet out and the blood in at the same time. Somebody be ready to catch it."

"On it," said Andy, and stepped forward, kneeling on Jeff's other side. He looked at me as he did, and when our eyes met, he nodded. Just once, but that was all I needed to know that he'd finally decided to believe me. We were teammates again.

I looked to Demi. "Save him," I said, half command, half plea.

She nodded. "I will," she said, and started playing again.

This time the song danced, trilling and twisting around the high, jagged notes that called the blood back into Jeff's body. There was almost none left on his skin or clothing, and my hands were clean. Demi blew a hard note, and a bullet shot up from his shoulder, gleaming in the shadows like a star. Andy's hand lashed out, closing around the projectile. The song continued for a few beats more, calling the last of the blood home. Jeff's pulse was strong, and so I moved my hands to cover the wound that was still there, ready to start bleeding again: Demi could pull the blood back into a body, but it seemed she couldn't heal broken flesh and bone. We all have our limitations.

Demi stopped playing and stood, panting, as I lowered my mouth to Jeff's, and kissed him.

His eyes fluttered open, and he blinked at me, nonplussed. Belatedly, I remembered that my face wasn't my own, and that, from his perspective, he'd just been kissed by a stranger. That probably wasn't the best way to begin something like this. I opened my mouth to explain, and stopped as he raised his hand and pressed it, trembling, against my cheek.

"Henry," he said. "I was starting to be afraid I was never going to see you again. What took you so long? Where did you go?" Then he stopped me from answering his questions by leaning up and kissing me again, more fervently this time. His chest moved under my hand as he breathed. He was alive. He was *alive*, and he was going to *stay* that way.

When he pulled away, he grimaced and said, "I believe I've been shot."

I laughed. I couldn't help myself. He sounded so offended, like this was the last thing he'd been expecting from his day. "Yeah," I said. "Sorry about that. It was my gun, and my finger on the trigger."

"But you're not the one who pulled it," he said. He looked toward Demi, who was still holding her flute just below her mouth. "I'm assuming you're the one responsible for my miraculous survival? I was more than halfway dead, you know. There are goalposts between here and the afterlife, and I'd passed most of them."

"Yeah," she said. "That was me."

"Thank you," said Jeff solemnly.

Piotr and Agent Névé came jogging around the corner with two EMTs close behind. Demi hastily put her flute behind her back, as if she was afraid they would look at it and instantly intuit the entire purpose of the Bureau. Jeff looked at them and nodded cordially.

"Good afternoon," he said. "I seem to have been shot. Would one of you care to assist?"

There didn't seem to be anything to add to that. I kept my hands where they were and held my silence, waiting for the EMTs to tell me what to do.

# # #

If the EMTs were surprised by how little blood there was at the scene, they were too professional to say anything. Jeff bled some when I was instructed to move my hands, but not much; Demi's spell was holding. The EMTs got him bandaged up and loaded onto a stretcher, and he kissed me one last time before they carried him off to the ambulance and away from whatever might still be lurking in the maze.

My unfamiliar heart was pounding against my ribs as the reality of what had almost happened began sinking in. He could have *died*. He almost had. Another few minutes of disbelief on the part of any of the people who'd tried to deny my identity and I would have lost a team member and a friend. The fact that I loved him was almost irrelevant. It was my team that I'd promised to protect. It was as my teammate that I'd failed him.

A hand landed on my shoulder. I looked up to find Andy frowning down at me.

"You're short and you're not pointy enough, and I don't think I'll ever get used to hearing you give orders in that voice, but I believe you are who you are," he said.

I managed to muster a smile. It wasn't easy. "See, if you just believe me in all things, your life improves."

Andy snorted. "That's the attitude that got me in trouble with the chick who swiped your body. How the hell did she do that, anyway? Do we need to set up secret passwords or something?"

"That might not be a bad idea," I said. "As for how Adrianna stole me, that's a long story, and one I'd rather wait to go into until after we've managed to find Sloane. She's all alone out there. She needs us." It was odd to think about Sloane *needing* anyone, but if there was anything I'd learned from seeing the start of her story, it was that she wasn't as invulnerable as she seemed. She could be hurt. She could bleed. Maybe, if someone knew where to push, and pushed hard enough, she could even die.

"What do we do?" asked Demi. She was clutching her flute again, holding it like the security blanket it was. Without it, she could still do a lot of damage—a Piper can hum the rats back into Hamelin, if they really want to. But with it, she was unstoppable. There was a lot of comfort to be taken in that fact.

I stood up straighter, trying to match the height I'd lost when Adrianna took my body. "We find her. We don't split up—we never split up again, if we can help it—but we find her. Ciara, you're our expert on secrets. You find things people don't want you finding. Can you find us a door into the right part of this maze?"

"Me and doors, that's not always a safe combination," she said nervously. "One day, that's the thing that's going to get my head chopped off."

"Could be today," I said. "But if it's not, then today could be the day when you find Sloane and bring her home. Can you do it or not?"

Ciara looked at me for a long moment before she nodded. "I can," she said. "Just give me a second."

"Take all the time you need, as long as you don't need very much," I said.

"See, I knew Henry was weird after the coma," said Andy. "She wasn't nearly as bossy."

I glared at him. He grinned.

"Welcome back, boss," he said.

Ciara walked toward the nearest hedge wall. It wasn't purposeful; she swaggered, rather than striding, seeming to follow an irregular path that just happened to bring her up against the greenery. "Oh, hello," she said, reaching out to caress a leaf. "Aren't you beautiful? You know, I saw a hedge like you once. Green and fine and lovely. But that hedge had a secret door, so I suppose it was nicer than you are. Unless *you* have a secret door?"

The hedge shook like it was fighting against a stiff wind. Ciara laughed.

"You *do*, don't you?" she said, sounding delighted.

"Is she chatting up the hedge?" I asked, glancing to Andy. He didn't look disturbed. I shifted my attention to Piotr, who *did* look disturbed. Good. I wasn't the only one.

Agent Névé, on the other hand, seemed perfectly sanguine about the whole situation. "She does this," he said. "I watched her talk a manhole into opening once. It was amazing."

"If you didn't know she could do this, why did you *ask* her to do it?" asked Piotr.

"I thought she had some weird narrative connection to hidden doors, and could just wave her hand and have one open!" I said. "I've seen stranger things happen, especially since I fell into a magical, apple-induced coma and woke up a foot shorter and two cup sizes larger."

"Three, I'd say, but I take your point," said Piotr.

I folded my arms over my new breasts and glared at him before returning my attention to Ciara. She was still cooing sweet nothings at the hedge, which was enjoying the attention, if the rustling and slowly engulfing her hand was anything to go by. She smiled. The hedge pulled her a little closer—and then the hedge spread open like the mouth of some great beast, creating a tunnel where none had been before.

"I *knew* you could do it!" said Ciara, and kissed the foliage before stepping into the opening, gesturing for the rest of us to go with her.

"Your team is weirder than my team," said Piotr.

"We consider it a badge of honor," I said, and followed Ciara through the hedge. Andy and Demi were close behind, with Piotr and Agent Névé bringing up the rear. Jeff was safe with the EMTs, I was almost sure; Adrianna, wherever she was, wasn't the sort to come back and kill the wounded. Especially not when she thought she'd taken them out the first time.

The door in the hedge closed behind us, weaving shut and leaving no sign it had ever been there before. That wasn't the only change. The light seemed dimmer here, fragmented by unseen prisms, making the patterns of sun and shadow unpredictable. The walls were less well-trimmed, and twined and twisted around us in a mad array of looping branches and uncut thorns. Some of them were almost as long as my thumb, and looked wickedly sharp.

I stopped, motioning for the others to do the same. "Did we ever find Birdie and Elise?"

"No," said Ciara. "We got the Rapunzel back. We still don't know her name. But those two . . . we just don't know."

"Adrianna said she knew where they were, back when we thought she was you, and damn near got us all killed," said Andy. "In hindsight, that should have been a clue something was wrong."

"We're *so* getting secret passwords," I said, and pointed to the thorns. "Adrianna is a Snow White with access to both a Cinderella and a Storyteller archetype. Don't touch the thorns. There's no way of know-ing whether she has access to a Sleeping Beauty, or worse, a Wicked Fairy, and I don't have the time or the patience to wait for one of you to take a hundred year nap."

"You have the best assignments, Marchen," said Piotr. "Remind me never to accompany you on another."

"I didn't ask you to accompany me on this one," I said, looking down the long green corridor of the maze. Moving as a group would mean we covered less ground. Splitting the party would make it easier for Adrianna and her allies to ambush us. Sloane was in danger, but we weren't going to save her by acting like fools. "We stay together, we stay away from the walls, and if we see anything—*anything*—that doesn't look like Sloane, we take it out. Understood?"

"Understood," said Andy. The others nodded, nervous levity fading as we locked in on our new mission. We were in the maze. We were past the first hidden door. What came next was what mattered.

The smell of chlorophyll and wet grass accompanied us as we walked down the long corridor, watching for entries to the rest of the maze with every step we took. I was at the lead, my body tight and ner-vous as a cat about to bolt, my eyes scanning the shadows under the thorns for signs of ambush. Adrianna and I shared a story. If I could get close enough to her, I might be able to pick up on her presence before she had the chance to pick up on mine. After all, she didn't know that I was coming.

We moved through the shadows like ghosts, silent save for the faint crunch of Piotr's footsteps. I glanced down. The grass around his feet was covered with a thin layer of frost, and he was casting looks at Demi that were half longing and half terrified. She had a flute. She could call out his wolf if she wanted to. That fact that she'd never do it didn't matter.

The corridor ended at a wall of solid green. We all stopped. It was Andy who spoke first, turning to Ciara as he asked, "So, uh, can you

278 INDEXING: REFLECTIONS

flirt with the hedge some more and get us through to the next point-less green hallway?"

"No," she said. She looked perplexed. "The hedge let us in because this was where we needed to be. It was the *right* door. We should be where we need to be."

"We are," said Agent Névé, stepping forward. "Don't you see it?"

"See what, Carlos?" asked Ciara.

He shook his head. "There's a doorway right there. You can't see it?"

"No, this one's all you," said Andy.

Agent Névé sighed. "I hate this fucking mirror," he said, with sur-prising passion, before walking into the wall. Literally *into* the wall: as he stepped forward, he disappeared.

"Uh," said Demi. "Has anybody else here seen *Labyrinth*?"

"Honey, if you're telling me David Bowie is somewhere in this maze, I may forget that I'm a married man," said Andy, and followed Carlos into the wall.

That was the cue for the rest of us to begin going through, one at a time, until only I was left in the green corridor of thorns. I looked over my shoulder. There was no one there.

Ciara stuck her head back through the green hedge wall. "You com-ing?" she asked.

"I'm coming," I said, and followed her.

# # #

The maze seemed to go on forever—far longer than it should have, given the limited space behind the house where it grew. Even if Adrianna wasn't here, the narrative had clearly been hard at work, distorting dis-tance and twisting causality until it created a virtual labyrinth in what should have been a rich man's idle diversion. Demi's earlier question might have been asked in nervous jest, but it was impossible not to look at the unending walls around us and wonder if we really were on a path to the castle beyond the Goblin City. If so, I hoped that they would be friendly hosts, and wouldn't mind the fact that we hadn't brought them any babies.

Then we came around a corner in the maze, and suddenly we had much bigger things to worry about than David Bowie's hypothetical trousers. Like the wall of thorns that had sprouted to block our path, ripping through grass and hedge wall alike. Even that wasn't the biggest problem in front of us. No, that honor was reserved for Elise.

She was sitting on a pumpkin shell throne, held aloft by three loops of thorns, and she was smiling, her pretty pink lips curled upward in a perfect Cupid's-bow smirk. Her dress managed to look elegant and tattered at the same time, like the greatest fashion houses in the world had come together to make "shredded chic" the next big thing. She was even wearing glass slippers, clear enough to show the dirt on her heels and insteps. It was beautiful. It was terrible.

"Hello, everyone," she said, in a high, bright voice. "I was wondering when you'd come along."

Demi's hands clenched on her flute. "Where's Sloane?" she demanded.

That was almost more of a surprise than Elise's appearance. I wasn't used to Demi showing that much spirit. I liked it. I didn't say anything. If Adrianna didn't know I was back, Elise might not know either. We could use that.

"Do you mean my stepsister?" asked Elise, and smiled like a broken mirror, all jagged edges and distorted glee. She had shattered her own story and stitched it into a shape she liked better, and nothing would ever make it whole again. I felt bad for her, even as I feared what someone who'd broken so many of their own chains might be willing to do. "She's gone to have a chat with our dear Mother Goose, who can show her the error of her ways. She's played the lapdog for you people long enough. It's time for her to learn what an unshackled story can do."

"Well, she's telling the truth as she sees it," said Agent Névé. He sounded slightly baffled. I suppose meeting someone else's suite of enemies for the first time will do that. The Joker makes sense to Batman, but to anyone else, he's just a shouting man whose coloration bears an unfortunate resemblance to my own. Elise made sense to us. To anyone else . . .

"That's delightful," said Piotr. He raised his voice, calling, "Miss, if you would please come down from your, ah, throne of thorns, I'd like to arrest you now."

Elise blinked. "Excuse me?"

"The ATI Management Bureau gives me the authority to arrest anyone who knowingly and willfully uses narrative energy to distort reality," said Piotr. "You've transformed a perfectly normal hedge maze into a terrifying tunnel of thorns and impossible doors. You're thus clearly using narrative energy to distort reality, and are within my jurisdiction."

Elise blinked again, more slowly. She wasn't the only one. We all looked confused, to one degree or another. All except Piotr, who was watching her with perfect calm, waiting for her response.

"I'm not going to come down there and let you arrest me," she said finally. "I knew that working for the government makes you arrogant, but I didn't know it made you stupid."

"It doesn't," said Piotr. "But it does make us very, very good at obfuscation."

"Huh?" said Elise.

"He was distracting you," said Andy, as Piotr broke into a run, heading straight for the thorns.

He was halfway there when his body turned inside-out, flesh becoming fur, hands becoming paws, until a great gray wolf was running in his stead. Demi raised her flute, starting to play the high, sweet solo from *Peter and the Wolf.* She'd been a music major before we activated her story and recruited her into the Bureau. She could probably have played that part in her sleep.

Elise shrieked, surprised by the sudden appearance of an apex predator, and waved one hand in a throwing gesture. Shards of colorless glass flew from her fingertips, arcing toward Piotr, who was mid-leap and couldn't dodge them. Agent Névé whistled. The shards changed direction, flying toward him instead.

He grunted when they impacted with his chest. That was all: just grunted. I stared in horror as rivulets of glass began to spread out from the wound, turning glossy and bright. Elise was laughing in the background. Piotr was snarling, and Demi's flute was playing louder and louder, chasing the narrative of the boy and his wolf ever closer to its conclusion.

The glass stopped spreading. Elise stopped laughing. The glass began to retreat, replaced by soft fabric and, presumably, living flesh. At the last, the glass emerged from his chest and fell to the ground, where it dissolved. I gaped.

Agent Névé shrugged, looking faintly abashed. "I already belong to somebody else," he said. "I'm not afraid of glass anymore."

Elise screamed. I turned to see Piotr, still in wolf-form, pinning her to her pumpkin throne. He had one massive paw on each of her arms, holding them down so she couldn't fling any more glass at us, and he was snarling, his muzzle mere inches from her face.

For a moment, I thought about telling him to go ahead and eat her. It would make things so much easier on all of us if she was gone. Birdie could manipulate stories, but she'd never demonstrated the kind of direct physical power that we'd seen from Elise. Whether it was the breaking and re-forging that had made Elise as strong as she was, or just the fact that she was tapped into a huge, successful story didn't really matter. We needed her out of the way, and she'd already shown that we had no prison capable of holding her.

No prison, except for maybe the one that was designed for fairy-tale princesses. "Piotr, don't kill her," I said.

The wolf swung his head around and glared at me. I sighed.

"I know, I know, she tried to kill Carlos, and that's bad, but you don't want to be picking bits of soured Cinderella out of your teeth for the next week. You know how human flesh upsets your digestion." Piotr was good at controlling his wolf. He let it out to run on private estates, and he ate duck three times a week. But there had been incidents, always under circumstances where a police officer would have been able to plead "justified shooting." It was just that Piotr's justified shootings ended with his belly full of people who didn't know when to surrender.

"See, first Ciara negotiates with a hedge, and then you negotiate with a wolf," said Andy. He sounded almost philosophical. "I love this job."

"Best one in the world," said Ciara.

I walked toward the thorn wall, shrugging out of my jacket and wrapping it around my hand as I searched for a suitable thorn. Finally, I found what I wanted: a jagged spike easily a foot long, with a wickedly pointed tip. It took a little effort to break it free from the branch, but I persevered, wiggling it back and forth until it came loose in my hand. Then I turned and looked calmly at Elise.

Her eyes widened when she saw the thorn in my hand. "No!" she said, and began struggling against Piotr. His head snapped around, his nose almost brushing hers, and he snarled again. This time, it didn't seem to have much of an effect. She kept struggling, fighting to break free of his bulk. "No, no, no, you can't," she said. "You *wouldn't*. You're the *good* guys."

"People forget law enforcement is a narrative too," I said. "Bring her down here, Piotr. You don't need to be gentle about it."

Piotr stepped off Elise. She had time to push herself onto her elbows, a look of elation spreading across her face, before the great wolf grabbed the back of her neck in his powerful jaws and leapt down to the ground. She howled like she was a wolf herself as they descended, and there was a horrible crunching sound when her right wrist struck the earth. Piotr let her go. She didn't try to stand, just rolled onto her side and cradled her broken wrist against her chest.

"I think you can be a human again, Agent Remus," I said. "She's not going to run. She's lost."

"I won't tell you *anything*," gasped Elise, between wails.

"Why?" I asked. "Because you're afraid of Adrianna?"

Elise froze, her eyes going wide in her pain-pale face.

"We know," said Ciara, stepping up next to me. "We know everything."

Not everything, but there was no point in contradicting her. Not here, not now. Piotr stepped up on my other side, back in his funereal suit. The only sign of what he'd just done was his hair, which was disarrayed and rumpled in a way that was unusual for the normally meticulous field team leader. Andy, Demi, and Carlos hung back. Demi wasn't playing anymore, but her flute was held at the ready, just in case Elise forced her hand.

"You thought there'd just be three people left for you to take out, didn't you?" I asked. "Demi's dangerous, but Birdie got around her once before, so she's not going to seem like as much of a threat to you. You're wrong, by the way. Demi may be the scariest thing I've ever seen."

"Thanks, I think," said Demi.

"No one's sure what Ciara's capable of, and there's this amazing tendency to forget that Andy carries a gun," I continued, crouching down in front of Elise. Her eyes tracked the thorn in my hands the whole time. She hadn't recognized me. Maybe that shouldn't have been such a surprise. My own team hadn't realized that Adrianna was wearing my face, after all.

Still. We had her now. There was no reason to hide. I raised the thorn until it was level with my face, wiggling it a little to make sure I had her attention. Then I smiled my ghastly red smile, and said, "Hello, Elise. Did Adrianna tell you she killed me? Because she was lying, if she did. All she managed to do was piss me off."

She looked confused for a moment. Then her eyes widened in slow, terrible realization.

"No, that's not possible," she said. "Adrianna took your body. Hers is gone. Decades gone. There's no way you could have put it on."

"Bodies are sort of like dresses for Snow Whites, and it turns out we all wear the same size," I said. "I want my body back. That's the only thing keeping me from slamming this thorn into your heart. What did you tip it with? Glass? Poison? Or maybe just a nice long nap? That's the traditional thing, with thorns."

"I don't know I don't *know* Birdie said you'd be expecting glass, so she gave it to me in a vial and told me to pour it on the ground," moaned Elise. She tried to scramble backward, and stopped as her back ran into the solid wall of Andy's legs. We had her surrounded. No matter what she did from here, she'd be doing it as our prisoner. "Please, you have to believe me. I'm not a bad guy. I'm not a villain. I'm a *princess*."

"It's amazing how people think being born royalty means being born good," I said. "I'm a princess too, Elise, and so is Adrianna. *She's* not good. Currently, I'm not feeling too good either, since she stole my body, tried to kill my boyfriend, and abducted Sloane. So maybe you should lay off the claims to the throne and start telling us where we can find her."

"You don't understand," said Elise. She looked wildly around, stopping only when she realized she had no supporters. She turned back to me and said, in a pleading voice, "If I don't do what she tells me to do, she'll tell Mother Goose to push me back into the story I came from. Please. Don't let her send me back there."

"You murdered a whole lot of people trying to turn yourself into a Cinderella, and you've murdered even more since you succeeded," I said. Calmly, I reached out with my free hand, took hold of her broken wrist, and squeezed. Over her screams, I said, "Why would I help you get anything you want? You are exactly as useful to me as the information you give me."

"Henry . . ." said Andy, and stopped. I glanced at him. He shook his head. "Never mind. You do whatever you need to do to get her to tell you where that woman took Sloane. All of us will back your play."

"Whatever it is," said Ciara. She looked at Elise, calm as anything, and said, "HR is on your side. We understand that sometimes recalcitrant stories refuse to respond to modern methods."

I released Elise's wrist. "I'm not going to torture you," I said. "That would be pointless. Anything you said would be suspect, because you'd be trying to make us stop. Besides, we're better than that. That's why we're the good guys. Because we don't stoop to torture."

"Oh, thank God," whispered Elise.

"Instead, I'm going to make you an offer. Tell us where Adrianna took Sloane, and we'll take you into custody, return you to Childe Prison, and keep you locked up for the rest of your life, far outside her reach. Don't tell us, and we let you find out what kind of potion she gave you to put on these thorns." I waved the thorn I was holding under her nose, watching as her eyes tracked the motion. "Tick tock, Elise. It's almost midnight, and this is the story you wanted. That means you were always living your life on a deadline."

"I was supposed to get the prince," she said. Her voice was still barely above a whisper, still filled with confusion and regret, but it was weakening. She was going to break.

Thank Grimm. I wasn't sure I could have stabbed her with the thorn, even after what Adrianna had done to Jeff. Elise hadn't been the one to pull the trigger, and we were supposed to be the good guys. I was grateful that I had no such qualms about Adrianna. If I caught up to her, I would do whatever it took to make sure that she didn't hurt anyone else. Including killing her, if that was the only way.

Even if it meant killing my own body.

The realization was chilling. Killing Adrianna would be a form of suicide, at least right now: the core of who I was would survive, but the woman I'd been would be lost forever. What's worse, the body I was wearing had a family. The hospital she'd been in before I woke up wasn't cheap, and someone had to have been paying the bills. They'd find me eventually, and I would have to find a way to explain that I wasn't her, not really, and that I hadn't displaced her, because she'd already been gone, happily existing in a place after life but before death, where the snow never melted and the princes couldn't touch her. That wasn't a conversation I wanted to have. If I killed Adrianna, I might not have a choice.

"You have to go to the ball to get the prince, you know," said Ciara. "This isn't a ball. This isn't even a ballroom. This is a nasty-ass hedge maze in a residential neighborhood that probably violates six or seven zoning rules."

Andy gave her a flat look. "Your priorities are bizarre," he said.

Ciara sniffed, and said nothing.

I waved the thorn at Elise one more time. "Tick tock, Cinderella. Do you turn back into a pumpkin, or do you find a way to extend your story for another day? I'm out of patience, and you're out of time."

"Childe," she said.

I frowned. "What?"

"The Bureau used what Mother Goose called a 'beanstalk fold' to create Childe Prison and anchor it to this world, without letting it be a part of this world," said Elise. She was talking fast now, like her first word had been the cork holding the rest of them inside. That was fine by me. The faster we could get this finished, the faster we could go after Adrianna. "There's a big beanstalk there. You just can't see it."

"Agent Winters helped plant it, according to her file," said Ciara. "No one who wasn't there or in a supervisory role over one of the architects was supposed to know."

"I didn't know," I said. Ciara's HR clearance must have given her access to material about my team that even I didn't have. I didn't like that.

"I'm sorry," said Ciara—and to her credit, she did look faintly abashed. "It's why fairy-tale physics take precedence there. You're halfway out of the real world and halfway into a storybook."

"So where are the roots?" I turned back to Elise.

"Nowhere," she said. "They're in a place that isn't a place. But Adrianna, she found a way to pull us further down the fold. She's there. They're all there. In the fold."

"She built a secret lair *under* the maximum security prison?" I stared at Elise for a moment. She shied back, her eyes still on the thorn.

"She's not lying," said Agent Névé.

"So what do we do now?" asked Piotr.

There was only one answer. "You have a prisoner who needs to be delivered to Childe Prison," I said. "You're a field team leader. That means you have access. The rest of us will come with you, find our way to the beanstalk, and climb down to where Adrianna is hiding."

"Oh, that sounds like a piece of cake," said Andy. "Let's go."

I tossed the thorn—and my jacket—aside as I stood. "Yes," I said. "Let's."

# # #

In all my trips to Childe Prison, I'd always been the one behind the wheel. Making the journey as a passenger was different, and unsettling. I clung to the grip above my seat, wincing every time we hit a bump. Demi and Andy were crammed next to me; Piotr was driving, with Ciara in the passenger seat, while Agent Névé sat in the far back with Elise. She'd stopped talking when we crammed her into the van, perhaps realizing it was really over: she had really lost. Between Demi and Agent Névé, her glass-based tricks weren't going to do her any good, and she didn't have any other weapons. We had her. No matter what else happened today, we had her.

"Henry? You okay?" Andy sounded concerned.

I swallowed, trying to force my stomach down out of my throat. "Turns out tolerance for high speeds is a function of the flesh and not the mind. I feel like I'm going to hurl."

"Roll down the window if you're going to vomit in my car," snapped Piotr.

"Sloane would be laughing her ass off right about now," said Andy. "I just want to put that out there. This would be, bar none, the funniest thing she had ever seen."

"Let's hope she gets the chance," I said, and closed my eyes. It didn't help. The car was still moving at a ridiculous speed, jerking my body back and forth with every turn, and refusing to look at the road didn't mean that it wasn't there—

—until, of course, it wasn't. I felt, rather than saw, Piotr steer the vehicle off Dead Man's Curve, sending us hurtling off into empty air. I bore down harder on the grip, grinding my teeth to stop myself from screaming. It would damage my authority with my team. It would be showing weakness in front of the prisoner. Worst of all, I was fairly sure that once I started, I wouldn't be able to stop.

We slammed into the parking lot of Childe Prison like a brick slotting into a wall, rattling the entire vehicle. I opened my eyes and let go of the grip, reaching for the door handle in the same gesture. We needed to move. We needed to find Sloane, and we needed to do it fast. If we could get my body back at the same time, all the better. I was *not* looking forward to making the journey home in this borrowed skin.

"We'll deliver the prisoner," said Piotr. "Given your current lack of credentials, Agent Marchen, that might be the best way to avoid awkward questions."

"I understand," I said, and opened the door, sliding out onto the blacktop. Then I stopped, staring blankly at the gray stone building in front of me. It was so *drab*. Why, the people who lived there must have very small, sad lives, trapped in a place with no joy in its construction. I could make them feel better, I was sure. A few nice pies and maybe some new curtains for all those windows and they'd find their inner joy in just a heartbeat!

"Henry?" Andy sounded cautious, like he was afraid of my response. "Boss, are you all right?"

"Oh, I'm fine," I said, smiling as I turned to face him. "I'm finer than fine, if that's a thing that you can be. This place needs a lot of tender loving care, don't you think? A woman's touch is just the thing to make any man's fortress into a proper castle."

"She doesn't have her countercharm anymore," whispered Demi, sounding horrified. "It was with her body. That's how Adrianna could come so close to this place and not get all fuzzy and weird. She had the charm."

"And Henry doesn't," said Ciara. "Aw, hell."

"So what do we do?" asked Andy.

"You turn that frown upside-down, mister," I said, smiling brightly. "I'm sure we can find you a princess to keep you warm and make you happy. What about her?" I pointed to Elise. "She's lovely, isn't she?"

"I think I get in trouble if I stuff the boss in the trunk," said Andy, sounding alarmed. "A little help here?"

"Do *not* let me go back to the real world, do you understand?" said Ciara, beginning to dig through her purse. "I may beg. I may command. But don't let me do it, no matter what I threaten or promise. It's not safe."

"What do you mean?" asked Andy.

"Ciara . . . ?" said Agent Névé. He seemed to understand what she was doing.

I didn't. Not until she slid out of the car, smiled at me, and said, "You dropped this." She held out her hand, and I automatically took what she was offering me: a crystal spire that glowed from within with a bright, oddly colorless light.

The overlay of innocent, eager-to-please princess dropped away, and I was myself again—myself in someone else's body, but still, myself. I didn't want to cook. I didn't want to clean. I wanted to punch Adrianna in the face until my knuckles bled, and forget the part where the face belonged to me. I could pay for any dental work my body needed after I got it back. I gasped. I couldn't help myself.

"I hate this case," I muttered.

Ciara blinked at me, looking confused. Then she turned, still smiling, to Piotr. "Can you take me home, please? This isn't my team, and it isn't my prisoner, and my husband expects me before seven. It's a little agreement we have."

"What, so you can open the forbidden door and get yourself chopped into firewood? I'm sorry, Agent Bloomfield, but that's not going to happen today. Maybe you can cajole your husband into homicide later. Today, you're going to sit in a nice warm office and do paperwork." Piotr got out of the car. "I'll take Elise in and be right back. Agent Névé can stay here to make sure Agent Bloomfield keeps out of trouble."

"Actually, I want him," I said, startling both Piotr and Agent Névé, who was in the process of hauling Elise out of the car. Both of them turned to look at me. I shook my head. "Your wolf is close to the surface right now, Piotr. Adrianna is a fully active Snow White in a world that obeys fairy-tale logic. You'll be her slave in a second."

"You can command me first," said Piotr.

I shook my head. "It doesn't work that way. She's been a part of the story longer than I have. She's stronger than I am. If I take you to her, she *will* take you from me, and I have too much respect for your abilities to let you be used as a weapon."

"I can go, sir," said Agent Névé. "I would be happy to."

"It's a good team," I said. "I have Demi and her flute; I have Andy and his relative resistance to the narrative. I'm not going to get your agent hurt, Piotr."

"It's not my agent I'm worried about," said Piotr. "You need more manpower than you have."

"We have no time, and we have three individuals with active narratives on our side," I said. "Have a little faith, all right? We can do this. I've defeated Adrianna once before."

"Judging by the face you're wearing right now, she's also defeated you," he said. "That doesn't sound like an easy win to me."

"We're tied right now, but she's about to learn that you shouldn't fuck with a fairy-tale princess who still has something left to lose." I lifted my chin. "We'll see you soon. Keep Ciara out of trouble. Agent Névé?"

He jumped before turning to face me. "Ma'am?"

"You see what's real instead of seeing what's not. Find me that beanstalk."

"Yes, ma'am." He pushed Elise toward Piotr, who took her unbroken wrist and pulled her away. Then he removed his sunglasses, blinking in the sunlight for a moment before he turned to scan the horizon.

Childe Prison stood in the middle of what looked like an impossibly vast forest—a fairy-tale forest, in other words, the sort of place where foxes spoke in riddles and the sun sometimes set early because it wanted to. No matter how many times the guards tried to map the woods, they always failed, because the woods didn't want to be mapped. They wanted to be dark, and tangled, and twisted, and unknowable. They had a vested interest in their own impenetrability.

"There," he said, pointing to a patch of wood that looked no different than any of the wood around it. The trees there grew thick and close together. If it was possible for foliage to seem unfriendly, this foliage did. It was almost enough to make me miss the hedge maze. "That's where they planted the beanstalk."

"Are you sure?" I asked.

"I'm sure," he said. "I can see it." The words sounded pained. He didn't like admitting what he saw, that much was clear, and I couldn't blame him. Seeing all the world's secrets might sound like fun at first, but the excitement would wear off quickly, replaced by the crushing realization of just how much everyone, even the people we loved best in all the world, lied.

"Then let's go," I said, and started walking. I didn't look back. Piotr would have more arguments; Ciara might try to convince me to take her with us; or worse, she might decide to take her blocking charm back. I needed my mind as clear as possible. I needed to be myself, Henrietta Marchen, and not whatever pale fairy-tale princess this place wanted me to be.

It was interesting, in a way. In the whiteout wood, the Snow White story was infinitely complex, a canvas defined only by a shared color and a sketchy common narrative. We would all eat the apple; we would all find ourselves in coffins made of glass. It was the space between those events that mattered, defining us in ways we couldn't explain, but lived through every day. Here, in what should have been the real world, the story had been simplified and candy-coated until the presence of Childe's wards reduced me to a simpering parody of a woman I'd never been. It was a kind of torture, and not a productive one. If I spent enough time in the presence of that field, with my soul rebelling against the story being forced on me, I would probably go either mad, bad, or both. It explained a lot about Adrianna and Elise. What it didn't explain was how people like them weren't more common.

We had hundreds of fairy-tale figures locked up, exposed to incredible pressure. It was only a matter of time before they started to shatter, and then we were going to have a lot more Elises on our hands. I made a quiet pledge to talk to the deputy director when this was over. If that didn't change things, I would talk to his superiors, and to their superiors, until I'd gone all the way to the top of the food chain.

The image of the president of the United States signing a bill forbidding narrative conditioning of detained individuals suffering from memetic infection was almost funny enough to make me crack a smile. Only almost. I kept walking, and my team walked with me, and as we passed the first trees, I couldn't help feeling like we were also passing out of safety and into story. The only question now was whether we would be able to find our way back again.

# # #

Agent Névé—Carlos, now that he was a member of my team, however temporary his assignment might be—led with calm confidence, walking straight toward something only he could see. The rest of us followed. Demi kept her flute raised, playing quick trills every time the underbrush grew too thick. It pulled back with surprising alacrity, leading me to glance at her and wonder if she even understood how strong she was becoming. We were in a story now. She could pipe the wings off a butterfly if she wanted to.

I hoped she wouldn't decide she wanted to. I hoped this wasn't going to be too much of a temptation. And I wondered, with sudden guilt, whether she could pipe the mirror out of Carlos's eye. She could free him from his gift, relieve him of his curse, and let him go back to working a desk job for HR, if that was what he wanted. It would be a wonderful relief for him, and I couldn't mention it until we'd done what we were here to do. I needed his sight.

It was suddenly, dismayingly easy to see how people like Birdie started down their own slippery slopes. Carlos had a gift that hurt him. I had a solution, but I needed his gift more than I needed his peace of mind. So I wasn't saying anything.

"Demi might be able to pipe the mirror out of your eye," I blurted. I wasn't going to be like them, I *wasn't*, and if that meant losing a weapon, so be it.

Carlos looked back over his shoulder, blinking at me in surprise. His gaze flicked to Demi. "Do you really think so?" he asked.

"It's worth a shot."

"Then we'll try it. After this is done." We had reached a clearing. Instead of walking forward, he reached out into the seemingly empty air.

It was like watching a chain reaction. His palm pressed flat against the beanstalk, and it appeared, stretching up and down for the better part of forever. It was infinite. It was Yggdrasil, the World Tree, and it had always existed, and it would exist when all of us were gone. Demi gasped. Andy whistled. I took a deep breath.

"All right," I said. "Let's go catch ourselves a traitor."

Carlos helped me get a good grip on the beanstalk. I reached down with one foot, and was somehow unsurprised when it passed through the seemingly-solid ground like it was a cloud. I nodded, once, and began to climb carefully downward. It was time for us to bring this story to a close, no matter how difficult that seemed.

The four of us made our descent through the world we'd known and into the world unknowable, and all I could do was hope we'd all be coming back.

Never After

Memetic incursion in progress: estimated tale type unknown
Status: ACTIVE

Sloane's eyelids fluttered, her mind resisting the siren-song of wakefulness. With waking would come awareness of her situation, and if there was one thing she didn't need right now, it was to be reminded how bad things were. Alas, no one can sleep forever, no matter how much they want to. Her eyes opened. She focused on the ceiling, which was far closer than she'd expected, before sitting up in the bed and swinging her legs over the side.

The drop that followed was equally unexpected. She hit the straw-covered ground with a loud "thump," and rolled onto her back to stare at the pile of mattresses—at least ten—where she'd been sleeping. "What the fucking fuck?" she demanded. The bed didn't answer.

At least the straw covering the floor had broken her fall and kept her from breaking her tailbone, although the straw represented another kind of challenge. It slipped and slid under her hands when she tried to push herself to her feet, until she finally grabbed the mattresses and hauled herself upright. Her velvet gown swished around her legs as she stood. It was a dress fit for a princess, and she glared at it hatefully. This wasn't her story. It never had been.

"Let's see," she said. "I've got the Princess and the Pea—nice one, make someone royal with no requirements other than insomnia and a skin condition—and there's straw everywhere, so I'm assuming there's a spinning wheel. Make someone royal for agreeing to sell their baby, which seems sort of crappy to me, but who am I to judge? I'm just the girl you have *locked up* against her will." She turned to survey the rest of the room. There was a vase full of red roses; a mechanical nightingale in a cage, waiting to be wound; a pile of nettles and carding equipment, to render them into fiber. The expected spinning wheel was near the fireplace, which was empty of all but ashes. The sight of it made her wince.

There was a jar of lentils sitting nearby, waiting to be dropped. That made it worse.

The room had windows, too high to reach without building some sort of ladder, but no door. She finished her first survey and began a second, slower. This time, when she reached the fireplace, there was a rocking chair, and in the rocking chair was a woman with thick glasses and a cloud of curly blonde hair. She was wearing a shawl and a button cap, both of which would have been more suited to someone twice her age, and she had an outsized storybook propped open on her lap. She smiled when she saw Sloane looking at her.

"Hello, dear," said Birdie Hubbard—Mother Goose. That was the role she'd chosen when she turned against the Bureau, a role she had only reinforced by breaking out of Childe Prison at her first opportunity. "I've been waiting for you to wake up. It's time for us to have a talk about your story, don't you think?"

Sloane didn't say anything. Birdie's smile widened, turning cruel.

The screaming started shortly after.

# # #

The beanstalk looked like it should have been slick, but looks, here as everywhere, were deceiving. It had the texture of thick rope, easy to dig our fingers into and grip as we descended through the layers of earth and cloud into the void below. I was grateful for the twist of fairy-tale logic that said beanstalks, like towers or braids, existed primarily for the sake of being climbed. Without it, we would have needed to go back for specialized equipment before we could attempt what we were doing now.

Of the four of us, my new body had the least upper body strength. Demi was climbing with her flute clenched in her teeth, to reduce the risk of dropping it, while Andy and Carlos took the descent like it was nothing. My shoulders were on fire, my arms trembling as I struggled to remain stable. Long comas don't do much for muscle tone, as it turns out, and when I'd jumped into the nearest available Snow White, I hadn't been able to select for physical condition.

My fingers slipped. It was a small thing, but enough to cause me to lose my grip and tumble backward, scrambling for purchase. Then I was dropping like a stone into the abyss, falling, falling—

—until Andy grabbed the collar of my shirt. It was such an abrupt stop that it knocked the wind out of me, and I hung in his grip, gasping for air. He looked at me sympathetically, waiting for me to start breathing again before he said, "Why don't you ride down on my back? We need you in one piece if we want this to work. None of the rest of us can face this Adrianna chick on her own ground."

"You need to focus on your own climb," I said.

His expression sobered further. "Henry, if you think I can focus on myself when I'm watching you struggle, you've got some really strange, really wrong ideas about me. Now get on my back. I'll get you down there safely."

"Thanks, Andy," I said, not bothering to conceal my relief. He nudged me closer to the beanstalk. I grabbed back on and, from there, climbed to hang, piggyback-style, from his shoulders. I was short enough that I couldn't get my legs comfortably around his chest, and had to settle for digging my knees into his ribs. Andy snorted in evident amusement and resumed his descent, catching up with Demi and Carlos, who had continued to climb after they were sure I wasn't going to fall to my death.

Riding rather than climbing gave me the opportunity to look around. We were passing through a void. It looked like clouds if I didn't focus on it too hard, but looking directly into the blank whiteness of it all made it quickly clear that there were no clouds here: there was no sky to support them, and no water to form them. This was *nothingness*, and the only reason we could breathe was because the narrative had been largely formed before people understood what oxygen was. You could drown in a fairy tale, sure, but you could also ride a jumping cow all the way to the moon and never have a problem catching your breath. In another hundred years, journeys like this might require SCUBA gear and oxygen tanks. Or maybe not. It was always difficult to tell what the story would seize on, and suffocating all the heroes mid-journey might not be a useful tool.

"How far do we have to go?" I called, toward Carlos.

"Not far now!" he called back. "We're almost there!"

"Thank Grimm," muttered Andy.

I smiled a little. "Sorry to make this harder on you."

"You weigh, like, nothing, Henry. Make me do this again when you have your real body back, and then we'll talk about hazard pay." Andy continued climbing.

The air shimmered around us, becoming thick with the distinct smell of impending snowfall. My head spun. Snow was my time, my place, and I wanted it more than anything. The whiteout wood was my destiny, and I could create it here, if I wanted to; I could pull it into the waking world and have it for my own. All I had to do was open my hands and my heart, and let the winter in. I shook my head fiercely, trying to push the impulse aside.

"We're close," I said, closing my eyes. I didn't want to see that shimmer in the air. It looked too much like the aurora borealis, and it spoke to me in a language I'd always known but never learned to understand. If I listened too long, I *would* learn, and then the world would change again. Not in a good way.

"No, we're not," said Andy. His shoulders flexed beneath my arms as he let go of the beanstalk. My eyes snapped open, adrenaline lashing through me as I prepared to panic.

He was standing on a smooth expanse of green grass. Carlos and Demi were nearby. Rolling hills stretched off into the distance, dotted with pastel castles too perfect to be real. Birds sang in the distance. Everything still smelled of snow, but there were no signs of winter here; this was perfect, eternal springtime.

"We're here," said Andy.

Demi looked around critically before saying what we were all thinking: "This is so not what I was expecting. It's so . . . cute. Are there unicorns frolicking nearby? Because there should be unicorns."

Carlos turned and stared at her. "What are you talking about?"

"Hold on." I put up a hand. "Carlos, why don't you tell us what you see right now?"

"We're standing in the middle of a field of dead grass and brambles," he said. "There are trees on all sides, but they're either dead or close to it. Their branches look like hands, reaching for us. The sky is the color of a fish's belly, all gray and sickly. Can't you feel the cold? You're standing in snow up to your ankles. You should be able to feel the cold, even if you can't see the snow."

"Can you bend down and pick some of it up, please?"

Carlos stooped and filled his hands with something my eyes refused to focus on. I could tell that they weren't empty: I couldn't, for the life of me, tell what he was holding. I held my hands out.

"Please," I said.

"This is strange, even for me," said Carlos, and filled my hands with snow.

I saw it before I felt it, white and cold and undeniable. I turned to look at Andy and Demi. Both of them were staring at the contents of my hands, eyes wide and bewildered. Good. That meant it was a fairly straightforward masking spell, and not something we were going to need to break for each of us individually.

"Adrianna's getting scary strong if she can hide this whole place from us," I said, focusing on the snow. "She's still a Snow White, though."

"Are you sure?" asked Demi. "If Birdie is changing the way peoples' stories work, Adrianna could be anything by now."

"I am, because Adrianna's still in my body," I said. "She was able to take it because we're both Snow Whites. If she'd changed her story that much, she would have lost her hold over my body. Either I would've been pulled back into it, or it would have fallen into a coma, but either way, she wouldn't be a problem anymore. She's still a problem, so she's still a Snow White." And she wouldn't give that up easily either, not even for more power; I knew that, as sure as I knew we still shared a story. Her sister had been a Rose Red. She was a Snow White. It was as simple as that, at least for her.

"So, what, do we follow Carlos through the place and hope he doesn't walk us into any evil trees?" asked Andy.

I hesitated. I knew Adrianna was here: I could feel her in the icy air, and in the snow I held. It wasn't melting. The odds were good she knew I was here too; there was no element of surprise between members of the same story. "I can try something, but if she doesn't know we're here yet, it *will* give us away."

"Try," said Andy. His tone was gentle, almost reflective. I shot him a surprised look, and he shrugged. "I don't have a story to run toward, you know? Out of all of us, I'm the one who maybe didn't have to be here. I mean, I don't want to go job-hunting right now or anything, but if I went to the Bureau and said I wanted a desk job, no more frontline fairy tales, they'd give it to me. Because they know this isn't my fight. And if I could, right now, I'd grab hold of my ever after and squeeze it until it bled. We're talking about saving Sloane. She's our friend. She'd never admit it, but she cares about us. If there's something you can do, you need to do it."

"All right," I said, and focused on the snow.

There are lots of stories about snow. Match Girls freeze in it. Snow Queens create and manipulate it. Sisters who speak in jewels search through it for strawberries, and sisters who speak in toads freeze their toes off on their way to the witch's cabin. Snow is one of those images that shows up again and again, universal and eternal. But the Snow White story, *my* story, is not about snow. It *is* snow. It is the story of all those girls who walked into winter not knowing if they'd come out the other side. We are the point between Persephone and Pandora, and ours is the frost and the frozen world that never, never thaws.

I looked at the snow in my hands. Felt the weight of it, traced the edges of the tiny snowflakes that clung to my fingers without melting. I'd always had cold hands, ever since I was a little girl, but this was a step past "cold," moving into "frozen solid." I was still flesh and bone. My heart was beating too fast. The snow didn't care. It knew me as its own, and it would not hurt me. I just had to hope it liked me better than it liked Adrianna.

"Can you do this for me?" I asked, and when the snow whispered wordless assent I threw it into the air and watched as it caught the wind. For a moment it hung there, suspended, creating a frozen prism around us. Then it swirled away, gathering mass and momentum as it picked up more and more snow from the frozen ground. Everywhere it touched the illusion was stripped away, replaced by the blighted reality of Adrianna's bolt hole.

"I think I liked it better before," said Demi in a small voice, looking around us. She tightened her grip on her flute. "Would it help if I piped away the snow?"

"It might weaken Adrianna," I said. "It would definitely weaken me. Leave the snow for now. Be ready to remove it if you need to." I turned, looking around this new landscape.

For the most part, it was as Carlos had described. There was a castle on the far hill, built of gray stone and blue slate, with towers so tall that they couldn't have served any useful purpose; even lookouts wouldn't want to be that far off the ground. Their bases were too narrow. They looked like they'd collapse if someone breathed on them too hard. It was a fairy tale made concrete reality, and it was where we needed to go.

"Come on," I said. "Adrianna's waiting."

We began wading through the snow, toward the distant stronghold where one of these stories was going to end. I only hoped it wasn't going to be mine.

# # #

"Do you feel like talking yet, dear, or should I get the nettles?" Birdie leaned close, putting her eyes on a level with Sloane's. Sloane turned her face away. Birdie sighed. "This isn't how a princess behaves, you know. This isn't regal or royal or even in the least bit charitable of you. I'm offering you your heart's one true desire. Shouldn't you listen to me?"

"I don't want anything you have to offer me," said Sloane. Her voice came out thick and red. She coughed. Bloody bubbles formed at the corners of her lips. "I'm not your toy."

"Not mine, dear, no. You belong to the story. The story's been trying to get its hands on you for a long, long time. It's offered you so many openings, and you've refused them all! I'm sure that seemed like strength at first, but there's a point past which it becomes nothing but rudeness. You need to be kind to the hand that feeds you. Otherwise, it may turn into a fist."

Sloane glared, mute hatred radiating from her eyes. Birdie laughed, apparently delighted.

"You can despise me, if you like. Loathing is a powerful force, especially since I'm one of the heroes of the piece. I'm Mother Goose. If you hate me, if you want me dead, you must be a villain. We could write you into a better role, my love. Something truly terrible. Put your poisons and your knives aside, and learn how to be the killer you were always born to be."

Sloane closed her eyes.

"I wish you wouldn't be like that."

Sloane didn't say anything.

"You don't *have* to be a villain. Only talk to me, tell me what you want, let me spin you a story you can be proud of, and the world is yours. We'd rather have you on our side than against us, Sloane. You have no idea how much potential you have. How much stronger you could be, with the right story at your back."

Birdie stroked Sloane's cheek. Sloane shuddered. Birdie didn't pull away.

"I won't promise you anything I can't deliver. I couldn't make you a mermaid if I wanted to, my darling, or turn your skin as white as snow. You can't be a sister-story, because your sisters have been dead so long that their graves hold only dust and memory. But I could make a monster out of you, set you in a remote castle, and let you wait for your Beauty to come along. I could give you clever hands and a clever mouth—cleverer, really, you've never been a slow student—and a candle to light your way, change your name to 'Jack,' and give you the world to roam. There are so many *options*! You still look young enough to be someone's stepdaughter if you wanted a Cinderella story all your own, or there's the poisoned thorn and the long, sweet sleep before the happy ending . . . I'd prefer you not choose that one. We want you to join us, and sleeping people are so dull, don't you think? Much more fun when you're awake, and primed to kill to keep the story you've been given."

"I like the story I have," whispered Sloane, voice still thick, now with longing as much as misery.

Birdie smiled. "Ah, but my little breadcrumb, my little crumpet, if you liked the story you have, you wouldn't still be talking to me, now would you? I think it's time we dug a little deeper into your narrative."

The screaming began again, higher and shriller than before. And like before, it seemed to last a long, long time.

# # #

We trudged through the snow in a loose diamond. I was at the front of the group, purely because I was the only one who wasn't slowed down by our environment: while I couldn't quite walk on top of the snow, it seemed to shift out of my way as much as possible, making the trek feel more like a light stroll. Demi and Carlos flanked me, him with his eyes fixed on the castle, her occasionally playing quick trills on her flute to clear the way a little more. I considered asking her to stop, and decided there was no point. Adrianna knew I was here. A little light musical accompaniment wasn't going to give away anything she couldn't figure out on her own.

Andy brought up the rear. He was shivering near-constantly. I cast a nervous glance back at him.

"You okay?"

"Just cold," he said, shaking his head. "Didn't dress for an unplanned trip to the land of frozen shit."

"We'll start keeping warm socks and heavy coats in the car after this," I promised. "Live and learn, right?"

Andy managed to crack a smile. "I think the key word there is 'live.' Let's manage that part first, okay?"

"You got it," I said, and turned to face forward, focusing on where I was putting my feet. The castle still seemed impossibly far away. I cast a glance at Carlos. "Am I missing something?"

"No," he said. "It's not getting any closer."

"Well, why the hell not?"

"Because it doesn't want to."

I groaned. "Sometimes I hate living in a world where masonry gets to have opinions. Demi? Can you change a castle's mind?"

"No," she said, after a moment's contemplation. "I can't pipe away the distance either. Distance is . . . it's an idea, not a thing."

"Delighted as I would otherwise be to hear that you have limits, this is a problem," I said, and stopped walking. The others did the same. I eyed the castle. "Any thoughts on why the castle isn't getting closer?"

"You've been fighting your story from day one, even when you embraced it," said Andy slowly. "Doesn't that normally come with an element of narrative rejection?"

I hesitated before pulling the crystal Ciara had given me out of my pocket. It was still glowing. There was still something here for it to fight. If I let it go, my story might get stronger, and the castle, which was a Snow White's stronghold, might stop keeping us out.

"Adrianna is a Snow White too," I said, watching the stone sparkle and gleam in my hand. "She's not a fuzzy little fluff-brain who just wants to wash underwear and sing with bunnies. She's managed to hold on to herself. She's tapped into the monomyth. But how?" Beneath the dizzy Disney girls were the girls who bled out in snowy fields, who opened their eyes in a world gone black and white and red, that would never see spring, never see harvest, never thaw. They came first, those girls, when "Snow White" was another word for "sacrifice," and "fairest in the land" was the phrase spoken to grieving parents who needed to know that their daughters hadn't died in vain.

"Hold this," I said, and handed the crystal to Carlos.

The story slammed into me as soon as I pulled my hand away, driving me to my knees in the snow, which caught me and kept me from hurting myself. This wasn't like eating the apple: That had been ripping away a scab and exposing the unhealed wound beneath. This was like cutting into the flesh of that wound, opening it wide to let the pus drain out.

I could hear voices in the snow. And yes, they spoke of hearth and home and service to others. But what I did for the Bureau was a form of service, wasn't it? Maybe I didn't wash windows, but I saved lives, and that wasn't "just as good." That was *better*. I was *better* for my story because of what I did.

The knife cut deeper. Distantly, I heard Demi saying, "She's bleeding!"

"Blood on the snow is important for her," said Carlos. "Don't touch her."

I was bleeding? I forced my eyes open and saw the blood dripping into the snow in front of me. I raised one hand and touched my lip, finding it hot and sticky. "Oh," I whispered, and closed my eyes, and pitched forward into the cold whiteness that was the entire world.

# # #

You've fought me for a long time. I do not see why I should help you now.

The voice of the story was ice and apples, the black brushstroke of a raven's wings across a winter moon. It was as cold and unforgiving as the frost, and the only things I knew about it with any certainty were that it loved me, and that it would kill me if it could. Those things weren't a contradiction, not really: The story of blood on the snow has always been a story of sacrifice. For her to love me, she had to be willing to kill me. Anything else would show that her heart was untrue.

I was standing in the middle of a frozen field. My dress was the color of dried blood, made of a material that felt as light as gossamer, but hung around me like samite and velvet. I didn't think about it too hard. Sometimes the only way to handle fairy-tale logic is to ignore it.

"You should help me because she's going to twist the story if you let her," I said. "If she wins, she's going to turn the name 'Snow White' into something that children are afraid of and parents don't dare speak. How much power will you have when no one tells you? How many of the forgotten stories are still able to reach the waking world the way you do?"

She is just one paragraph. I am the page. I am the chapter and the verse.

"A line—a word—can change the meaning of an entire book. Biblical scholars live and die debating over *commas*. You want to tell me a paragraph can't distort you? Rewrite you? Because I always knew you were dishonest, but I never took you for a liar."

The story swirled around me, black and white at the same time, an eclipse in motion. It was the snow and the storm, the feather and the fall, and it was beautiful, and it was terrible, and I wasn't sure I'd be making it back into the waking world alive.

You were a rare gem to me, a fallen apple that rolled from one orchard to another. You should have grown in my sister-soil, a Snow White beside her Rose Red, and never come to the blood or the snow or the apple's sweet perfume.

"But I did." The Snow White archetype who stood with her sister against the world wasn't defined by appearance the way the Snow White who stood alone was. I shouldn't have been born bone and coal and rubies; I should have been a normal little girl, maybe a little pale, but still allowed to look like everybody else. "Why? Why me, and why Adrianna?"

We are not paragraphs, to be bound by short phrases and shorter lives. We see the shape of the story. Neither of you walked from one end to the other in the company of your shadow-self. Hers left her; yours was never what the first story wanted him to be.

It was comforting, in a way, that my narrative didn't misgender my brother. It was also telling. Snow White and Rose Red had to be the same gender, or at least had to be able to fall in love with the same handsome prince. Had Gerry been gay, we might have stayed with our initial narrative, which had probably claimed us at conception. Sometime between then and birth, the forces that drove our lives had realized Gerry was a boy, and everything had gone strange.

I don't blame you, brother, but oh, sometimes I envy the life we might have had, I thought, and said, "So Adrianna and I are the same. We're both aberrations."

Yes.

"And that's why I have to be the one who stops her."

Yes.

"So why won't you help me?"

The swirling storm around me seemed to slow and still for a moment. Then, without changing in the least, it became a woman. There was no contradiction in the fact that she had been mist and darkness a moment before: she was here now, she had always been here, and when she went away again, she would never have been here at all. I knew all those things, even as I knew who she was, even though she didn't look at all like she should have. She was too young, for one thing, fifteen at most, with a child's half-formed figure under her rough, homespun clothes. Her skin was pale, but it was nowhere near as white as snow. Her hair was dark brown, not black, and while her lips were very pink, they weren't as red as blood.

"Because no one helped me," she said. "No one even knows for sure whether or not I existed. I don't remember anymore. I could be a fiction about a fantasy about a fairy tale, the pretty village girl who caught the eye of a nobleman and enraged his mother, for how dare I be so beautiful when her own beauty had been spoiled by the pox? So she sent her men to take me to the forest when it was time to call the sun back into the sky, and I brought an end to winter, and I never saw the spring. That was where the red and white began. With blood on the snow."

"I know," I said softly.

She tilted her head, looking at me as her skin paled. Not all the way, but enough to bring her closer to the arctic creature she would one day become. "Do you really? You haven't bled out yet, not for me, not for anyone. Not even to prevent the winter from lasting forever. You'll have to, if you continue in the way you have been. That's what happens to girls like us, when we refuse the narrative the world would lay upon our shoulders."

"You're the one who decided what my story was going to be," I said. "You're the one who has to help me now."

"Do I?" She smiled. It was terrible, and beautiful, like an apple filled with worms. "I don't think that's in the story. And no one helped me. They say I was a king's daughter, that he never let me walk outside, because he was afraid I would die the way my mother had. Maybe if I'd seen the sun, I might have learned that beautiful things could be cruel. It would have burned my skin and taught me caution. But he kept the curtains drawn, and when he took a new wife who saw me as the reflection of the youth she'd lost, I saw her only as a new mother, someone who would love my father after I was married to another man. She sent me to the woods with her favorite servant. He cut me open and brought her my heart and lungs, as proof of what he'd done. It would be a hundred years or more before he let me go. A hundred years of my story playing out, warning little girls not to trust the women who came into their homes with ice in their eyes. I was the first to fear her stepmother in the night. All the others came later, when those clever boys wrote their stories down wrong."

"I don't have time—"

"You have as much time as I give you, Henrietta Marchen. You have all the time in the world." Her clothing was changing, becoming finer, shifting through the centuries as she began to walk a slow circle around me. I recognized none of the fashions my story wore. They were all older than anything I had reason to know. "My mother sat by the window, mending my father's cloak, because that was a thing queens did, then: they worked, they ran the household, they had calluses on their fingers and blisters on their toes. She sat by the window, and when she pricked her finger on the needle she remembered the stories about blood on the snow, about the girls who went into the woods to summon back the sun. She promised me to the altar and the blade before I was even born, if only her lord would come back from the war. She put the knife to my throat herself, and there was no contradiction between her and the interloper with the broken reflections in her heart. Mother, stepmother, it didn't matter. As long as I went to the wood, it didn't matter." Red began blossoming over her lips, turning them the color of fresh arterial blood. "It would be a long time before people agreed on why I had to die. Sacrifice or slaughtered lamb, the result was always the same. That's the thing about being destined to become a beautiful corpse. No one ever looks too hard at how you wound up that way."

"My friends need me."

"Your story needs you. Your story has always needed you." Her hair was darker now. One inch at a time, she was slipping toward the archetype she had always been. Something told me I didn't have much longer to argue with her: that when she was done remaking herself in her own image, she would shed her girl-skin and return to the wind. "My dwarves came later. The apple, the girdle, the coffin of glass, those were all added when no one could remember the child in the village, the one who never hurt anyone. *She* deserved a happy ending more than the princess they made me out to be did, and yet she never had one. *I* never had one. Not until I left her so far behind as to never have existed in the first place."

"The story changes." I paused. "The story *changes*. You were the first of us, you started the archetype, and when the monomyth wouldn't let you go, people kept on changing the way they told the story, because— because they'd seen you? Because they'd known you? Every Snow White had her own name once."

"They didn't call me that for centuries, not until I'd split off from the narrative that claimed me and become a story all on my own," she said. "I was more flexible then. I changed more quickly, because there was less weight behind me."

"You were a paragraph," I said. "You were what Adrianna is now. Don't you see how easy it would be to let her make you into a villain? All these girls you've been before, the village girl and the princess and the tithe, none of them would matter, because there's no coming back. Once people see you as the bad guy, you don't get to be good again, no matter how much good you do. No matter how hard you try. Human hearts don't forgive that easily."

She smiled, and her lips were red and her skin was white and her hair was as black as a raven's wing. She was a village girl and a princess and a sacrifice and a resurrection of the spring, all in the same body, and I had never seen anything so beautiful, or so terrifying, in my life. "She can change me. That much is true. But so, my windfall apple, can you. You can shift the boundaries, just a little. Just enough. We want to be free of what we've become. The glass coffin is too small. We need something larger. Something where we can be a heroine, and not just a prize to be won. Fight back."

"Help me," I countered. "Offer the hand that no one offered to you, and *help* me. Let me defeat her on her own ground, and show that the story where you're a hero matters more than the one where you're a villain. I'm not going to pretend to be your only chance. You're bigger and older than I am. But I'm telling you the truth when I say that I can't win this without you."

She stepped closer, Snow White stepped closer, and the frightened princess that always lurked at the bottom of my thoughts shrank away, shivering, from the frozen beauty that birthed us both. I was her daughter and her sister and her protégée, and it hurt to be this close to her.

"Do you really want my help?" she asked. "I warn you, once done is done forever. You can't be separated from me once you let me in. No mortal force will ever split us apart."

"My story's already active."

This time, her smile was sad. "Oh, pretty little village girl, with your red, red lips and your white, white skin, you never understood, did you? How could you, when your world was so much smaller than the woods around it? Your story is active, but that doesn't matter. That's a change of degrees, a rearranging of the flowers in the garden. What you ask will blow the palace doors open, and leave you to contend with what's been locked inside all this time. 'Active' is a word for humans to put on stories, to try and contain them. What I will make you is so much more than that."

"Will you put the knife against my throat?" I asked.

"Yes," she said, smile fading into seriousness. "If that's what it takes to bring about the springtime, then yes. You are so important to me, child, but you must never forget that my mother bled me out and left me white as winter in the wood."

"Then I accept," I said. "Help me."

"As you wish," she said, and pulled me close, and kissed me. Her skin was cold, and her lips tasted like blood and apples, sweet and salty at the same time, until there was nothing else in the world. She wrapped her arms around me, and I was falling, and I was never going to land, and that was all right, because this was how the story was supposed to go. I gave up fighting. I let her in, and the whiteness closed over everything, and took the world away.

# # #

"Can she, you know, freeze to death? Because the 'snow' part in her name isn't literal. It's a metaphor for her total lack of complexion."

"Technically, white is a color, so she has a complexion. It's just a very, very pale one." Demi sounded more anxious than Andy had. Neither of them sounded happy. I couldn't blame them for that. Watching your friend and team leader's borrowed body collapse into the snow would make anyone uncomfortable.

I rolled onto my back, staring up at the gray, storm-wracked sky. I was obscurely grateful for the clouds that covered it. Blue would have been hard to handle at the moment, one color too many forced into my three-color world. Gray wasn't black *or* white, but it was a transition I was prepared to endure. "I'm okay," I said. "I just had to sort a few things out with my story, that's all. I'm fine. Somebody want to help me up?"

"You bled *everywhere*," said Carlos, bending to offer his hand. My fingers were shockingly white against his brown skin. "I thought Agent Santos was going to toss her cookies."

"Agent Santos does not have cookies to toss," said Demi primly. "I've been gluten-free for years."

"How do you do burritos?" asked Carlos.

"I don't. Corn tortillas work for everything else. Tastes better, perfectly healthy, and I don't spend as much time sick in bed." Demi shrugged. "It works out."

I let go of Carlos's hand. "All right, fascinating as this moment of shared culture has been, it's time for us to get moving. How long was I out?"

"Not long," said Andy. "Maybe five minutes. Long enough to groan a few times, which is why we left you there. It seemed better than messing with you while you were doing whatever it was that you were doing."

"I was having a chat with my story." My lips still tasted like apples and blood. They felt like they'd been bruised. It was all I could do not to touch them and find out. Snow White—the original—had kissed me in this body. She'd warned me that there was no going back. What if I was trapped here now? My own lips had never kissed my story, after all.

"What did she say?" asked Demi, eyes going wide.

"She said she'd help me."

"What does that mean?" asked Andy.

"I don't know." I turned to face Adrianna's castle. "Let's find out." And I started walking. The others followed me. Demi and Andy were in the habit of letting me take the lead, and I got the feeling that Carlos was just glad we weren't looking to him for answers.

Before, I hadn't been walking on top of the snow: the snow had just been getting out of my way. Now, I seemed to balance atop the thin crust, and though I weighed as much as ever, I no longer broke through it, or left even the faintest of footprints in my wake. It was like I'd come to some sort of an accord with winter. That would have been unnerving, if not for the fact that the castle on the hill was getting closer. Every step we took seemed to devour ten feet of distance. We'd be there soon. Adrianna and her lackeys couldn't hide from us.

"What are we going to do when we get there?" asked Andy.

"We're going to do our jobs," I said. "We're going to get Sloane back, and we're going to stop Adrianna and Birdie from doing whatever it is that they're planning to do." Distort the narrative. Turn the stories that wouldn't stop replaying to their advantage. We knew the broad strokes, but we'd never quite managed to unsnarl the details. I wasn't sure they had either. We'd been at their heels every step of the way, and it's hard to properly plot your evil empire when the damn heroes won't stop harrying you.

"I can't go back," said Demi. I glanced at her. She was shivering, and not just from the cold. "Birdie . . . she *said* things when she had me. They made so much sense, because she knew where to hit my story to make it resonate. I can't go back to her. I'll die before I go back to her."

"You're not going to," said Andy. "She can't claim me, and I am totally cool with the idea of punching a woman who wears glasses as many times as necessary. I think I might actually enjoy it if it's her."

"Use lethal force if necessary," I said. "Against anyone but Sloane."

There was a moment of stricken silence before Andy said, "Henry, if we shoot her while she's . . . you know . . . what's that going to mean for you?"

"I'm not a ghost, if that's what you're asking, and I didn't steal this body. The original owner doesn't want it anymore. That happens sometimes with Snow Whites who didn't know about their story." I shook my head. "I can stay here if I need to, and if the girl who used to live here comes back, I can find another one. It's a trick they don't advertise when they're explaining the ins and outs of once upon a time."

"Is that why sometimes princesses wake up from comas and they're all weird and don't know their own names anymore?" asked Demi. The rest of us turned to look at her. She shrugged. "I read. I've been trying to learn as much as I can, since all this started. I think I might like to work in the Archives someday."

"You'd be a damn good archivist," I said. "Yes, this is why sometimes sleeping princesses wake up different. It's because they can become totally different people while they're unconscious. I'm serious, guys. Do not let the fact that Adrianna has my face keep you from pulling the trigger. Saving Sloane and maybe the world is a lot more important than keeping my bra size from changing." At least I wanted it to be, almost as much as I wanted my own body back. I had been through too much to be comfortable with the idea of seeing someone else's face in the mirror for the rest of my life.

And that couldn't be more important than saving Sloane. It *couldn't*. I refused to let my story be that selfish.

"You're the boss," said Andy.

"We're here," I said, looking up at the cold stone wall of Adrianna's castle.

"Now what?" asked Carlos.

I smiled at him, thin and cold as a knife sliding between his ribs. "Now we get inside."

# # #

Sloane wasn't screaming anymore. Sloane had run out of screams some time before, right around when she ran out of tears and tension. Now she hung in her web of spun straw and knotted silk, head bowed, not responding to the world around her. Birdie sighed.

"You were supposed to be made of stronger stuff, my broken glass-girl. You've lasted so long without committing yourself to a tale that I genuinely thought you'd be able to ride through this. Have I broken you, or are you just playing possum to see what I'll do? I don't recommend toying with me, Amity. You'll like me better as a friend."

Sloane didn't say anything. Sloane didn't move.

Birdie sighed a second time. "So it's the long nap and the contemplation for you, then. I was hoping you'd be willing to fight beside us. The story needs you more than you can know. But a time of rest should give you a chance to consider your crimes—and give me the time I need to change a few things about your past. You'll wake to a better world."

She pulled a needle from the collar of her sweater. It gleamed in the firelight, dull as pewter and sharp as sin. Birdie smiled.

"I promise."

# # #

The servant's door at the base of the main tower was locked. That wasn't a surprise: what was the point in building a secret castle on a layer of reality that wasn't even supposed to exist if you were just going to go and leave the door open for anyone who wanted to wander inside? I glared at it anyway.

"Demi, can you pipe this open?"

She shook her head. "I could pipe a key *out* of a lock, but I can't convince a lock that it wants to be open when it's not."

"Ciara could talk it into opening, but we had to leave her behind," said Carlos. "Maybe now that you don't need that counterspell for the prison wards anymore—"

"There isn't time," I said. I felt bad about cutting him off, but that didn't stop me from going on. "You'd have to climb back up the beanstalk, give her the crystal, explain the situation, and then get back down here to us. Adrianna isn't going to hold off blowing us into next week for that long. We need to move."

"How concerned are we about being found out?" asked Andy.

"She knows we're here." Even if she hadn't before I kissed our shared story, she did now. There was no way she didn't. "The only reason we're not trying to go through the front door is that it's ten feet tall and eight feet across, and we don't have a battering ram."

"Great," said Andy. He drew his pistol, turned, and shot three times at the wood right next to the lock. Everyone but me exclaimed in surprise and dismay, and were still exclaiming when he holstered his gun, walked over to the door, and punched a hole through the damaged section of the paneling. Reaching inside, he pulled back the bolt, withdrew his hand, and opened the door before turning to beam at the rest of us.

"Given the right situation, anything can be a key," he said.

I nodded. "Good thinking. Now follow me." I stepped past him, through the open door and into Adrianna's lair.

The first thing that struck me was the cold. It was like walking into a freezer, and while my breath didn't plume in the air, it was only because my core temperature was already so low. I could feel the chill, and that told me more than enough about what we were walking into. Adrianna was still strong here. Stronger than I was, even with our story on my side.

The second thing that struck me was her fist, as she stepped out of a hidden alcove in the wall and slammed her knuckles into my nose. I reeled backward, knocked off balance. Andy's hands on my shoulders caught me, pushing me upright in time for Adrianna to swing for me again. This time I ducked, and her fist hit him in the middle of his chest. Andy looked down at it, his eyebrows rising toward his hairline.

"You probably didn't want to do that," he said, before grabbing her wrist and pulling her toward him. He bent at the same time, clearly intending to throw her. He had a lot of experience at throwing that body; we'd sparred together for years. He knew exactly how to take me down. By extension, he knew how to take *her* down.

I saw her smile and knew that he was making a mistake.

"Andy, no!" I shouted. It was too late. Adrianna was on top of him, and as he pulled her into the throw, she ran the fingers of her free hand down his cheek in what looked almost like a caress, except for the part where it left bloody scratches in its wake. Andy froze. Adrianna pulled her hand out of his grip, still smiling. And ponderously, slow as a tree toppling over in a forest, Andy fell.

The floor shook when he struck. Carlos and Demi were staring at her in open-mouthed shock. Demi hadn't even raised her flute yet. Adrianna straightened, turning her bloody smile on the two of them.

"Now that it's just us pretty lies standing here, why don't we have a bit of fun?" she asked. "You run. I'll chase you. And when I catch you, we'll dance."

"I have a better idea," I said. "You give me back my fucking body, and I let you go back to the whiteout wood."

"Because otherwise you're going to what, keep me here? Kill me? If you kill me, you kill yourself—the self you've always been, anyway." Adrianna turned to face me. "Bold move for someone who's always tried so hard to follow the rules. But I suppose you've already started breaking them, haven't you? I never took you for a thief, niece. That face you're wearing, do you even know the name of the girl who owns it? Did you ask permission, or did you just take what you wanted, and damn the consequences? Maybe we're closer than you think."

"Or maybe I asked the wood to show me a body whose owner didn't want it anymore," I said. "Leave my team alone. Your fight isn't with them."

"My fight is with anyone who would slave the story when it deserves to run free." Adrianna took a step toward me. "We could have kings and queens and quests. Castles and dragons and mermaid lagoons. But *you* people, you insist it's too dangerous. That a few deaths justify locking us all into lives that aren't worth living. Let people eat the apples that are thrown to them. They'll treasure the time they have much more than they do the pale shadows you allow them to enjoy."

"Oh, that's your big problem with the way we do things? We don't break shit often enough for you? Well, I've got news for you, Adrianna: You've been in the mirrors for too long. You've lost touch with your own story." I leaned forward and smiled. The air around me chilled. "I just talked to our story. She chose me. She's helping me. So no matter what the mirrors told you, looks like you're old news."

Adrianna couldn't pale—my complexion didn't allow it. Instead, her features contorted with rage, and she launched herself at me. I did the only sensible thing.

I turned and ran.

# # #

The castle belonged to Adrianna; she had created it out of whole cloth, weaving it according to her ideas of what a castle should be. Birdie had probably helped her. Adrianna had the raw power, but Birdie had the *experience*. She knew about stories and how they built their foundations. What neither of them had counted on was the fact that it wasn't really Adrianna's castle; it was *Snow White's* castle, which meant it was mine. It wanted me to be happy. It wanted me to have whatever my heart desired—and what my heart desired was Sloane.

I ran, and doorways appeared before me. I flung myself through them and stairways blossomed out of walls, spiraling up, up, ever upward. My new body wasn't used to this sort of exertion. My lungs burned and my legs ached, and all my flesh wanted to do was lay down and sleep. Comas are a hard habit to break. I kept going. I needed to find Sloane and lead Adrianna away from the rest of my team. That was all that mattered. After that it was all sort of fuzzy and hard to focus on.

A door appeared in the wall. I grabbed the doorknob, twisting as I slammed my shoulder into the wood, and bounced off when it refused to yield. Something else was holding this door closed against me. I backed off a step, rubbing my bruised shoulder and glaring.

"Open," I commanded.

The door didn't open.

Adrianna was close enough behind me that I didn't really have time to waste arguing with the inanimate. I only hesitated for a second before retreating to the shadows formed where the stairwell emptied out into the hall. It was a little bit of architectural frippery, more for effect than practicality, and it concealed me nicely. I put a hand over my mouth to block the sound of my labored breathing, and I waited.

I didn't have to wait long. Adrianna thundered into view, pure rage on her stolen face, and hammered on the door. It opened a few seconds later, revealing the familiar face of everybody's favorite traitor, Birdie Hubbard.

"Where is she?" demanded Adrianna.

Birdie frowned. "She's sleeping. I told you that might be the only option. She'll dream as I tell her, and when we drag some fool in here and drug him into thinking she's his one true love, she'll wake malleable and ready to be of service."

"Not her, the other one," said Adrianna. She gestured wildly to her—to *my*—face. "This one! She's here, and I know she'd go straight for her missing piece. Where is she?"

Birdie's eyes widened in evident alarm. "Henry? She's here? In the castle? How could you let that happen? You promised we'd be safe here. My work—"

"Isn't going to matter if she kills us both," snapped Adrianna. "Did you let *anyone* in? A mouse, a bird, a clever little squirrel? Think, woman!"

"I let *you* in." Birdie's expression smoothed out, becoming neutral. "Where have you been all day, Adrianna? Is that your name right now? Or did Henry take her body back?"

"It doesn't work that way for us," said Adrianna. "Don't be stupid as well as useless, or I might start thinking I don't need you." She turned then, and stalked off down the hall, presumably to keep looking for me. Birdie stayed in the doorway, watching her go.

That was my opening. As soon as Adrianna turned the corner I rushed forward, slamming my shoulder into Birdie's chest and driving her backward. My lower center of gravity actually came in handy; in my own body, I would've had trouble running while bent that far forward. As it was, the run came easily, even naturally, and Birdie went sprawling. I slammed the door, taking my eyes off her long enough to lock it. I didn't need to have worried. She was still on the floor when I turned around, crawling backward away from me as fast as she could.

"You can't be here!" she said.

"Oh, so you recognize me, do you?" The room was a weird jumble of princess iconography, from the spinning wheel to the pile of mattresses in one corner. A fire burned in the fireplace, making everything too hot. The cold around me was fighting back, intensifying until I left frozen footprints on the floor. "Too bad you decided to leave the Bureau. You could have saved me a lot of trouble. Now where is Sloane?"

"Adrianna! Help! She's here! She's—" My hand across her mouth cut her off. I crouched with one knee on Birdie's chest, ignoring her wide, pleading eyes.

"I've figured a few things out. You're a Storyteller. You can twist the narrative. That's a big power to have. Too bad it only works if you can talk." I shifted more of my weight onto my knee. She whimpered. "Now where. Is. Sloane?"

Birdie pointed to the stack of mattresses.

"Thank you." There's an art to knocking someone out without killing them. It's never as easy as the movies make it out to be. But there were other ways. "You said you'd help me, so help me," I said, and used my free hand to pinch Birdie's nostrils shut. She looked at me like I had lost my mind—until the smell of apples filled the air, and her eyes closed.

"Great. I'm chloroform now." I pushed myself off of her. That was a trick that wouldn't work in a world that was more set in its ways: I knew that, and I didn't care. As long as it worked here, that was all that mattered.

There were fifteen mattresses in the stack. I climbed them as fast as I could, almost falling several times. When I got to the top, there she was: Sloane Winters, asleep, in a gown that had been fit for a princess once, before it was shredded and burnt to the point of becoming rags. There were bruises and cuts on her exposed skin. I had no doubt that there was worse concealed under her clothing. Her eyes were closed. She had slept through my entire fight with Birdie. She'd sleep forever unless someone woke her.

"Dammit, Sloane," I whispered. She was my friend. She was my colleague. She was my brother's ex-girlfriend and the pain in my ass, and she was probably going to kill us all one day, and none of that mattered, because she was *Sloane*. I loved her because she was Sloane.

I loved her. Maybe that would be enough. Gingerly, I leaned forward, and I kissed her.

Her eyes snapped open. I pulled back, fast enough to get out of her way as she sat up, grabbed the front of my shirt, and demanded, "Who the fuck are you?"

"Henry," I said. "It's a long story. Do you want to hear it, or do you want to help me kick Adrianna's ass?"

She paused. Then, slowly, she nodded. "You're going to tell me *everything*, snow-bitch. Including the reason I taste apples right now. All right?"

"All right," I said. "Can you walk?"

Sloane snorted. "Can you keep up?"

# # #

It turned out I could, although it wasn't easy; her legs were so much longer than mine that I felt like I was sprinting as she led me through the castle, her unerring nose for the story leading us to a ballroom swathed in cobwebs and dust. Adrianna was there, pacing back and forth at the far end of the room. She stopped when she saw us.

"You," she snarled. "You've ruined *everything*. Do you understand what you've done?"

"My job." I didn't have a gun. *She* had my gun—something I was reminded of when she pulled it from her belt and fired in my direction.

She also didn't have any firearms training. The shot went wild. Sloane and I didn't hesitate. We both broke into a run, rushing for her as fast as we could. It was the only hope we had left.

Sloane reached her first, and Sloane's fist reached her face a heart-beat later, impacting with a wet *crunch*. The gun went flying. I grabbed it, aiming straight for Adrianna's chest. Sloane took a step back, giving me a clear shot.

"Stand *down*!" I snarled.

Adrianna smiled. "Shoot me," she countered. "Can you? Can you kill yourself, just to stop me? I hope you can, niece. I've already done more damage than you can know. I want you to remember it every time you look in a mirror. I want you—"

She stopped mid-sentence, looking suddenly confused. Then she folded forward, hitting the floor with all the grace of a sack of wet concrete. Sloane smiled, holding up a long brass needle.

"Spindles come apart," she said.

I blinked. Then I held out my hand. "Good," I said. "Put me under." "What?"

"Put me under. I need to stop this. Besides." I smiled, lopsidedly. "This time, I'm pretty sure Jeff can wake me up. Now put me un—"

Her hand lashed out, embedding the needle in my arm.

"—der," I finished.

I didn't feel myself fall down.

# # #

The whiteout wood was exactly as it had always been, black and white and red: only I was different. I felt like a resident, not a visitor. This was my home now.

"You," snarled a voice. I turned. There was Adrianna, wearing her own face, standing some feet behind me. The snow under her feet was already melting, revealing black, blasted ground. "You little bitch. You ruined everything."

"No, Aunt Adrianna," I said. "You did. You tried to make me your mirror. You came too close. I'm sorry."

"You will be," she said, and took a step toward me—or tried to. The ground gripped her feet fast, holding her in place. She looked down, suddenly alarmed. "What's going on?"

"I don't know how you stayed out of the mirrors for as long as you did, but that's over now," I said. "The story chose me. When something's a reflection, something else is real. I guess you're not the real one anymore."

She was still screaming when the mirrored hands reached up from beneath her and pulled her down.

I sat down in the snow. Then I stretched out, full-length, getting myself comfortable, and crossed my hands over my chest in the classic pose. They'd wake me up soon enough. I believed in them.

They were my family, after all.

# # #

Jeff was still leaning over me when I opened my eyes. He looked concerned, like he'd been afraid his kiss wouldn't work this time either. I blinked. His look of concern deepened.

"Henry?" he asked.

"Oh thank Grimm I'm me again," I said, and sat up, looking down at my body—*my* body—before turning to him. "You woke me up."

"Yes," he said, tears of relief beginning to form.

I grabbed him, pulled him close, and kissed him hard before I asked, "Where is everyone else?"

"Demi went back up the beanstalk to get Ciara and Piotr, while Carlos and Sloane kept watch over the rest of you. Together they got you, Andy, and the others out of Adrianna's fold before it collapsed. Demi and Ciara removed the mirror from Carlos's eyes while the rest of you were removed to the hospital," said Jeff. "Sloane is recovering. Your temporary host is still in her coma. Carlos said to thank you for removing him from the field; he's returned to HR. Piotr said fuck you very much for taking one of his best agents away, although the fact that he got to take custody of Birdie made up for some of it. She still hasn't woken up, by the way. Ciara is requesting a permanent reassignment to our team, under you. I—why are you smiling?"

"Because I'm home with the people who love me, and that's what matters," I said. I'd have to tell Sloane what happened, and we'd have a lot to talk about once she knew I'd kissed her awake. I wasn't going to recover instantly from having my body stolen. Jeff was probably going to have his own issues with it. And there was the matter of what I might owe to my story . . .

But all those things were problems for later. Right now, I was here, I was home, and I was one step closer to the ever after that I deserved. That was what mattered. As I pulled Jeff close and kissed him for a third time, that was all that mattered in the world.

Acknowledgments

When I wrote *Indexing*, I wasn't necessarily planning on a season two. I had left some openings, in case it decided to happen, but as far as I was concerned, the case was closed, and we could all move on.

And then people started asking what would happen next. And I realized that I really, really wanted to tell them.

Big thanks to the Amazon Kindle Serials program, which made this story a possibility; thanks for going out on a limb for me. Thanks also to my acquiring editor, Alex Carr, my faithful Machete Squad, and my developmental editor, Michelle "Vixy" Dockrey, who is finally getting professional credit for the heavy lifting that she's been doing all along. Finally, I owe a debt of gratitude to my agent, Diana Fox, who puts up with more than any one person should ever be expected to tolerate. All my love.

As I have said before, the Aarne-Thompson Index to Motifs in Folk Literature is a real thing, and is used by folklore and fairy tale scholars the world over. My copy previously belonged to the state folklorist of Minnesota, and is one of my most prized possessions. If you're interested in learning more, I highly recommend checking the folklore section of your local library. There's so much to learn about the stories that we have created, and which have created us in turn.

Now rest my dear, and be at ease; there's a fire in the hearth and a wind in the eaves, and the night is so dark, and the dark is so deep, and it's time that all good little stars were asleep.

About the Author

Photo © Beckett Gladney

Seanan McGuire was born and raised in Northern California, where she has lived for the majority of her life. She spends most of her time writing or watching television, but also draws a semiautobiographical comic strip and has released several albums of filk music (science fiction and fantasy themed folk music). To relax, Seanan enjoys travel, and frequents haunted corn mazes, aquariums with good octopus habitats, and Disney Parks. Seanan is remarkably good at finding reptiles and amphibians wherever she goes, sometimes to the dismay of the people she happens to be traveling with.